Amulet of the Goddess

A NOVEL BY

John Darr
Book Three

Copyright © 2017 John Darr Books
All rights reserved.
ISBN-13: 979-8985232714

A special thanks to my critique group and all the help, advice, and gentle corrections you've provided.

Thank you to my friends for feedback and needed encouragement.

Last, I dedicate this third novel of the series to all those who've faced the scary demons from their past and came out a stronger person. Time heals all things.

Table of Contents

Amulet of the Goddess

CHAPTER ONE
GRIM PLAN

The Grim Reaper's summons tugged on Deyanira's soul, signaling the end of her exile. As if to underscore that fact, her Master's ship-of-bones arrived soon afterward to carry her to his Grim Keep.

Growing anxious, Deyanira quickly boarded and glanced up the ship's spiral stairwell. It led to where the steersman, and her fellow KIN, stood. The steersman's blood-red robe blew in the wind and his hands gripped the large ship's wheel made of bones.

"Hurry," she urged.

The steersman nodded and whirled his wheel. The large ship, the skeletal remains of a long dead leviathan, lurched into motion. Vibrations along the hull of the vessel increased until they hurtled over the ice floes of this area of the Afterworld.

Strong gusts of wind buffeted the craft and frigid air whistled through the portals: the eye sockets of the skull. Bits of ice crystals stung Deyanira's skin, forcing her brilliant, emerald eyes to mere slits.

Why would her Master call her back into his presence now? *Something must have happened.* She tilted her slender chin up, letting the bracing wind caress her pale skin and whip her lone, red braid around. The cold made her ritualistic scars ache, a pain she welcomed. *Better to be alert.*

The first signs of the Keep–double rows of towering, hooded figures–came into view. Ancient statues, a hundred feet tall, stood facing each other, scythes crossed. The rows of silent sentinels dwarfed the ship-of-bones as it zoomed between them.

The bulky shadow of the Grim Keep appeared against the bleak grey of the overcast skies. Its central complex was a mountain of rock, towering a thousand feet above the dreary surrounding. The various outer segments grew from solid rock in twisting patterns like roots jutting out of the frozen tundra.

As the Keep loomed ever closer, the awe-inspiring outline of a huge skull appeared out of the gloom. Carved into the rock face, the skull blazed with red fire. *Only the most powerful could summon that color of supernatural flames.* Deyanira shuddered at the display of raw might.

Soon, the bulk of the Grim Keep blotted out the dreary sky. The ship-of-bones slowed as it entered a natural overhang that created a cavernous opening at the base of the central formation. Turning from the eye-socket window, Deyanira descended the steps to the exit.

A dull, grating vibration reached her feet as the skull's maw opened. The flowing, red carpet, like a living tongue, had already extended to the guardhouse platform and solidified into a shallow ramp. Breathing in the frigid air, Deyanira pulled her hood over her head and marched off the ship.

A Grim Guard waited at the main gate, blocking her path.

"Well?" Deyanira said, gazing into the guard's bone-white mask. "Our Master has summoned me. Either lead me to him or move out of my way."

The guard turned and marched through the gate, Deyanira right behind. Once they entered the sheltering walls of the Keep, the sound of wind died away and the cold disappeared, replaced by the warm, moist air of the interior.

She followed the guard through the heart of the mountain until the corridor narrowed and closed in on each side. Adding to the oppressiveness of the place, veins of red rock meandered in the natural stone like blood dripping down the surface.

They reached a wide set of shallow steps cut into the rough stone, worn to glassy smoothness from centuries of use. As Deyanira prepared to climb the five stories to the arena, her mind raced.

Convocations of the KIN took place in the arena. A chill traveled down her spine because the arena was also used for special executions. She swallowed, calling on her long-repressed anger to push away the fear. If she had to die today, she would stand tall and not cower.

The sky had darkened to a sooty grey by the time Deyanira entered the arena. Black poles lined the outside of the circular area. Angel script, etched into the surface and glowing, covered each pole. On top of the poles rested onyx bowls filled with blazing, red fire.

Grim Guards stood in the darkness between each pole like living shadows. Their skull masks gave off a faint, white glow and the eerie, green illumination of their scythes produced a strange counterpoint to the red glare from the fires.

Deyanira's escort marched toward the center of the arena before coming to a halt and moving aside. That's when she noticed a person huddled on the ground, sobbing. He wore the grey robes of a Hunter, an agent of the Grand Oracle. *What's he doing here?* Her Master would reveal the answer, she decided, lifting her gaze to a high dais about twenty feet beyond the man.

The Grim Reaper stood robe-less with his head tilted back and his arms thrown wide. His bare arms were like corded, barren tree limbs, stripped of the bark. The red tint of his flesh had the smeared look of melted wax. It was not a product of reflected firelight, she knew. Something he'd done to himself long ago permanently marred his skin and turned his complexion a reddish bronze color. Even though his face was turned from her, the ritualistic scars were still very visible like jagged cracks along his bald head.

After a long moment, the Grim Reaper's back heaved and he lowered his arms, sated. A servant scurried forward with a robe. As soon as the Grim Reaper donned the garment, the hem writhed and moved as if alive.

He turned. All that was visible of his face was the glow of his angry-red pupils beneath the hood.

"Tell me why I shouldn't kill you, Deyanira?"

His voice curled around her, holding her in place until the guard gripped her shoulder and forced her down onto her hands and knees. The mortal in the Hunter robes jerked his head to look at her and Deyanira grimaced because she finally recognized the man. *Agent Hunter!* The once-arrogant man was little more than an emaciated figure now. According to the reports, Jonah Blackstone had sucked all the power from him, rendering him into this pathetic and frail husk.

Tremors rippled through the Afterworld at that news. Only a Deliverer could wield that kind of power. Hunter's eyes, once so full of pride, showed abject fear now. He flinched and squealed at the eerie sound of a scythe cutting the air.

But the weapon came to rest against Deyanira's throat, not his. The ceremonial weapon's super fine blade cut into her flesh, drawing blood. She grunted, willing herself to remain still despite the hard, uneven stone gouging into her palms.

Her Master drew closer. When he spoke, his voice sounded like stone grinding against stone. Anger and fury radiated from him. "Tell me why I shouldn't banish your soul to everlasting oblivion!"

Deyanira gulped, feeling the scythe bite into her neck, followed by a stinging wetness. "I helped you kill the traitor, Isaiah Blackstone." She paused. "I found the ring…"

"And you lost it."

Deyanira wanted to protest. It wasn't her fault the Grim Reaper had allowed Jonah to defeat him.

The Grim Reaper glided closer while tracing a circle in the air with the index finger of his right hand. The hem of his robe reacted, reaching out to touch her face. "There are some who would have me kill you."

"That's easy for them to say," Deyanira replied while resisting the urge to recoil from the robe's touch. She spoke through a clenched jaw. "They hide in the shadows, throwing stones. Could the others do any better?"

The Grim Reaper stepped past her, balling his hand into a fist. The hem of the robe curled back on itself. A moment later, the guard withdrew the scythe, leaving a line of blood across Deyanira's throat. She risked a glance and found the Grim Reaper watching her.

He gestured. "Stand up. I called you here because I also wondered if someone else could perform better than you have done."

Deyanira stood at once and scanned the arena. They were still alone with the mortal, the servant, and the Grim Guards–until a single KIN entered the space. Per custom, KIN had to expose their faces to their master. When the newcomer didn't follow the ancient protocol, Deyanira's lip curled in disgust.

The Alliance mole bowed to the Grim Reaper. When he straightened, he threw back his hood to reveal a masked face. Deyanira noted that his form wavered from an enchantment that concealed his general features and made identifying him more difficult.

When he turned toward her, his filtered voice carried clear disappointment. "It's good to see you in one piece."

Deyanira didn't bother to acknowledge the taunt. She held her own chin high as she addressed the Grim Reaper. "Master, you were saying?"

"We are ready to proceed with my plans for the Wraiths, even a little ahead of schedule." The anger evident in his voice permeated the chilled air. "Our person within the Alliance expressed concern that you'll interfere again."

"What's this?" Deyanira overcame her caution and whirled on the mole.

The man crossed his arms and despite his masking magic, Deyanira could feel his smugness. "You prevented me from capturing the courier and ending the Afterworld rebellion."

Fury caused Deyanira's ears to ring, but self-preservation stayed her desire to protest. If the Grim Reaper had allowed this fool to say these things, she'd risk instant death to belittle it now. "Master, it's not true. I stopped Hunter from taking Blackstone to the Grand Oracle." She pointed a slender finger in the mole's direction. "This fool had lost control of Hunter by that point."

"And because of your feelings for the dead father, you helped the brat escape," the mole interjected. "Tell me, witch, is young Blackstone the son you always wished you had?"

Before she could stop herself, Deyanira had conjured green flames. "I warned you about calling me witch!"

"Enough!" The sky crackled overhead and the Grim Reaper's voice rolled over Deyanira and the mole like a tidal wave.

He made a hissing sound as he paced around them. "That isn't our most pressing problem. The half-breed has the Deliverer's Tales. That ancient book should have been locked away in the Central Archives."

A shudder went through Deyanira. If Jonah Blackstone had possession of that book, he could find the rest of the rings and… the Medallions. She wondered if the universe were playing a cruel trick on them. After more than two thousand years, this young boy burst on the scene and no one could stop him.

The Grim Reaper spoke just over Deyanira's shoulder, startling her out of her dire thoughts. "Now you understand the urgency! The mole has informed us the boy's friend is a Seeker! We must move ahead with our plans before they can grow stronger."

Even though Deyanira had a feeling deep inside that the plan would fail, what choice did they have? Well, she reasoned, clutching at a ray of hope, she could eliminate the troublesome mole when he returned in shame.

As if sensing her thoughts, the mole pointed at her. "Master, I humbly request you forbid Deyanira from interfering this time."

The Grim Reaper's glowing eyes bored into her soul and his will smashed against her mind. "You will remain in my Keep until the mission is over."

Deyanira sucked in a ragged breath. "Yes, Master." The oath wrapped around her body, binding her to the Grim Keep. To try and leave would mean instant, painful death.

The Grim Reaper gave a satisfied nod and turned to the mole. "If you fail, the leeway I showed Deyanira will not befall you."

The mole bowed.

"Either we control the boy," the Grim Reaper began while making a slight gesture with his left hand before the scythe whistled through the air again. It was followed by a heavy thud and then several wet splats. Deyanira turned, staring at Agent Hunter's headless body and the trail of blood leading to his head as it rolled a few feet away.

"Or you will bring him to me so I can personally witness his head roll." The Grim Reaper chuckled as he strode toward the exit, taking his Grim Guards with him. The mole paused long enough to glare at Deyanira in triumph before he followed.

Cold air wafted through the empty space and Deyanira breathed it in, calming her apprehension. After a backward glance to be certain she was alone, she held out her right hand toward the closest pole.

With a muttered counterspell, the pulsing, amber etchings faded to black. From the moment she saw the glowing symbols, she knew the Grim Reaper had found a way to prevent young Jonah from eavesdropping on their meeting. Now that she'd broken the protection, Jonah could see, or at least, hear her. Deyanira focused her thoughts on the source of all their fears.

Far away, in the mortal world, Jonah Blackstone jerked awake in his bed. Despite the throbbing in his temple, he was sure he'd dream-walked again. Well, almost. This time, he'd been blocked until the very end, when he saw an open-air arena under a dark, clouded sky, lots of red flames and... *Deyanira*.

Jonah's Death Sense spiked as one sentence hammered into his mind. *Beware, young Blackstone.*

CHAPTER TWO

MORNING VISITOR

Why did Deyanira warn him? Jonah wondered, rubbing his aching, sweaty forehead and scrunching up his face. He slumped back onto his pillow and stared at his dark bedroom ceiling. The evil Reaper had tortured him earlier this summer. However, Deyanira's Grim Hound managed to save his life, protecting him from Agent Hunter.

It made no sense. He closed his eyes, but true sleep eluded him. After tossing and turning for another hour, he glanced at his bedside clock and groaned. It was still a bit early to rise and dress for school. The chilled October morning hadn't even dawned yet.

Screw it, he thought, throwing off the warm covers. He rolled out of his twin-sized bed, which had become a little short after growing a few inches taller during the summer. Jonah was lankier and within half an inch of his cousin, Robert, in height now, which he thoroughly enjoyed.

As he left his bedroom and crossed the quiet family room, he stretched in that unrestrained way you can't help doing in the morning. Rubbing the sleep from his eyes, he entered the kitchen and stopped.

Aunt Imma and Uncle James were already seated at the round kitchen table. They each held a steaming cup of coffee and were talking to a stranger.

"Uh, good morning," Jonah managed as he wrapped his arms around his middle, trying to cover his rumpled t-shirt. The two inches of exposed skin below the hem of his sweatpants also embarrassed him. Only now did his mind register that he could hear the low rumble of a quiet conversation while approaching the kitchen.

The stranger had a well lined, deep chocolate face. His hair, a short afro, was salt and pepper. Dark blue mechanic's coveralls were visible beneath his opened, pale tan coat. And the man's serious expression morphed into a smile as he continued to scrutinize Jonah.

When he spoke, his baritone voice filled the quiet kitchen. "My God, he looks just like Janice. No denying him, huh?"

Uncle James stood and grinned, but the hand holding the coffee cup shook a little.

"Good morning, Jonah," his uncle began, already dressed for work in his trademark sports coat and slacks. Like Jonah's mom, Uncle James had a thin face, pecan tan skin, and brown eyes. This morning, his round eyeglasses were temporarily placed on the table. "This is your Uncle Amos Peacock." Uncle James gestured at the visitor.

Jonah waved but his Uncle Amos rose, leaned over the table, and thrust out a calloused hand. "Nice to meet you finally!"

"You too," Jonah said. He couldn't hide the confusion on his face.

Aunt Imma sighed and added, "This is your Aunt Ruby's husband."

An involuntary pit formed in Jonah's stomach. His Aunt Ruby was the woman in the pictures over the mantel. Ever since Jonah had arrived in Mount Vernon, almost two years ago, he experienced dread any time he looked at the woman's image.

He came out of his reverie in time to notice the furtive glance exchanged between the adults. There was something going on, and he didn't need his Reaper Stare to sense that.

Uncle James motioned toward the door. "I'll see you out, Amos."

Blinking in surprise, Uncle Amos waved to Aunt Imma. "Thanks for the coffee." He flicked his gaze to Jonah. "Good to meet you."

With that, the men exited the kitchen. Jonah tried to listen to their low conversation but Aunt Imma intervened.

"How about a big breakfast?"

Jonah gave up trying to eavesdrop. "It's not even Sunday morning."

"Oh, that doesn't matter," Aunt Imma said in false cheeriness as she stood. She was a short, solidly built woman and at least a head shorter than Uncle James.

"It's nice to change up the routine from time to time." She loudly pulled out pans, cooking trays, and pots. In short order, she had grits bubbling on the stovetop, buttered slices of bread toasting in the oven, and strips of bacon crackling in the pan.

She asked Jonah to retrieve plates from the cabinet and also to prepare the orange juice. All the while, he couldn't help thinking she was keeping him busy so he wouldn't ask any questions. As if to prove it, each time he caught her gaze, Aunt Imma would turn to do something else.

Jonah's uncle returned with the morning paper, which he plopped on the table. After a quick word with his wife and a kiss on her cheek, he waved goodbye to Jonah and left for work. Jonah's aunt placed a big plate of scrambled eggs on the table, and another stacked high with buttered toast, along with a third plate full of crispy bacon.

She stood back, tightened the belt on her duster, and let out a long, satisfied sigh. "That should do it. Wake up your cousins, Jonah."

With that, she topped off her cup of coffee and hustled away to her room.

Jonah didn't need to fetch his cousins because the aroma of the hot breakfast had already worked its magic. Lynn strolled into the kitchen first, dressed in a new sweater. And to Jonah's surprise, she wasn't wearing her mid-top sneakers. This morning, she wore a nice pair of boots and her shoulder-length braids hung free, swaying as she deftly pulled out the newspaper's sports section.

It always amazed Jonah to watch her checking the scores as she ate breakfast. But this morning, she paused, paper in hand, and her eyes narrowed as she took in the big breakfast.

Her twin brother, Robert, appeared behind her a moment later, yawning. He was thin and lanky like his sister, and sported a perpetual bushy afro with neatly trimmed edges.

Robert stared in disbelief at the food arrayed on the kitchen table. "What's all this?"

Jonah shrugged. "Aunt Imma wanted to make a big breakfast." He grabbed a plate and piled food on it.

"It's not even Sunday," Robert said, his voice still full of questions. "What gives?"

Lynn prepared a buttered muffin and tea, then scooped some fluffy eggs onto a plate before she sat down. She eyed Jonah. "What happened?"

Jonah gulped down his first mouthful and said, "I caught them talking to Uncle Amos."

Lynn's eyes widened in response. Robert jumped up from his chair and rushed into the dining room to peek out the front window. He came back and slumped in his chair, frowning. "I can't believe he was here and didn't even bother to say hello to us."

Jonah didn't have an answer. He never even knew he *had* an Uncle Amos.

Lynn stared straight ahead, her butter knife tapping the edge of her saucer. "It has to be Aunt Ruby."

"Duh," Robert said around a piece of bacon that hung from his mouth. "We know he's married to her."

"Think, Robert." Lynn glared at her brother as if she were willing him to catch up. "It's been seven years…" she prompted.

Robert stopped chewing and his jaw dropped. "No way. But…"

"But what?" Jonah asked when Robert didn't elaborate.

Lynn put her butter knife down. "Aunt Ruby's been in a State Mental Institution for seven years."

Twirling a finger around his right ear, Robert also made coo-coo sounds.

"Robert!" Lynn admonished him. "But essentially, he's right. She ranted about the end times and the dead rising up to destroy the Earth."

"That went over well at family reunions!" Robert snorted, adding, "No one wanted her around. Uncle Amos argued with Dad and your mom. He accused everyone of choosing sides."

"Whoa," Jonah said, his breakfast now forgotten.

"Of course," Robert continued, "that could have been just old sibling rivalry. Aunt Ruby always hated your mom, as well as my dad, but more so, your mom."

"Why?"

"Because Aunt Ruby didn't have the Sight," Robert made air quotes, "like your mom. That drove our aunt crazy." He gulped. "Well, you know what I mean."

The story stunned but also fascinated Jonah. "So, what happened next?"

"She got worse," Lynn continued. "Uncle Amos tried to hide Ruby's condition until she hurt several innocent people. By then, he couldn't do anything to keep her from being arrested." Lynn rose, discarded her tea, and crossed to the refrigerator. Inside, she had a large container of her custom sports drink mix. She loaded some into a squeeze bottle and returned to the table.

Jonah waited, eager to know more about his aunt. "And?"

Lynn sipped from the squeeze bottle before she continued. "Like I said, she got sentenced to a mental institution."

"Can we talk about something else?" Robert finished his second plate of breakfast before he leaned back in his chair.

"Fine." Lynn focused her attention on Jonah. "So, what do you think of our idea?" She raised a questioning eyebrow, waiting.

"About Aunt Ruby?"

"No. Advertising our services," Lynn corrected him.

Jonah glanced out the kitchen window, stalling for time. He had successfully managed to avoid giving Robert and Lynn his opinion on turning the Mount Vernon Social Club into a detective agency. Wick had taken a few cases because of the increase in ghosts and Wraiths being spotted around town. Wick said it was because Halloween was only four weeks away.

The young mage was the only one brave enough to advertise his interest in the supernatural. However, things hadn't gone so well with the first ghosts he encountered, so Wick reasoned that Jonah's unique ability to talk to spirits could be the clincher.

Basically, he wanted help in sending any lingering spirits on their way. But Jonah wasn't remotely interested in welcoming any further strangeness into his life.

Lynn nudged his chair with her foot. "Well?"

"Aren't you afraid of Aunt Imma and Uncle James finding out?"

"No." When Jonah raised a skeptical eyebrow, Lynn pursed her lips. "The way I see it, if anyone at church asks for our help, well, they aren't likely to mention it to Mom."

"Yeah," Robert agreed. "That goes for church and non-church folks. A lot of people claim they don't believe in the supernatural, but they really do." He nodded sagely.

Jonah frowned at his cousins, searching for another way out. "Lynn, you know the Tolerance Club's taking a lot of my time."

Lynn nodded. "Yes, I do, but we can walk and chew gum at the same time."

Robert, who had added a bowl of cereal to his morning helpings, snorted and shot milk and bits of cereal out of his mouth and across the table. "You sound just like Dad."

Lynn held her chin higher. "Well, it's a good saying." She tossed her brother a few napkins before turning to Jonah. "We're not talking about a case every day."

"Okay. Whatever. It's fine with me." As soon as the words left his mouth, Jonah suspected he would regret his answer.

"Good," Lynn said. "We'll put the ad in the next blog and post it on all the social sites."

"And we'll pass around flyers," Robert added, wiping up the spilled milk and tossing the sodden napkins into the trash can. "That reminds me." He ran to his room and returned with a printed sample of the latest blog in his hands.

He waved it in Jonah's face. "I did a nice job on these."

Jonah took the sample. He noticed the ad but the main article drew most of his attention. It was about sightings of a large, black cat around Mount Vernon. His friend, Danita Jackson, had written the article. A ninth grader like Jonah and Mike, she was also the leader of their reading group.

He lowered the flyer to stare at Lynn. "Danita wrote an article for you?"

"Yes, she did, and it's excellent. She explained the background behind all the misunderstandings of black cats throughout history. The Ancient Egyptians revered cats because they represented Pakhet, the Goddess of the Hunt, or something like that."

Robert grinned at his sister. "Lynn's just impressed because Danita looks up to her. That's why she wants Danita to join the Summit team."

"She's also intelligent and a good writer," Lynn protested.

"Well," Robert continued. "I say no. She's too nosy, Lynn. How would we keep our other business away from her?" He elbowed Jonah. "Right? You know her."

Jonah's face warmed. Danita was brilliant, every bit as smart as Mike, even. But she was also scornful of anyone's belief in the supernatural. "Let's just deal with the ad first."

Lynn surprised Jonah by nodding. He was grateful when she let the matter drop. That allowed his thoughts to return to the significance of his Aunt Ruby release and Deyanira's warning. Was it just a coincidence that on the same morning he received the cryptic message, he also found out his Aunt Ruby had been released from a mental ward?

No, Jonah decided. Things were always connected when it came to him.

Robert caught his worried expression and patted him on the shoulder. "Little cousin, you need to get out more often."

"Ha ha."

"Seriously. I know a couple of girls who might be interested."

It was Jonah's turn to snort. "So do I."

When Robert laughed and went back to eating his cereal, Jonah slumped in the chair, brooding. Without warning, the title from an old, dark, fantasy novel his reading group covered last month popped into his head: *Something Wicked This Way Comes.*

CHAPTER THREE

HUMAN LIE DETECTOR

"Can you read his mind or not?" Brandon sneered as he crossed his arms and stared at Jonah. Besides being the local rich snob, the varsity boy's coach wanted to recruit him for the basketball team, something rarely done for any freshman.

Great, Jonah thought, *just what Brandon needed.* He squirmed in his seat as more of the kids milling around the Commons during this lunch period moved closer after hearing Brandon's challenging tone.

"Of course he can't read your mind!" Danita retorted, pushing her thick black-rimmed glasses up on her nose. She, along with Mike Littleton, Lorraine Hughes, Rodney Elkins, and Anthony Freeman, had commandeered one of the numerous lunch tables.

"Don't be ridiculous. That kind of thing doesn't exist," Danita insisted, sounding sure and superior. Anthony, who made valiant attempts at impressing Danita, nodded his agreement.

Before Jonah could respond, Mike rose from his chair. Like Jonah, he had grown a few inches by the time school started. "I told you, Brandon," he said while giving Danita an exasperated look, "Jonah doesn't read minds."

"Really? Then how can he tell if I'm lying?" Brandon's focus never wavered from Jonah. "I knew you were a freak, DC. You gonna open a palm-reading shop? I hear it runs in the family." The boy's buddies laughed at the stupid remark. "Go on, tell me if I'm lying." Brandon held out his palm.

"He doesn't read palms, either." Mike waved his thin arms into the air with visible irritation. "You have to ask him a question."

"Mike!" Danita shouted, her short afro puff shaking as she stood. "You shouldn't encourage such nonsense." But many of the kids sneered at Danita and motioned for her to sit down. She did, but seemed put out. "It's ridiculous."

Brandon didn't appear to mind as he scrunched up his face, presumably thinking.

Nearby girls watched him with dreamy attention. Jonah shook his head. Even with his face screwed up, the girls thought Brandon was so handsome. Jonah wanted to gag.

"I got one," Brandon said.

Mike held out his slender right hand and patted the palm. "Pay first." Jonah stared at Mike as if he'd grown a second head. His buddy winked. "Don't worry."

Jonah wasn't worried; he was irritated. Mike had goaded him into using his ability on a tenth-grade girl. Despite all assurances, the little demonstration soon spread around the school like an internet virus. He expected the same to happen with this demonstration.

Brandon made a big show of opening his wallet and pulling out a crisp, five-dollar bill from a large wad of cash.

Mike scanned the immediate area for an adult, then he slid the money into his neat, tan pants. "Okay. Jonah's ready. Ask your question."

Brandon hooked a thumb at his friend Drew, who hovered in the background. "Does he like April?"

Danita frowned at Mike but she also couldn't hide her interest in anything that concerned Jonah. Lorraine let out a squeal of excitement and sat forward, more than eager to hear the answer. The large group of kids crowded closer to witness the show.

Jonah decided not to punch Mike and instead, put all thoughts out of his mind and focused on Drew. As a half-Reaper, Jonah could read the aura that people's emotions projected. It was how he determined the first student had lied. That use of his ability had also spawned rumors, causing some kids to consider him freakish, but most appeared pretty cool with the whole idea.

At least Lorraine, Rodney, and Anthony didn't seem to mind. Like Jonah, they were also members of the disbanded Teen Center Practice Club. They were coincidentally around a few times when strange things happened to Jonah. That collective experience created a bond among the four club members, one that the other kids didn't share.

However, Danita wasn't a club member and she often voiced her doubts about his ability clearly. Jonah avoided her glare and focused on Drew, doing it purely for show. In truth, he didn't need to hear the answer nor scan the boy's emotions again.

Each time Drew glanced at Lorraine, Jonah sensed the boy's intensifying interest. But Drew would never let Lorraine know that, not with Rodney around.

"Yeah," Drew answered. "I do like her." He tried to smile. "She's not bad." A few girls whispered to each other, ensuring the comment would reach April's ears at warp speed. The rest of the kids waited to hear Jonah's verdict.

He gave Mike a scathing look because Drew wouldn't like the answer. The other kid who played this little game didn't like what he had to say. Convinced he was lying about his ability, she turned angry when he caught her in a lie.

"Well? Is he lying?" Brandon asked.

Without taking his eyes off his lunch, Jonah muttered, "He's lying."

The crowd erupted in catcalls and jeers. Brandon pounded his friend's shoulder but Drew appeared mortified. Jonah met the boy's anguished expression. *Wait for it*, he told himself.

Like clockwork, Drew's reaction turned to anger. "You're the only one lying!"

"He busted you." Brandon laughed even harder. "Who do you like?"

Drew's pudgy, caramel-colored face darkened with embarrassment. "I told you." He thrust his hand toward Mike. "Brandon wants his money back."

"No refunds." Mike crossed his arms and stood his ground.

Brandon wouldn't let it go and slid an arm around Drew's shoulders. "Who do you like, Danita?"

Danita gasped and Drew grew more embarrassed and angrier. When their gazes met again, Jonah thought he saw pleading in Drew's frantic expression.

"Can you tell?" Brandon asked, catching the brief glance between the boys.

An African-accented voice called out, "He doesn't read minds." The speaker's voice sounded muffled, like the person spoke through a filter. When the crowd parted, Jonah understood why. A tall, thin girl in a niqab approached the table. The veil that made her headscarf into a niqab was a black, mesh fabric that draped over her face, letting only her eyes show.

Murmurs broke out as she came to a stop only a foot from the table, clasping her coffee-colored hands together. "He senses the emotions of other people." She turned her covered head, speaking to Drew. "So it's not a good idea to get too emotional around him."

Jonah's insides went cold. It was one thing for people to think he was a little strange or for Brandon to pick on him. But to hear someone explain how his ability worked was something else altogether. Jonah caught the narrowed look Brandon gave him. The boy was a snob and a bully, but Jonah had to remind himself that Brandon wasn't stupid.

Last summer, Brandon and his friend, Antwan, had spied on Jonah at the request of a rogue GBI agent. Antwan caught Jonah phasing—moving from one location to the next in the blink of an eye. The Alliance, a secret coalition of human and supernatural beings that governed what people like Jonah could or should do, had to intervene.

There were Alliance members called Memory Charmers, who modified the boys' memories as a safety precaution. As a result, Brandon and Antwan were left with a one-hour gap in their respective memories. And of course, they became even more suspicious of Jonah. This girl had just given Brandon another piece of that puzzle.

Drew's face darkened to a shade of purple as he muttered, "Mind your own business!" Brandon, looking uncharacteristically cautious, gripped his friend's shoulder. But Drew shrugged him off. "It's not Halloween yet."

A few people laughed but most hissed.

"Hey!" Mike shouted as he thumped the yellow Tolerance Club ribbon pinned on his chest. "We don't allow intolerance or bullying around here."

Jonah wanted to slump in his chair because if this went any further, someone would want the real answer, and he didn't want to go there. Lorraine and Rodney had enough issues already. One moment, they couldn't get enough of each other. Then, the very next day, they would argue or pretend the other didn't exist. Rodney had already cast suspicious glares at Drew.

That's when something unexpected happened. Drew let out a yelp when an invisible force yanked his feet from under him. He landed on his back with a painful thump. People gaped at the boy and cast glances at the students closest to him. But Jonah knew better, having detected the crackle of magic in the air.

The mysterious girl's left hand fluttered slightly at her side just before Drew fell. *She had to be magical,* Jonah decided.

Although Brandon, too, glared at the girl, he seemed reluctant to say anything.

Her eyes remained fixed on Jonah as she crossed her arms. "I expected more from the son of Isaiah. You're supposed to be The One."

Jonah rose to his feet. "Who are you?"

The girl's intense eyes bore into his. "You never answered the question. Who does Drew like? Surely you can sense the *emotion* coming from him."

Drew's eyes widened as he scrambled to his feet and shoved his way through the crowd. Brandon chased after him.

The mysterious girl watched them leave, her own shoulders shaking with quiet laughter. "Pathetic." She whirled back to Jonah. "And you, playing parlor tricks."

Jonah stared at the girl in confusion. *Palm readers and parlor tricks?* Why were people mentioning those things? His parents, both dead now, worked as archeologists. His uncle was a newspaper publisher and his Aunt Imma, a very religious woman, was a hairdresser and wouldn't go near anything supernatural–or *Satanic*, as she often referred to it.

He pointed at the girl's left hand and whispered, "You're one to talk after what you did."

"Touché." The girl inclined her head before she turned and slipped through the gawking crowd of students.

Mike, who had watched the entire disaster in visible astonishment, stirred and leaned close. "Jonah, was she…"

Jonah nodded. "Do you know her?" Seeing Danita trying to fend off Anthony and listen to their conversation, he moved to the trash bin to throw out his tray.

Mike followed. "I haven't seen her around. She would stick out. The other Muslim girls don't cover their faces."

Mike scanned the students in the Commons. "Maybe she's really conservative."

"No." Jonah surprised himself with how sure he sounded. "She didn't want me to see her face."

"Oh." Mike's eyes narrowed as he watched Jonah. "Yeah. It's always about you!"

Jonah would have argued but just then, a small, anxious-looking, ninth-grade girl stepped beside the table.

Mike waved her away. "We're closed for business."

"Mike!" Danita objected as she smacked his arm. "Be nice."

Mike's shoulders slumped. "Sorry. Jonah has to get to class."

The girl eyed Jonah for a moment, clutching a folded bill in her right hand. Jonah opened his mouth to ask if he could help her when the amulet she wore sparkled in the sunlight. It was an ankh with a brilliant, green stone embedded in the circle.

The girl jumped at the same time a cold sensation ran down his back. It felt like someone had just opened a door to the chilly outside air. Spinning around, for a fraction of a second, he thought he saw the form of a boy. When he blinked, however, the effect vanished.

Jonah would have thought the boy was just a reflection in the window if not for the cold chill. When he turned back to ask the girl, he caught a glimpse of her running out of the Commons. *That was odd.*

Danita huffed and picked up her books. "Didn't you recognize her, Jonah?"

"No. Should I have?"

"She's Latrell's little sister. You know, the boy who killed himself? You volunteered the Tolerance Club to help at his vigil."

"Yeah," Jonah said. He recalled hearing that Latrell had a little sister. "I didn't realize she was in our grade." His face warmed.

Anthony, still trying to impress Danita, blurted out, "Everyone knew that."

Jonah wanted to punch the boy.

"I'll talk to her," Danita offered, "and tell her not to waste her time on supernatural nonsense." She aimed a sad glare at Mike, who was too busy rooting around in his book bag to notice. Peeved, Danita hurried out of the Commons, taking Anthony in her wake. Lorraine and Rodney trailed behind them.

Once Jonah was sure no adults were watching, he punched his buddy in the upper arm. "I don't like playing the human lie detector."

Mike winced as he rubbed his bicep. "That hurt."

"Good."

Mike balled his hand into a fist, then decided against punching back.

Jonah pulled his book bag over a shoulder and headed for the stairs. "Did you see what just happened with that ninth-grader? Something scared her away."

"Yeah, I did," Mike said, falling into step with him.

"No, I meant something supernatural."

"Jonah, have you had any dream-walks lately?"

The question caught Jonah off guard and he paused at the bottom of the stairs.

Except for Deyanira's warning, his sleep had been undisturbed since before school had started. He decided not to mention the evil Reaper to Mike.

"No. Everything's cool. Why?"

"That girl in the niqab," Mike began as he climbed up the steps. "She worried you."

"Well, yeah. She called me *Son of Isaiah*." Jonah couldn't miss the anxious face Mike pulled. "I didn't tell anyone about that, not even my godfather. So how could she know that name?"

"You're right. But now you're saying there was someone else in the Commons?"

"There was."

"I don't doubt you," Mike added. "I just hoped for more time before strange things started happening."

Jonah could sympathize. His own life had been turned upside-down with the death of his parents two summers ago; not to mention everything else that happened. His first school year in Mount Vernon was quiet and ordinary.

Naturally, Jonah hoped this school year would also pass by with just the regular, mortal teenager stuff.

"Maybe the year will be quiet." Mike tried to make his voice sound hopeful. He spotted a tall boy beckoning him from the doorway of a classroom. "Oops. I'm late. See you later."

As Jonah watched his super busy friend hustling off, he too wished this school year would remain quiet, but sincerely doubted that would happen.

CHAPTER FOUR
THE TOKEN

Lorraine cornered Jonah at the end of the school day. She wanted the club members to wear bright orange ribbons complete with pumpkin heads at Latrell's vigil.

"Not only will it make a more visible statement than our regular yellow ribbons," she concluded, "but Halloween is in just four weeks. So it's seasonal too."

Lorraine beamed at Jonah and held up a sample ribbon. "Rodney designed the pumpkin heads. Each one is unique." She remained quiet and waited for his decision.

Jonah appreciated the amount of work–as well as Lorraine's barely contained enthusiasm. "Sure, why not?" he said.

Lorraine gave him a quick hug. "We'll bring them to the vigil tonight."

With the last bit of business done, Jonah headed out to his bike, his mind filled with homework, club schedules, and other things. He didn't pay attention when he dropped his book bag beside his bike as he'd done many times. Reaching out to unlock the chain, a shadow fell over him. The next moment, a large boy in a hoodie grabbed his book bag and ran.

"Hey!" Jonah shouted.

The boy sprinted across the sloping, grass hill and toward the outside patios where students ate lunch during school hours. Jonah shot off after him, trying hard to swallow the fact that someone stole his book bag! Though frayed and smudged, the bag was also one of the few things that remained from his old house in Virginia. Everything else had burned to the ground.

Jonah's rage at the boy propelled him forward and he gained on the thief despite being shorter. But as the boy reached the tall spruces screening the south side of the patio area, he dived into the thicket of bushes and phased.

"No! Wait!" Jonah shouted. He reached the spot where the boy disappeared and without stopping to think about his actions, he too, phased.

When he inhaled the mist of the aether, he recalled his training and focused. Soon, he felt a pinpoint of heat, the faint trail left behind by every person who phased through the supernatural realm. He concentrated on that, willing his mind to go in that direction.

The regular world snapped into existence around Jonah as he reappeared in an empty parking lot. He did it! He actually followed someone through a phase on his own. The reality of the situation caught up with him and Jonah paid closer attention to his surroundings.

The mysterious guy was several yards away. He still had Jonah's book bag slung over one shoulder as he headed for a pimped-out, former cop car.

"Hey," Jonah called out.

The guy froze for a second, then he sprinted for the car. Instead of getting inside and speeding away, the guy phased just short of the vehicle.

Jonah charged after him, pursuing the guy into a phase once again. In the aether, he felt the pinpoint of heat and willed himself to follow it. When the mortal world appeared around him again, Jonah was in for a shock: he was standing in his parents' hideaway.

The entire place, a lower, brick courtyard, and upper, smaller courtyard garden, once belonged to his parents. Back when they were still alive, they came here to get away and meditate. Now gone, they left the place to Jonah.

Jonah stood in the main courtyard. Before he overcame his shock, the hairs on the back of his neck bristled. A second later, the guy grabbed him from behind and pulled him into a bear hug.

"Let me go, perv!" Jonah shouted.

The guy laughed, his voice muffled by the face mask. "Perv? That's nice," he said in an amused tone. "You get too distracted, little man."

Jonah's eyes widened and he twisted around. "Kevin! What are you doing here?"

Kevin threw back his hood and yanked off his knitted face mask. The boy's deep brown eyes squinted in genuine amusement. "Why'd you call me a perv?"

"I..." Jonah slugged the Fallen Reaper in the chest. "You stole my book bag."

Kevin didn't budge from the punch. He was almost six feet tall and very muscular. But he frowned and rub the spot where Jonah hit him. When Jonah reared back for a second punch, he held up the book bag as a shield. "Just wanted to see if you could follow me through a phase, so cool it."

"You know I can." Jonah snatched the bag from Kevin and dropped it at his feet. "Rex told you." His irritation and surprise changed to a grudging happiness at having Kevin there. "Are you back?"

Kevin hunched his big shoulders and shoved his hands into his pockets. "No. Mandara is still pissed with me."

Jonah's annoyance flared at the mention of the Alliance's lead Fallen Reaper's name. "If Mandara is still mad, then how did you get here?"

"I asked Marcus if I could check up on you."

"My godfather said yes?"

Kevin nodded. "He's covering for me, but I have to get back to my assignment. That reminds me." Kevin pointed to the short row of brick steps that led to the upper courtyard. "There's something I want to show you."

Jonah only hesitated a moment before mounting the steps to the smaller, upper courtyard. An uneven, brick-covered path led from the stairway straight to the far side, disappearing into the surrounding forest. A second path bisected the first before vanishing into the trees.   A sculptured rhododendron bush in a large, brick planter was placed at the center of this area.

Off to the right was an alcove, and that's where he spotted the shiny, brown box resting on the alcove's bench. He hurried over and discovered the box had a genetic lock.

It was just like the one on the birthday cylinder his father had left him.

"It's not my birthday," Jonah said.

"I know that," Kevin groaned. "Your mom's old office at HQ is being cleared out. Marcus had her stuff boxed up for you. But he thought you might want this now."

Jonah's hands trembled as he lifted the box. Sitting down, he rested it on his lap. This close, he noted the script that covered the surface, the same script as on Robert's archive box. He touched the small button, which he assumed was keyed for him. Sure enough, the symbol glowed and the genetic lock clicked.

When Jonah stared at the box without moving, Kevin asked, "Are you going to open it?"

"Yeah. It's just that, well, it's been locked since…"

"You don't have to look."

"But I want to." And Jonah opened the lid. The first thing he saw was a 4x6 color photograph. He reached inside to pick it up and realized it was the front of a small photo album. Jonah suspected, without opening it, that it contained his mother's photos of her family. These were the pictures she never displayed at home.

Jonah opened the album. The first picture was of his mother, father, and a small baby boy. They were all standing in front of a wooden bench with a brick wall behind them. He recognized the place. They had taken the picture right here in the hideaway. He wondered if that was the same time when they put his baby handprint on the alcove wall. At once, the tender memories caused tears to sting his eyes.

Kevin sat down beside him and rested his chin on Jonah's shoulder, pressing their cheeks together. "You'll be all right."

Jonah nodded, letting Kevin's physical touch strengthen him. He wiped his eyes and turned to the next photo. This one featured two young girls and a young boy. They looked just like Robert and Lynn. But Kevin pointed to the small date written in the bottom corner.

"That's your mom and uncle and–"

"My Aunt Ruby."

Jonah's stomach lurched and he made a small sound in the back of his throat. Every time he thought about her or saw a picture of his Aunt Ruby, fear prickled his insides.

Jonah flipped to the next photo, glad to get to other relatives, including his grandparents on his mom's side. The last picture was a very recent one of his mom and Uncle James. They must have taken it just before his mom disappeared with his dad. Did she come here to see her family before that trip?

Kevin reached into the box and pulled out a small, sealed, manila envelope. Jonah hadn't noticed it beneath the photo album. He took it, being careful not to rip the paper, and opened it. Several pictures spilled out. He caught them, wondering why his mom would seal them up instead of putting them inside the photo album with the others.

Jonah gasped when he turned over the first photo. It was of Aunt Ruby. Her hair, a tangle of long curls sticking out in all directions, reminded Jonah of Medusa. She also wore a brown shawl over her shoulders and large, beaded earrings. Jonah could imagine the things clinking and clanking every time she moved her head.

His aunt and uncle had five kids in all, which were neatly arrayed around them. They looked like Jonah and his twin cousins. While gazing at the pictures, Jonah realized that his aunt never smiled. Instead, she smirked at the camera.

The final picture was of a small storefront with a strange, T-shaped doorway and a large, wooden ankh positioned above the door. The words, *Ankh of Life*, glowed in bright, neon letters across the left front window. Although the photo was black and white, Jonah could easily imagine garish colors on the letters.

He gazed at the picture, trying to decide if it were a bookstore or… she was a palm reader. That's when he spotted a neon palm in the lower right corner of the right front window.

The last things in the box were a folded note and three pieces of lacquered wood. He held those up. Viewed together, they displayed a beautifully drawn map. Seven locations of different terrains including a plateau, a forest, a valley, hilly land, and a meadow, were marked with a detailed drawing of stars.

Jonah grinned. "It's a triptych."

"A what?" Kevin frowned.

"A triptych. You know, a piece of art divided into three separate parts. Together, they make one picture or scene."

Kevin reached out to run a finger along the surface of one piece.

"This is cool," Jonah said, placing them inside the box, "but why did my mom lock them up?"

Kevin shrugged and didn't offer an opinion.

Jonah decided to show the triptych to Mike later. That brought him to the final object in the box, the note. He opened it and read.

I'm sorry I couldn't stop Ruby before she hurt others. Don't blame yourself for what happened to her and Jonah. There's no way any of us could have known. Isaiah's furious and won't let you take Jonah back to Mount Vernon, but at least he's safe now and will grow up in peace. – S

A shudder went through Jonah, but he didn't know why. Who was S? Why had his dad been angry? Whatever the cause, Jonah wasn't surprised it had to do with Aunt Ruby.

Kevin nudged him. "You all right?"

"Yeah." Jonah slid the pictures into the envelope. He didn't blame his mom for not placing them in the album. He didn't want to see them again and he put the envelope and the note back inside the box. As soon as he closed the lid, the locks clicked into place.

Kevin settled his chin on Jonah's shoulder again and ran his fingers over the designs on the box's lid, remaining quiet.

Jonah welcomed the closeness with the young Fallen Reaper. But he could tell that Kevin was thinking about something. He nudged the older boy.

In response, Kevin pulled a small, wooden token from his pocket. "Here."

Jonah took the token. "Is this…"

"Yep. It's a way to call for help. Trueblood made that. We all have one. That's yours. We're working on something else, but it's top secret for now. Hold the token tightly in your hand," Kevin said. Jonah did, closing his fist around the object. "Then say or whisper 'Help' and it sends an alert to all the others with enchanted tokens."

The implications of the token registered on Jonah and he met Kevin's gaze. "You think something's gonna happen?" He feared Kevin would confirm his own feelings. First, Deyanira's warning, then learning about his aunt being released, and now this box with a note about his dad being angry over something that happened. "You do, don't you?"

Kevin shrugged. "Just being careful. Marcus, Rex, and Trueblood are traveling to the Afterworld to talk to the rebels. Mandara actually suggested they represent the Council."

"He wants Marcus out of the way," Jonah said, hating the man he had never met.

"We know." Kevin tapped Jonah's token-holding fist. "That's why you have that."

Jonah swallowed, trying to hold onto the brief spike of happiness. But it wasn't working because he knew Kevin would leave within minutes. He rose from the bench, gripping the box in both hands.

Kevin seemed to sense his disappointment. The Fallen Reaper remained seated but reached out to toy with the zipper on Jonah's jacket while staring at him in the eyes. "You okay? Everything all right?"

"Yeah. Why wouldn't it be?" Jonah caught himself because he didn't have to lie to Kevin about anything. He told the older boy all about Deyanira's warning and the weirdness at lunch with the mysterious girl.

Kevin gnashed his teeth together as he listened. His voice was tight when he said, "Deyanira could be playing with you. And that girl could have guessed about your abilities."

"No." He knew Kevin was just trying to cheer him up, and he didn't want that. "Tell me the truth."

"Well, why would Deyanira warn you? She hates you, remember? And the girl didn't set off your Death Sense. Just be careful." He tapped Jonah's hand again. "You have the token if you need more help."

Jonah nodded. "I'll take it with me tonight, to the vigil."

Kevin scowled and shot to his feet when he heard that. "I don't think you should go to the vigil."

"No choice. I'm representing my club tonight."

"Let the other kids do it."

"Why?"

"Because I can't be there to protect you, that's why."

Jonah gulped, moved by the pain in the boy's voice. "Kevin... I... you know, trouble finds me no matter what I do."

Kevin snorted. "That's the truth." But his hunched shoulders didn't relax.

Jonah hefted the box in one hand and opened his other palm to show Kevin the token. "Like you said, I'll have this in case anything happens. That's why you gave it to me." His words didn't reassure Kevin. Jonah could still sense the boy's tension. Something had him spooked. Why else would he risk getting in more trouble with his boss? "Why didn't you call me or text?"

"They stuck me in places where I couldn't use my phone." Kevin's hands balled into fists. "Mandara does it on purpose, to keep me away from you." He let out a sigh. "Watch out for his spy."

Jonah had all but forgotten the Alliance sent someone else to keep an eye on him. "Do you know who it is?"

Kevin scowled. "Marcus won't tell me."

Jonah didn't trust himself to respond because of the looming goodbye.

Kevin pulled him into a weak headlock and ruffled his picky afro. "Well, be careful, little man."

"I will," Jonah said, pulling free. He and Kevin walked down to the main courtyard in a comfortable silence.

Once there, Kevin lifted the book bag and held it so Jonah could slip the straps over his shoulder. When he did, Kevin turned him around and smirked. "Now you look like a regular nerd." He narrowed his eyes. "Wow. You've grown too."

Jonah grinned. "Oh, you noticed?"

"It's about time. I'll have to stop calling you *little man*."

Jonah toyed with the box, slightly nervous but willing to go further. "I thought I would always be your little man?" He glanced up into Kevin's face.

The young Fallen Reaper grinned. "Yeah, I guess so." He toyed with the strap on Jonah's book bag, lingering.

Jonah's heart beat faster as he gripped Kevin's hand and slid his fingers between the boy's larger ones.

Kevin wiggled his hand. "Jonah, I gotta go." He pulled his hand free of Jonah's, stepped back, and, as if mustering all of his courage, darted forward and kissed Jonah.

The first time was quick, the second longer. Jonah had never felt anything so wonderful. It was better than anything he could have imagined.

He hated it when Kevin pulled away. "I'll be back soon."

"Okay," Jonah whispered as Kevin phased. He closed his eyes, savoring the moment and the sensation of his first real kiss.

CHAPTER FIVE
THE VIGIL

The Tolerance Club had a table from which members could hand vigil attendees candles that were already lit. Jonah arrived later than he intended, but was proud to see his crew already taking care of business.

Sidling up to the table where Lorraine, Danita, and Anthony worked, he clipped on the new, pumpkin-head ribbon. "Everything going okay?"

"Yes," Lorraine answered. "Oh, Mike and his friend are passing out candles at the other entrance."

Jonah glanced at Danita, thinking she would know Mike's friend. She and Mike had grown up together on Morningside Drive. But Danita gazed back at him with a curious expression, like she was gauging his reaction to the news. Jonah didn't get that.

To avoid Danita's piercing gaze, he turned and peered through the gathering crowd, hoping to spot Mike.

Anthony cleared his throat. "I think we should walk through the crowd and hand out club pamphlets." Despite being his usual, take-charge self, he courteously waited for Jonah's decision.

"Sounds like a good idea," Jonah said.

Growing more curious by the second, Jonah scooped up a handful of pamphlets and skirted the edges of the gathering crowd. Anthony moved in the opposite direction. Suspicions blossomed in Jonah's mind about Mike as he walked. Aside from eating lunch together at school and their mutual club duties, he and Mike weren't hanging out as often anymore. In fact, they hadn't been to a movie together since school started.

With Kevin popping in and kissing him, the usual vivid awareness of being alone was absent. So why did he feel so moody now when he was practically walking on air after Kevin's visit?

His negative emotions spiked, forcing him to stop in his tracks. In addition, his Death Sense, the ability to detect mortal danger to himself or his loved ones, also prodded him with a painful twinge.

A raised conversation alerted Jonah that the crowd had grown thick around him. After handing out a few pamphlets, he tried to move to a more open area but bumped into another kid.

"Watch it," the boy warned. He turned and, seeing Jonah, added, "Oh. I didn't realize it was you."

Jonah blinked at the kid's surly tone. He also recognized the boy as the one who waved to Mike in the hallway at school. "You know me?"

Before the boy could answer, Mike slipped through the crowd to stand right beside him. "Jonah, this is my friend, Patrick."

Jonah remembered him from somewhere else now. "Aren't you in my Physical Science class?"

"Yeah." Patrick reached out to shake hands without any enthusiasm. When he did, his light coat slid up, exposing blue and yellow wristbands.

Jonah glanced at Mike's wrist, only to find the same colored bands there. A cool realization settled in Jonah's gut. The reason for Mike's absences and frequent tardiness to club events instantly crystallized. Mike had found a boyfriend. Jonah's new, turbulent emotions settled on a burgeoning dislike toward Patrick. He reached up to rub his aching forehead.

Mike stepped closer. "Jonah? We need to talk."

"I have to get back to the table," Jonah lied, angrily pushing his way through the crowd before Mike could say anything else. The more he thought about it, the more enraged he became.

In between the flares of his emotions, he wondered at the sudden mood change. This feeling of irritability and fury with his friend and the world was… odd. Still, seeing Mike with someone else didn't help matters one bit.

Rodney dated Lorraine. Anthony was vying for Danita. And now Mike and Patrick? It reminded Jonah how alone he was, even in the middle of a stupid crowd! No, he corrected himself, he and Kevin were moving forward. *So why am I pissed?*

In his rush to get away, he stumbled in the wrong direction, and was now headed toward the back of the field. When his Death Sense suddenly spiked, it only added a severe headache to his roiling emotions and Jonah clutched his head as he stifled a loud groan. Turning on the spot, he lifted up on his toes to see over and around the nearby people. It felt like a fiend was deliberately drilling spikes of tortuous pain into his skull. He thought of Kevin's warning and wondered if Mandara's spy could have been the reason for it.

That's when he saw her. A lone woman in a long, traveler's cloak stood near the stone dugout. The hood was drawn forward over her head, hiding her face in the shadow.

The crowd erupted with applause at something the vigil sponsors said. Jonah ignored the ensuing speeches and pushed through the press of people. By the time he stepped clear, the woman had vanished, along with some of the pressure on his mind. He searched around but didn't see her anywhere.

But how? he wondered, kneeling on the spot where the woman was standing. *Was she the reason for his emotional spikes?* Without warning, a sudden vision of a quiet train yard exploded in his mind. Jonah stifled another moan and grasped his head, knowing that's where the woman had gone.

Again, the question of *how* returned when it occurred to him that phasing was a Fallen Reaper power. But it wasn't the only way for supernatural beings to travel. Mages used vortices. Wraiths, in their gaseous form, could fly away on the air. There were also the portals and the Seeker's compass.

Jonah didn't know how the woman did it, but one thing was clear. She wanted him to follow her.

The raising of the candles surprised Jonah. With everyone's attention focused on the event, he had the perfect opportunity to get away. Throwing caution to the wind, he ducked behind the dugout and phased.

*

Even though Jonah wasn't following someone who had recently phased, he barely sensed the faint trail of magic in the aether. Rex, a friendly Fallen Reaper working with Jonah's godfather, never told him about that. Jonah filed it away, intending to mention it to the Fallen Reaper later. Right now, he concentrated on the magic, just as he did with Kevin's heat trail, and the real world exploded into view around him.

He was in a train yard, exactly as it appeared in the vision. Jonah whirled around, expecting an attack. When nothing happened, he took a moment to catch his breath.

The only sounds were the rattle of a train moving along tracks somewhere out of sight and the background drone of trucks rumbling on the distant overpass. Many of the rusted rail cars in this section sported broken wheels. It was more like a train junkyard.

His irritation peaked and he said, "I know you're here."

Something crashed against the side of a nearby train car. Jonah jumped at the sound and reached inside his pocket to grip the token Kevin had given him.

"Jonah Blackstone?" a woman's voice echoed, making it hard to pinpoint. But Jonah guessed it came from his left.

"Jonah?" This time, it was much closer and came from his right.

As he turned, trying to spot the slippery woman, he felt a familiar pressure. She was using a vortex to jump from one place to another around him while keeping out of sight. Her toying actions only compounded his frustration. "What do you want?"

"What do *I* want?" The voice was taunting. "You followed me. Brave, aren't you?"

Jonah felt her presence behind him as he pulled the token free of his pocket, preparing to activate it before she rushed past in a blur, brushing against his shoulder without attacking him.

The woman stopped at the far end of a boxcar and faced him. She was little more than a tall shadow but she made Jonah's Death Sense spike. The woman meant him harm, but not right now. He sensed mostly intense hate.

"I knew your father, young man," the woman continued, sounding like someone Jonah should have known but failed to place. "Despite all his faults, Isaiah was a powerful Fallen Reaper. He would have been proud to see his son using his abilities so adeptly."

Jonah took two steps closer toward her despite the danger. "Who are you?"

The woman laughed, sending a chill down Jonah's spine. Her heavy voice turned thoughtful in a mocking way. "Or perhaps you're more like your mom. Poor, poor Janice! Now she–" The stranger stopped and let out a low laugh. "I see your friends have arrived."

Jonah detected the telltale pressure at the same time a light flared behind him and a vortex opened. To his surprise, four huge men in black uniforms charged out, rushing into the train yard. Two flew by a stunned Jonah as they hurtled toward the woman.

Instead of opening a vortex, the woman wove her hands through the air before she vanished in an outpouring of dark, thick vapor. Jonah strained to catch a glimpse of her face in the reflected light from the spell, but it was useless.

The large men charged to the spot where the woman disappeared and studied handheld devices that glowed with a pulsing, eerie, orange color. Jonah wondered if the devices could detect magic.

A third guard remained by the open vortex with a young mage; while the fourth guy was standing right beside Jonah, regarding him with undisguised curiosity.

This close, Jonah needed to crane his neck back to see the man's brown face. All the men were well over seven feet tall and their muscled upper bodies were almost out of proportion with their lower halves. Each held an advanced club weapon in two-handed grips. Power sizzled along the length of the weapons, which made the hair on the back of Jonah's neck stand on end.

The man beside Jonah wore a black, military-style vest with the Alliance symbol on the left breast pocket. Below that were two short, horizontal, gold bars. Jonah recognized the commanding aura about the man as he touched a button on the side of his helmet.

"We have him, sir. The enemy fled upon our approach." He listened to a response Jonah couldn't hear. Then he clamped a large, gloved hand on Jonah's shoulder. "Come along."

Jonah didn't resist, but he gulped as he asked, "Who are you?"

The man blinked in surprise. "I'm the captain of the Alliance Guards."

Oh no, Jonah thought. Although he never knew anything about the Alliance Guards, he imagined their being here now couldn't be a good thing.

The Guard Captain nodded. "There's a Council member waiting to have a word with you."

This is it, Jonah thought. Visions of the intimidating mage, Rubio, waiting on the other side of the vortex, formed in Jonah's mind. Or worse, what if the perpetually mean-spirited Mandara finally showed up?

With those thoughts in mind, he let the Guard Captain lead him to the vortex. Jonah spared a glance at the young mage who produced the magical opening. The boy couldn't have been any older than Robert and Lynn. It amazed Jonah someone so young could already be an Alliance mage. And then he noticed the lack of an Alliance symbol on the boy's royal blue tunic. But he had to have been powerful and talented just to open and maintain a vortex like this one.

Maybe he's a trainee?

The boy didn't acknowledge Jonah but kept his chin up and his eyes forward with an important air about him.

The Guard Captain gestured at the magical opening. "After you, sir."

Jonah glanced back at the guard, screwed up his nerves, and cautiously entered the vortex.

CHAPTER SIX
THE HONORABLE COUNCIL MEMBER

Traveling through a vortex differed from phasing. For one thing, it took several more seconds because you had to walk or run to the next location. For another, the vapor that obscured your destination clung tenaciously to the body almost like cobwebs. And the vapory mist inside a vortex always managed to come into contact with every part of your body, despite the clothes you wore.

Jonah shivered, although he wasn't cold. Maybe he was biased, but he preferred phasing. Within seconds, the mist parted and he stepped into the Teen Center's attic clubhouse. Jonah paused, causing the huge Guard Captain to bump into him.

"Sorry," Jonah said, moving further into the familiar space.

In quick order, the other three guards stepped through, followed by the young mage, who closed the vortex.

The Teen Center, a renovated, old, Southern mansion with a commanding view of the hilly surrounding neighborhoods, was a popular destination for young people from all over the county.

Per an agreement with the administration, Jonah and his cousins were allowed to use the attic as their base of operation. It comprised two areas. The area to the right, the Summit, contained all the computers and monitors his cousins used to write their blog and maintain the center's website. Stray papers and computer parts littered the top of a smaller worktable, situated just beyond the computers. It was where the twins composed their blog.

On the left side of the attic was an old, slightly sunken sofa, two mismatched armchairs that faced the sofa, and a battered, brown steamer trunk in between. This is where the club regularly met.

Jonah's hopes rose when he saw a tall man in the blue tunic of an adult Alliance Mage. Slowly releasing the breath he held, Jonah felt relieved. He didn't have to face Rubio nor the mysterious Mandara, a Fallen Reaper who would have worn a Reaper's long coat. But that didn't mean he wasn't in big trouble.

The mage talked with an aide, keeping his back toward Jonah. His shoulder-length dreads bobbed as he emphasized something. When the conversation ended, the Alliance member turned and Jonah received a pleasant surprise.

The mage was Native American and his chiseled facial features looked very familiar. The man wore a genuine expression of relief as he bounded over to Jonah's group.

"Thank the ancestors you're safe!" He extended his right hand. "I'm so glad."

Jonah shook the mage's hand, feeling a little confused.

The mage stood back, taking in Jonah's appearance.

When he didn't introduce himself, the Guard Captain cleared his throat. "This is the Honorable Council Member and Mage, Symon Trueblood."

Trueblood frowned and shook his head, causing his dreads to sway around. "I wouldn't call myself *honorable*."

Jonah's jaw dropped. "Trueblood? You're related to Mage Trueblood? I mean…"

"That's right," the mage said. "Eleanor's my little sister." He spread his arms wide. "Yeah. It's hard to believe a guy as young as me has an adult kid sister." He laughed at his own joke.

The Guard Captain shook his head and the young mage trainee frowned.

Jonah suspected they all had heard that joke before. He grinned, never expecting an Alliance Mage to act like that.

Trueblood folded his arms across his chest and stared at Jonah. "That was a foolish thing to do."

Jonah's shoulders slumped, and he nodded. "Yes, sir, but…"

"But…?" Trueblood raised an eyebrow.

"She didn't attack me."

"True. What if the situation had turned south and she decided to hurt, or, even worse, *abduct* you?"

Jonah gulped because the mage's earlier playfulness was gone. In its place was a deep concern for him. Something worried the mage. Jonah reached inside his pocket and withdrew the token. "Kevin gave me this, in case anything happened. Plus, I can phase and fight."

The Guard Captain grunted in a satisfied way, eyeing Jonah with what looked like an approving gaze.

Plucking the token from Jonah's hand, Trueblood inspected it. "This is my sister's work." He winked at Jonah. "I showed her how to do it."

"Oh, really?"

"Yes." Trueblood dropped the token in Jonah's hand. "It's good to see you learning your powers," the Council member continued, "but following a stranger wasn't a good idea."

"She didn't mean me any harm." Jonah's face warmed at the obvious craziness of the statement. The woman definitely meant him harm. *Just not tonight.*

Trueblood raised a finger. "First, how did you follow her?"

Jonah averted his eyes, unsure of how the mage would take this part. "Well, I… I think she sent me a vision of where I had to go."

The Alliance people stirred. Trueblood rubbed his jaw, frowning as he peered at Jonah.

Jonah refrained from mentioning the woman had also spiked his emotions tonight. Instead, he asked, "Do you know how we follow someone through a phase?" The mage nodded. "When I phased, it was weird, but I could sense her magic trail and I followed it. I didn't need the images she sent."

"I've never heard of a Fallen Reaper who could do that," the mage said, sounding amazed. "That's remarkable, Jonah."

"You think so?" A cautious optimism crept into Jonah's voice. Unlike so many others, who got spooked when they learned of his unique abilities, Trueblood's amazement was genuine.

"Of course. You will do a lot of things no one else can. The Council knows that." Trueblood waved Jonah to the clubhouse section and then into an armchair. The mage sat on the arm of the sofa, trying to affect a relaxed air but failing.

"Tell me. What did she want from you?"

"Nothing. She was showing off and talking about my parents," Jonah confessed. "I never saw her face and…" The sudden sense of dread and worry that rolled off the Alliance mage stopped Jonah mid-sentence. "Do you know who she was?"

Trueblood made a dismissive gesture with his right hand. "She could have been anyone. The important thing is that you're safe."

Once again, Jonah wondered why an Alliance Council member would show up with his guards. "I'm in big trouble, huh?"

Trueblood smiled. "No, not as long as you show better judgment."

Feeling bolder, Jonah asked, "Why did you come, if I'm not in any trouble?"

"Well," Trueblood said, "I had one of those rare free moments in my schedule. So I decided to visit the young man who's been causing our enemies so much anxiety."

Jonah welcomed the cheeriness he heard, but also suspected the mage wasn't telling the truth. Sure, he could imagine Trueblood wanted to see him. In fact, Jonah fully expected the Alliance Council to summon him long before now. He realized they were watching at the field.

"Why are you spying on me? I mean, my godfather does that, and I know the Council sent someone to replace Kevin and keep an eye on me."

Trueblood studied his face but didn't contradict anything he said. "I thought it best if I saw the situation firsthand. And," he added, "you are the Deliverer."

An idea occurred to Jonah. He was the Deliverer, so why couldn't he ask for things? Kevin insisted he shouldn't do that, but for the first time, a Council member, someone besides his godfather, was right in front of him.

"Can Kevin come back?" Jonah asked. "You're on the Council. Couldn't you order Mandara to do it?"

Trueblood let out a roar of laughter but stifled it when Jonah frowned. "You need to learn more about Council politics. You don't order Mandara to do anything! Not unless you're the chairperson. Which I'm not." He chuckled to himself. "That being said, I'll see what I can do."

"Thanks," Jonah replied, somewhat reassured.

The mage sobered and leaned forward, scanning Jonah's face. "You look just like Janice." His smile was rueful.

Jonah blinked. "You knew my mom?"

Genuine amusement lit up Trueblood's face. "We were best friends. Me, her, and Omar."

"Omar?"

"Yeah. We all joined the Alliance at the same time. Janice escaped small town Mount Vernon to attend school in Atlanta. I was just off the reservation, all full of myself, young and stupid. And Omar was thousands of miles away from his home and everyone he knew and loved. We formed our own little mutual support pack." Trueblood's eyes had a gleam in them as if he vividly remembered old adventures. "We also had our share of trouble."

Jonah couldn't believe it. His mom had always been so…what? Could she have been like him and his cousins?

Trueblood seemed to read his thoughts. "Your parents would be proud of you, Jonah."

Jonah met the mage's gaze. "You were friends with my dad too?"

"Yes. He was one of the bravest men I ever met. And he sponsored my membership on the Council."

The sad truth of that statement hit Jonah with a sudden heaviness. "They never had a chance to tell me anything about the Council or…"

"I miss them too," Trueblood said. He pointed at Jonah's chest. "But you carry both your parents inside you. Whatever your father and mother were, so are you, now and forever. Never forget that."

The Guard Captain intoned, "Ashe."

The other guards and the young mage repeated the word in hushed voices.

A surge of pride, history, and belonging swelled Jonah's chest. He sucked in a breath and his lip trembled as he nodded. No one had ever said or done that to him. He wondered if the mage could have cast a spell on him, but suspected otherwise. There was no magic, just an energy more basic and powerful than anything else.

Suddenly, Jonah wanted to ask the mage about so many other things.

Trueblood intervened with, "I bet you're interested in how we followed you, right?"

Jonah hesitated, forcing himself to shift his thoughts to the new topic. "Well, yeah. I guess."

Trueblood snapped his fingers. "It was a location spell."

Jonah had been around Wick long enough to understand how those spells worked. "You needed something of mine. Like…"

"A piece of hair?" Trueblood laughed. "Let's just say not all the hair clippings at the barber shop end up in the trash."

Jonah didn't know how he felt about people keeping pieces of his hair. If the good guys could use it, couldn't the bad guys, too?

"I can guess what you're thinking," Trueblood added. "We made sure you left none of your hair behind. We are always aware of when you get your hair cut." He squinted at Jonah's afro. "Speaking of which…"

"That's okay," Jonah blurted out, causing the mage to smile.

The captain tapped his earpiece and drew Trueblood's attention with a nod.

The mage refocused on Jonah. "We should get you home."

Jonah only had a second to wonder if they would open a vortex to his backyard. Eleanor Trueblood had done that once and it was freakin' cool.

The mage stood and called out to the young trainee, "How late am I for my meeting?"

The boy glanced at his watch. "Ten minutes."

"Excellent." Trueblood grinned at Jonah. "If you're gonna be late, then do it in style." He shook Jonah's hand. The Council member had extraordinary strength in his grip and he didn't release his hold as he said, "I don't want you wandering around all alone in the evenings. That's an order."

Jonah gulped. "Yes, sir."

"Sir?" Trueblood pulled a scandalized expression as he released Jonah's hand. "Don't call me *sir*. Makes me feel old." After an exaggerated shudder, he waved to the young trainee-mage. "Mr. Pledge, have you met Mr. Blackstone?"

The serious boy turned his attention to Jonah and shook his head.

Trueblood smiled. "Well, then, Thomas Pledge meet Jonah Blackstone."

Thomas's nod was formal and quick. Caught off guard, Jonah returned the gesture.

Trueblood frowned at the young man until Thomas strode over and offered to shake Jonah's hand. "Nice to meet you."

"Same," Jonah said. Like Trueblood, Thomas had a strong handshake.

"Mr. Pledge is finishing his trials and will become a full-fledged Alliance mage soon, and," Trueblood stage-whispered to Jonah, "his mom is on the Alliance Council."

Jonah's awe of Thomas instantly went up a notch. He was already on course to be an Alliance member and had a mom on the Council. No wonder the young mage carried himself so seriously.

But Thomas looked rather embarrassed at the sudden attention. He shuffled in place while staring at anything but Trueblood and Jonah.

"You two represent the next generation and should know each other," Trueblood continued. He patted the young mage on the shoulder and motioned toward the space in front of the attic window.

Thomas seemed relieved to do his job. He moved to the window and reopened the vortex with a practiced wave of his hand.

Jonah took a step toward the opening but the Guard Captain stopped him.

Mage Trueblood waved goodbye and then turned to the vortex and said to Thomas, "You think I have enough time to put a war stripe on my face? You know how Mandara hates that."

Thomas let out a moan and shook his head. "No, sir." Trueblood laughed as he stepped through. The Guard Captain removed his helmet and outer vest and handed those to the other guards. They exited through the opening next.

Thomas nodded to the captain and then, for a moment, he locked gazes with Jonah before stepping through and closing the magical opening.

Once they exited, the captain detached his weapon from its holder. He touched a button on the side, and it collapsed into a foot-long, black, octagonal cylinder. He reattached that to his belt and nodded toward the attic steps. "After you, sir."

At first, Jonah didn't like the large guard escorting him through the Teen Center. But he understood why the man got rid of his helmet and vest. Without them, he looked less like he was wearing a uniform.

Still, his size drew everyone's attention and Jonah hated that because it also made him the center of attention. However, the upside of the situation presented itself when Brandon and Antwan moved to block his path.

Brandon folded his arms. "What's up, freak?"

Jonah didn't hesitate to step toward the boy who didn't have the height advantage anymore. Before he could say a word, the Guard Captain pulled him back and planted himself in front of Brandon.

"Is there a problem here?" The captain's deep voice rolled across Brandon.

The bully stumbled backward while staring up at the imposing man. "Um, no." He hurried off with Antwan.

The Guard Captain snorted and motioned Jonah down the east wing and toward the side exit.

"You didn't seem afraid of that boy." The Guard Captain kept his eyes on the other kids as they neared the exit. "Admirable."

"I wasn't afraid of him." Jonah let his anger seep into his voice.

The captain nodded. "Good. It's important to stand up for yourself."

Jonah noted the tone of pride in the man's voice. He glanced sideways at the guard. "Do you think I made a mistake tonight?"

"You were brave, that's for sure," the captain didn't hesitate to reply. "But always remember to have a second person with you, to watch your back."

Jonah nodded, taking the man's advice to heart. They reached the side exit to the Teen Center, and a large, black SUV was parked at the curb outside. The captain sprang forward to open the back passenger door.

Jonah paused before getting in. "My bike's still at the ball field."

The captain smiled. "It's in the back of the truck."

"Oh," Jonah said, looking stunned as he got in.

The captain slid into the front passenger seat and they started off. Jonah sat in silence, brooding about the sudden upsurge in his protection. He'd never seen these types of guards before. Even when Agent Hunter was in Mount Vernon, Jonah never had an escort.

What was Mage Trueblood afraid of? It had to be connected to the mysterious woman he followed. When the vehicle slowed to leave the center's parking lot, Jonah glanced out the window and jumped.

Across the parking lot, in the shadows of the tree line, two bright, red eyes stared back at him. But as soon as the truck started into motion again, the eyes blinked and disappeared. Jonah searched the gloominess as they zoomed by, sucking in a quick breath when he glimpsed the eyes bobbing through the trees, tracking his course.

Anyone else would have been terrified, but not Jonah. If he weren't mistaken, those eyes belonged to a Grim Hound. With his Death Sense quiet, he knew the beast wasn't there to harm him.

Soon, the SUV turned down a street with little tree cover and houses on both sides and the Grim Hound's eyes were lost from sight.

What the heck was going on?

CHAPTER SEVEN

MYSTIC WORLDS

Jonah's biggest fear was that Lynn or Robert would spot him getting out of the SUV. Once he put his bike in the backyard shed and entered through the kitchen entrance, the only person he saw was Robert, who was watching TV.

After nodding to his cousin, Jonah scooted through the family room and toward his own bedroom, feeling relieved. He should have known better. Lynn's hand gripped his shoulder before he could even enter his room. She spun him around.

Jonah guessed his cousin had been looking out the front window.

"Who was that?" she demanded. "Why'd they give you a ride home?"

Robert leapt off the sofa and was at their side in a second. "What did he do now?"

"He hasn't confessed yet." Lynn narrowed her eyes.

Giving in to the inevitable, Jonah waved his cousins into his room. He plopped on the bed while Robert leaned against the desk.

Lynn closed the door and rested an elbow on Jonah's chest of drawers. "Okay, spill it."

Jonah gulped and launched into his story about the vigil, the mysterious woman, and following her to the train yard.

"That was stupid, Jonah," Lynn hissed in frustration. "What if she had attacked you?"

"I had this." Jonah showed the token to his cousins. "I got it from Kevin, in case I need to call for help."

Robert took the token from him. "Kevin? When did he come through?"

Jonah told them about Kevin's visit, but he hesitated to mention the box. It rested on his memento shelf beside his dad's golden Alliance badge, although neither of his cousins seemed to have noticed it.

Robert let out a low whistle and passed the token to Lynn. "You've been busy today."

"You don't know the half of it," Jonah admitted.

Lynn tossed the token back to him. "So, what happened next? Why the ride home?"

Jonah avoided their inquisitive gazes by looking at the token. He turned it over in his hands. "Alliance Guards showed up and took me to the clubhouse. I met another Council member, Mage Trueblood's brother." He told them that Trueblood often hung out with his mom back in the day.

Robert gaped at him.

Lynn remained on point and asked, "How did they follow you?"

Robert laughed. "It had to be a location spell, right, Jonah?"

"Yeah. They had some of my hair."

"Dang!" Robert looked stricken. "Wick warned me not to leave my clippings behind! I thought he was just being paranoid."

Jonah shrugged. "I guess not."

"The more important question," Lynn continued, "is why a Council member would show up with his guards?"

"I didn't know they had guards," Robert added, scratching his head in confusion. "You don't think it has anything to do with our dear aunt, do you?"

Lynn pursed her lips. "Yes, of course I do! The mage is right: You shouldn't go out alone at night. Not until we know more. Got it?"

Jonah wanted to say, "Yes, ma'am," but feared he'd end up in a headlock. So he nodded and didn't mention the Grim Hound. When his cousins left him alone, Jonah pulled out his books and finished his homework.

Sometime later, he turned in. As he slipped under the covers, he realized that Mike's wish for an uneventful school year probably wasn't gonna happen.

*

During the night, Jonah had regular dreams about the brief image of Deyanira and the strange arena. By the next morning, he had an idea of how to interpret the sorceress's warning. Maybe she would be at her old store. He hadn't thought about the place or gone there in two years. But there was a chance he could find out the true reason for her warning.

When he told Robert and Lynn about his idea during breakfast, they all agreed to visit Mystic Worlds after school.

Jonah went through his day while avoiding awkward questions about his early disappearance from the vigil. Danita was the only club member to press for more information. Mike, catching Jonah's silent plea for help, came to his rescue and distracted her.

Free of Danita's questions for the time being, Jonah was fixated on getting to Mystic Worlds. As the time rapidly approached, Jonah prepared himself to face the dangerous sorceress and get the answers he sought.

Robert and Wick, who first jumped at the chance to come along, surprised Jonah by opting to remain at the mall. Lynn mumbled about them having something up their sleeves but she didn't elaborate. In fact, while they walked the few blocks from the mall to Mystic Worlds, Jonah suspected his cousin was in a sour mood. Something must have happened at school because Lynn wasn't that way during breakfast.

But he refocused his attention when they reached the location that used to be Mystic Worlds. Jonah let out a surprised groan at the sight of the brand-new sign above the store's front door. Mystics Worlds was now a New Age bookstore.

Jonah pressed his face against the front window to peek inside, fearing their trip had been for nothing. He relaxed when he spotted Deyanira's former clerk.

Glancing at Lynn, he nodded. "Let's do this."

The pleasant ding of the door chime made a strange counterpoint to the low buzzing of his Death Sense when he entered the store.

Unlike Mystic Worlds, which had dark walls and shelves filled with strange knick-knacks, this new store featured pale blue walls. The bookshelves contained as many odd things and statuettes, but very few demons, dragons, or Reapers. Overall, the ambience was less oppressive and much more calming.

The configuration of the floor space hadn't changed, nor the chest-high shelves of books of all sorts. And the back counter was now soothing earth tones of green with a brown top instead of its former midnight black. The clerk finished with a customer and froze when he saw Jonah and Lynn.

The trio stared at each other for several tense moments until the clerk cleared his throat and smiled. "Ah, Jonah, isn't it? You're here to buy more books?"

Jonah didn't need his Death Sense to realize he was encountering the same noble Egyptian Wraith which had possessed the clerk before. But he wore different clothes now: loose pants, a flowing, colorful dashiki, a skull cap, and sandals on his feet.

Lynn nudged his arm and Jonah asked, "Why are you back here?"

The Wraith stood tall with a regal posture. "The host invited me in."

Jonah shuddered, failing to understand how anyone would willingly accept Wraith possession. He put that aside, however, and peered around at the half dozen customers in the store.

"Where's Deyanira?" When the clerk didn't answer, Jonah subjected the man to a Reaper's stare even though he had never tried using it on a Wraith-possessed person.

The clerk spread his hands as if he had nothing to hide. "I assure you," he answered, "since I've owned this store, Deyanira has never been in here."

Jonah didn't sense a direct lie to his question. But that didn't mean the clerk was telling the whole truth.

Lynn must have concluded the same thing because she took out her Reaper blades. In their current deactivated stage, the blades were eight-inch cylinders. But when transformed, they were fifteen-inch, razor-sharp, silver blades covered in Angel script. In addition, the weapons could hurt anything supernatural.

She pointed one inactive blade at the clerk. "Why would she warn Jonah?"

The clerk slowly retreated and moved to a corner display of calendars, further away from the other customers. His eyes remained fixated on the cylinder as he said, "Deyanira doesn't tell me her plans, young warrior."

"Why not? I thought you were her pet Wraith."

The clerk merely nodded as he shifted his gaze to Jonah. "She eventually deduced I helped you, young Blackstone, and has never fully trusted me again."

"Too bad," Lynn said before whirling on Jonah. "Well? Is he lying?"

Jonah nodded. "He's cherry-picking his words."

Lynn glanced around and activated one blade. Holding it close to her body, she shielded it from the view of anyone else. "I say we send this Wraith packing."

The clerk lifted an eyebrow. "In the middle of my store? I think not." He reached behind and underneath his dashiki. When he withdrew his hand, he was holding an ancient short sword very low at his side. "I've too much to accomplish to let you send me back to my realm."

Any other day, Lynn would have shown more common sense. But she stepped toward the clerk.

Jonah feared his cousin wouldn't back down, so he tapped her forearm. "Lynn, don't. He helped me with Deyanira."

Lynn shook with frustration as she deactivated the blade. "If anything happens to my cousin…" she warned before turning toward the door.

Jonah followed but stopped when his eye caught a display of potions books. He reached out to take one and held it toward the clerk. "You sell potion books?"

"Ignorant people erroneously assume that potions and natural remedies are no more than witchcraft." The clerk's voice adopted an eager tone.

Slipping the book from Jonah's hand, Lynn read the back cover and scowled.

"You should buy it," the clerk urged.

Lynn scoffed and dropped it back on the shelf. "You have got to be kidding."

The clerked slipped his sword into the scabbard he had hidden beneath the dashiki and moved closer, ignoring

Lynn's harsh glare. "Your parents were researchers, were they not, young Blackstone? Surely they trained you to value knowledge in all of its forms."

Lynn gripped Jonah's shoulder and turned him toward the door before he could respond. "Let's get out of here."

Jonah gave the eager clerk one curious glance before he exited the store.

*

Lynn fumed all the way to the mall, causing Jonah to worry about her surly attitude and distracted behavior.

"What's wrong with you today?" he asked as they entered the mall.

Lynn's stride never faltered but her brow wrinkled. She glanced sideways at him and let out a breath. "It's Rico. We had a big fight today."

With anyone else, Jonah would have assumed a fight meant an argument. But since this was Lynn, and Rico was also her regular dueling partner, he wanted to be accurate. "You do mean an argument, right?"

"Yes, an argument," Lynn said, a little too loud. A few people glanced in their direction and she lowered her voice. "I didn't see it coming."

"Well, that happens," Jonah said, but added to himself, *I guess.* He had no real clue about relationships.

"But not with me!" Lynn paused at the top of the first escalator and pulled Jonah to the side when he bumped into her. She waited until the people behind them passed before saying, "I've always been able to tell when we were heading for a fight and managed to avoid it. Most of the time."

Jonah nodded, pretending to follow her, and then suddenly, he got it. "You're using your intuition?"

Lynn's jaws worked as she mounted the next escalator. Jonah hurried to follow, eager to hear the answer to his question.

After leaning against the escalator's rail, Lynn finally said, "Yes, I was. But it didn't work this time. In fact," she glanced around, "Mom beat me in cards last night. Can you believe that? Normally, I could tell which cards not to play."

Jonah couldn't believe it. Not only was his cousin using her power–in her case, a super-strong intuition–but she had been using it regularly in her everyday life! What astounded Jonah even more was that Lynn watched him, waiting for his reaction, like he should have known the answer.

"Uh…" Jonah scratched his head as they reached the end of the escalator and moved down the concourse. He let it go when they approached Robert and Wick, who were waiting for them.

Robert sat on the bench with a couple of pretty girls leaning over him. Wick, who had a girlfriend, never shied away from performing. He stood beside Robert, creating balls of beautiful blue flame in his palms for the small crowd. Jonah didn't fail to notice that Wick scanned the area for mall security each time he did it.

The onlookers clapped and Wick snuffed out the flames before passing out cards. "Don't miss my show at the Teen Center this Saturday night!"

One of the girls made an awestruck sound as she took a sketch from Robert and showed it to her friend. Wick patted Robert's shoulder. "My friend's a part of the show." He flashed his lopsided grin at the small group.

Lynn slipped behind the bench and peeked over her brother's shoulder.

The girl who had received the last sketch watched Robert with an intense gaze. "Do you do private sessions?"

The sly grin on his cousin's face let Jonah know that Robert had indeed been doing private drawing sessions.

"No, he doesn't." Lynn clapped him on the shoulder. "Or at least, he better not be."

The girl's comical frown quickly changed as she took Robert's sketch pencil and wrote her number on a blank sheet of paper. That done, she flashed Robert a brilliant smile before strolling off smugly with her friends.

Lynn poked her brother in the head. "Seriously?"

Robert took his time tearing out the page with the number and folding it. "You're really gonna go there? I'm sure you and Rico are just studying when you two disappear." He glanced up at his sister, smirking. "And I know you must use your intuition to find the best spots for your *studying*."

Jonah's jaw dropped while Wick laughed like a maniac, enjoying the sparring.

Robert seemed to score the point because Lynn didn't have a comeback.

Wick's laughing stopped as he studied her face. "I guess the bookstore visit was a bust."

"Yes, it was," Lynn answered.

"He knows something," Jonah offered.

Lynn huffed. "Jonah wouldn't let me send the Wraith back."

"Why not?" Robert asked as he began to sketch again.

Lynn glanced down at what he'd drawn and hissed, "Robert! You're sketching random people's thoughts?"

"Yeah." Robert avoided looking at his sister.

Jonah saw the jumbled, yet distinct, images.

"How long have you been able to sketch peoples' thoughts without them concentrating?" Lynn pressed him.

"Not long," Robert hedged.

Lynn threw her hands up in frustration. "It's unethical."

"Come on. I'm not digging for anything personal, just…" Robert's voice trailed off.

"I don't think you should do anymore sketches for a while."

Robert and Wick objected, Wick being the louder. "Lynn, he's part of my show! People are coming just for that. And we're starting to make good money."

Lynn crossed her arms. "Speaking of that, I think you're getting a little too flashy with your power. What if someone notices it's real?"

"Hey," Robert said, standing up, "just because your intuition is acting up, don't spoil our fun."

"Yeah," Wick chimed in. "I know what I'm doing, Lynn."

Robert peered at his sister and said, "Or are you getting a bad feeling about this?"

Jonah realized the taunt had rattled Lynn when, instead of punching her brother, she let her shoulders slump in a way he'd never seen.

Robert's expression changed in an instant. "I didn't mean that."

"We'll be fine," Wick added. "You'll see. And whatever's happening to you will soon pass."

Lynn stood tall and crossed her arms. "Maybe. But I still say we should be careful."

Wick nodded, but Robert watched his sister with a concerned expression.

Jonah thought she had a point. Wick and Robert were using their abilities more often than ever, and he had the Human Lie Detector gag at school. To top it all off, he chased after that woman at the vigil, even though it was, no doubt, a stupid thing to do.

Once again, Deyanira's warning came back to him. *Beware, young Blackstone.*

CHAPTER EIGHT
THE UNKEMPT CLERK

Jonah rapped on Mike's bedroom window and waited. Nothing. Everything was quiet inside the Littletons' split-level home. After several more taps on the ground-level window, Jonah gave up with an irritated huff.

While his cousins and Wick headed off to the Teen Center, Jonah searched for Mike to thank him for helping with Danita. And to apologize. Besides, he wanted Mike's opinion on everything that happened. But Mike wasn't home.

Images of Mike and Patrick, secluded somewhere while making out, popped into Jonah's mind, stoking a sudden jealousy. He was sure Patrick was keeping his buddy away from him. For a moment, Jonah fantasized about phasing the boy to the top of a tree or the middle of a busy highway!

Jonah gritted his teeth, waiting for the fit of jealousy to pass. What was wrong with him? The mysterious woman wasn't even nearby. Besides, why shouldn't Mike find someone? Especially after everything that happened with Trevor?

But Patrick? Jonah didn't get that one. He shook his head in bewilderment as he hopped on his bike and rode off.

At the entrance to Mike's cul-de-sac, Jonah stomped on the brakes. An idea suddenly occurred to him. Mike could have gone to work at his uncle's bookstore. It was still open.

Ten minutes after leaving the Littletons' home, Jonah rolled up to the front of Hackett's Book Emporium. The store was located inside a one-story house that had been rezoned for commercial use. An old-fashioned wooden sign hung above the front door.

Although Mr. Hackett could be a little intimidating, Jonah liked visiting the store. It smelled like a real bookstore and reminded him of the wonderful times his mom took him to little, out-of-the-way, secondhand shops. That was where he'd find the best books—the old ones with crinkled covers, smudges on the inside pages, and even underlined passages.

This evening, he was on a mission when he entered. Jonah glanced at the cash register, expecting to see Mike. But the counter was empty. A few customers milled around, cautiously avoiding the teetering stacks of books at the end of every aisle. Jonah moved further into the cramped store but stopped when someone directly behind him spoke.

"Can I help you?"

Jonah turned to find a short man with strange, sunken eyes, the kind that rarely blinked, staring at him. Sporting a mustache and goatee, the man wore a pale shirt and shabby, green slacks that covered his rail thin body and yellowish skin. He wasn't someone Jonah would have chosen to invite for dinner.

The man reached up to push a strand of his disheveled brown hair out of his face. "Yes?"

"Oh. I'm looking for Mike."

"He's not working today."

"Thanks."

Jonah edged around the stranger and headed toward the door when the man asked, "Are you a friend?"

"Yeah." The man's silence stretched on, growing uncomfortable, so Jonah added, "I'm Jonah."

The answer produced a sudden smile and the short man stood straighter. "You're Jonah Blackstone? Mr. Hackett told me about you."

Jonah nodded.

"My name is Alastor. Mr. Hackett hired me to look after the store while he's away." Alastor held out a thin hand.

Jonah hesitated because the man's overly long nails were uncut with mucky traces of dirt underneath. But he didn't see a way out when Alastor glanced down at his proffered hand.

As soon as Jonah touched the man, he wished he hadn't. The palm felt clammy. He yanked his hand away and stoically resisted the urge to wipe it on his pants. "So, Mr. Hackett told you about me?"

Alastor tilted his head to the side, studying Jonah. "You like the Occult section, no?"

Jonah nodded, wondering if Mr. Hackett had also told Alastor to keep him out of that area. "I guess we can't go back there."

Alastor smiled. "Hmm, I approve of anyone's healthy interest in things beyond what you can see with your eyes." He gestured toward the Occult section of the store.

"Oh, no. I need to talk with Mike."

"He seems more focused on his social life these days."

Jonah blinked at the man's sharp tone. "Mike's cool."

Alastor retreated two steps while staring at Jonah's balled fists.

"I meant no offense," Alastor hastily added.

Jonah's ringtone, a sci-fi movie theme, blared out through the quiet store. He fumbled to answer the call while several customers glared at him. "What's up, Lynn?"

"Get to the Summit."

"Why?" Jonah whispered as he retreated toward the front door.

"We have a client. I'll try to wait, but hurry."

Jonah pocketed his phone and glanced back.

Alastor was watching. "Come back anytime, Mr. Blackstone."

Jonah nodded and slipped outside. There was something very off about Alastor. He wondered if the man were a Fallen Reaper. Or maybe even an Archivist. Jonah couldn't tell either way because fallen supernaturals didn't set off his Death Sense, not unless they meant to do him harm.

That thought didn't offer Jonah much comfort as he headed toward the Teen Center.

*

"Jonah!" Danita called out when he reached the door to the clubhouse.

Having taken over a bench outside one of the administrative offices on the second floor, she had her school textbooks perched on her lap, a spiral notebook in one hand and a highlighter in the other. Danita snapped the book closed and cradled it and the notebook in her right arm while tugging her heavy book bag over to him.

"What are you doing out here?" Jonah inquired. He offered to hold her bag open so she could cram her things inside. The backpack was already bursting at the seams.

"I was waiting for you to show up," Danita said, a little flushed. "I tried to persuade Latrell's sister not to come and see Wick, but…" She waved at the attic door.

It bore two signs: one for the Summit and a second one for the Mount Vernon Social Club. "So *that's* why they called me."

"Yeah." Danita dropped her book bag on the ground. "Are you gonna use your," she lowered her voice, "your hypothetical talent to help Wick?"

Jonah wasn't surprised Danita remembered every little thing she learned. "You really don't believe in anything that can't be tested and measured?"

Danita looked scandalized. "No, I don't, and neither should you."

"I don't get it," Jonah stammered, unable to resist entering the argument. "You're the leader of our book club! We read science fiction and fantasy books."

Danita sighed in a patronizing way that never ceased to rankle Jonah. "Those are books, stories, and fairy tales. And that's where those things belong! Not where people start believing them in the," she made air quotes, "real world!"

Jonah smirked at her. "You know, most myths are based on actual facts."

"Yes, regular, boring, explainable, and provable facts," she insisted. "It's just sad when people rely on mysticism to explain things they're too lazy to attempt to process with their brains and logic."

"Right," Jonah said, rubbing his forehead. "Anyway, I need to go–"

"Wait!" Danita gripped his forearm. "I asked Lynn about joining the editorial team for the Summit. She's all for it, but," she frowned, "I'm not sure about your cousin, Robert. Did she ask you yet?"

"Well, yeah, but–"

"Did you support me?"

Jonah tried to avoid her expectant expression. "We haven't decided on it yet."

"Jonah, you know me." Danita opened her bag and pulled out a small notebook with frayed edges from extensive use. "I'm working on a second part to the black cat story." She flipped to a page and showed him. Jonah looked down at a badly drawn map of Mount Vernon and a big star near a north corner. Above the drawing, in bold ink letters, were *Black Cat Sightings*. "I've discovered several sightings of the cat in a park on the north side of town."

She closed the notebook and pushed up her glasses while giving Jonah a defiant look. "I'm gonna prove without question it's just some kids poking fun at people's superstitious beliefs."

That not only surprised Jonah, but also worried him. "Ah, that's not a good idea."

"Why?"

"It could be dangerous."

"I plan to go there during the day." Her uncertain glance belied her confident tone. "Just in case it's more, I would like you to go with me."

"Me?"

"Yes."

"But... But what about Anthony? He likes you."

Danita threw her hands up as if she were dealing with a little child. "Of course he does, Jonah. Anyone can see that."

"Well, then...?"

"He's okay, but I don't want him doing something stupid just to impress me."

Jonah snorted with laughter until Danita narrowed her eyes. He racked his mind to find a way out of the request, but failed. "I'll think about it, okay?"

"Thanks." She gave him a quick hug.

Jonah's face warmed. "I, uh, really have to go. They're waiting for me."

Satisfied with his answer, Danita nodded, grabbing up her book bag before she headed for the steps.

Jonah used his key to open the attic door while wondering why everyone seemed to be seeking his help or advice.

*

Robert and Lynn sat on the club's sofa, their backs to Jonah as he entered the attic. Wick stood beside them. Jonah's attention, however, was fastened on Latrell's sister, Alicia, who sat in one of the ratty armchairs.

Wick ruffled his twists as he sat down on the steamer trunk. "We believe you." He sounded reassuring.

"Oh." The girl's voice was small and fragile, Jonah thought. "No one else will. My mom gets angry with me."

"We understand," Lynn chimed in. "I'm glad Danita didn't talk you out of visiting us."

"Actually, I heard about Jonah at school." She paused as he slipped into the armchair opposite her and watched him for a quiet moment.

"Yeah," Wick said, giving Jonah an approving nod. "The Human Lie Detector. We should add you to the magic show." He grinned as he leaned forward over the trunk. "So, Alicia, tell us about it. You're seeing a ghost?"

"Yes," she said in an uncertain voice. "My brother."

Robert exchanged an eager glance with his sister. "He talks to you?"

"Yes."

"How?"

"He appears in his room sometimes and other places where I go." Alicia shivered and hugged herself. "My brother used to be nice, and we'd often talk, just like we did when he was still alive. But now he's scary. He yelled at me because I wore his ankh. He got so mad until I put it back."

"That's when he stopped appearing to you, right?" Wick asked. When the girl nodded, he snapped his fingers in triumph. "It must be the ankh! I bet he's attached to it."

Jonah was glad when Lynn ignored Wick and asked, "What happened next?"

"He's haunting the basement, and tearing it apart. My dad keeps insisting that someone's breaking in, but I know better. And I think my mom does too." Tears glistened in her eyes. "I miss my brother."

Lynn moved to sit on the arm of the chair the girl was in, placing her own arm in a comforting way around the visitor's shoulders. "I wonder why he's staying around? Did he tell you?"

"He said he has something to do." She wiped her tears. "But I don't know what. He won't tell me."

"And you're the only one who can see him?"

Alicia shrugged. "I think my mom might sense him, but Latrell won't appear to her."

"Well, then, it's our job to find out why he's hanging around." Wick's confident voice seemed to relax Alicia for a moment.

"Oh," she squeaked, digging inside her pocket and withdrawing neatly folded bills.

Wick and Robert sat straighter, staring at the money.

Lynn spared them both a glance before saying, "You don't have to pay us."

"I want to."

"Yeah, Lynn," Wick seconded.

Lynn raised a fist and Wick slumped in defeat.

"I'll tell you what: Just pay us for the cost of the gas and we'll call it even."

Alicia nodded as she held out the cash. Lynn plucked out two bills and handed them to Wick. "Now, give us your address."

The girl did as Lynn asked while Wick scribbled it all down and Jonah listened. Alicia's parents were taking her to a family doctor the next day after school. Jonah had little doubt the doctor would be a grief counselor or psychologist. He recalled dodging his own bullet by not having to see a *doctor* after his parents died.

Alicia pulled out a house key and passed it to Lynn. "We always go out for dinner afterwards. We won't be home for a while."

Lynn nodded, all business. "Don't worry. We'll figure this out." She stood and motioned for Alicia to come with her.

Wick whirled on Robert as soon as Lynn and Alicia exited the attic. He frowned while holding up the limp bills. "A few bucks for gas?" He glared at Robert. "Your sister's gonna cheat us out of making any serious money."

Jonah agreed with him. "Why advertise if we're not gonna get paid for our services?"

"Thank you, Jonah." He turned to Robert. "Well, Bobby?"

Robert gave him a helpless shrug and kept sketching. Curious, Jonah leaned over to see what his cousin had drawn. The page showed a cluttered basement with things thrown around and turned over.

"That's her basement?" Jonah asked.

Wick came over to see it and whistled. "That looks serious."

Robert nodded. "Tell me about it." He glanced over his shoulder and said, "Lynn doesn't want to charge money because of how it'll look."

"How what will look?" Wick asked, confused.

"If our parents ever find out, she wants to say we were just using our abilities to help people. Charging for services will seem like, well…" He met his best friend's gaze. "… Like we're taking advantage of them."

Wick was dumbfounded. "We're helping people too."

"I know, but she doesn't want to be considered a cheap, charlatan palm reader." Robert stared at his drawing, unable to meet his friend's mutinous expression. "It's a thing with her." When he heard the attic door close, he hastily whispered, "I'll talk to her."

"You do that," Wick said before plastering a practiced grin on his face.

Lynn leapt up the steps a second later, snagging her squeeze bottle from the computer desk and sipping from it as she came over. "Can you do that spirit trap you're always talking about, Wick?"

"I need to get my stuff together, but yeah. Easy."

"Perfect. If her brother really is dangerous, I figure we can trap him long enough for," she patted Jonah's shoulder, "Reaper boy to do his thing."

"Don't call me that," Jonah fumed.

Besides his desire to use Jonah's ability to talk to dead people, Wick had also speculated that Jonah could open a rip or tear in the barrier dividing the realms. In doing so, he could send dangerous Wraiths back to where they came from. So far, all the ghosts Wick had encountered were less dangerous souls with unfinished business.

As a result, Jonah never bothered to try the technique. That didn't daunt him. It would be just his luck that on their first case, they'd get a real Wraith or an angry spirit.

Jonah glanced at the picture of the ruined basement again. That was exactly what he didn't want in his life: more weirdness. He would have asked Lynn if she had a bad feeling about this first job for the Mount Vernon Social Club, but he caught himself while the instinctive question was still perched on the tip of his tongue. Lynn's intuition was acting up now and she couldn't reliably sense anything.

A new, chilling thought occurred to him. What if her loss of intuition was deliberate? That woman at the vigil managed to spike his dark emotions. Could she have done something to Lynn? That threat frightened Jonah so much that he kept it to himself.

Besides, Robert and Wick were okay. And as far as he knew, all his powers were also fine. He realized he was just trying to cheer himself up.

When he noticed Lynn watching his reaction, he offered her a confident nod and said, "Let's do it!"

CHAPTER NINE
PECK OF POLTERGEISTS

Jonah sensed something was off. Latrell's spirit loomed in front of him, floating in the dark, damp basement. Yet the ghostly boy wasn't raving mad, nor did he appear even slightly dangerous.

Jonah whispered over his shoulder to the others, "What do you think?"

Robert and Lynn stood back. Wick, who wore his trademark fatigue pants, muscle shirt, and unlaced combat boots, was much closer. He reached up to ruffle his short twists as he peered over Jonah's shoulder. "I don't know, Padawan. Maybe he's stuck here because of unfinished business and isn't a Wraith at all. Talk to him."

Wick had already set up his spirit trap as planned. Robert drew a perfect circular sigil on the ground with red paint, and Wick set up a series of iron poles. As a precaution, Wick also linked all the poles with a single iron chain, since iron could hurt supernatural creatures.

But Latrell caught them all by surprise, appearing before the trap was even completed.

Tapping a pole with his boot, Wick said, "I guess I won't be needing this."

Robert called out, "Hey, I spent a lot of time drawing that sigil!" He pointed a spare pole at Latrell. "He has to be the one haunting this basement. Look around."

Lynn raised her chin while watching the apparition. "He can hear you talking about him," she said. "Do your thing, Reaper boy."

Jonah glared at his cousin. "You know I don't like that name."

"Tough. Find out what's going on and then send him packing."

"He's not–" Jonah stopped because Latrell flickered out of sight before he reappeared right in front of him. His first impulse was to back away, but Jonah held his ground.

Wraiths, ghosts, and spirits came in all guises, depending on the period in which they perished. In Latrell's case, death had occurred two weeks ago. Except for the black tunic and pants, he looked like any other kid at school.

However, the boy's haunted, unblinking eyes thoroughly unnerved Jonah.

He gulped and asked, "Are you the one haunting this place?"

Latrell shook his head and opened his mouth to say *no*. As a ghost, the boy didn't produce actual sound waves. Instead, Jonah heard the reply in his own head.

The plan to use his ability to talk to the ghost and help him with any unfinished business seemed straightforward.

Now that he faced Latrell's ghost, however, Jonah had no clue where to begin. Could it be as easy as passing along a last word to a living family member?

What worried Jonah most was the information Wick had learned from his grandmother, a professional ghost hunter. According to her, all human spirits remained until after their funerals and their spirits were laid to rest. Others might linger a little longer to settle unfinished business but they too, eventually moved on.

Wraiths were different. They didn't have unfinished business. They were stuck. Period. That's why they grew so mean and violent. If left unchecked, a Wraith could turn into a dangerous poltergeist–or worse, a Phantom.

Jonah didn't know if Latrell was a Wraith or a regular spirit because the boy's funeral was still a day away. He glanced around the cold basement, rubbing his arms as the nagging doubt crystalized.

Narrowing his eyes, Jonah asked, "Do you have unfinished business here?"

Latrell nodded.

"I can help." Jonah waited but Latrell didn't explain. So Jonah waved his hands around, gesturing toward the ruined basement and the old, moldy boxes. The contents, mostly important papers and family photos, littered the damp basement floor. "Who did this, Latrell?" After seeing the boy, he didn't think the ghost could have been responsible for all the damage.

The young ghost shuddered and opened his mouth in a quiet scream while pointing behind Jonah. The next moment, Latrell flickered out of sight before he reappeared across the basement.

Robert yelled and Wick jumped away from his spirit trap.

An older spirit, a Wraith, clad in a black judge's robe and a powdered wig, stood in Wick's trap, glaring at the kids. The Wraith looked very solid as it sucked in a deep breath and bellowed at Latrell. *Don't tell the Reaper anything!*

Jonah winced, envying the others because they couldn't hear the Wraith. "I'm not a Reaper."

Liar! The Judge-Wraith tried to move and growled in pain when its body touched the iron chain. Dark welts appeared on his legs and wisps of ethereal smoke rose into the air. He whirled on Wick. *Release me!*

Wick blinked at the ghost. "Ah…"

"He says to release him," Jonah translated.

"Yeah, I kind of guessed that." Wick stood taller and peered into the Wraith's angry eyes. "No."

The Judge-Wraith went crazy, moving into a frenzied blur as he threw himself against the invisible container wall created by the trap. His thrashing was so violent that the floor shook beneath their feet.

Jonah's Death Sense spiked as six more Wraiths barreled up through the basement floor.

The trapped ghost pointed at Jonah and the others and shouted, *Attack!*

Wick whirled his hands and conjured green flames to fling at the Wraiths. The tactic caught one ghost by surprise. Jonah winced at the spirit's agonized howl when it disappeared.

Robert swung an iron pole at anything that approached him. A few times, he connected with a Wraith, causing sparks to erupt across the spirit's body.

Lynn grappled with a large Wraith, dressed like an inmate. The ghost grabbed her by the shoulders and pressed her against a wall. She struggled in its grip as it hoisted her into the air.

"Take out the idiot in the wig," she yelled to Jonah. "The one who looks like an old judge!"

Wick blasted a second Wraith with diminished fire that injured the spirit but didn't vanquish it. "Do it now," he said, risking a glance at Jonah. "I can't keep this up."

"Yeah," Robert shouted between swings of his pole. "Do something."

"Do what?" Jonah asked.

"You're a Reaper," Robert answered. "Command them to leave. I don't know." A Wraith dodged Robert's makeshift weapon and knocked him into the mildewed boxes.

"Robert!" Lynn reached into her pouch and drew out her Reaper blades. "That's it. I've had enough."

In a fluid motion, Lynn brought her blades up, slicing through the body of the Wraith that was attacking her. The ghost screamed and its body flared before it exploded into ethereal fragments.

Lynn dropped to her feet and rushed to defend Robert. She cut the Wraith that was menacing him in half. As it burst into flames, Lynn whirled around. "Get your butt in gear, Jonah."

In the confusion, the Judge-Wraith dislodged an iron pole. It gouged out a section of Robert's constraining sigil.

"Oh, no!" Wick exclaimed just as the powerful Wraith broke the barrier, sending poles in every direction. The freed spirit slammed a solid fist into Wick's chest, hurling the young mage into a basement support column. Wick sagged to the ground, dazed.

The sight of his friends and family in trouble galvanized Jonah. He leapt on the old Wraith's back without thinking. He expected the Wraith to disappear, but it remained solid, allowing Jonah to wrap his hands around its gaunt face.

The Wraith tried to buck him off, but Jonah held on while mentally exploring Wick's idea about creating an opening to the Wraith realm. Since the basement lay in a direct line with the nexus point at the Crossroads, Wick theorized Jonah could do it.

The problem was that Jonah didn't know how to open a doorway between the realms. He agreed to try, however, because he preferred not to kill the Wraiths. His options were somewhat diminished anyway after Lynn and Wick managed to dispatch half the Wraiths.

Jonah closed his eyes. *Leave. Leave. Please, leave!* He repeated that over and over in his mind, but nothing happened.

His desperation increased as the Wraith turned on Lynn after it failed at trying to dislodge him from its back. Unlike the other Wraiths, this one was smarter and more powerful. He raised a hand and yanked boxes and other objects off the ground to hurl at Lynn and Robert.

Reaper blades weren't designed to deflect old pieces of kitchen appliances, but Lynn succeeded at it quite well. The Wraith upped the ante and went for an old sofa. The entire thing bucked and vibrated before rising into the air.

"Jonah!" Lynn shouted.

He concentrated, struggling to bypass his mounting fear as he imagined the magical energy source running beneath the floor of the basement. He reached out with his Reaper side and touched the power.

Jonah thought, *Leave.* Still, nothing happened.

Meanwhile, Lynn pushed Robert back but the sofa levitated in the air and followed them until they collided with a stack of boxes against the back wall and had nowhere else to go.

In anger over his failed attempts, Jonah shouted, "I command you to leave!" The Wraith wavered in its attack, the sofa poised to crash down onto Lynn and Robert.

Jonah felt a tug on his body and twisted around to see a rip forming in the air. The pull grew stronger by the second.

That's when he realized Robert was right. He was half-Reaper, and Reapers commanded spirits. Confidence and power surged into Jonah's body as he summoned his Reaper half. When he spoke again, his voice was deeper than normal and he knew how to phrase the command. "Go back to your realm."

The Wraith bucked and shouted beneath Jonah, but the pull of its own realm was too overpowering. Just as its body stretched thinner, Jonah slid from the apparition's back.

No longer fearing the Wraith, Jonah pressed a hand to the body and shouted once more, "Go back!"

The rip widened like a weird, blossoming flower. The pull increased, sucking the angry Judge-Wraith and the three remaining spirits through it and swallowing them into the other realm. As soon as they disappeared, the crack between realms closed with a snap! The sofa, no longer held aloft by the Wraith's power, crashed to the ground, merely inches in front of Robert and Lynn.

Jonah collapsed to his knees, his chest heaving as a wave of dizziness overcame him. He felt hollowed out from the exertion required to keep the rip open.

"Way to go, Jonah," Wick whooped despite being a little unsteady on his feet. "I knew you could do it."

Lynn snorted before she deactivated her blades and pulled her brother from among the smashed, wet boxes.

Robert lifted his damp shirt away from his side. "This sucks."

Wick laughed at his buddy and didn't notice that Lynn's posture stiffened. She reached for her blades while glaring into the basement's far corner.

Jonah turned in that direction and realized Latrell had remained behind. That sealed it for him. The boy wasn't a Wraith like the others. "So, do you have unfinished business?"

Latrell didn't answer but stared at Lynn, his eyes widening. *Reaper blades.*

"She won't hurt you," Jonah said to the boy in a soft voice.

Latrell shook his head with a violent motion and jabbed a finger at Jonah. *You're a Reaper.*

"I'm not a Reaper." Jonah was quickly growing tired of saying that. Then something became obvious to him. "Wait. Is that why you set us up?"

I didn't set you up. My sister wasn't supposed to go to you, not like that.

Jonah stepped toward Latrell but the boy disappeared and didn't return, leaving them alone in the cold basement.

CHAPTER TEN
THE FUNERAL

Jonah, his cousins, and Wick all huddled in the Hightowers' den, talking about the Wraith attack. Latrell's odd behavior continued to baffle all of them.

Wick resorted to pulling his trusty lighter out of his fatigue pants, a sure sign of his churning thoughts.

Lynn crossed her arms, watching him. "Seems you were right."

"At least we got rid of the Wraiths haunting the basement," Wick agreed. "But now we're stuck with a new mystery."

Robert, who had changed into a dry shirt, added, "Maybe not now, but I know a way to find out."

"You mean Latrell's funeral?" Lynn tapped her bottom lip, considering the idea. "If it's a trap, I can't tell."

She strode around the living room in an agitated circle. "I hate this."

Robert's eyes widened. "Hey, what if dear old Aunt Ruby's involved?"

Lynn hugged herself while turning on the spot. "That's impossible."

"Why?" Jonah asked.

"First," Lynn said, holding up a finger to tick off her points, "Aunt Ruby's up in Titusville, staying with a friend."

"How could you possibly know that?" Robert asked, incredulous.

"I, unlike you, dear brother, did the proper thing and called our cousins to see how they were doing. They talked to their mom right after she got out." When her brother made a disgusted face, Lynn glared at him. "Robert, no matter how we feel, she's still their mom."

Robert shook his head. "I wouldn't have done it."

"Right, whatever." Lynn frowned at her brother in dismay. Then she turned back to Jonah and held up two fingers. "Second, our aunt had no real magical abilities. That's why she hated your mom. She couldn't have been the woman you followed to the train yard."

"Oh," Jonah said.

Robert snorted but gave his sister a begrudging nod.

"With that question settled," Wick said as he snapped his lighter closed, "I think Jonah should go to the funeral."

"Why?" Lynn looked ready to argue.

"Think about it," Wick continued. "We weren't supposed to go to Latrell's house. It threw off their plan, whatever it was."

"Didn't I say so earlier?" Robert asked.

"True, Bobby," Wick admitted.

Lynn wasn't convinced. "The Wraith told Latrell to keep his mouth shut. So, he won't show up at the funeral."

"Yes, he will," Jonah answered for Wick. He understood where his friend was going. "He can't help it. Remember what Wick's grandmother said about spirits? Latrell's stuck here until after the funeral."

"And Jonah can talk with Latrell while knowing there's something up," Wick finished.

Despite Lynn's frown, Jonah nodded his agreement, liking the plan.

*

Oak Hill Cemetery was within a short bike ride of the Hightowers' home. Only after he arrived at the cemetery did Jonah realize he had no clue where to go. He found the groundskeeper and asked about the funeral.

When the grey-haired man gave him a once-over, Jonah was glad he put on the black pants and white dress shirt that he normally wore to church. His plan was to find a hiding spot to watch the funeral, unobserved. But if he couldn't do that, he'd have to blend in.

The groundskeeper pointed out a prepared site. It was on a level spot, halfway up the adjacent, gently sloping hill.

The grave reminded Jonah that this was his first time in a cemetery since his parents' memorial service. As he coasted by the gravestones, he wondered if any ghosts would show themselves, aside from Latrell, of course.

He paused long enough to read the words on the substantial marble headstone already in place above the open grave. Latrell's birth and death dates sobered Jonah. The boy was only sixteen, the same age as Robert and Lynn.

The very thought of losing Robert or Lynn was unimaginable to Jonah, even though they had all been in extreme danger at times. As always happened, Marcus's warning to him about being careful took on new meaning.

He turned from the headstone, glancing around for a good spot to hide. Beyond the grave, at the crest of the hill, was a thick tree line. *Perfect.* Rolling his bike up to the thicket of trees, he chose a large pine and huddled behind it in his windbreaker. The day was crisp, but also bright and comfortable.

Nearly half an hour passed before a black hearse made its slow way up the curving cemetery road, followed by a long line of cars. It was like a living, mechanical snake. As soon as the hearse stopped at the base of the hill, a group of men exited the other cars and hurried to the hearse's rear door. Jonah felt a chill as the men pulled out a black casket, hefting it onto their shoulders, and carrying it to the gravesite.

A woman, whom Jonah suspected was Latrell's mom, exited the limousine with her husband. She was in tears while the father remained stoic, walking with stiff jerks of his legs. Latrell's sister, Alicia, trailed behind, solemn and quiet.

Within a short time, a sizable crowd of people had gathered, shifting on their feet. The minister, in a long, black robe and multi-colored stole, opened his Bible and the ceremony began. But Jonah wasn't interested in that. Instead, his eyes searched the surrounding land.

A weather-beaten angel stood fifteen feet away, near the crest of the hill. Jonah paused when he felt a slight twitch in his Death Sense, but nothing happened. He continued his search until the twitch in his gut happened again. This time, when he turned to the angel statue, Latrell stood there, watching his own funeral with an unblinking gaze.

Out in the bright sunlight, Jonah noted Latrell's features. He was a little taller than Jonah, with his hair cut in a box fade that seemed to accent his thin, handsome face.

Once he was sure no one was looking in his direction, Jonah left the hiding place and made his way toward the teen. He was only a few feet away when Latrell's head snapped around to look at him. The move was so sudden and eerily inhuman that Jonah stopped short.

What are you doing here? Latrell asked, his voice echoing in Jonah's mind.

"Tell me what's going on."

Latrell fixed his eyes on the funeral. His ghostly jaws worked. *What are you?*

"I'm a half-Reaper. Why?"

I didn't know there were half-Reapers. Latrell gave a strange, hollow laugh. *I didn't know a lot of things until after… I died.*

"It's a long story," Jonah said. "So, are you gonna tell me what's happening?"

Latrell seemed on the verge of speaking when a sudden, low groan escaped his mouth. His little sister had placed a flower on the casket. A tear ran down Latrell's cheek, surprising Jonah. He never imagined a disembodied spirit could cry. He averted his eyes while searching for a way to get the boy to talk to him.

"I'm sorry about what happened." He peeked at Latrell. "I know how it feels, not having anyone to talk to."

You're gay? Latrell asked, focusing more closely on him.

Jonah hesitated. No one had ever asked him that question directly, not even Mike. They both kind of revealed themselves to each other during the Agent Hunter mess, the way two friends do when they suspect the truth in each other and just accept it.

For Jonah, something strange happened now. He didn't fear answering that question. True, Latrell was a ghost and not likely to tell anyone, but still, Jonah thought it revealed something about himself. At once, he realized Latrell waited for an answer, and he nodded.

Well, at least you didn't kill yourself.

"Maybe if we'd met each other, you wouldn't have done that?"

Pain flitted across Latrell's semi-transparent features. *I… wasn't all alone.*

Without conscious effort, Jonah opened his senses to his Reaper Stare. Feelings of sadness and regret rolled off Latrell. Jonah could understand the emotions, but if Latrell did have someone to talk to, why couldn't he have survived the bullying?

He reflected on his own run-ins with the bully, Brandon. In those moments, he relied on his cousins and friends to help him. Then again, no one ever bullied *him* for being gay, Jonah readily admitted, although others had been cruelly taunted. It was one reason he decided to start the Tolerance Club. Not only did he want to help other kids going through similar torment, but the club also grounded him to his mortal side.

After his recent experience in the Afterworld, Jonah harbored a deep fear that he could turn into a true oddball, someone unable to understand what normal people experienced. And he couldn't ignore the knowledge that something like suicide wasn't an option, not for himself, anyway. His godfather, Marcus, once told him that the Alliance wasn't certain what would happen if he died. Jonah might even turn out to become a super Reaper.

A commotion arose at the funeral that broke Jonah's train of thought. Latrell's mom had flung herself across the casket, wailing. His dad tried to pull her off, but his first attempts nearly overturned the coffin. The little sister looked too stunned to help.

Finally, one of the teenagers sprang from his seat behind the family and helped to pry the grieving mother's fingers from the lid. The rest of the crowd shuffled in nervous agitation as Latrell's mom slumped back into her chair.

During the entire episode, lights kept flashing from a photographer and a reporter who were standing among the mourners. The suicide already had several stories written about it. Some insensitive people even claimed that Latrell deserved what he got because of his sexual preference.

Jonah noted the boy's angry expression. "What's wrong, Latrell?"

The ghost pointed toward the crowd. *I can't believe they came.*

Jonah thought he meant the reporters. "I saw a decent article about you in the paper. Not everyone's a jerk."

No, Brandon's parents. How can they dare to show their faces?

Jonah scanned the crowd and spotted four people standing slightly away from the rest of the group.

Brandon Warner, Senior, was a tall, light-complexioned man with a head full of wavy, black hair, peppered with gray. He wore an expensive, long coat and his demeanor was arrogant and dismissive, even when he was just standing still.

His wife was half a head shorter than him and thin. She also wore an expensive, long coat and clasped her gloved hands together in front of herself. With her chin tilted up and standing rigid as a plank, she watched the ceremony with a bearing that reminded Jonah of a movie queen.

The other couple, the Edwards, wore clothes as expensive as the Warners', but they seemed more resigned than arrogant. The man had a round face, glasses, and a short, neat afro. He was stocky, and essentially an older version of Drew. The mom was slender, with a thin neck that attractively showed off her pearl necklace.

Just behind and to the left of the couples stood Alastor, the clerk from Hackett's Book Emporium. He wore all black, but his hair was still unkempt. The truly eerie thing about the short man emerged when he looked straight at Jonah. As soon as he grinned, Jonah's Death Sense throbbed in unwilling response.

He thought of ducking behind one of the larger gravestones, then realized it was useless. Alastor nodded as if to emphasize that very fact before refocusing his attention on the memorial service.

A lot of kids bullied me. Latrell's voice shook with anger as he continued. *But Brandon and Drew were the worst.*

A pit of bitterness exploded in Jonah's stomach. Were Brandon and Drew's parents aware of what their sons had done? The graveside service ended while Jonah mulled that over.

Most mourners uttered soft, banal words to the stricken couple. Brandon's parents didn't even bother with offering their condolences. They, along with Drew's parents, retreated to an expensive sedan and hastily drove off.

Latrell's dad helped his mom out of her chair and led her toward the waiting cars. With the crowd steadily dispersing, Jonah grew anxious Latrell wouldn't linger. He fought to get his own anger under control so he could focus on what he needed to know. "Where does Brandon live?"

Why? Latrell's eyes narrowed. *What are you going to do?*

"Nothing. I was just wondering."

Latrell cocked his head to the side, studying Jonah. *He lives on my street. I'm not sure about Drew.*

The boy lived in Brandon's neighborhood. That explained the expensive headstone. It also explained why the Warners came. They had to know Latrell's parents.

Those connections only caused Jonah to feel the need to examine Latrell's situation even more closely. Not only did the boy fail to reveal anything about what was happening, Jonah still didn't know if Latrell was a ghost or a Wraith. "Are you going to move on?"

Latrell's eyes widened and he shook his head no. *I have unfinished business.*

"What?"

The ghost shrugged, looking like any other kid at that moment. *Maybe to do something about the bullies.*

Jonah heard the uncertainty in Latrell's voice. "I started a club at school to help kids that are being bullied."

That's cool. Latrell smiled. *You should help people like me… I mean, us.* He stepped closer to Jonah.

"Can't you tell me anything?" Jonah asked, searching the boy's ghostly eyes. They were a light brown. "Please."

I have an ankh in my room. It's on my dresser in a jeweler's box. Get it.

"Why? What's so important about that?"

The guy who gave it to me was the same one who talked to me before I died.

Jonah's jaw dropped. "Someone talked you into killing yourself?"

No.

"But–"

Never mind that. He had several custom-made ankhs. There's a sticker on the bottom of the box.

Jonah wanted to hear more about this person, but it finally occurred to him what the boy was asking him to do. "I can't break into your house. I mean, we still have a key–"

Everyone's heading to our house for the post-funeral gathering, Latrell said. He gestured at Jonah's clothes. *You'll fit right in.*

"I don't know…"

Jonah let out a breath and nodded. He'd come there to get more information. At least this was a lead. "Okay. What's the address?"

Latrell told him and then paused with a curious expression on his face. *Who are you?*

"Oh," Jonah said, thinking the boy must have heard his name in the basement. "My name's Jonah. Jonah Blackstone."

CHAPTER ELEVEN
MOTHER'S SORROW

Jonah's jaw dropped when he got off the bus and caught the first glimpse of Latrell's neighborhood. The homes along the beautiful, tree-lined street were grand–some with columns on the front porches–and all featured large front yards.

Kids didn't run up and down Latrell's street, shouting and playing with each other like they did in his own neighborhood. The sensation that enveloped Jonah as he walked along was a subdued peace. The impressive homes brought back Robert's comments about this neighborhood. Most of Mount Vernon's black lawyers, doctors, and other professionals lived here.

For the first time, Jonah wondered about Latrell's mom and dad's occupations. Drew's father, a successful dentist, had remained on the Hightowers' side of town. That impressed Jonah despite their son being such a bully. Maybe that's why Brandon treated Drew like a second-class friend.

Latrell's house was easy to spot because of all the cars lining the street and the curving driveway. Jonah's insides also knotted as he recalled the reception at the Garretts' after his own parents' memorial service. He hated the gathering and stormed off through the neighborhood. He wondered if Latrell's sister would do something like that, but didn't see the lonely girl as he proceeded up the driveway to the house.

Like all the others, this one was two stories, but all brick. As he drew closer, his Death Sense buzzed just before Latrell appeared in a second-floor window. He beckoned to Jonah, who almost pointed at his own chest in that hesitant way when a person's unsure they are the one being addressed. At the last moment, Jonah stopped in mid-motion. Latrell was invisible, but people might still have noticed him.

Latrell pointed down toward the front door and Jonah's heart climbed into his throat. *Remember the mission*, he chided himself. The front door was open behind the thick-paned, glass storm door. People moved in and out of sight beyond. Jonah screwed up his courage, opened the storm door, and entered the house.

The atrium was spacious with a long staircase to the right. Directly in front of Jonah was a huge funeral arrangement of flowers. The clashing, sharp scents tickled his nose, so he moved further into the house. To his left was a large living room filled with somber, black-clad adults. Straight ahead was a family room, much larger than the Hightowers'. Sunlight streamed through a row of windows that opened out to the backyard where more people had gathered.

His nerves tingled as he moved into the crowd, expecting someone to pounce on him, asking why he was there. Couldn't any of these people hear his heart pounding in his chest? *This is crazy*, Jonah thought, sliding through the adults. Without any conscious effort, he reached a table laden with food. Not the least bit hungry, Jonah turned away and that's when he saw kids outside on a large patio.

They were all his age and talked in little, nervous groups. In fact, Jonah realized there were more kids here than at the funeral itself. A boy, the one who had helped Mrs. Dickerson at the funeral, glanced inside, saw Jonah, and moved toward the patio door.

Jonah backed away and slipped into the midst of the talking adults when he discovered Alastor among the guests–watching him. Jonah considered just leaving until he spotted a second stairway that led to the second floor. Latrell stood on the midway landing, again beckoning to him. Once he had Jonah's attention, he disappeared.

As soon as Jonah mounted the first steps, someone tugged on his arm.

"Where're you going?" It was the boy from outside. He peered at Jonah.

"Uh, to the bathroom."

The boy pointed down a short side hall. "It's right there." When Jonah hesitated to respond, the boy added, "You started that Tolerance Club. Well, too bad it didn't help Latrell." His voice rose with his words.

Jonah didn't see a way out of this until Alastor arrived and placed a hand on the boy's elbow. "Excuse me, but I wondered if you could help me in the kitchen. The family wants to put out more ice."

"But…" the boy stammered, trying to extricate himself from Alastor's firm grip.

The little man must have been stronger than Jonah suspected because he hustled the boy away and into the kitchen. At the last moment before entering, Alastor glanced back at Jonah and nodded.

Despite the help, Alastor ignited a firestorm of questions for Jonah. He suspected the man had seen Latrell at the cemetery. Supernaturals could see ghosts and Wraiths, which meant Alastor was one. Jonah just didn't know what kind. He also realized he had stalled for too long, and hurried up to the second floor.

The first thing Jonah noticed was that Latrell's bedroom was neater than his own. He wondered if the boy's mom or a housekeeper had tidied up the room after the boy's death.

Latrell's full-size bed had a sea blue cover and multiple pillows on it. Jonah was envious of that, considering he still slept on a twin-sized bed. He shifted his gaze to the walls, where the boy tastefully hung black-and-white photos, all framed and neatly arranged. Judging from the expensive digital camera on the dresser top, Jonah guessed Latrell was really into photography.

A pang of regret hit Jonah and he wished he had only met the boy before his death. He crossed to a low worktable with a sleek reading lamp positioned in front of the room's main window. A closed laptop sat next to the lamp, with a couple of notebooks stacked off to the side.

This is where he'd seen Latrell. He reached out to touch the laptop when the boy spoke from behind him.

I thought you might not show.

Jonah spun around and hesitated before speaking fearing that someone might hear his voice.

Latrell nodded as he moved to stand right beside Jonah and point out the window. *That's where Brandon lives.*

Jonah leaned over the narrow desk to peek outside. The Warners' mansion sat further off the road and behind a slate wall and wrought-iron gate. *It must be nice*, Jonah thought.

"Thanks." He glanced at Latrell.

The boy peered back, frowning. It doesn't seem fair. His supernatural body shuddered. *I should have been stronger. My sister will miss me.*

Jonah didn't know what to say until he realized he could be honest. "I still miss my parents, but I have to keep going." He lapsed into silence.

Latrell reached out his hand. The movement surprised Jonah and he stepped back before he could stop himself. Latrell jerked his hand away and instead crossed to stand beside the bed, his arms wrapped around his waist as if he were cold. *I didn't mean to try that.*

"It's okay," Jonah said, worried that he might've offended the ghost. When Latrell continued to stare at the floor, Jonah asked, "Where's the ankh?"

Latrell pointed at his dresser.

A small, wooden box with a handle carved into the shape of a mallard duck sat on the dresser. Jonah opened that to find five different neck chains and a small, black jewelry box. As Latrell said, the jewelry box contained the ankh amulet with the bright green, embedded jewel in the loop.

"I've seen this on your sister."

A rueful smile touched the Latrell's ghostly face. *I had to scare her to get it back.*

Jonah sucked in a breath. "That was you at the school when your sister came up to me." Latrell stared without answering. Jonah turned the box over. The small, white sticker attached to the bottom displayed the name of the jeweler in tiny letters.

"Cool. Got it." He turned to put the box back.

What're you doing?

"All I need is the clue," Jonah said, stopping before replacing the jewelry box in the larger box. "I can't take the ankh."

I want you to have it. Latrell came closer. *Please. Wear it, but not here. Wait until you get home.* Latrell's head tilted to the side as he listened to a silent call. He focused on Jonah. *Slip the box in your pocket. Hurry!*

Latrell's mom appeared in the doorway. Her eyes were puffy as she clutched a handkerchief in her boney hands. Her gaze skewered Jonah. "Why're you in my son's bedroom?" She looked around the room like she suspected he'd stolen something.

"I…" Jonah made the mistake of holding up his hand, the one with the box.

Latrell's mom shot into the room and snatched the box from Jonah's grasp. "What are you doing with this?" she demanded. "It belonged to my son."

Her voice cracked as she sat on the edge of Latrell's bed. Her shoulders shook with quiet sobs, leaving Jonah feeling like an idiot. She wiped her eyes with the handkerchief and sucked in a shaky breath.

Her sad eyes met Jonah's again and she held up the box in a trembling hand. "Did you… did you give this to him? Were you… his friend?"

Jonah didn't want to lie to Latrell's mom, but he needed to explain why he was in the room. Before he could answer, Latrell appeared, near the doorway. He met Jonah's gaze, pleading with him to say yes.

Mrs. Dickerson stiffened. "He's here. I know it! I can feel him."

The words shocked Jonah. And her raw, emotional pain got to him, fueling his anger toward Brandon and Drew. Looking for something to say, he focused on his prepared excuse. "I run a Tolerance Club at school. We're setting up peer groups in honor of Latrell."

He didn't know how the woman would respond. She searched his face, her eyes tearing up before she dabbed them again. Without warning, Mrs. Dickerson rose to her feet. "Thank you. It's important to stand up to the bullies." She held out the box.

Jonah took it, unable to avoid feeling guilty for the slight deception.

"Do you hear me? Stand up for the others before it's too late." The woman's voice wavered at the last. She turned and fled.

Latrell disappeared as soon as Jonah opened his mouth to speak to him.

Left alone in the room, Jonah wanted to be anywhere but there. He hurried down the stairs, thankful he didn't run into Alastor or the troublesome boy before exiting the house. Only after he ran down the long driveway and rounded the curve in the street so he couldn't see Latrell's house did he finally slow his pace and relax.

When he reached the bus stop, he leaned against the kiosk and let his mind replay that brief encounter with Latrell's mom. Her words still burned inside him, causing another mission to take form in his mind. Brandon and Drew needed to pay. And Latrell thought his unfinished business had something to do with the bullies.

The boy at the house was so right. What good had the Tolerance Club done Latrell? The way Jonah saw it, going after the bullies was just fulfilling the Mount Vernon Social Club's mission. Of course, that was assuming Latrell was a ghost and not a Wraith. Jonah ignored the nagging doubt for now. Even Latrell's mom thought he should stand up to the bullies. The problem was he didn't know what to do.

CHAPTER TWELVE
PERPLEXED PROPRIETOR

Jonah returned to school for the last half of the day with a determined frame of mind. When the time came to patrol with his anti-bullying crew, he hurried to his assigned trouble spot, eager to catch Brandon and Drew stepping out of line. But the bullies weren't around.

"I haven't seen them all day," Lorraine said as she finished her last shift.

"Oh, thanks." He waved goodbye to her and Rodney before catching sight of Mike heading down the bisecting hallway. Jonah reached the corner and spotted Patrick waiting by the exit. Wanting a word with Mike first, he leapt forward and grabbed his buddy's arm. "Hey, I'm telling Lynn and the others about the funeral. You should be there too."

Mike seemed hesitant as he glanced between Jonah and Patrick. It gratified Jonah to see real doubt in Mike's expression. But he also knew what his friend would say.

"Sorry, Jonah. I've already made plans, and I have a lot of work to do. Just tell me later."

Jonah checked his immediate irritation with his buddy. Mike looked tired, like he hadn't slept. He opened his mouth to ask about it, but Mike cut him off.

"Just call me later. Okay?" He joined Patrick before Jonah could even answer. The boys exchanged a few words before heading outside.

Jonah didn't get it. Mike acted like he didn't want to be around them anymore. *Or around me.* His frustration over the situation bubbled to the surface. He didn't need Mike's help to deal with the bullies, anyway. This was his decision.

Adding more fuel to his stewing anger, he believed the bullies only used Latrell's funeral as an excuse to skip school.

That thought was galling to Jonah, especially considering they were responsible for Latrell killing himself. A small voice of doubt popped into Jonah's head. *What if Latrell was lying?* But Jonah rejected that idea. Latrell's own anger was convincing enough at the funeral.

He would deal with that, but first, he already had a job to do for the club. The first place to start was finding out more about Latrell's ankh.

*

Jonah, Lynn, and Robert stood just inside the entrance to the jewelry store at Green Oaks Mall. The compact establishment, wedged between a vitamin store on one side and an electronic shack on the other, looked unremarkable to Jonah.

The jewelry store owner stood on the opposite side of the display counter, dressed in an immaculate, dark grey suit. "You interested in buying something for a pretty girl?" he asked Jonah.

"My cousin? Date someone?" Lynn asked. "I seriously doubt it."

Jonah glared at her. "You don't know that."

Lynn pulled a shocked expression. Robert, who was further back with his sketchpad open, cracked a smile.

"Well?" the jeweler asked.

Jonah shook his head. "No."

The jeweler sighed dramatically as he rested his hands on the edge of the display counter, careful not to smudge the glass itself. "In that case, what can I do for you?"

Lynn produced Latrell's small jewelry box. She opened it to reveal the ankh inside. "Did you make this?"

The man's eyes gleamed with pride. "Yes, I did. Exquisite, isn't it? That's real gold, by the way. And the stone is jade. They weren't cheap either."

Lynn snapped the box closed, smiling. "How many did you make?"

The man's demeanor changed as he peered at Lynn. "How did you get it?"

"We wanted to know who ordered it," Lynn pressed.

The jeweler's eyes narrowed. "Customer records are strictly confidential."

"But it was a birthday gift," Jonah said. "I simply wanted to send the person a thank you note." When the guy flashed a skeptical expression, Jonah added, "My aunt's insisting on it. She says it's the proper thing to do for such a nice gift."

"Well, uh," the owner stammered. "I can't. I value my clients' confidentiality."

Jonah gestured to a display of Halloween-themed rings. Some had little dragons engraved on them; others were embedded with blood-red, sparkling jewels, among other items. "What if I buy one of those?"

That offer seemed to irritate the man and he puffed out his barrel chest. "You can't bribe me and I won't give you any information." He leaned on the counter. "I suggest you leave immediately before I call mall security."

Jonah gulped. Mall security had recently chased him and Mike only a few months ago when Agent Hunter came after them. He doubted it would be wise to cause another incident so soon.

But Lynn crossed her arms, poised to test the man. "It's not illegal to ask questions."

Robert let out a startled yelp from behind. Jonah turned to find his cousin rubbing his forehead, like he had a headache.

"It may not be illegal," the owner said while taking out his cell phone, "but the mall security doesn't like its business owners being… ack!" The man stopped in mid-sentence, his expression instantly going vacant.

At the same time, Robert let out an anguished grunt. "His mind is… blocked all of a sudden," Robert hissed.

And Jonah's Death Sense also spiked. He pushed between Lynn and Robert as he spotted the niqab-wearing girl from school on the opposite side of the concourse. Instinctively, he opened his Reaper Stare. The colors of her emotions were darker and riddled with something inky black, like a virus. *It's the evil intention behind her magic!*

He blinked, shutting down the enhanced sight, and pointed. "She put a hex on the owner." With that, he took off around the curved end of the concourse without further explanation.

The girl turned and dashed in the opposite direction. Halfway down the concourse, she darted into a service hallway between two stores and burst through the metal door at the end.

Jonah ran after her, angered by the girl for more than one reason. Not only had she interfered with their case, but she was hiding under a niqab even though she wasn't Muslim. She was a sorceress, Jonah concluded, and he wanted to expose her.

He pushed through the doors, dimly aware of Lynn telling him to be careful. But his determination lent him speed and the corridor blurred. He was at the stairwell and leaping down at full velocity.

The girl had already reached the bottom, but Jonah landed right behind her a second later.

Shocked, she conjured a spell and hurled it at him.

Jonah dodged the attack, letting the walls absorb the impact of the spell with a surprisingly solid bang! that echoed in the enclosed space. He was fast, always had been, but he failed to consider the confined space. As a result, he hit the wall rather hard, temporarily dazing himself.

The girl laughed as she wove her hand and conjured a second hex. Jonah froze, knowing he couldn't dodge it this time.

That's when Lynn landed in front of him. She swiped her activated blades and shouted, "*Kulinda!*" The deflected hex responded with a low, snapping boom!

The slight hesitation in Niqab Girl's movement revealed her utter surprise at Lynn's unexpected arrival. She recovered quickly, however, and flung another spell. It was merely a distraction so she could open a vortex, the weakest one Jonah had ever seen. The edges were ragged and they undulated like it could collapse at any moment. Plus, it was very small. Yet the girl dived through anyway, head first.

Lynn's voice rang off the drab walls when she shouted, "Coward!"

Jonah rose to his feet. "How did you learn to do that?"

"Oh," Lynn blinked, looking a little embarrassed as she deactivated the blades. "When Rex came down to work with you, I asked him about the deflection move. He taught me how to do it."

Her answer impressed Jonah and made perfect sense. Rex was the only adult member of the Alliance who didn't hide everything from them. "Well, at least whatever's bothering your intuition isn't keeping you from successfully doing that spell!"

Lynn's eyes widened. "Robert!"

Jonah understood and he raced up the stairwell behind his cousin. They found Robert waiting at the entrance to the back hallway, looking spooked.

Lynn hurried to him. "Are you okay?"

"Yeah," Robert said, although he still rubbed his forehead. "What about the girl?"

"She got away."

Robert's expression fell. "We won't get anything from the store owner. She muddled his mind. I doubt he even knows his own name."

The news sickened Jonah. It was their fault the girl even attacked the store owner. "Maybe we should tell someone?"

Lynn stared down the concourse at the jewelry store and the owner. The man paced back and forth, talking to himself. Her shoulders sagged. "Hold on." She speed-walked over to the owner of the adjacent business, a woman dressed in a sheer, flowing, Indian fabric of vibrant reds and yellows.

After a brief conversation, the woman checked on the jewelry store owner. Lynn slipped away and came back to Jonah and Robert. "There. She's gonna call his brother."

"That's good," Jonah said, but he couldn't shake his sense of guilt and feeling responsible.

"We didn't know this would happen," Lynn offered, not looking any happier than he felt. After a moment, she nodded. "Come on."

Jonah thought they would leave the mall. However, once they descended the escalator, Lynn walked to the other end of the mall. She pulled her brother to an empty bench and plopped down beside him. Robert seemed to understand because he flipped open the sketchpad without being asked.

Jonah crowded in close to see what he had drawn. The partial picture showed two customers standing at the jewelry store counter from the owner's point of view. The problem was, the faces weren't completed. Just the general shape and a few lines.

The dimensions of the two people were easy to see. One person was a man, as massive as a walking tank. He had thick arms and almost no neck.

The other person was thin and wearing a cloak just like the shadowy woman's cloak at the vigil. His inability to see her face only made Jonah more certain. Something caught his attention: her slender fingers and long nails. And Robert also included a fair bit of a strange amulet she wore around her neck. It depicted a woman dressed in Egyptian clothes, but her head was that of a lion with a solar disc for a crown.

The hairs on Jonah's neck bristled. He was sure he'd seen that amulet before, in an old book his parents had.

Lynn studied the drawing, then sat back, frustrated. "You drew the ugly amulet in detail! Why not the faces?"

Robert frowned at his sister as he rubbed his forehead. "I think they purposely obscured their faces while they talked to him. It was easier to focus on the amulet first. How could I know the girl would attack?"

"Well," Lynn said, "I can't tell anything about the woman, but," she tapped the drawing, "I saw that huge guy. He bumped into me at the store about a week ago. Knocked all my groceries out of my hands and didn't stop, nor did he apologize. The jerk!"

"You never mentioned that," Robert said.

"Until now, I didn't see the need to." Lynn wore a puzzled expression. "I wonder if he hit me on purpose."

"Could be," Robert said.

"Well, I've seen that woman," Jonah cut in. "She was at the vigil."

"Are you sure?" Lynn said. "You never saw her face."

"It's definitely her. Who else could it be?"

Lynn didn't have an answer for that.

Robert closed the sketchpad with an annoyed flick. "I'm sorry I couldn't get it all."

"That's okay." Lynn leaned into him. "It seems I'm not the only one they're attacking."

"Attacking?" Robert's eyes widened in horror at the idea.

"Yes, Robert. The more I think about it, the surer I am that something's deliberately being done to impede my abilities. Someone is doing it on purpose."

CHAPTER THIRTEEN
NIGHT PROWLER

Jonah's spirit was low when he returned to the Teen Center with his cousins. The woman who bought the ankhs was the same person from the train yard, but how did that help them? Who was she? And where could they find her now?

Lynn and Robert stopped just inside the atrium when they spotted Wick outside the West Hall, talking with the center's director. He held a poster advertising his magic show in one hand.

Not looking forward to rehashing the events for Wick, Jonah headed upstairs. "I'll catch you guys later."

He entered the attic and discovered Mike sitting at the editor's desk in the back corner. Jonah's buddy glanced up from his work, squinting through the eyeglasses he always wore when reading or studying. "Hey."

Jonah crossed to the desk, pulled a computer chair around, and sat. He hesitated a moment before saying, "Sorry about the vigil. I was–"

"A jerk?" Mike gave him a tired smile. "It's okay. I'm used to it."

"Funny," Jonah grumbled.

He avoided Mike's gaze and looked down at all the spiral notebooks, pencils, pens, and crumpled pieces of paper scattered over the desk. Mike even had the thick *Deliverer Tales* book, given to them while in the Afterworld, on top of the desk.

Jonah's godfather suggested Mike keep the book at the clubhouse. That arrangement also provided a space for Mike to work on the translations. The desk was the obvious choice.

The book's author recorded the tales in coded Angel script, and Mike was the only one who could decipher it. He intercepted the mind boost meant for Jonah. As a result, the incident transformed Mike into a Seeker, a Pathfinder, and a dutiful companion to a Deliverer.

After his awesome transformation, the Alliance Council had no choice but to allow Mike to translate the book. Of course, Mike had to travel to Alliance HQ and report his progress. Jonah used to keep up, but Mike hadn't mentioned any recent trips.

As Jonah watched his friend, he thought of all the times Mike claimed to be too busy to hang out. Work on the translation was always the favored excuse, but now that Jonah knew about Patrick, he felt certain that Patrick had become the real reason.

He grabbed a notebook and peeked inside. Mike's small, precise words covered every page, front and back. He felt a bit guilty about his lingering doubts. Mike had spent a lot of time in the attic working on the translations.

The situation raised a different question. When did he find the time to meet a new boyfriend? A spike of jealousy flared, giving him pause. He couldn't blame it on the supernatural attack by the mysterious woman. She wasn't here now, yet he was still jealous.

Why? He and Kevin had successfully attained a new point in their relationship before the Fallen Reaper returned to his Alliance assignment. And that's when Jonah hit on the problem. While Mike managed to find someone right there in Mount Vernon, Jonah couldn't even talk to Kevin.

And the older boy's whereabouts were also a secret. Kevin had accused Mandara of doing it on purpose. His incessant frustration with the Alliance also fueled Jonah's irritation. He dropped the notebook on the desk.

Mike glanced up from the laptop screen at him. "Jonah, we need to talk about Patrick and other things."

"Fine, but later."

"Jonah…"

"I have something to tell you." And Jonah recapped everything for his friend. When Mike continued to type and write, Jonah thought his friend did it out of spite because he refused to talk about Patrick. "Are you even listening to me?"

"Yes, I am." Mike recited everything Jonah said, but in a more concise form. "Happy?"

Jonah blinked in awe. He should have known Mike's enhanced mind would allow him to do more than one thing at once. In a way, Jonah was a little jealous of that too. "Okay. You heard me." He slumped in his chair.

Mike spared him a severe look. "I understand you being down because of the mall. But you have another lead."

"Yeah, yeah. The Niqab Girl."

"So, why are you acting pissed?"

Jonah chose his words carefully. "Brandon was one of the people bullying Latrell."

Mike pulled off his glasses. "That's news to me, but I'm not surprised." With a sad huff, he replaced his glasses and continued writing.

Jonah understood his friend's reaction. Mike had been on the receiving end of Brandon's bullying once. That made Jonah even angrier. "The Warners had the nerve to show up at the funeral. I'm surprised Brandon didn't come there just to gloat."

"He was in Atlanta on a tour of the State House." Mike paused in his writing and tapped the pen against his bottom lip. "His dad made him go in order to meet lawmakers and other important people. Brandon hated it."

"Why? I thought his snobby butt would love stuff like that."

"Brandon wants to play basketball, Jonah. And he's good at it; he even got accepted on the varsity team. That–"

"That rarely happens," Jonah finished. "Everyone's talking about it. So what?"

Mike exhaled, like he was trying to stay calm. "His dad thinks basketball is beneath his son's future career as a lawyer."

"Really? Oh, wow," Jonah said. For the first time, he didn't envy Brandon, not with a dad like that. He opened his mouth to ask a different question when he registered

Mike's in-depth answer. "Wait a minute. How do you know all that?"

"They talked about the trip at school. Besides," Mike's oatmeal complexion darkened with embarrassment. "Don't get mad. Drew told me."

"You're still talking to Drew?"

"Sometimes. I'm trying to bring him back from the edge."

"He's one of the bullies!"

"Jonah, he only did that because Brandon made him do it." When Jonah gave him an incredulous look, Mike's shoulders slumped. "I know. He should have stood up to Brandon and told him bullying Latrell was wrong. I'm trying to get him to admit that, but it takes time."

Jonah wanted to tell Mike he was being stupid about Drew, but kept it to himself. This development changed his plans for scouting out Brandon's house. Knowing where the bully lived wasn't enough. If he ever intended to phase there, Jonah needed to see the inside of the house first.

For now, he would switch to Drew. That also fortified Jonah's resolve not to reveal his plan to Mike. Not only would he object, but Mike still considered Drew worth saving! As far as Jonah was concerned, Drew was even worse than Brandon.

"I'll see you later." Jonah stood. Then he remembered his mom's box. "By the way, my mom left me a triptych."

"Oh?" Mike gushed. "Was it in three pieces or all connected together?"

Jonah's earlier irritation evaporated at once. He loved how Mike knew what he meant without ever having to explain. Each could reference an obscure science fiction or fantasy movie and the other would instantly get it or even finish the quote. They were cool that way. Nerds. Best friends. "It was in three pieces."

"I want to see it." A real fire glimmered in Mike's eyes.

Jonah's face warmed with shame over his earlier shortness. "We can talk now, if you want to."

Mike seemed as if he wanted to do that. Jonah waited him out, hoping, but in the end, Mike said, "That's okay. I know you have other things on your mind. And I need to catch up on this work."

Jonah nodded. "Well, the triptych is in my room. I'll show you later?"

"Yeah, that's cool." Mike continued watching him. "Where's your book bag?"

"At home. I'll finish my homework there." That was true. He needed to finish his own work and then prepare for his first scouting mission. "Check you later."

*

One benefit of focusing on Drew was that his family lived on the same side of town as the Hightowers. This neighborhood was older than Jonah's and had two positive attributes: Large tracks of undeveloped forest that ran along the back border of the neighborhood; and many of the mature trees near the homes had thick trunks. Perfect for hiding behind.

In the gathering dimness of evening, Jonah found several places around or near the Edwards' huge home to which he could phase. Jonah's sense of purpose increased as he headed home.

That night, around midnight, he snuck into his backyard. Having learned the year before that he couldn't phase into nor out of the Hightowers' property, due to the magical protections, it made things trickier for Jonah, but not impossible.

Situated beside the shed and out of sight of prying neighbors, Jonah phased to Drew's fenced-in backyard. He appeared beside the Edwards' shed, which he spotted earlier. After a few minutes, he determined which window belonged to Drew's bedroom: second floor, east side of the house. Jonah exited the backyard through a squeaky gate and snuck up behind a tree outside Drew's window.

He was too low to see inside the house, but that wasn't a problem. Jonah gazed into the tree's branches, allowing his eyes to adjust to the dimness. Once he was sure he had the spot in mind, he phased and reappeared on a thick branch. With a little shifting, he had a direct view into Drew's window. Thankfully, Drew had his blinds open and fully retracted.

Jonah concentrated, noting the placement of the bed, the chest, and desk. He shifted to see into a corner of the room. He had just decided on a space to phase—at the foot of Drew's bed—when the boy walked by the window and stopped.

Panicked, Jonah shifted behind the tree trunk, hoping the darkness concealed his movement.

The window clicked and slid open. "Hello? Who's there?" Drew stared right into the tree where Jonah hid. "Mike, is that you?"

Jonah's eyes widened and he phased to the ground but continued to stay flat against the tree. Then he felt a chill along his back at the same time Latrell's ankh amulet grew warm against the bare skin of his chest. "Dang it!" he whispered.

Jonah only wore the ankh to honor Latrell on this scouting mission. Now he realized that was a mistake because of the ghost's attachment to the piece of jewelry. The ghost could appear wherever the person with the ankh went.

He spun around to face Latrell's glowing form. "What are you doing here? Go home!"

Drew's window snapped closed like a gunshot in the quiet evening, startling Jonah. He suspected the boy would come outside to investigate and waved at Latrell. "Go!"

He can't see me.

"That doesn't matter. Now–" Jonah's Death Sense spiked as a low growl came from the adjacent yard.

Two bright orange cat eyes stared back at him from the darkness between the trash cans. That seemed to frighten Latrell, and the ghost disappeared. Jonah prepared to phase when he heard Drew's approaching footsteps, crunching the autumn leaves.

Oh no! If he phased away, whatever was stalking him would attack Drew if the stupid boy came into the side yard. Drew reached the backyard gate and stopped to turn on a flashlight. Jonah ducked behind the tree, barely avoiding the beam of light as Drew searched the side yard.

"Mike?" The boy's voice shook with uncertainty.

Please go back inside. But the gate creaked as Drew opened it. Jonah turned to see the orange feline eyes narrowing to slits. His Death Sense spiked harder. The creature would attack any second.

What could he do? Rush Drew and phase the boy to safety? That was the only option. Omar or someone else from the Alliance would have to modify the boy's memory afterward.

"Who's there?" Drew asked again.

Just as he stepped through the gate, a chilling howl from a Grim Hound pierced the night air. Drew swore, followed by a heavy grunt of pain, and then Jonah heard the unmistakable metallic clack! of the flashlight hitting the brick steps.

A steady vibration reached Jonah's feet. Those were the heavy footfalls of a charging Grim Hound. The cat screeched out an angry feline growl before it leapt away, knocking over the neighbor's trash can. Seconds later, a huge, darkened shape rumbled across Drew's side yard, galloping right past Jonah and into the next yard, trailing the cat.

The beasts growled at each other as they raced off into the night.

"What the…" Drew said in a shaky voice. His rapid breathing was audible.

Jonah realized his own heart pounded away in his chest. Drew retrieved the flashlight, lingered a moment at the gate, and then hurried away. Once Jonah was sure the boy was back in the house, he phased to his own backyard.

Hidden in the shadows beside the shed, he slumped against the tree and tried to let his heart calm down as he regulated his breathing. Jonah had to credit Drew's willingness to come outside and investigate, even though that was dumb.

That was also too close.

Was the cat following him or Drew? Why would a Grim Hound suddenly appear to protect him? Unless it was Deyanira's Hound? Jonah didn't want to think about that. The Reaper's warning was strange enough. Would she send her Grim Hound to Mount Vernon?

And then there was Latrell. Jonah would have to talk to the boy and tell him not to follow him around. Of course, he could stop wearing the ankh. But that seemed a little rude if he were intent on helping the boy's ghost complete his unfinished business.

With everything that had just happened, Jonah harbored doubts about his plan for the bullies. He was prepared to save Drew's life instead of letting the cat have him. Marcus's comment from their Afterworld mission came back to Jonah. *You're not a killer.*

No, he wasn't a killer. But as the nervous excitement waned, his resolve to do something about the bullies stubbornly remained.

CHAPTER FOURTEEN
DIPLOMATIC RELATIONS

Brandon returned to school on Friday. But he and Drew acted subdued, preventing Jonah and his people from having any chance to report them. Jonah wondered if Brandon was down about having to come back to school on a Friday instead of staying in Atlanta. At least, Jonah hoped that was the case. *Or maybe his dad wanted him out of sight on the day of the funeral.*

Somehow, Jonah suspected Drew wouldn't mention his little scare from the night before. That didn't matter. He saw what he needed. Besides, the person Jonah really wanted to find was Niqab Girl. He didn't know what he'd do or say when he found her. He couldn't accuse her of attacking the store owner. If he did, she might try to hex him again.

As the school day wore on and none of the club members spotted her, Jonah wondered if she walked around *without* the niqab to hide in plain sight. Sensing his interest in the girl, Danita checked with her big sister, who often volunteered in the main office.

She stopped Jonah in the hallway before his last class. "No go. My sister refused to do it," Danita huffed, looking put out.

"That's okay." Jonah tried to cover his own disappointment. The girl was the only lead they had.

Danita perked up and said, "Guess what? People saw the cat on our side of town last night."

"Really?" Jonah winced at his failed attempt to sound surprised.

She eyed him. "Yeah. I want to go to that park and soon." When Jonah frowned, she added, "You promised me."

"Okay. I'll hit you up later."

Danita grabbed his wrist. "You're still coming to the movies tonight, right?"

Jonah wanted to say no. He already had visions of Anthony constantly puffing out his chest for Danita while Rodney and Lorraine kissed in the darkened theater.

"Mike's coming with his friend," Danita said. Once again, she subjected Jonah to her calculating gaze.

"He is?"

"Yes."

For the first time, Jonah wondered if Danita knew about Mike and Patrick. That thought reminded him why he hesitated to go. Not only would he be the odd man out, but the person he liked couldn't be there either.

*

Jonah rode with Danita, Anthony, Lorraine, and Rodney to the movies. His desire to put the events of the previous night out of his mind was the primary motivation for going.

When Mike arrived with Patrick, Jonah noticed the two boys were careful not to reveal they were dating. Whenever Jonah joked with Mike, Patrick scowled at Jonah. It was as if the boy feared he liked Mike. That thought jolted his awareness about Danita's strange stares.

Not only did she know about Mike and Patrick, she was watching to see Jonah's reaction. A distinct surge of irritation with the whole situation overcame Jonah. He took a calming breath and made sure that he didn't sit near Mike during the movie.

Two-and-a-half hours later, Jonah was grateful for the mindless fun of the movie because it took his mind off Drew, Brandon, and everything else. As the group paused in the busy lobby of the theater complex, Jonah heard Brandon's snobbish laugh. He spotted the boy and Antwan near the games, talking to some girls.

"Let's hit the ice cream shop," Mike said, glancing out the atrium's glass windows. Patrick crossed his arms, glowering.

But when Danita and the others agreed, the boy didn't have a choice. They started for the exit but Jonah tapped Mike's arm.

"I need to use the bathroom. These are nicer than the ice cream shop's."

"Fine," Mike said, giving Jonah a curious look. "We'll get a table."

Jonah made his way through the crowd and headed in the general direction of the bathroom. Once his group had moved off down the sidewalk, he changed course and aimed for the sitting area adjacent to the games. He peeked around the wall separating the spaces. He didn't have a good reason to eavesdrop, plus, he really had to go to the bathroom after drinking his large soda. But he waited anyway.

Antwan craned his thin neck to look outside. "Our ride's here." His clipped African accent sounded irritated.

Brandon waved off his buddy, taking his time with the girl.

"My cousin's waiting in the car," Antwan insisted. "You know how she gets."

Brandon scowled at Antwan, but finally said goodbye to his little fan club. Despite needing to take a pee, Jonah's curiosity got the better of him and he exited the theaters behind the boys. A driver, of all things, waited by a large, black SUV with the door open for Antwan and Brandon to settle in.

Jonah's Death Sense spiked. The front passenger window rolled down and a pair of brilliant, brown eyes peered out of the darkened interior. It was Niqab Girl! Seeing her, Jonah did something he never expected to do: He stepped toward the vehicle.

The girl's eyes narrowed and Jonah could sense that she grinned at him. His Death Sense continued to throb. Despite that, he took another step, drawn by the mystery of this girl. That's when the SUV drove off. Jonah reached the curb and, remembering Lynn's advice, noted the license plate. That presented another problem because the SUV had a Diplomat's plate.

*

A regular nightmare about the Niqab Girl interrupted Jonah's sleep. She chased him through the streets of Morningside Drive, firing hexes at him. Nothing Jonah did could deflect the attacks. Each strike was more painful than the last. Then, as he watched in horror, the girl transformed into a huge, black cat.

Sprinting at full speed to his house, he made it inside the front door right before the cat pounced on him. He slammed the door and leaned against it, breathing hard. Instead of pounding or colliding with the door, there was a quiet *knock, knock, knock…*

That terrified Jonah even more.

Again, *knock, knock, knock.* Jonah jerked awake in his bed, his covers tangled around his legs and ankles. He sat up, blinking and listening. This time, the knock was louder and harder at his bedroom door.

"Yeah?" Jonah mumbled.

Robert's muffled voice came from outside. "Get up, sleepy head. It's a beautiful Saturday morning, perfect for selling pumpkins."

Jonah groaned. "I'm coming." A faint glow came from his curtain, indicating it was near dawn. He shook off the weird dream as he tumbled out of bed and headed toward the shower.

After dressing, he slipped Latrell's ankh amulet around his neck. He wanted the ghost to show up so they could discuss his sudden appearances. At the last minute, he remembered his promise to Mike. Unlocking his mom's box, he took out the triptych and the mysterious note before placing both in his string bag.

*

Mike was just as sleepy as Jonah when they stopped by his house to pick him up before dawn. Wick, who sat in the front passenger seat, was wide awake like Robert. Once Mike settled in, they set off for the church.

Jonah was about to open his bag and show Mike the triptych when Robert took a corner too fast and a long, curved case in the rear of the van tumbled off the rear seat. "Robert?" Jonah asked, peeking over his seat at the case. "What's that?"

Robert glanced at Jonah in the rearview mirror. "Nothing."

Wick punched his buddy in the upper arm. "Tell him."

"Yeah, tell me," Jonah prompted, leaning forward to peer between the front seats. Mike even opened his eyes, looking just as interested.

Robert gave them an embarrassed glance. "I'm taking archery lessons, okay?"

"You are?"

"Yes." Robert narrowed his eyes as if daring Jonah to say something smart.

But Jonah thought that was the coolest idea. "Can you show me the bow?"

"Not now."

"When do you practice?" Mike asked.

"I go to the old Practice Club field on the weekends mainly," Robert confessed. He slowed as he reached the church and turned into the parking lot and glanced at Jonah. "I'll show you later, after we finish."

"Cool." Jonah looked forward to that. He never expected Robert to learn something like how to shoot an arrow from a bow. He wondered if Wick or Lynn would have suggested it or if the idea solely belonged to his cousin.

Jonah didn't have time to consider Robert's new skill because a huge truck was in the church's parking lot, its back wide open. The deacons and other young men from the congregation were lining up to unload the vehicle.

The boys went straight to work and soon dozens of pumpkins were littering the empty parking lot. A consignment of miniature pumpkins, good for making pies, was even included. Wick took charge of those. He caught Jonah's puzzled expression. "They're for the bonfire."

"Oh, cool."

By the time the sun was high in the sky, the south-facing lawn of the church that bordered the main road was adorned with neatly placed pumpkins. Jonah had to admit it was an impressive sight. Already, cars were slowing as people admired the grand display.

A second crew of guys hung around during the sale to help customers by carrying the pumpkins to their vehicles. Done with their shift, Jonah and Mike headed to the Hightowers' van and climbed inside to wait for Robert and Wick.

Jonah took advantage of the opportunity to open his small bag and pull out the triptych.

"Wow," Mike gushed again as he took all three pieces and examined them. "It's beautiful! Did your mom make it?"

"I don't know."

Then Mike did something Jonah never thought to do; he connected the pieces. They made audible clicks as if the ends were magnetized. When he finished, the entire surface of the triptych glowed.

Mike's jaw dropped. "Very nice."

Jonah leaned closer to look. The seven stars pulsated as if they were animated. And fainter stars appeared below those, almost like reflections. The 3D effect was amazing. Then Jonah's own mouth dropped open when a label appeared beside each star. There were seven names in all: Phantom's Passage, Spector Ridge, Apparition Valley, Haunted Forest, Mirage Lake, Soothsayer Meadow, and Harbinger Plateau.

The names represented the terrain depicted at each location on the map. To Jonah, it was like looking at a video game fantasy world.

"It's been enchanted," Mike said.

Jonah waved his hand over the artwork. "Yeah, I can feel it too."

Mike glanced out the front window when they heard Wick's laugh. "You want to show them?" He raised a questioning eyebrow.

"Let's figure it out on our own." Jonah said it before he remembered that he and Mike didn't hang out as often anymore.

Mike nodded absently while running his thin fingers over the surface of the triptych. His eagerness to discover the map's secrets replaced his generally tired appearance. The work had driven away Jonah's morning yawns, but Mike still had puffy bags under his eyes.

Jonah wanted to ask if his buddy were sleeping at night, but Mike pulled the first piece of the triptych apart. The enchantment vanished, leaving the sections inert. However, Jonah could still sense the magic at a low, power saving mode.

Mike stacked the pieces and cradled them in his hand. "How's the case going?"

"Fine. Why?"

"Sorry for not helping more. I've been busy."

Jonah swallowed his taunt about Patrick and instead told Mike about the encounter at the mall with Niqab Girl. "And I found out last night she's Antwan's cousin! Can you believe that?" Jonah finished.

Mike's brow furrowed. "We were at the movies last night. How'd you find that out?"

"Oh, I saw Brandon and Antwan on the way to the bathroom." Jonah's face warmed a little. "I followed them outside and saw the girl in the car."

"Jonah!" Mike elbowed him. "That's why you had us wait for you at the ice cream shop?"

"Yeah. This is an important clue."

"Maybe." Mike scrunched down in the seat.

Jonah ruffled his afro, thinking. "We can watch Antwan's house and catch her."

"No, you can't." Mike turned in the seat to face him. "Don't forget, Antwan's dad is the brother of an Ambassador and a member of the royal family from his home country. Their house sits on a big piece of land on the north side. You can't even see it from the road."

Jonah's burgeoning enthusiasm waned. "I didn't know that."

"Yeah. And before you ask," Mike added, "Antwan had an older brother in school here and a couple of other cousins. Everyone knew about them."

When Jonah slumped back in his seat, Mike nudged him. "I'm sorry. His cousin is probably an exchange student. She could hide out in their house forever."

"So much for that idea." Jonah frowned, thinking about the girl. Without warning, his dream popped into his head. "Hey, is there a park near Antwan's house?"

"Yeah. A really nice one. Our seventh-grade class had a cookout there. I think Brandon's mom arranged it. Why?"

"No reason."

Mike punched him. "Don't lie. Tell me."

"Okay." Jonah told him all about the dream and Danita's research into the sightings. "It's crazy, I know."

But Mike didn't laugh. He looked thoughtful. "Considering everything we've seen, that wouldn't be too much of a stretch."

"I wasn't serious, Mike. I was just wondering if Niqab Girl's a trainee with that woman in the train yard. Deyanira had a pet Grim Hound. What if that woman has a pet cat?"

"Or the girl?" Mike traded a look with Jonah. "Yeah, that's a definite possibility. But you're still stuck. Why not search for the big guy Robert drew? It couldn't be easy for him to hide."

Jonah agreed, but he didn't want to confront a guy that huge. Not unless he had a couple of those Alliance Guards with him. Besides, his suggestion couldn't work either. The Alliance, or more accurately, his godfather, would shut down anything he and his cousins were doing.

The club would have to find another way to discover what was going on, and fast.

Robert and Wick returned to the van and clambered inside. Jonah noticed that Wick had a small box with several of the miniature pumpkins inside.

"Who wants to see Robin Hood practice?" Wick asked as he grinned at Robert.

"I do!" Mike and Jonah chorused at the same time.

CHAPTER FIFTEEN
FAILED MAGIC ACT

Robert was fantastic at archery. "I started just after Lynn got her blades from Jonah's mom," he said.

Wick thumped Robert on the shoulder. "Tell the truth. You were chasing a girl who was into archery. Who knew you'd be so good at it?"

Robert grinned. "Thanks. I think."

Jonah didn't care why Robert chose the bow. He was simply impressed with his cousin's skills.

"This is a recurve bow," Robert explained as he held out the bow for Jonah and Mike to inspect. "My teacher has an authentic hunting bow from Tanzania. That one's a long bow. He's gonna let me borrow it for the bonfire."

"Why do you need a bow for that?" Jonah stopped fingering the bow to gaze at his cousin. "What are you wearing to the bonfire?"

"You'll see in three weeks."

"We have a lot of things to finish before the show tonight," Wick reminded him.

Robert put the bow away and stowed the case in the back of the van. "Let's go."

As they rode home, Mike asked to see the triptych again. He held the pieces in his hands, turning them over and examining the artwork. "Can I borrow this?"

"Yeah." Jonah didn't hesitate. Mike was a Seeker, after all, and Jonah trusted him more than anyone else.

"Cool." Mike slipped the precious pieces into his jacket pocket.

When Robert pulled to a stop in front of the Littletons' house, Mike hopped out of the van and turned back to Jonah. "I'll meet you at the Teen Center tonight."

There was enough of a question in the statement to let Jonah know Mike sensed his persistent irritation.

"I'll walk home," Jonah told Robert. He got out of the van and stood beside Mike at the top of the Littletons' curved driveway.

Robert honked the horn as he and Wick drove off.

"Oh, boy," Mike said. "I know that look. You have to come tonight."

"Don't get me wrong," Jonah began, "I want to see Wick's show."

"But…" Mike prompted.

"I'm tired of being the odd person out, watching everyone else with their dates."

Mike blinked at him and didn't respond for several seconds. "Jonah, when are we gonna talk about things?"

"I don't want to talk about Patrick, okay?"

"I meant Kevin. I know there's something there."

Jonah realized he had a chance to do what he really wanted: talk to his best friend. "He kissed me," he blurted out.

Mike was stunned for several moments and then he laughed. "He did!?" When Jonah nodded, Mike shoved him. "Jonah, that's great!"

Jonah shrugged.

"How was it?" Mike asked, grinning at him.

"Good." Jonah couldn't resist smiling. "Really good."

Mike playfully shoved him again. "I knew it."

When Mike continued to stare, Jonah's irritation returned. "You want me to go and just watch you all having a good time? What about me? I don't even know where Kevin is. Sometimes I wished he hadn't kissed me. At least that way, I wouldn't still be thinking about it."

"Jonah, you don't mean that. And I'm sure that Kevin will show up. Marcus won't let Mandara keep him away. You just watch and wait."

"Maybe."

"But Jonah, we're all your friends. If you back out, people might get the wrong idea about you. Think that you're anti-social."

"I don't care."

"Yes, you do," Mike pressed. "Everyone likes being around you, Jonah, even if you don't notice or appreciate it."

Jonah pretended to be fascinated by the tuft of yellowing grass he worried with his foot.

"Jonah…"

"What?"

"You were different after our trip to the Afterworld. You were driven, always in charge. You started the club and a lot of kids joined just because of you. Don't start back-pedaling now."

The more Mike said, the more Jonah knew his friend spoke the truth. And that exasperated him even more. "I hate you."

Mike laughed again. "I'll see you tonight." He started down his driveway without waiting for a response.

"I'm not going!" Jonah called after him.

Mike reached his front door and went inside.

Jonah kicked at the tuft of grass one last time before he set off for home.

*

Jonah's group arrived early for the show because Rodney and Anthony were part of the band scheduled to perform as an opening act. Rodney played the keyboards and Anthony was a dancer as well as an announcer for the group.

Helping Rodney take his keyboard and equipment up to the stage was fascinating for Jonah. He volunteered to help wherever needed as the band members began setting up.

Lorraine and Danita hung around the front of the stage, assisting the guys in any way they could.

After a while, the band's leader thanked Jonah for his kind assistance. Not feeling needed any longer, he decided to get a hot chocolate in the Cyber Café. The show wouldn't start for another thirty minutes or so and kids were already entering the hall.

His thoughts were on Mike's comments about Kevin as he bought a steaming drink. When he turned to find a place to sit, someone called his name.

"Jonah!" Alastor waved to him from a nearby table. "Over here."

Jonah hesitated.

Alastor continued to stare at him, seemingly forgetting the paper in his hands. Jonah didn't think he could just leave the guy hanging, so he crossed over to the table and sat down.

If Alastor sensed his hesitation, he didn't comment. Instead, the strange man leaned on the table and subjected Jonah to an oddly intense stare, one every bit as penetrating as a Reaper's Stare. Finally, he blinked and said, "You look like a man with a lot on his mind."

"Actually, I do…"

Jonah trailed off as Alastor lay down whatever he'd been reading. It was a story about Latrell's funeral in the Summit newsletter. Jonah had completely forgotten that Robert and Lynn had already covered the suicide.

"It's a sad story," Alastor continued. "I can't imagine being bullied so much that I'd take my own life."

Jonah tore his gaze away from the newsletter. "Yeah. I know." He focused on Alastor, a question coming to mind. "Why'd you help me at Latrell's house?"

"You seemed like you wanted to get upstairs."

"Yeah, but you didn't know why."

"I assumed you knew Latrell?"

"No. But my Tolerance Club started peer groups because of what happened."

"I heard. That was a very noble show of solidarity. Too bad something can't be done about the bullies." Alastor sipped from his iced mocha.

Jonah shrugged, his new doubts bubbling to the surface. "Bullies always get away with it."

"But just once, I wish someone had the power to do something. You know what I mean?"

Jonah shifted in his chair and faked a laugh. "Where's a superhero when you really need one?"

"I don't know," Alastor replied, his voice thoughtful. "I mean, if I had the power, I'd make the bullies pay. Shake them up a bit." A hardness came into the man's face and tone. "I'd show them they can't pick on people like that. Screw the consequences." He subjected Jonah to a brief, intense stare before sitting back and spreading his hands. "Listen to me. It's not like I was anything special in high school."

Alastor grinned, but the gesture seemed odd, like the man wasn't used to doing it. And this conversation was too close to the things Jonah already had occupying his mind.

Even so, he leaned back in his own chair and said, "You can't bust into the bully's house and jack him up."

"Of course not." Alastor frowned at him. "That would be foolish. The bully would claim to be the victim in that case." He paused, tapping his finger on the edge of his cup. "However, if the bully didn't know the identity of the person…"

As soon as Alastor said it, Jonah realized he'd need a disguise or a mask. He ignored his recent doubts while working through the various ways he could accomplish that. He had a full-faced mask that he planned to wear to this year's Halloween Bonfire. If he added a hoodie, Drew wouldn't know who he was. *Yeah, that could work!*

The distant sound of Rodney's band starting up reached the café. The thumping bass of whatever song they played vibrated the floor beneath Jonah's feet.

Alastor grimaced and stood. "I should go. You have a show to attend?" When Jonah nodded, the man waved. "Nice talking to you, Mr. Blackstone."

As Jonah watched the peculiar guy exiting the café, his thoughts returned to the plan forming in his mind. He could do this. In fact, he called it justice. A small voice in the back of his head warned him that he should be wary of Alastor. There was something suspicious about the man that Jonah couldn't nail down.

But this has been my idea all along, Jonah reminded himself. And he'd already scouted out Drew's house at substantial risk. All he needed now were the final details.

Jonah checked his watch, finished his hot chocolate, and headed for the hall.

*

He was shocked when he entered the West Hall. Not only did the wall of sound hit him but all the kids were packed in, creating a darkened mass of bobbing heads and swaying arms. The crowd moved in time to the opening band's music, which blared from a set of on-stage concert speakers.

Anthony danced around the stage with glowing strips attached to his gloved hands and the sleeves of his special shirt. His movements created lingering light shapes and swirls in the air.

The entire setup impressed Jonah, and he regretted not attending one of Wick's shows until now. Clearly, he had missed out on a lot. He went up on his tiptoes, searching the crowd before he spotted Danita and Lorraine in the glare of lights from the stage. They were right up front, dancing. And not far away, he recognized Rico and Lynn.

One of the disbanded Practice Club boys, wearing a black t-shirt that said CREW in white letters, paused on his way past him. "What's up?" the older boy asked. He noted the direction of Jonah's gaze and added, "You want an escort up front to where Lynn's standing?" He grinned. "We'll push the people out of the way."

Jonah laughed, thinking his fellow club member wasn't serious until the boy motioned to another of the older boys.

"Oh, no. That's okay."

"You sure?"

"Yeah. I'm… waiting for my friend, Mike," Jonah lied.

The boys nodded and exchanged quick handshakes with him before moving on, patrolling the crowd. There were others from the club, all wearing the same black t-shirts. It was a subtle dig at Brandon's crew, who served as security for the event. They were the official Teen Center's sponsored group ever since Brandon's dad had Jonah's club disbanded. Tonight, the guys wore their dark blue polo shirts with *Security* written on the left pockets.

Jonah ignored them and pressed further into the mass of chattering and dancing kids. He began to search for Brandon and Drew. But he didn't see either bully, which he found peculiar. Brandon never missed a chance to ruin their gatherings at the Teen Center. Yet tonight, he seemed noticeably absent.

Anthony went into a complicated series of turns, creating a vortex of multi-colored lights. When he stopped, he stood right behind the center microphone. People cheered as the band reached a crescendo and suddenly cut out, except for the continued thumping of the background drumbeat.

"Are you ready for the greatest magician in Central Georgia?" Anthony shouted into the mic. The crowd roared its eagerness and approval.

Jonah had to admit the boy's normal, show-off personality fit the occasion. He joined in the hooting and yelled "Yeah!" with the rest of the kids.

"Are you sure?" Anthony made a show of cocking his ear toward the crowd.

Jonah thought he'd go hoarse as he yelled with everyone else again.

"Then give it up for Magician Extraordinaire, Wick Jean-Baptiste!"

The place exploded in applause at the display of colored smoke that erupted from small tubes situated all along the front of the stage.

Wick emerged from the midst of the smoke just as the music kicked into high gear again. Anthony launched into his complicated moves with the light sticks and Wick joined in, like synchronized choreography, while producing amazing, syncopated puffs of blue fire in time with the music. It was spellbinding to watch. Wick was really quite good.

The talented, young mage ended with a burst of purple-colored fire over the heads of the crowd. Several ducked but others yelled with unbridled delight when it became clear the brief flare of fire was harmless.

Jonah was about to whistle when someone pressed in beside him. He turned to find Antwan's cousin standing there. She wore a hoodie to cover her head, but the mesh mask was still in place over her lower face.

"Pathetic," she said and her muffled voice was dripping with hate.

Jonah bristled at her comment. "Don't be jealous."

She turned her intense eyes on him. "Jealous? That fool is using real magic in front of mortals. He must know how dangerous that is." She pointed at the stage. Wick was into his regular opening magic trick, but mixing in real spells. "Look at him!"

"What about you?" Jonah asked. He kept his voice low, which made it hard to talk when people started clapping and cheering. "Dumping Drew on his butt and hitting that jewelry store owner with a hex."

He felt the girl's anger radiating out toward him, causing his Death Sense to throb. "Those were insignificant, subtle uses of magic."

"Yeah. Right! I bet that shop owner's still out of his mind. And you attacked Drew in front of a whole group of kids." Again, he sensed the girl's annoyance so he leaned closer to prod her more. "We almost caught you at the mall."

The girl laughed. It was strangely beautiful and very much at odds with what he was beginning to understand about her. He wondered if her laugh would remain that way or eventually become more sinister, like Deyanira's.

"Your cousin, Lynn, is far more adept with the blades than I thought," she said.

A grudging compliment was the last thing Jonah expected. He grasped for something else to say. "I know you're working with that sorceress."

"Your friend should be more careful," the girl said. She nodded toward the stage where Robert had begun his segment of the show. "Accidents often happen."

Jonah's insides froze at the threat. And his Death Sense spiked as Antwan's cousin spoke. He almost expected her to hex Wick and Robert at any moment.

But she remained still as she watched Robert drawing all kinds of things he'd taken from the first volunteer's mind.

Although his Death Sense finally quieted, Jonah's mind raced with the girl's cryptic threat. Now, more convinced than ever that she was a young sorceress-in-training, he had to stop her from completing whatever mission she came to do. The problem was that when he turned toward her again, she was gone, almost like she used a spell to vanish. Jonah knew better than that because he didn't sense any residual magic.

He searched the surrounding crowd, which proved hopeless in the darkened room. Closing his eyes, he summoned his Reaper Stare. But that too turned out to be a mistake. There were too many people pressed too closely beside him. Plus, the souls of young people were like brilliant stars and the vibrant colors of their emotions were more than enough to make him dizzy.

He couldn't search for the girl that way, but he could focus on her magic. However, each time he tried, Wick used a spell on stage, most often in between Robert's drawing stunts. Jonah's senses spiked so hard that he had to relent.

The situation provided further proof that Wick was summoning a lot of real magic in his show. A nagging doubt that the girl was right began to bother Jonah.

Focus, he warned himself as he opened his senses to detect the magic again. He was trying to filter out Wick's use of spells, but after a while, he just gave up. Not only did the process exacerbate a growing headache, but as far as he could tell, the girl wasn't using any magic.

Did she have a way to conceal herself? Jonah suspected the mysterious woman, whoever she was, must have trained the girl to be sneaky and hard to catch. He snapped his fingers as something the girl told Drew came to mind. *"You should be careful being emotional around him."*

Of course! All she had to do was calm her own emotions. That was the big downside of his Death Sense. Unless he were being directly threatened, or someone desired to hurt him or someone close to him, Jonah couldn't sense the person's true intentions.

At the same time, he realized the girl may have thrown off her hoodie and face mask to blend in with the crowd. In fact, she could have been standing right beside him and he wouldn't have recognized her.

Jonah let out a low growl of frustration and his heart raced with growing worry. A young sorceress in the crowd was a disaster just waiting to happen.

Robert's part ended and Wick let loose with an impressive, crowd-pleasing display of flickering, blue flames, set in time to the music. That's when it happened. The spike of magic produced a bright, hot flash of warning from Jonah's Death Sense. Wick's display of blue flames suddenly changed into green fire and surged outward in all directions. Unlike the purple and blue variety, these flames produced real heat and they bellowed out like lethal ripples, moving recklessly into the unsuspecting crowd.

Oh, no! Jonah thought as he watched the scene unfold in abject horror.

CHAPTER SIXTEEN
TOKEN CALL

If Wick's sudden fumbling around on stage weren't the first sign of trouble, the intense heat of the bright green flames must have been the next clue. People not only ducked, but they screamed and tried to run away. Those caught at the front of the crowd pressed into the ones behind them. In no time at all, the green flames ignited parts of the stage, and everyone panicked before the real stampede for the doors began.

Jonah shoved his way to the wall to let the jostling kids press past him. For the first time, their club members and Brandon's crew were actually working together. They shoved the doors wide open just in time for the kids to dive through. Jonah had to give the boys credit for wading into the crowd to help the unlucky ones who fell.

Shouts came from the front, where a few kids got knocked down. Jonah tried to edge toward the commotion, but it was difficult at best.

Meanwhile, Wick stood with hands outstretched toward the flames now threatening the stage and shouted, "*Washa!*"

Jonah had never heard Wick use the fire-casting word before. To his relief, the roaring green flames instantly became the harmless blue variety before they could burn anyone. As the hall emptied, Jonah observed several injured kids.

Helping one girl to her feet, she gingerly tried to place her weight on her left foot. She winced as Jonah lowered her to the ground. Another kid, a boy, cradled his arm while one of Brandon's team held paper towels against it. The other kids seemed mostly dazed rather than seriously hurt.

Once again, Jonah's Death Sense spiked. Off to the side of the stage, hidden in the shadows, he saw Antwan's cousin hurling a hex at Robert, who yelled before he dropped to the floor near one of the large speakers.

Jonah phased without a second thought, not caring if anyone saw him. Just as he reappeared at the side of the stage, from the corner of his eye, he saw the large speaker falling. Robert's shriek of pain followed.

Before Jonah could alter his focus and help his cousin, his Death Sense spiked again. The girl flung a hex at him, but he dodged it, plowing into a stack of chairs. Seizing the opportunity, Antwan's cousin raced out the back door and fled into the night.

Jonah rolled to his feet as a bright flash of reddish light came from outside. He felt the slight pressure of a vortex being opened.

Too late to stop the girl, Jonah stumbled onto the stage as Rico heaved the huge speaker off Robert. Lynn knelt down and muttered continuously to her brother who had tears streaming down his face. A pit formed in Jonah's stomach when he saw Robert's bloodied right hand. At least two of his fingers were bent at unnatural angles.

"Oh, my God!" Jonah whispered to himself.

Lynn met his gaze. "We need some ice."

"I'll get it," Rodney said, leaping off the stage and hurrying out of the hall.

Wick leaned over Robert, saying, "I'm sorry, Bobby. I'm sorry." He confronted the shocked faces of the other kids who remained inside the hall. "It was all my fault."

Robert's face had turned a ghostly pale by the time Rodney returned with the ice and the Center's Resource Officer.

Lynn took the ice and used her own scarf to wrap her brother's hand, securing the ice in place. She glanced up at the officer. "He needs to go to the hospital."

"I've already called the EMTs and the fire department. They should be here soon."

True to his words, the sirens sounded outside. EMTs entered the hall along with another officer, the firefighters, and, to Jonah's dismay, the Teen Center's director. After the last fiasco at his birthday party, Jonah was sure the woman would ban them permanently from the premises.

The professionals checked all the kids. The girl Jonah helped earlier did have a sprained ankle. Aside from the boy with the cut arm, the rest had only minor bumps and bruises from being trodden on. Brandon's security goons talked with the director and the Practice Club guys offered to help wherever needed.

In any other situation, Jonah would have expected Brandon's people to bad-mouth Wick. But judging from their nervous looks and shaky voices, he knew they weren't doing that.

Activity around Robert brought Jonah's attention back to his cousin. The EMTs were trying to move Robert toward the exit, but Lynn was stubbornly objecting.

"I need to stay with him!" she shouted.

When a second officer attempted to stop her, the Teen Center's officer waved to his buddy. "Let her go. I'll talk to them later."

Jonah tried to follow, but the Resource Officer stopped him. "You have to give a statement."

"But that's my cousin."

"I know." The officer withdrew a pad.

Jonah wanted to object until Rico came up beside him, looking just as pissed about not being allowed to go with Lynn. They exchanged a mutually sad glance before each told the officer what they witnessed. Jonah had to weave around what really happened. Even so, it didn't look too good for Wick.

The shattered, young mage was talking to the second officer and once or twice, he raised his voice. "I wasn't using explosives in my show." Wick darted to a box at the rear of the stage, throwing back the lid, and pulling out several small cylinders that looked like large firecrackers. He showed them to the officer. "These make a lot of harmless, colored smoke, that's all."

Wick and Robert had already planned for a way to explain the supernatural fire if the need arose. That impressed Jonah. He wanted to tell Wick it wasn't his fault. An evil sorceress-in-training had been here, acting on someone's orders. But Jonah never got the chance. Before he knew it, parents had already arrived.

Wick's mom and dad had the same dark chocolate complexion as their son and they spoke with pronounced Jamaican accents. Wick's mom exuded a regal bearing, and she patted her son's slumped shoulders while her husband did most of the speaking. Her eyes surveyed the damaged stage, the toppled speaker, and finally, Jonah.

Jonah didn't know what to do, but he couldn't break her gaze until she nodded and turned back to the conversation. Since Wick's grandmother was a ghost hunter, Jonah wondered if the mom was also aware of magic and other things.

When she spoke, however, Jonah was sure of it. "My son knows his craft. He wasn't responsible for this."

"Then how do you explain the fire?" the Teen Center officer asked.

"Sabotage. I believe there were hard feelings between some of the kids here."

The officer looked stunned and Brandon's crew stirred. Wick's father stepped in, raising his hands in a placating gesture. "It was a simple accident, nothing more." He met his wife's gaze. She nodded.

Jonah recognized that look. There would be plenty of arguing later. Personally, he wanted to thank Wick's mom because she knew at once that something unusual had happened.

Perhaps the only thing that helped Wick was the fire chief's comment after examining the smoke makers. He agreed that the devices couldn't have started the fire, but he also couldn't determine what did.

Eventually, Aunt Imma arrived to take Jonah home. Rico tagged along, looking lost and uncertain.

"What about Robert?" Jonah asked as they climbed into their minivan.

"Your uncle is at the hospital." She sighed, like all the air was leaving her body. "Honestly, I always worried something would happen to Lynn, not to Robert."

Jonah hated that he was unable explain the real cause of the mess to his aunt. He rode home in silence while blaming himself for not stopping Antwan's cousin when he had the chance.

*

The long wait in the Hightowers' kitchen reminded Jonah of the time he, Robert, and his aunt were waiting for Lynn to come home after her mishap. She suffered a severe cut while saving Mike during the summer. This time, it was Robert who got injured.

Marcus's warning to Jonah, that his friends and family would get hurt, came back to him with a vengeance. Sure, he could also get banged up, and he did so way too often. But owing to his dual nature, Jonah had the ability to heal at a rapid pace. Unfortunately, Lynn, Robert, and Mike were mortals who didn't share that advantage.

It was at times like these when Jonah wanted to call his godfather. He needed to hear Marcus's calm voice assuring him that everything would be fine and the Alliance would handle it. Where were the Alliance adults right now?

Didn't they have someone here watching him? Where was that person? Jonah had never felt more alone and exposed than he did now and he wished Kevin were there. He bet the young Fallen Reaper would have caught Antwan's cousin with no problem.

The token. Jonah shoved his hand into his pocket and withdrew the small piece of wood. He rose and started for his bedroom before he changed his mind. His aunt would think he was upset and call after him.

Instead, he hurried to the bathroom at the end of the hall, closed the door, and sat on the closed toilet while gripping the token in his right hand. He concentrated and said "Help" three times, like Kevin had instructed him.

In response, the token grew hot in his palm for a few seconds and then it cooled. Was that it? What should he do now? Well, he couldn't stay in the bathroom all night! Without warning, the token went from cool to red-hot in a second. "Ouch!" he said, dropping it onto the floor.

After a shocked moment, he reached over and touched it with a hesitant finger to make sure it had cooled. He clutched it in his hand again. That must have been a response, but from who?

He flushed the toilet and ran the water to make it seem normal. As he exited the bathroom, his cell phone rang. He didn't recognize the number but suspected it had to be someone from his godfather's group.

Aunt Imma and Rico watched him with curious expressions as he crossed over to the patio door and stepped outside. "Hello?"

"We received your warning," Mage Symon Trueblood said. His voice carried a trace of urgency. "Are you in immediate danger?"

"No. I'm okay, but…"

"Are you somewhere alone?"

Jonah didn't expect that question. "Yeah. I'm outside my house, on the patio."

"Hold on."

Jonah only had to wait a few moments before a vortex opened near the back shed. Symon Trueblood exited through the opening and quickly closed it. He walked over to Jonah but stopped in the shadows, avoiding the light that streamed out through the sliding doors.

"You were saying?" Trueblood prompted him.

Jonah told Trueblood everything that happened. By the time he finished, the mage had moved to the edge of the patio. There was a short silence.

"I suspect there's much more magic being used than you can appreciate, Jonah." Trueblood sounded as if he were selectively choosing his words. "I'll send someone else down to investigate as soon as I can."

"Who? Kevin?"

"He's on assignment again."

"You'll come, won't you?"

"I may not be able to. We rotate all the members of our group to camouflage our collective support for Marcus."

Jonah wanted to scream. Kevin had warned him and Mike about Alliance Council politics, but he hated hearing the harsh reality of it. "How soon?"

"Soon."

"What about the person the Council sent to watch me?"

Trueblood frowned. "You'll find no help there."

"You know who it is?"

"Yes, but we've taken an oath not to reveal anyone's identity."

"You mean you can't tell me? That's not fair."

"I am sorry." Trueblood sounded more somber than usual.

Just then, Aunt Imma let out a small sound of dismay from inside the house. Robert, Lynn, and Uncle James had just returned home. Robert's right index and middle fingers were bandaged and wrapped in a brace to keep them immobilized. His face was still pale and he looked tired and miserable.

Jonah scrambled for the sliding door and opened it just as his Uncle James loomed in the doorway. The man's eyes were furious as he gazed over Jonah's shoulder and saw Trueblood.

Jonah backed away and let his uncle exit the house. "Ah, Uncle James, this is—"

"I know exactly who he is, Jonah!" Uncle James narrowed his eyes in pure anger. "That man is Symon Trueblood, a mage who works directly for the Alliance."

CHAPTER SEVENTEEN
ROGUE'S GALLERY

Jonah couldn't believe his uncle recognized Trueblood. "You know about the Alliance?"

"Go inside and pull the blinds," Uncle James ordered.

"But–"

"Do it now, Jonah!" His uncle took a breath and added in a softer but final tone that didn't invite argument, "Please do as I say."

"Yes, sir." Jonah obeyed without another word.

"Who's that?" Aunt Imma asked Jonah as he reentered the kitchen.

Jonah blinked, reaching for a good cover story, and decided to be as honest as possible. "One of my godfather's coworkers. I told him what happened."

"Oh, that was thoughtful."

As soon as Aunt Imma turned to Robert, Jonah closed the blinds.

"You should lie down," Aunt Imma urged her son.

"I don't want to lie down," Robert objected. "I need to talk to Wick so he doesn't go crazy or keep blaming himself."

"You can do that later." She forced him to sit down on the sofa. "You lie back down for now." She read the pain medication directions.

Lynn watched from the entrance to the foyer, her arms crossed as her entire body kept trembling.

Rico had an arm around her shoulders. He whispered, "He'll be okay. I broke my fingers once when I flipped over the handlebars of my bike after running into a pothole."

"Not helping," Robert muttered. "I broke my fingers, not my ears."

Robert's sour mood seemed to affect Lynn the most. She shook her head from side-to-side. "I should have known. I should have felt this before it happened."

"Not that again," Rico sighed.

Lynn whirled on her boyfriend. "I sense when bad things are gonna happen. It's not my imagination!" She pulled away from Rico, marched down the hall to the front door, and dashed outside.

"Lynn!" Aunt Imma called.

"I'll go after her," Rico said and he followed Lynn.

Robert met Jonah's worried gaze as he rose to his feet again. "I'm tired and I don't need help."

Aunt Imma ignored his protest as she trailed him to his room. With the den cleared, Jonah returned to the patio doors and opened them a crack to listen. Uncle James and Trueblood had moved off into the darkness of the backyard, but their voices reached Jonah's ears.

"...told me you would protect my sister," Uncle James said.

"I *did* protect her."

"Really? Then what happened? Now my son and daughter are getting hurt. I won't have it!"

"We told you that Robert and Lynn would have to develop their skills."

"When they're eighteen. Until then, I'm responsible for them and Jonah."

A silence followed that comment. Then Trueblood said, "Jonah's not your son. You know what Janice and Isaiah wanted for him."

"He is my son, just as much as Robert!"

That statement touched Jonah. He still thought of his cousins as his cousins though, and not his brother and sister.

"I won't have you endangering my kids," Uncle James said.

"They are who they are, James."

"Not again."

When Trueblood spoke, there was real pain in his voice. "I miss Janice too. Every day."

"Don't mention my sister. It was your foolishness that provoked Ruby. And what happened to poor Jonah..."

"He's fine."

"No thanks to you! At least Jonah's godfather is level-headed and responsible. He wanted Jonah to stay out of all the trouble and that's why he sent him here."

"That was his parents' decision, and Marcus was only honoring their wishes. Jonah's becoming exactly whom he's destined to be. You can't stop that. No more than you could stop your sister."

"Get out of my yard."

"Fine, James. Tell Jonah I'll contact him later."

Jonah saw a brief flash of light when the vortex opened and quickly closed. Uncle James seemed to appear out of the darkness, walking purposefully toward the house.

When he caught Jonah listening, he let out a sigh and entered the house. "You heard?" Uncle James asked.

"Not everything," Jonah said. "I'm sorry."

"It's not your fault. None of this is." He looked very tired.

"So, you know about Lynn and Robert and me?"

Uncle James nodded and leaned against the breakfast bar to calm himself.

Jonah pulled out a kitchen table chair and sat.

Before Uncle James continued, Aunt Imma emerged from Robert's room, muttering about the state of his bed linen. She hustled to the hall closet and came back with clean sheets. Uncle James gave his wife a weary smile and pulled out a bar stool. Without warning, he said, "I always thought fate cheated the males in my family. Then Imma pointed out how I could make the right decisions on little information."

"You mean, you have the gift?" Jonah winced at using the word.

Uncle James looked thoughtful. "The gift. That's what your aunt–" He stopped, his eyes widening.

"Don't worry," Jonah said. "I found out about Aunt Ruby."

Uncle James blinked several times and then released a low breath. "Lynn and Robert have been talking too much."

"It's okay."

"No, it isn't. Listen to me, Jonah: Don't you worry about Ruby. Whatever happened is over."

If that were true, Jonah wondered, why was his uncle yelling at Trueblood and blaming the mage for his mom's death? Jonah hated the doubt that crept into his mind at his uncle's words. Did he not know what happened? Or was his uncle only trying to protect him?

A simple Reaper Stare would have done the trick, but Jonah resisted that idea. It didn't seem proper to use it on his friends and family.

"I can't deny that Robert has a variation of Lynn's ability," Uncle James said. "And his magic trick…" He looked Jonah squarely in the eye. "Given my sister's abilities, and your father's nature," he raised an eyebrow, "I realized you would be special, Jonah."

It was clear to Jonah that his uncle knew a lot but was also fishing for information. When he didn't answer, Uncle James rose. "Lynn's angry about losing her intuition, but it's really for the best. Those types of things always lead to unnecessary pain and suffering."

"Yes, sir."

Uncle James cocked his head to the side. "Have you called your godfather?"

"He's on a business trip. That's why I called Mage Trueblood."

"Business trip? I can imagine." He started for Robert's room but paused on the other side of the breakfast bar and said, "Steer clear of Trueblood and all this other business, Jonah. If the Alliance insists on sending someone while your godfather is away, tell them to send someone else. I'll tell Robert and Lynn the same thing. Better safe than sorry."

His uncle was wrong. When it came to the supernatural, things had a way of forcing him into the very middle. If Trueblood were right, events were already in motion. No, he couldn't steer clear from it even if he wanted to. And he didn't want to, either, because there was something he had to do.

*

The rest of the evening passed quietly. Lynn didn't return home before Jonah headed to bed. Uncle James spent a long time talking with Robert. Far longer than he did with Lynn after she got injured. When Jonah peeked in on his cousin, Robert was fast asleep.

So Jonah slumped off to bed, his mind in turmoil. He liked the Truebloods. The sister had kicked butt in the Afterworld and saved his and Mike's life more than once. He couldn't imagine not being around either mage.

Feeling strangely keyed-up and anxious, Jonah slipped under his covers, put in his earbuds, and listened to music well into the night. Finally, his exhaustion overtook him and he slept.

Dream-walks, when they happened, seemed to occur just after Jonah closed his eyes. In this one, he stood in front of an impressive stone site with seven tall stone pillars evenly spaced around a large round platform of granite. Words, in an unreadable language, were etched in the flat faces of the pillars.

Too bad Mike isn't here, he thought. The place reminded him of the Georgia Guide Stones site, a granite monument in North Georgia. This monument was even bigger and it covered more area. At the center was a large, horizontal slab of stone.

For some reason, Jonah thought it was a sacrificial table. The idea popped into his mind on its own, along with sharp flashes of images of previous sacrifices. At first, he thought they were from some movie he shouldn't have watched. Yet the images seemed too real. But that couldn't be. He'd never seen a sacrifice in real life.

The flashes and thoughts left a sour taste in his mouth and an ache in the pit of his stomach. He shook his head and would have stepped onto the marble platform but he caught a slight distortion in the air in front of him. He stopped, knowing that it must have been a ward or some other kind of barrier. Jonah had learned that even during a dream-walk, any ward reacted to his astral body.

He took a step back and for the first time noticed someone moving in the shadow of a pillar. As he narrowed his eyes, peering into the darkness, he managed to make out enough details to identify Antwan's cousin, the girl in the niqab! She was still wearing the face mask and hoodie she wore at Wick's magic show.

Jonah's hands curled into fists. *Why was she here?* In answer to his unspoken question, someone in all black phased onto the marble platform.

It was the Alliance mole. Jonah remembered the traitor from a previous dream-walk in which the man had argued with Deyanira. Like then, he wore his Reaper long coat but also a hat and a mask to hide his true identity. And his outline seemed to waver as if it were distorted.

A flash of purplish light appeared, and the sorceress stepped through. It was her own version of a vortex, and very cool and frightening to witness.

The hulking man from Robert's picture came through the misty opening behind her. His eyes were a glowing, milky white, a sign of Wraith possession. As he lumbered around the center stone slab, he cast angry glances at everyone else.

But Jonah shifted his attention to the woman. Like the girl, she concealed herself in the shadows between the pillars. Jonah hoped she would lower her hood, but she didn't. Even with his ability to discern small details in the shadows, her hood was drawn too far forward to allow him to make out her face.

When she spoke, her voice sent chills down Jonah's spine. "You called us here, mole. Why?"

"I'm concerned with the mission's success," the mole replied with his slightly distorted voice. "Thank goodness tonight went exactly as planned." He waved a finger at the huge Wraith. "Your failure to control your brethren threatened the entire operation. They should have never attacked the Blackstone brat and his cousins."

"He banished my brethren back to the Underworld! A Wraith requires a long time to recover from that." He smacked his huge fists together. "I should have snapped the brat's neck."

"You'll be lucky if he doesn't send you back too," the mole scoffed. "Because of you, this girl had to take care of the store owner in broad daylight. And she also had to deal with the cousin tonight."

Niqab Girl stirred. "I did what I needed to do."

"Yes, but I've been working overtime to make sure everything else remained on track."

"You just want to keep your head neatly attached to your body," the Wraith taunted.

"We should all be concerned with surviving, idiot!"

The Wraith growled and pounded the stone slab with his fist. The thing didn't budge, but it did creak.

"As for you," the mole continued to Niqab Girl, "are you even sure this barrier will keep the brat from eavesdropping?"

Jonah winced at being called *brat* yet again, but he didn't move a muscle.

Niqab Girl raised her hands. Magical energy crackled around her fingertips. "Deyanira trained me to do my job well."

The tension between the group was palpable, even to Jonah in his spirit form.

Then the woman laughed. It was low and mocking.

Niqab Girl turned her head toward the woman and lowered her hands.

The mole nodded and addressed the sorceress. "You, at least, must understand that careful, slow revenge is the best revenge of all."

The woman nodded and threw back her hood. But Jonah couldn't discover her identity because her face glowed, obscuring the features. When she spoke, her rich voice filled the air. "When it's over, Jonah Blackstone will belong to me, or–" she suddenly turned and looked right at Jonah. Her brilliant, orange eyes met his when she added, "You will die, young one!"

She waved her hand and pain engulfed Jonah's mind. He woke up in his bedroom, both hands clamped over his head. "Ow, ow, ow!" The severe headache lasted for several minutes, leaving Jonah on the verge of vomiting until the pain subsided.

As he tried to recall the meeting, a residual ache made his head throb. Had she put a spell on him to make it too painful to remember? He kept trying and when the pain finally subsided, he concluded that wasn't the case.

Eventually, he replayed the dream-walk and one thing became clear: The woman's eyes had vertical pupils, just like the cat that stalked him outside Drew's house.

CHAPTER EIGHTEEN
DARK AVENGER

Robert and Lynn were already in the kitchen when Jonah entered. Aunt Imma had prepared her normally huge Sunday morning breakfast. She was in her room getting ready for church while Uncle James sat on the patio, sipping coffee and reading the Sunday paper.

Robert looked so disgruntled and helpless in his hand brace that Lynn took pity on him and fixed him a plate of food.

When Robert held his spoon awkwardly in his left hand, Lynn's patience wore thin. "You can feed yourself."

"I know that, Lynn," he barked.

Lynn glared back until Robert slumped a little and added, "Thanks."

She nodded before starting on her toast.

Jonah sat down and piled his plate with hot food. Before he ate his first forkful, he glanced at his cousins. "Did Uncle James talk to you?"

Robert grunted but kept eating.

Lynn gave an angry huff and put down her toast. "Yes, he did. We're not stopping what we're doing."

"Cool." Jonah had assumed as much, but it was good to hear it all the same.

"Why didn't you tell us Trueblood came by last night?" Lynn asked.

Jonah nearly choked on his food. "Uncle James told you that?" Lynn nodded and waited for him to continue. Jonah told them everything he heard.

Even Robert stopped eating to stare at him in shock. "Wow. They really went at it. Our dad?"

"Yeah." Jonah waited. When his cousins didn't say anything else, he asked, "You're not surprised he knows about your powers?"

"No," Lynn answered. "Your mom was his sister. With all those gifted women on his side of the family, our dad had to know what was up."

"Then why keep the club a secret?"

"Because as you heard, our dad doesn't like the supernatural stuff. He knows about our powers but not how often we're using them."

Jonah nodded, wondering if the death of his mom and dad had anything to do with his uncle's opinion. But that brought up another subject. He put down his fork. "Did you find out why my mom stopped bringing me here?"

Lynn and Robert exchanged a worried look. "It had something to do with Aunt Ruby," Lynn finally admitted.

"What happened?"

"I'm not sure. But I remember the arguments. Instead of watching you, my dad asked Aunt Ruby to do it. When your mom arrived and found out, she went ballistic." Lynn's voice sounded hollow. She gazed across the kitchen, like she was recalling the critical moment. "When your mom came back with you, she looked tired. And you were asleep, I think. She and my dad argued again."

"Yeah, I remember that part," Robert chimed in. "Your mom cut her trip short and insisted on leaving that night." He pushed his plate away and leaned on the table. "That was the last time we saw you."

"Well, that is, until you came to live with us," Lynn said. "All this happened a few months before Ruby went totally crazy. But now that I think about it, her change started right after that night. Sorry."

He didn't want them to apologize. This was more information than he ever had before. To keep the conversation going, he described the note from his mom's box, one that he suspected came from Mage Trueblood.

Lynn nodded. "No wonder my dad was angry with the mage. But…" She faltered. "I think Dad also blames himself. Maybe that's why they can't stand to be around each other."

"Maybe." Jonah was bummed because he had no way to find out. His mom was dead. His aunt was in another part of the state, although Jonah had no intentions of talking to the woman anyway. If Trueblood knew something, Jonah doubted the mage would tell him. And then there was Omar, who insisted he ask Marcus. But Jonah's godfather was in the Afterworld.

Jonah wished he could have hit something. Adding to his frustration and anger were Robert's broken fingers and

Lynn's diminishing intuition. Their last clue, Niqab Girl's location, was a bust because the girl stayed out of reach.

Jonah needed to act, but he wasn't sure how to do that. *Well*, he corrected himself, *that wasn't exactly true*. He already had a plan forming in his mind.

*

After church, Jonah spent the late afternoon in his room assembling his disguise. He intended to wear a black hoodie, black pants, gloves, and a full-face mask made of resin. It looked like a Komainu, a lion-like creature with boney ridges on the forehead and spiked cheekbones.

He pulled the mask on, adjusting the elastic straps. The material began to mold itself to his face. When Jonah glanced into the mirror, he was startled by his reflection. The only features about him that were still identifiable were his eyes. And the effect of narrowing them in mock anger was downright menacing.

A slow smile creased his lips. This was perfect! Drew wouldn't know him at all. Just to be sure, he positioned the hoodie over his forehead and moved his head from side-to-side. The mask remained firmly in place and the hoodie covered his afro.

Satisfied with his perfected disguise, Jonah stripped down and stowed the clothes in the closet. His judicious eavesdropping at school on Friday, plus, seeing Drew for himself in his room, revealed the boy stayed up late playing video games. Jonah bet Drew would do the same tonight. That suited him because he wanted the bully to be fully alert and scared when he suddenly appeared.

Jonah acted normal during dinner and even played video games with Robert afterward. He allowed his cousin to win, which was hard, given the adverse effect of Robert's brace on his usually adept gaming skills.

Late in the evening, Jonah sat at the kitchen table to go over his homework for the next day. He faked a wide yawn after a couple of hours and announced, "I'm going to bed."

Choosing a nice playlist of quiet songs on his phone, not the usual movie scores, to settle his pounding heart, he slipped under the covers. Falling asleep was the last thing on his mind because of his nervous anticipation.

Lost in his thoughts of what he had to do, it took him a moment to realize how much time elapsed. It was now ten until midnight, the time he selected to be sure his aunt and uncle were settled for the night.

Throwing off the covers, he put on the clever disguise, being careful not to make too much noise. He grabbed the mask, saving it until he got outside the house. At the last minute, he grabbed a handful of butterscotch candies and stuffed them into his pants pocket. Since his time in the Afterworld, he didn't get dizzy while phasing. But he planned to do a lot of it tonight, and that might take its toll. Better to be prepared.

The time on the clock radio changed to midnight. Jonah snuck out of his room, through the den, and, after turning off the alarm, he stealthily slipped out into the backyard. The autumn night sky was cloudless and there was a slight nip in the air. As he entered the shadow of the big tree near the shed, he shivered slightly, thinking the temperature felt even chillier there.

Jonah put on the mask and pulled the hoodie's drawstring tighter. Then he lowered his head, dropped his hands at his sides, and took deep breaths, settling his mind. *It's now or never. There's no turning back once I show up in Drew's room.* Jonah called up the images of Latrell, a troubled Lynn, disillusioned Wick, and finally, an injured Robert. The images pushed away any lingering doubts. That done, he mentally nudged himself into a phase.

*

Drew was exactly where Jonah expected to find him. In fact, the boy was reaching over to type something on his computer keyboard when Jonah suddenly appeared. Drew's eyes bugged out of his head and he stared at Jonah for a horrified moment, too shocked to say anything or even move.

Jonah took advantage of the surprise, lunging forward, and grabbing the front of the boy's t-shirt before phasing them both away.

They reappeared a second later inside the lower hallway of the high school. As soon as Jonah released Drew, the boy screamed and scrambled away to press his back against a wall.

"How did I get here?" Drew shouted.

Jonah watched, allowing the silence to build.

"Who are you?" The boy grew more frantic.

Jonah raised his arms and gestured at the surrounding hallway and the nearby bathrooms. It was a hotspot that the anti-bullying club often patrolled, and something else.

He once noticed during one of his shifts that it was invisible to the motion detectors. He and Drew could move around without setting off any of the alarms.

"This is where you bullied him," Jonah said, careful to change up his voice. In fact, he spoke in a low and measured tone, trying to sound like Marcus.

Drew's eyes dilated even wider. "Latrell! Is that you?"

"No!" Jonah stepped toward him. "What did Latrell ever do to you?"

The bully cringed against the wall. "We were just having fun."

"Fun?" Jonah loomed closer.

Drew jerked away. "We never thought he'd kill himself."

Anger surged through Jonah. He grabbed Drew and hurled the boy against the opposite wall of lockers.

Drew cried out when he hit the wall and slid to the floor. "Please don't hurt me!" he begged as he curled into a defensive ball.

Jonah only dimly registered that he'd just thrown the hefty kid like he weighed nothing. It seemed like a spike of power must've entered his body. The lingering effects of the surprising extra strength suffused Jonah as he stood over Drew.

In desperation, the boy jumped to his feet and threw a punch, but Jonah easily blocked the attack. Moving with practiced grace, he gripped Drew and flipped the boy over a shoulder and onto the hard floor.

"Ow!" Drew squirmed in pain and tried to crawl away. "Please. I'm sorry!"

"No, you aren't!" Jonah gripped him by the ankle and phased again.

They reappeared outside Latrell's house this time, in the middle of the quiet street. Before Drew could react, Jonah hauled him to his feet and clamped a gloved hand over his mouth. Again, power augmented his movements, allowing him to hold the stocky boy with no problem.

"Did you tell his parents you were sorry?" Jonah hissed in Drew's ear. "I think you laughed it off with Brandon." Drew mumbled against the glove, but Jonah wasn't prepared to let him talk. "Did you tell Latrell you were sorry?"

Jonah phased them again to the roof of the high school, perching on top of the solar energy array. He hustled Drew toward the edge and a four-story drop. "Maybe people will think you took *your* own life."

Drew howled against the gloved hand before wetting himself.

The pungent smell hit Jonah a moment later. "Nice," he said, shifting to avoid being splashed by the growing puddle at their feet. Then he phased them again, sooner than planned, to get away from the mess.

They reappeared in Oak Hill cemetery. Drew let out a muffled scream when he saw the headstones. Jonah pushed him to the ground, right in front of Latrell's grave. He felt a savage satisfaction at the bully's raw fear. *Let him think he's gonna die.*

"I'm sorry!" The words tumbled out of Drew's mouth between wet sobs.

"Tell that to Latrell," Jonah growled.

Drew reached out his shaking hands toward the headstone. "I'm sorry, Latrell. I'm so sorry."

Jonah stood behind him. "Tell that to the principal too. Confess your crime."

"I will. I swear. Please don't kill me. I don't want to die."

"Latrell didn't want to die either, not until you and Brandon made his life utterly miserable."

Drew broke down into more sobs.

Jonah was sick of him. Besides, the dizziness had increased and he still needed to get himself home. He gripped Drew by the back of the neck and phased to the boy's bedroom, where Jonah shoved the bully onto the bed.

"Remember," Jonah said. "Confess." With that, he turned and phased.

*

The mask and hoodie were suffocating Jonah. He stripped them off as soon as he entered his room and collapsed on his bed. His heart was beating so fast that he became light-headed and dizzy. Unwrapping a piece of candy proved difficult, as his hands shook. Once he managed that, however, and popped it into his mouth, he lay back on the bed and closed his eyes.

Several minutes later, the excitement wore off but his hands trembled again. He pushed himself pretty far tonight. Too far, if he were being honest.

No, the angry voice in his head answered. Drew deserved it. Brandon did too. He just hoped that Drew would come forward and snitch on Brandon. Then he intended to deal with Antwan's cousin separately.

After his head cleared, Jonah rolled off the bed, undid the black pants, and put them and the rest of the disguise inside a large shopping bag with handles. He pushed it into the back corner of his closet. As he lay in bed again, the events of the previous night caught up to him.

Did he do anything to give himself away? Jonah doubted that. But what if Drew told someone instead of confessing? *What would happen then?* Jonah wondered. Well, apart from Brandon, perhaps no one would believe the kid.

Jonah enjoyed the pleasant image of the snobby boy wetting his own expensive pants. He smiled to himself for a brief moment before a sobering fear intruded.

What if he had really hurt Drew? He threw the boy across the hall. Where did the sudden burst of strength come from? For once, Jonah wished he could go to Alliance HQ, sit down in one of their libraries, and read all about the powers of a Fallen Reaper. Well, there was Hackett's, but he didn't want to face Alastor right now.

Besides, he wasn't totally clueless about Fallen Reapers. It made sense that his Reaper half could provide him with extra power. But since he never was able to call on it before, he could only wonder why now? Jonah fumed because his godfather never explained any of those things to him.

As much as he wanted to dwell on that aspect of the evening, his mind wouldn't cooperate. His thoughts returned to his original question. Did he really do that for Latrell?

Maybe I did it for myself? He was quite satisfied with his actions. Someone needed to confront Drew.

Although his anger had waned, the deeper frustration and sense of isolation remained. No one could know about what he'd done. Lynn would kill him if she ever found out and Mike wouldn't talk to him for months, if ever again. This was his own private, little war on the bullies and now he knew he'd have to fight it alone.

CHAPTER NINETEEN
BAD-TEMPERED BULLY

School was uneventful for Jonah on Monday, which was fine because he felt lethargic from lack of sleep. What worried him was Drew's absence. He hadn't hurt the boy, not seriously. So why wasn't he around? Brandon and Antwan didn't act as if Drew had confessed. Not in the hallways, nor at lunch.

Doubts began to assail Jonah. Did he do the right thing? The voice inside his head was sure he did.

Toward the end of his lunch period, Jonah strode to his locker alone, still trying to calm his mind and banish his uncertainties. He had just removed his book for the next period when Mike came up. Jonah was shocked. Mike's eyes were heavy with bags beneath them. And his posture was somewhat stooped.

He leaned against the adjacent locker, watching Jonah. Although he seemed tired, Mike's eyes darted around, taking in everyone who passed by. He fidgeted with his own book. In fact, his hands never stopped moving.

"Mike? Are you okay?"

He seemed to have forgotten Jonah was there, even though he just walked up to him. "Yeah. Why?"

"You look like you haven't been sleeping."

Mike snorted. "You're one to talk! You look like the walking dead." He turned, leaning his back against the locker. "I'm fine."

Jonah began to suspect his friend needed the locker for support. "Where's your ribbon?"

Mike glanced down at his shirt and his eyes widened. Fumbling briefly in his pocket, he withdrew a bent, orange ribbon, and attached it to his shirt. "Happy?"

Jonah couldn't believe it. Mike was neat to a fault. His clothes were always clean and pressed and he seemed so put together. Today, his shirt was wrinkled, causing Jonah to doubt that he ironed it—and he even suspected he might have slept in it.

"I'm fine, Jonah. I just want to complete the translation. It's a lot of work and…" His voice trailed off. He shook his head and seemed to snap back to attention, narrowing his eyes at someone over Jonah's shoulder.

Brandon and Antwan sauntered by and snickered at them.

"Aw, you're so cute with the pumpkin ribbons!" He and Antwan laughed as they walked away.

"Idiots." Mike smacked the flat of his hand against the locker while glaring at the retreating boys.

Jonah was reassured by his buddy's reaction, and that reminded him that Mike would probably know about Drew. "Hey, have you seen Drew?"

"Nope. Why?"

Jonah hid his surprise by hooking a thumb at Brandon and Antwan. "It's only been those two clowns today."

"Oh, well, maybe Drew came to his senses."

"I doubt it," Jonah said. Now that he was on the subject, he was sure he could persuade Mike to give Drew a call. He just needed to prod his friend without seeming too interested.

Before he could come up with a way to do that, Patrick arrived and Mike's attention refocused like a laser.

"See you later," Mike said as he waved. Patrick gave Jonah little more than a suspicious glare before they walked off.

Thoughts of visiting Patrick one night in the disguise became more appealing by the second. Jonah slammed his locker closed and turned for class. That's when he spotted Latrell standing, or rather, floating in the middle of the hall. Streams of students walked through his ghostly body.

It was interesting to watch the kids' reactions to his presence. Some shivered while others didn't seem to notice anything. And if the boy's presence wasn't weird enough, he turned and floated through the closed auditorium door. Jonah hurried after him.

The stage lights were on, shining down on semi-circular rows of folding chairs set up in concert formation. The band and orchestra agreed to combine for a one-time Halloween concert.

Despite the bright lights, Jonah had no problems spotting Latrell, who stood off to the side of the auditorium, near the back.

Jonah slipped down the row and stopped beside the ghost. "I know you're connected to the ankh you gave me." Latrell didn't respond so Jonah added, "What are you doing here?"

"I wanted to see you."

"You can't just show up unannounced." Jonah dropped into a seat while keeping an eye out for anyone who might overhear. "Why were you at Drew's?"

"Because you were." Latrell's ghostly eyes stared at Jonah's chest.

He wondered if the ghost could see the amulet beneath his sweater. "Well, stop doing that, okay?"

"I saw Brandon in the hallway. When you asked where he lived, I thought you'd do something to him."

"He was out of town. I..." Jonah hesitated, but was not sure why. "I visited Drew. I wanted to scare him into confessing his part in bullying you."

"You did that for me?"

Jonah nodded, expecting Latrell to smile. Instead, the boy looked worried. "What's wrong?"

Latrell didn't reply. After an awkward moment, he reached out to touch the pumpkin ribbon pinned to Jonah's chest. The semi-transparent finger passed through the fabric and chilled Jonah where it touched his skin. Meanwhile, the ankh around Jonah's neck flared with heat. The combination of cold and hot caused Jonah to suck in a startled breath.

Latrell pulled his hand away. "Sorry."

"It's fine." He held out his hand. Latrell hesitated before touching his palm to Jonah's. It felt weird, besides being cold. But Jonah imagined he could feel the texture of skin on Latrell's palm. "Can you make yourself more solid? One of the Wraiths in your basement did."

"That takes time and uses a lot of power." Latrell attempted a caressing motion with his hand but his fingers slipped through Jonah's. That seemed to sadden the boy and he withdrew his hand. "It's easier for a Wraith to share a mortal's body."

"You mean by possession?" Jonah shuddered. "No, thank you."

"But it doesn't have to be possession. That's forceful. A person can choose to share their body."

The eagerness in Latrell's voice worried Jonah. "I'm sorry, Latrell. I could never do that."

"Never?"

Jonah shook his head. In the back of his mind was a fleeting memory of something terrible that happened. It was connected to this subject. Despite the sense of dread that accompanied the notion, Jonah tried to call it up, but hit a wall. The more he tried, the more his head throbbed. He abandoned the effort.

Latrell moved closer, peering at him the whole time. "What was that? You looked like it hurt."

Jonah leaned away from the ghost. "I'm okay."

A band member walked onto the stage and moved around the back of the chairs. "My lunch period's ending," Jonah whispered.

Latrell nodded, then glanced down at his folded hands. "Thank you."

"You're welcome," Jonah replied but Latrell had already disappeared.

He stood and hitched his book bag in place while thinking about Latrell's cryptic request. He'd never let a Wraith share his body. Not even a sad boy like Latrell. Again, the wretched feeling that something terrible had happened to him pressed on the edges of his awareness.

Jonah's mind replayed the strange encounter all through his next class and afterward, until Mike came running up. He pulled Jonah to their first patrol spot, across from a boy's bathroom on the lower level. Jonah's face warmed because it was the same location where he had phased with Drew the night before.

He wiggled out of Mike's death grip. "What's up?"

"Drew!" Mike gulped and glanced around, lowering his voice. "He and his parents came to the main office this afternoon. I was talking to the secretary when they marched in." Mike's news was interrupted by two fellow ninth-graders being rough with each other.

Once they turned the corner, Jonah nudged his friend. "Well?"

"He confessed to the principal that he bullied Latrell." Mike folded his arms, looking disgusted. "I tried to talk to him, and then he goes and does that!"

Jonah acted as if he were shocked by the news. "Did he report Brandon?"

"No, but Brandon would just deny it, Jonah. He's not dumb. And his father's important enough to make a big stink about it." Mike paused as a couple of girls walked by. "Drew should've been the last person to bully Latrell. I can't believe hanging out with Brandon means that much to him."

Jonah shrugged. "Maybe it does."

"Well, at least there's some good in him."

"What do you mean?"

"He came forward and admitted it," Mike pointed out. "So it must have been eating him up inside."

Jonah wanted to tell his friend that Drew had no intention of confessing until after his private visit, which scared him into it. The way Jonah saw it, if Drew were truly sorry, he'd have no problem telling on Brandon.

The last period bell rang. Mike pushed off the wall, and Jonah followed.

Before the end of the day, the entire school knew about Drew's confession, primarily through texting and instant chat apps. Jonah wondered if the boy would ever show his face again. The whole situation scared him a bit. He'd been the cause of this development, but it also set his resolve. *One bully down, one to go.*

*

Brandon proved to be a difficult target to watch. Between Jonah's school work, Practice Club meetings about the coming Halloween Bonfire, Tolerance Club, and other obligations, he couldn't scout Brandon's house until late in the day.

The other problem was the Warners' house itself. As Jonah had discovered while visiting Latrell's room, Brandon's house had a wall around it. Jonah borrowed Lynn's binoculars so he could spy on the bully from a distance. To his mounting dismay, he found that wouldn't work because the houses on either side of Brandon's also had stone or brick walls, as well as screening shrubbery.

Jonah's frustration grew as his search for a suitable hiding place proved fruitless. Plus, he was afraid someone would notice him loitering around the upscale neighborhood. As if proving Jonah's fear, Brandon exited his front gate.

For a critical few seconds, Jonah froze, unsure of what to do. Then he dived behind a nearby SUV. If Brandon caught him, the entire plan would be ruined. Only now did it occur to Jonah to phase away.

Feeling a bit embarrassed, he prepared to phase when he heard Brandon speak. "I told you, I don't care about law school."

"Brandon," his mother's urgent voice cut in. "Quiet. You're making a scene."

"What do you expect?" Brandon's dad said.

Jonah peeked around the edge of the SUV. Brandon's mother glanced up and down the street, as if she were worried about the neighbors overhearing. She and her husband were dressed in elegant evening attire. The dad's expensive coat was folded over his left arm.

"Your great-grandfather, grandfather, and I have worked hard to build our firm to the respected establishment it is today. You have no idea what they had to go through to stay alive, literally, in the South." He stepped closer to his son, towering over him. "We didn't work this hard to see you go out and prove a stereotype about young black men only being fit to play ball or wave a microphone around on a stage."

"But I'm good and I worked hard at it. The coach wants me on—"

"I'll have a word with the coach and extend my regrets. You will not be on the team this year, nor any future year."

"Listen to your father," Mrs. Warner urged. "Our plans for you are much higher. A judgeship or even the State House."

Mr. Warner arched an eyebrow and his voice sounded dangerous. "You will comply with our wishes or you'll find out how hard things can be. Drew won't be the only one confessing. My protection for your chronic pattern of missteps will cease. Is that understood?"

"Yes, sir." Brandon sulked.

Seeing the arrogant boy so cowed was a new experience for Jonah. Again, he couldn't deny a smattering of pity for him. Just then, at the far end of the street, a black car came toward them. Jonah ducked under cover again as the car slowed, but not before noting it was a black limousine. The car pulled up until it was even with the Warners.

A huge man in a black suit that was stretched tight cross his large frame exited the front passenger side. Jonah sucked in a breath because he recognized him as the hulking man from Robert's sketch and Jonah's dream-walk. What shocked Jonah the most was the little, white skull the man wore on his left lapel.

Jonah had seen the small skull before. Mr. Warner had once escorted Agent Hunter and a serious-looking man in a dark suit and sunglasses around the Teen Center. Mike claimed the mysterious man was a security expert but Jonah remembered seeing the same small skull on the guy's suit coat.

So far, the only people Jonah had encountered wearing the small skulls were either Wraith-possessed or working with the Wraiths. That ignited a whole fury of questions about Mr. Warner.

What was he doing with this huge guy? Was Mr. Warner involved with the Alliance mole too? At least Brandon's dad didn't wear a skull on his expensive suit lapel.

The hulking guy gave the Warners a perplexed look. "You didn't have to wait here, sir. We coulda driven up to the house."

Mr. Warner glared at his son. "We were dealing with a minor problem."

The hulking guy shrugged and opened the back door.

Mrs. Warner got in, but Mr. Warner paused to speak to his son. "Your mother and I will be back this evening around ten."

Brandon's dad got into the car. The huge guy hurried around, moving quickly for his size. As soon as he closed his own door, the car drove off down the street.

That's when Brandon called out, "I know you're hiding behind the truck, freak."

Jonah's heart nearly leapt into his throat as he stood.

Brandon's face was a mask of fury. "I don't care what you heard–"

"I wasn't listening," Jonah lied.

"Then why are you here?"

Jonah moved around the vehicle to face the bully and gestured to the house across the street. "I was talking to Latrell's mom."

Brandon's face paled and he took a step away from Jonah. He seemed to realize he was showing fear and his face twisted in anger. "What did you do to me and Antwan?"

"I don't know what you mean."

Brandon jabbed a finger at him. "You did something to our memories." He moved closer. "I have a block. That's what Antwan's cousin said."

Uh-oh. Jonah was at a loss. He racked his brain, trying to stall and think of something to put the bully off.

Brandon noticed. "I knew it! What's going on?"

"Why don't you ask Antwan's cousin?"

To his surprise, Brandon scowled. "She won't tell me anything else about you, but she knows."

Jonah relaxed upon hearing that. He could be totally honest with Brandon. "I didn't do anything to you. I swear."

"Liar!" Brandon yelled after checking to make sure no one overheard him. "When I find out, you'll get it, freak." He spun on his heels and headed down the street.

With his original mission busted, Jonah decided to trail the bully. As he went along, he reflected on the unnerving conversation. Niqab Girl's willingness to keep Brandon in the dark was fortunate. *Maybe she didn't trust him either.*

Brandon reached a nearby park, and Jonah discovered it was the same one Danita and Mike had mentioned. *Too bad the black cat wouldn't show up and eat Brandon*, he thought with savage pleasure.

But he didn't have time to dwell on that pleasant prospect because he had to pick a spot to hide in. He chose a large tree close to the picnic table where Brandon stood, and phased. Jonah's placement was perfect because he could overhear the boy's phone call.

"Drew told me someone was outside his house. That was right before he went crazy and confessed. So what?" Brandon paused to puff on a lit cigarette. "Why does your cousin want me to be careful?" He paused again, then threw his cigarette butt away.

"I don't like her bossing me around, Antwan. She's hiding what she knows about Jonah. I just saw the freak in my neighborhood. If she wants me to leave him alone, she better talk–or else." Brandon frowned and swore under his breath as he listened. "Fine. Whatever."

Jonah ducked behind the tree when Brandon turned on the spot, checking the area. "We still heading to the party tomorrow night, right?" He paused again. "Yeah, yeah. I'll meet you at your place. I'll be there at seven. I want to leave before my folks come home."

Jonah smiled. He knew exactly where Brandon would be the next evening. If he could see the boy's room–even if it were only in pictures, it would work. The main problem was that he didn't have any pictures.

As Jonah headed home for the evening, it occurred to him that Drew might have the type of videos or pictures he needed. And since Mike still talked to the boy, Jonah thought he could persuade his buddy to help. It was a slim chance, but his only option at this point.

CHAPTER TWENTY

ONE DOWN AND ONE TO GO

Jonah's first sight of Mike's bedroom convinced him that something was wrong. Mike's eclectic group of posters, everything from music groups to famous black scientists, still covered the walls. And the model planes of the famous Red Tails still hung on near-invisible threads from the ceiling.

But his two calendars that were filled with marks and circled dates that normally hung on the wall near the window were missing. Jonah thought he spotted the corner of one under a pile of books.

Mike had half his collection of supernatural, mythology, and alternative history books scattered around the room. And the starscape bedspread, which Jonah loved, lay hidden beneath the clutter of loose pages and magazines.

Jonah dropped his book bag on the only clear space of floor he could find, beside a beanbag chair.

Mike moved from an open book on his desk, to a notebook on his bed, and finally to another book on his dresser. He only paused for a few moments in between each move. All the while, he tapped a pen against his bottom lip while muttering to himself. Jonah feared this could have been a side effect of the mind boost.

When Mike tried to cross to his desk to repeat the circuit, Jonah jumped in front of him, blocking his way. Mike blinked as if he just remembered that he had let Jonah into the house.

He tried to step around, but Jonah gripped his thin arms and shook him. "What's wrong with you?"

"Nothing." Mike squirmed out of Jonah's grip and backed away, crossing his arms. "I need to finish these projects and my homework before I go to the clubhouse to work on the translations."

"Are you sleeping?" Jonah doubted that, especially after seeing the bed. And that brought up another point. "How come your mom hasn't noticed?"

Mike's face reddened a bit. "I sneak out early for school and…" He gestured to the corner of the desk and a couple of plates with half-eaten food on them.

That explained the foul smell. Jonah wrinkled his nose. "Is it the Enhancer or the compass?"

Mike blinked. "No. I'm fine with the compass. I only use it when they call, like when Marcus and Rex crossed over."

"What?! You saw Marcus?"

"Yeah. I didn't tell you?" Mike scratched his head. "I forgot. He said to say hello to you." Mike tried to get to the dresser again.

Jonah blocked him. "Mike, are you on something?" he asked, considering for the first time it could have been drugs but hating the very notion.

Mike glared back at him. "No, Jonah! I'm not on drugs." He threw up his arms in irritation. "Why did you come over?"

Even though Jonah had rehearsed his response, he hesitated to answer. The problem was that he didn't know if Mike would insist on all the details of the plan or not. "I need to ask you about Drew."

Mike stared at him as if he were trying to understand what he said. "Drew? Not that again."

"No, not that," Jonah said. "I wanted to know if Drew ever showed you pictures of Brandon?"

The abrupt changes that washed over Mike's tired, light complexion would have been funny at any other time. At first, he was shocked, then curious. "Don't tell me you like Brandon."

"No." Jonah grimaced and lowered his voice. "I don't like Brandon."

"Then why do you want pictures of him?"

"I don't want pictures of *him*. I wanted to know if Drew ever showed you Brandon's–"

"Brandon's what?"

"His house, what else?" Jonah could feel his face warming.

Mike shook his head and sat on the edge of the bed. He ignored the dislodged papers that slid to the floor. "I don't get it."

"I want to see if he lied about how rich he is."

"He didn't."

Jonah searched the messy room and spotted what he looked for. Mike's laptop was on the desk underneath a stack of papers. Jonah pushed the pages off and opened the computer. "Did Drew ever show you pictures?"

"He's posted stuff before, yeah."

"Show me." Jonah pressed his hands together in a pleading gesture and added, "Please."

Mike let out a tired breath, came over, and called up a social website. He opened a private photo album that Drew shared with his friends. Inside were tons of pictures and numerous videos. Jonah grew impatient with flipping through the photos. They didn't show enough of the background.

"Try the videos."

Selecting one that featured Drew, Brandon, Antwan, and two other guys, Mike leaned back to let Jonah look.

"Happy?" Mike asked.

"Not really." The video, taken at Brandon's home, showed more detail, but only in the kitchen area. The boys' mindless antics bored Jonah. "Do any of the photos show his bedroom?"

Mike's eyes narrowed. "Why do you want to see that?" Losing his focus, his eyes settled on the open books.

Jonah felt a bit ashamed using Mike's distraction to his advantage, but he tapped the laptop to get his buddy's attention. "Just show me, okay?"

After refocusing on the computer, and a moment of shuffling through the posted videos, Mike found a clip of Brandon and his buddies in the boy's bedroom. It was larger than any bedroom Jonah had ever seen and featured a huge bed, a very expensive-looking desk, and a computer. The dark wood dresser had a large mirror. Brandon also had a sitting area and what looked like a huge plasma TV and game consoles.

Jonah had only seen a room like Brandon's in magazines about expensive houses. *Gee whiz.* A big part of him was envious and he wondered if that was why Drew hung around the boy. On the plus side, the huge space made phasing there safer.

He rewound the video back so he could take in details of the room again but Mike snapped the laptop closed.

Jonah snatched his fingers out of harm's way. "Why'd you do that?"

"You're not planning on phasing to Brandon's house, are you?"

Jonah wondered how long it would take Mike to connect the dots. "No," he lied. "Why would I want to go to Brandon's house?"

Mike lowered his gaze as he rubbed his hand over the laptop cover. "Jonah, you have powers…"

"And?"

"Well, I'm not saying you would ever do this, but some kids might try to use their powers for stupid purposes."

Jonah couldn't face Mike's piercing gaze, so he crossed to the window. Mike came over and slung one arm over Jonah's right shoulder and the other underneath his left arm, hugging him.

Jonah relaxed a bit into the embrace. The hugs had become a comforting gesture whenever something was bothering one of them. There hadn't been any recently.

Mike rested his chin on Jonah's shoulder and whispered, "Tell me you aren't doing anything dumb."

"Tell me what's wrong with you," Jonah countered. He waited, wondering if Mike would answer.

"I don't know. I just have to work all the time. It's like… I can't stop myself." Mike shook him. "When are we gonna talk? I figured we'd tell each other about anyone we met."

"Then why didn't you tell me about Patrick?"

Mike let out a long breath. It was warm against Jonah's shoulder. "I didn't think you'd understand. Patrick's not supernatural. And after Trevor, I couldn't face being with someone in that world."

Jonah tightened his jaw. "I guess I can understand."

"And he's not my soulmate either. That person is still out there."

"Soulmate?" Jonah gaped at his friend.

"Yeah. You know, the right one for me."

"I got that. But how can you be sure?"

"Because, whenever I use the compass, it's like I can see possible futures, and sense the possibilities. In all of them, someone's out there for me, just over the horizon."

Jonah's jaw dropped. "You've been using the compass a lot, huh?"

"The Alliance asks me to do things for them."

"Oh, the top-secret stuff you can't tell me about."

Mike ignored Jonah's jab. "Patrick's just…"

"An idiot?" Jonah offered.

"No. A break from the weird. True, he can be a pain. He wants to move so fast and do… everything."

"You mean, like go all the way?" Jonah twisted around to see his friend's face.

"Yeah."

"Did you…"

"No! Jonah, I told you, he's not the one!"

"So you're saving yourself?"

Mike eyed him. "Yes, I am. You think it doesn't work that way for us, too?"

Saving ourselves for the right person. The idea hadn't occurred to Jonah. He wasn't at that point yet. "Did you see anyone for me in your crystal ball?" Jonah snorted.

Mike shook him. "It's not hard to figure out your soulmate."

"Really?"

"No. It's Kevin."

Jonah couldn't deny Mike's words. The very thought of Kevin being his soulmate filled him with an old warmth deep inside. It was something from their first promise, and Jonah was reassured that it still remained. If only he and Kevin could be in the same state at the same time, things might be different.

Mike patted Jonah's chest. "Now, promise me you're not gonna do something dumb."

Jonah thought about it. What he had planned was the right thing. It worked with Drew, so it should work again. "I'm not doing anything wrong." His voice was steady because he was certain he was right.

Mike released him and crossed over to the desk.

For a moment, Jonah considered confessing everything to his friend. But his smoldering anger at Brandon and Latrell's subsequent suicide prevented him from doing so. Plus, Mike had gone back to shifting from one open book to another.

"See you later," Jonah called out as he grabbed his book bag and left.

Two hours later, Mike's questions still nagged him while he rode to the Teen Center. Jonah ignored the lingering doubt and locked his bike in the rack. He walked around the building and scrambled down the hill to the creek. As expected, no one was around.

With Brandon leaving his house so early, Jonah didn't have the luxury of waiting until midnight and sneaking out of his house again. So he chose the deserted area near the creek.

He pulled his disguise out of a newer book bag rather than his cherished older bag. He planned to hide the bag while he was away, but there was still a chance someone might find it. Better to lose the new one than his old one. After pulling the mask down over his face, he drew the hoodie forward to cover his head.

One thing was different: He wasn't nearly as nervous this time. Maybe that was because he'd already done this once, and gotten away with it. In fact, Jonah felt so cavalier, he predicted he'd be home in time for dinner.

He drew in a breath but froze when he heard the quiet crinkle of crushing leaves on the hill. He didn't move as he listened for additional sounds. It was a bird, he decided, hopping along the ground or a squirrel foraging for nuts. When he didn't hear another sound, he phased.

Brandon sat on his overly large bed, earbuds on. He was bopping his head to music when Jonah appeared. The boy let out a scream and jumped backward, slamming into his substantially hard headboard. Jonah smirked as he took a step toward the bed, delighting in Brandon's terror.

He reached out to grab the frightened bully when he suddenly felt a slight change in the air pressure. A dark shape appeared beside him. Jonah almost screamed, himself, when the newcomer grabbed his arm and phased him away.

CHAPTER TWENTY-ONE
INTERVENTION

As Jonah plunged through the aether, he struggled to come to grips with the sudden change of events. He was also aware of who grabbed him. *Kevin.* When the outside world reappeared, Jonah immediately recognized his parents' hideaway.

He jerked his arm free just as Kevin released him. Thrown off-balance, Jonah stumbled forward and sprawled on the patchwork bricks of the hideaway's lower courtyard.

"No more vigilante work tonight," Kevin's muffled voice said. The young Fallen Reaper removed his mask.

Jonah scrambled to his feet and shoved Kevin in response. "Why'd you do that?" His own voice was muffled and he paused to throw back his hood and yank off his mask. "You messed up everything!" He tried to shove Kevin again.

The older boy blocked Jonah's attempt and pushed him away with an irritated huff. "I'm making sure you don't bother another innocent person tonight."

"Innocent?" Anger surged through Jonah. "Brandon's not innocent!"

"It's not up to you to decide that!" Kevin shouted back. He darted forward and grabbed hold of Jonah.

"Let me go!" Despite his struggling, Kevin managed to turn him around and hold him in a one-armed bear hug.

Jonah growled in frustration when Kevin checked his watch.

"Let me go!"

"Will you shut up?" Kevin hissed. "I'm waiting for an Alliance Council member, okay?"

Jonah's insides went cold. It was one thing for Kevin to catch him, but if a Council Member were coming, Jonah knew he was in big trouble.

After another glance at his watch, Kevin's impatient breath came almost at the same time a pinpoint of light appeared before them. The glittering shape expanded and formed into an undulating Alliance symbol of three interlocking circles with a pair of wings above.

Jonah's squirming ceased as the beacon flared and faded away before a vortex formed in the air. *Oh boy*, he said to himself, fearing the extremely serious Mage Rubio would appear through the magical opening this time. He had used the Alliance beacon before to announce his arrival.

However, the person who appeared on the other side wasn't Rubio, nor, to Jonah's surprise, was it Symon Trueblood, either. This Council person was short, bald, with large, black-rimmed glasses and an oversized, curly mustache.

As he exited the vortex, the mage continued a conversation with a young woman who also came through. The short mage signed a form she held out for him.

"Yes, yes. I'll take care of that when I get back." He motioned the woman back through and closed the vortex with an impatient gesture. After adjusting his royal blue tunic, he took quick, little steps toward Jonah.

"You've pulled me from important Council business, Mr. Brown." He had a stern-sounding voice that wouldn't have been out of place in a strictly run classroom.

"Sorry, sir. I know you're busy," Kevin replied in an unusually subdued and businesslike voice.

"Well, some things can be overlooked when it concerns the Deliverer." The mage adjusted his glasses and peered closer at Jonah. When he continued to fiddle with the spectacles, Jonah wondered if they were enchanted.

"You favor your mother," the mage said, "that's for sure. But I also see Isaiah in you." He beckoned Kevin closer. "Come, come. I have a lot of work to complete before the evening is over."

Kevin shuffled Jonah closer. The man raised his right hand, the palm glowing. Jonah's first thought was that the mage would hex him.

As the short man waved his hand back and forth, Jonah realized what he was doing and squirmed even more fiercely in Kevin's grip. "Don't take away my memories!"

The mage's curly mustache twitched. "Really, young man, I'm not taking away anything. I'm not a Mind Bender."

Jonah stared at the mage in confusion. "A Mind Bender? What–"

"I'm merely determining if you've been hexed."

"What?"

"Be quiet," Kevin ordered, sounding more serious than Jonah had ever heard the boy before.

Jonah clamped his mouth shut and watched as the mage continued the examination, which consisted of a light pressure on his skull. The whole experience reminded him of the sensation he received when Robert read his concentrated thoughts. The instinctive thing for Jonah was to resist, and he did. *Get out of my mind*, he thought.

"He's clean," the mage announced, pulling his hand away with a jerk. "Thank goodness for that. You have a strong will, young man, as well as the maddening shortsightedness of all adolescents."

Jonah bristled at the dig. "Who are you?"

"I'm Council Member Mage Albrecht." He didn't offer to shake hands like Trueblood did and instead, Albrecht clasped his hands behind his back. "I work with your godfather from time-to-time."

"Where's Mage Trueblood?" Jonah asked.

Albrecht raised an eyebrow at Jonah's tone. "He didn't think it wise to return, given your uncle's feelings. And unlike me, he's not a certified Memory Charmer."

"Whoa." Jonah didn't know that members of the Alliance could do more than one thing. When his awe of the newcomer began to wane, he focused on the mage's original statement. "Why'd you think I was hexed?"

"Because," Kevin answered, "you went all Batman on Brandon and Drew."

Jonah was stunned and angered because that meant… "You were watching me the whole time?"

Kevin released him. "You bet I was! When I followed you to the creek, I thought you were sneaking out for a date. Then you phased away." Kevin wiggled an admonishing finger at him.

Jonah was about to argue his case when Albrecht cleared his throat to get their attention.

"As Mr. Brown mentioned," Albrecht began, "you can't use your powers for vigilantism. Marcus agrees."

"He's back?" Jonah's stomach churned at hearing that. "You told him?"

"Yes, we did," Albrecht answered. "Marcus is meeting with members of the Council." He glanced at his watch. "I really should have been there, but…" He gestured to Jonah.

"Sorry. I didn't mean for that to happen."

"Really?" Kevin chided. "You weren't sorry fifteen minutes ago."

Jonah wanted to jab the boy with an elbow but refrained with Albrecht watching him. "So, you thought I was hexed?"

"Given your ill-advised actions, yes." The mage's gaze penetrated Jonah, every bit as invasive as a Reaper Stare.

Jonah grimaced under the scrutiny. He boiled with anger at the thought of Kevin watching him without revealing he was even around. The situation reminded Jonah that there was another person secretly hanging around. "What about the Alliance person in town? I thought he was spying on me." Jonah sucked in a breath. "Did he tell you about Drew?"

"No, he didn't." Albrecht's voice carried definite tones of disapproval. "His name's Alastor."

"Alastor? The guy at Hackett's?"

"Yes. He's a Fallen Reaper," Albrecht added.

Then it all made sense to Jonah. The strangely intense stare that he thought was as strong as a Reaper's really was. Alastor had been scanning his emotions and goading him. The ensuing shame prevented Jonah from confessing to being fooled.

Albrecht cocked his head to the side but didn't offer any consoling words like Eleanor or Symon Trueblood would have done.

Maybe Kevin sensed his mood. He patted Jonah's shoulder and said, "We should have warned you about Alastor."

Jonah shrugged. "I thought you couldn't tell me about him?"

"As a Council Member," Albrecht cut in, "I have the authority to share that information with anyone I deem fit. I think you and Kevin should know."

This was so different from his godfather that Jonah perked up at the unexpected opportunity. "So, is he working with the mole?"

"We think so," Albrecht answered. "That person almost ruined our talks with the Afterworld rebels."

And killed Trevor, Jonah thought but didn't add. As his mind raced through everything he knew about the

Alliance insider, his jaw dropped. "I saw the mole arguing with Deyanira in a dream-walk one time." When Albrecht glanced at Kevin, Jonah wondered why the mage didn't know that bit. "I told Marcus about the dream-walk. The mole wore a Reaper's coat and covered his face with a mask and filter."

Albrecht shook his head. "With all that happened during the summer, that information was pushed to the side."

"Deliberately?" Kevin asked.

"That would be my guess. The mole wouldn't want the Council focusing on it."

"I can see that," Kevin added, "but why would he cover his face in front of Deyanira? She has to know who he is, doesn't she?"

"Not necessarily," Albrecht hedged. "But I think he covers his face in meetings with Deyanira because of Mr. Blackstone." He eyed Jonah, adjusting his glasses as he did so.

"Alastor knows about your dream-walking power and would have told the mole. Your recent experience seems to confirm it."

Kevin snorted. "And Alastor works for the Hardliners."

When Jonah nodded, Albrecht asked, "You know about them?"

"Yes, sir," Jonah answered. "They want to use me like a weapon."

"It's more complicated than that, but you are essentially correct. They know all about your various abilities."

"And the mole didn't want me to see his face," Jonah concluded.

"You would have told Marcus," Kevin explained, "and blown the mole's cover."

Jonah glanced between the two Alliance members. "Can't you do anything about Alastor or the mole?"

"We can't openly accuse Alastor of anything," Albrecht explained. "We're trying to gather evidence against him first, but he's very careful. If we move too soon, it could cause fractures on the Council. I fear that's the mole's ultimate purpose."

As the mage talked, something else occurred to Jonah. Agent Hunter had been ordered to leave him alone. Could this plan between the mole and his group have already been set in motion? *He knows all about your powers.* That thought scared Jonah. He didn't like strangers looking over reports on everything he could do.

Of course, he couldn't avoid telling Marcus everything, but he never appreciated the fact that his godfather reported to the Council, until now. Another, more ominous conclusion also became clear.

"Oh, my God," Jonah said. "If Alastor knew about my powers, he had to know about Robert, Lynn, Mike, and Wick."

"Yep," Kevin agreed.

Jonah began to pace back and forth, sensing he was on to something. "Alastor could have told the mole about Lynn's intuition. And they must've broken Robert's fingers so he couldn't draw what he sees in a person's mind." He paused to stare at Kevin and Albrecht. "Wick's magic act was ruined by Antwan's cousin. Everyone's been attacked except me!"

Kevin rubbed his chin while watching Jonah. "Well, they sent you out to get revenge."

"Taking advantage of my emotions? You mean they wanted to upset me about things? And attacking my family and friends…" Jonah's voice trailed off. He thought of every encounter he'd had over the past week, trying to fit it into the new information and awareness. When he came to the bookstore Wraith, he wanted to kick himself. The clerk urged him to buy the potions book. Had he been trying to help?

"Could they be using potions?" Jonah asked Albrecht.

"Potions?" Kevin snorted.

Albrecht twirled the end of his mustache. "Potions… Yes, that's a fair point, young man. But I don't think you've been affected by a potion."

Jonah's nervous excitement increased. "Not me. I think they got my cousin Lynn and…" Just now the final piece clicked. "Mike! We have to go and check."

Kevin and Albrecht didn't make any moves to phase, nor open a vortex. Didn't they understand his exigency? He was about to ask that very thing when he felt the change in air pressure.

He turned in time to see his godfather appear, accompanied by Eleanor Trueblood. Jonah was relieved to have his godfather there. But he paused when Marcus drew closer with a grim expression on his face.

CHAPTER TWENTY-TWO
POTIONS MASTER

Jonah braced himself for the lecture when Marcus gripped him by both shoulders. But instead of yelling, his godfather subjected him to a concerned gaze. "Are you okay?"

Jonah nodded. "I'm all right."

A relieved smile tweaked the corners of Marcus's mouth. He looked around the darkened courtyard. "Can we have some lights?"

In response, Eleanor Trueblood raised her hands and muttered, "Illumens." Flares shot into the air and expanded into a small grid of pinpoints. They flooded the courtyard with soft, pale light.

"Thank you."

Eleanor nodded before turning to Kevin and talking in low tones. Meanwhile, Marcus walked around to the opposite side of the courtyard, taking his time. Jonah followed while wondering about his godfather's reserved mood.

When Marcus faced him, it was with a frown. "I'm sure you know why I came down from Atlanta," he began. "Your vigilantism concerns me, despite Alastor's obvious involvement."

His godfather's words were as alarming as a bucket of ice cold water being dumped on his head. "Sorry."

"I understand the temptation to act. And God knows we all make mistakes, Jonah. But we should always learn from them."

Jonah nodded.

"That brings me to our second issue," Marcus continued, narrowing his eyes. "We need to discuss your knowledge about the bullies." An edge tainted his voice. "Latrell?"

"I talked to him at his funeral," Jonah confessed.

Marcus closed his eyes and massaged his forehead. "You shouldn't have done that."

"All I did was talk." When Marcus glared at him, Jonah suspected his godfather was scanning his emotions. "I've seen him a few times since then."

"This is certain to be dangerous, far beyond sending you after Brandon and Antwan." Marcus pointed an admonishing finger at Jonah. "Stay away from him."

"But–"

"I mean it. He's a Wraith and clearly working with the mole."

"What if he appears to me again?"

"Command him to leave at once!" Marcus said. "You're a half-Reaper."

"Okay," Jonah muttered, hoping that was the extent of his troubles but sadly suspecting it wasn't.

Marcus withdrew a thin, square box out of his inner coat pocket and held it in both hands. "You must learn to establish control, Jonah. There's a reason we have Memory Charmers like Omar and Albrecht readily available. We can't allow the larger world even a small glimpse of our existence. And we certainly can't tolerate our young trainees abusing their powers."

Marcus held up the box and cracked it open. Two wristbands gleamed inside despite the relative darkness. Both were a flat silver color with Angel script covering their surfaces.

"What are those?"

"I want to make sure you understand the seriousness of what you did." Marcus held the box closer. "Put them on."

Jonah's Death Sense prickled with a slight warning. When his hand neared the bands, he could sense the magic on them. For a moment, he thought they were shield bracelets, but his godfather wouldn't give him something with more power in it. Not as a punishment anyway.

"Jonah…" Marcus's voice took on an edge again.

Accepting that he had no choice, Jonah took the bands and slipped one over each wrist. As soon as he did so, the bands tightened and an unpleasant jolt shot up both arms and collided in his chest.

Jonah sucked in a breath, sensing that something vital had been stripped away.

"The bands nullify your ability to phase," Marcus explained.

A sense of betrayal overwhelmed Jonah next, followed quickly by shameful resignation. His shoulders slumped and his hands dropped to his sides. "How long do I have to wear them?"

Marcus's expression was unreadable. "I'd say a week should do it."

"A week?"

"It could be longer," Marcus warned. "Kevin will have to take you home." He turned and motioned to Trueblood.

"What about the Afterworld, and the rebels?" Jonah asked, ignoring the bands for the moment.

Marcus looked thoughtful. "They are well. It's dangerous work but it'll make a difference when things happen."

"What things?"

"Now's not the time to talk about it. We're due at Headquarters."

Trueblood reached them and graced Jonah with a smile. "It's good to see you again. I hope my brother didn't tarnish the title of mage."

"Ah, no, he didn't." Jonah stammered. "He's…"

"Different," Trueblood finished.

Marcus arched an eyebrow at Jonah. "Learn the lesson." His expression softened a bit. "I'll tell you about the trip some other time. Right now, go help your friend." With that, he placed a hand on Trueblood's elbow and they disappeared.

*

Mike radiated a tired excitement when he answered his front door. He peeked behind Jonah. "Where's Kevin?"

"Let's talk." Jonah raised an eyebrow and pushed his buddy inside.

After greeting Mrs. Littleton, who was up in the kitchen, Jonah followed his manic friend down the short flight of stairs to the split-level home's lower floor. Mike turned for his bedroom but Jonah grabbed his arm and pulled him toward the family room.

"Well?" Mike asked as soon as they entered the room.

"Kevin wants to come in through the patio door."

"The patio? Why?"

"He's not alone. A Council mage is here."

Mike's eyes widened in fear. "Not Rubio?"

Jonah shook his head and moved to the sliding doors. "No. Someone else." He slid open the door and stood back.

Mike's eyes were riveted on the short mage as he and Kevin entered the house.

Albrecht glanced around the family room, taking in all the details. "Will we do it here?"

"No," Jonah answered. He nudged Mike. "In your room."

As soon as everyone crowded into the bedroom and closed the door, Mike asked Albrecht, "Who're you?"

The mage cast a spell on the bedroom door before giving his name, as if that were enough of an answer.

"He's a Memory Charmer, like Omar," Jonah explained.

"Wow." Mike offered to shake Albrecht's hand, but once again, the mage refused to do so.

Albrecht's earlier claims of being busy seemed to suddenly vanish, and he took his time surveying the room. He even crossed over to the desk to peruse the books he saw laid out there.

"Excellent! You're a voracious reader." The little mage bounced on his feet as he placed a square, black case on the desk. He turned to Mike, raising his right hand.

"What're you doing?" Mike exclaimed as he reared back and bumped into Jonah.

"He's just scanning you." Jonah leaned against Mike to keep him from moving further away from Albrecht. "He did the same thing to me. It won't hurt."

Albrecht let out a startled sigh almost as soon as he began the probe. "He's been affected. But it's curious." The mage's brow furrowed and he flexed his fingers while skimming all the titles on Mike's bookshelf. "You wouldn't have a potions book, would you?"

Mike blinked several times before answering, "No."

"What's the problem?" Kevin asked.

"It's not what I expected." Albrecht stepped right up to Mike and adjusted his glasses.

Since he wasn't the object of Albrecht's attention, Jonah could study the man's glasses up close and he discovered he was right. The lens wavered and adjusted at the mage's manipulations. They were enchanted.

Albrecht motioned to Mike's mouth. "Open please."

Mike's face reddened. "I haven't brushed my teeth–"

"Do it," Albrecht ordered. Mike obeyed. The mage leaned closer and sniffed before nodding. "Yes, just as I thought." He moved to his small case and opened it to reveal rows of glass vials, all individually labeled. Each had a black, screw cap on top.

Mike hovered over the mage's left shoulder, fascinated by all the vials of mysterious liquids.

"I'll need two small glasses of water," Albrecht announced after removing three of the vials.

"I'll get them," Jonah offered before racing to the kitchen. He asked Mike's mom for a couple of glasses and then returned.

Albrecht placed a spell over the door again and began measuring small amounts of the contents inside the vials into one of the glasses. He swizzled the mixture around before handing the glass to Mike and saying, "Drink up."

Mike obeyed without any fuss.

That impressed Jonah. He expected a little resistance. "So that'll fix my buddy?"

"Yes, it'll counteract the potion." The mage began mixing another potion in the second glass.

Meanwhile, Mike blinked and glanced around his room. Jonah watched the dawning horror on his friend's face. It seemed the potion was working faster than anticipated.

Mike gripped the sides of his head as he stared at the mess. "What did I do to my room? I remember, but…"

"Given the effects of the potion, you couldn't stop yourself, young man," Albrecht said.

Mike turned to him. "Yeah, it was crazy."

"How do you feel now?"

"Better. I mean, I don't want to keep studying." He glanced at this room. "Maybe cleaning up would help."

"Sit down first," Albrecht suggested.

When Mike hesitated, Jonah ushered him to the bed and sat down beside him. Albrecht followed and handed Mike the second glass of liquid.

"What'll that one do?" Jonah thought to ask.

Mike didn't wait for the answer but gulped down the second glass of antidote. As soon as he did, his arm went limp and he dropped the glass. Kevin caught it before it hit the carpeted floor.

When Mike slumped sideways onto Jonah's lap, Kevin grinned. "That's what it does!"

"Something to help him sleep," Albrecht added, a slight tinge of humor in his voice.

"Oh," Jonah said. He rested a hand on Mike's shoulder as a low snore escaped his buddy's mouth. "Uh, maybe we should put him in bed?"

"Here," Kevin said. He lifted Mike off Jonah's lap and cradled the boy in his arms. Jonah hurried to clear all the things off the bed by shoving them onto the floor. Then he pulled the covers back so Kevin could lay Mike gently on the bed.

Jonah finished tucking in his buddy before turning to Albrecht. The mage had already returned to his inspection of Mike's books. "Excuse, me," Jonah called out. "What was the potion?"

"Oh, that? It was an infatuation draft," the mage said.

Kevin snorted. "You mean, a love potion?"

Jonah gaped at them. "A love potion?"

"There's no such thing as a true love potion, Mr. Blackstone." Albrecht frowned. "An infatuation draft is designed to merely increase an existing attraction or interest."

"Why'd the cure work so fast on him?" Kevin asked.

The mage had returned to his case and he briefly paused in closing it. "It must be the change he went through to become a Seeker."

"Change?" Jonah tore his gaze from his sleeping friend to stare at the mage. "The mind boost just enhanced his mind, right?"

"Mr. Littleton experienced more than simple mind enhancement. The combination of the mind boost and the activation of the Seeker's compass changed his very nature." Albrecht's voice assumed an excited quality, like he was explaining a successful science experiment in class. "He's no longer totally mortal. He's part supernatural now, like all of us." Albrecht snapped his case closed with a flourish. "I surmise that's why the initial potion didn't work as planned."

"I don't know about that." Kevin gestured at all the books and notebooks around the bedroom. "He really loves reading and doing research. It just pushed it to a crazy level." He shook his head, but a smirk tweaked the corners of his mouth. "Leave it to you nerds to be more interested in reading a book than… well, you know."

When Kevin couldn't hide his sudden embarrassment, Jonah knew at once the older boy was thinking about their last goodbye. Shelving that pleasant memory away for a later, more convenient time, Jonah concentrated on the true culprit. *Patrick.* Somehow, that fool successfully managed to infect Mike with a love potion.

Kevin waved a hand in front of Jonah's face. "What's up?"

Jonah confirmed that Albrecht was examining Mike's books again and then whispered, "I'll tell you who did it later." He glanced at Mike surreptitiously.

Kevin's eyes widened. Then his expression turned sly, and he whispered back, "It wasn't you, was it?"

Jonah slugged him in the arm. "No, it wasn't."

Once again, thoughts of phasing Patrick to the middle of a busy highway returned with exponential force. Jonah wanted to do that so bad now that he was already working out the details when two horrible realizations set in.

First, he couldn't phase Patrick (or anyone else) to any location as long as he wore the nullifying bands. Second, Mike described Patrick as non-supernatural. Presumably, that meant the boy didn't know anything about their world. So where would he get an infatuation potion?

The mole? No, Jonah decided. *It had to be the sorceress.* She was running around Mount Vernon and must have been behind all the attacks on his friends and family. Just when he needed his powers most, he was stripped of them.

CHAPTER TWENTY-THREE
PLAUSIBLE DENIABILITY

Jonah held the magic wristbands under the shower's spray, hoping they would short out. To his amazement, they repelled the water droplets. After drying off and dressing for school, he decided to test the bands while heading out back to the shed. He thought about the Practice Club clearing and tried to phase there. A sharp jolt ran up his arm and settled behind his eyes, resulting in an instant headache.

"Nice." Jonah squeezed one eye closed, making it difficult to roll his bike to the front yard. *That was stupid.*

"What's wrong with you?" Mike asked. He had just joined Jonah for the ride to school.

"Nothing." Jonah blinked his eyes, willing the headache to subside. "How're you feeling?"

Mike's smile was shy and slightly embarrassed. "Fine. I really needed the sleep."

Jonah could see that. Mike was once again as neat as ever and fully alert when they set off on the overcast, chilly morning.

Although Jonah was glad to have his buddy riding to school with him, he prepared himself. Mike must have had a lot of questions.

Sure enough, Mike glanced sideways at him and asked, "What happened to me?"

"Someone spiked you with a potion."

"What was it, Jonah? I don't remember anything after I drank from the second glass." He narrowed his eyes. "Tell me."

Jonah concentrated on the road ahead. "You sure?"

"Jonah!"

"Okay." Jonah took a deep breath and told him everything Mage Albrecht had said about the potion.

Mike paused at a crosswalk, his jaw working. "A love potion? That weasel!"

"Who?" Jonah acted innocent, but he knew exactly who.

"Patrick." Mike smacked a hand against his handlebar. "I'll kill him."

Jonah snorted. "You don't believe in fighting."

Mike glared at Jonah. His expression changed. "You could always phase him somewhere isolated and leave him there."

Jonah's insides froze. Mike didn't know about the vigilante stuff yet. "My godfather wouldn't like that," he said as they rode on.

They reached the high school a short time later. After securing their bikes, Mike leaned against the rack while gazing at the grey sky. "I'm not surprised."

"How so?" Jonah glanced around all the kids moving by.

"Well, he's pushy about making out," Mike answered in a low voice. "He's jealous of you and doesn't like us hanging out together."

"Tough." Jonah meant it. But talk of Patrick brought up another idea. "Maybe Patrick was supposed to distract you."

"Maybe." Mike kicked at the loose pebbles below the bike racks.

"Sorry," Jonah added.

Without warning, Mike slugged him in the arm. "You don't mean that. You hate Patrick."

"Well, yeah." Jonah rubbed his arm.

Mike hitched up his bag. "Anything else?"

Jonah feared how Mike would take the news that he was changed, so he just came out with it. "Albrecht said you're different now, like me and Kevin."

Mike grinned. "I already know I'm part supernatural. The Alliance Healers told me the last time I visited HQ for a checkup."

"That doesn't bother you?"

Mike stared off, thinking. "No. The mind boost is permanent." He gazed sheepishly at Jonah. "Well, now I got my wish to be like everyone else. Right?"

Jonah recalled Wick assuring Mike that everyone had a hero inside them. Seeing that his friend really was okay with the change, Jonah smiled. "The club's meeting after school with Kevin and Albrecht."

"What about?"

"We need to figure out what the mole is doing. I'm sure it's about me."

"It's *always* about you, Jonah." Mike shoved him. "I'll be there." He glanced at his watch. "We're gonna be late."

Jonah bowed and motioned for Mike to go first. "Lead the way, Pathmaker."

Mike laughed. As they headed inside the high school, they talked about Mike being a Seeker before speculating on everything that had happened so far. With all the other things going on, Jonah was glad to have his best friend back.

*

Alliance adults crowded the attic clubhouse. Not only had Kevin and Albrecht arrived, but Mage Symon Trueblood and Rex were also there.

The big, blond Fallen Reaper bounded over to Jonah and Mike, pumping their hands like he hadn't seen them in a long time. "How're you doing, young fellas?"

"We're fine," Jonah answered, suppressing a grin. "What are you doing here?"

Rex grinned as he scratched his reddish nose. "You kidding? This is serious business. Marcus wants as many of our group as possible to know what's going on."

"He's keeping the Council occupied with his information from the Afterworld rebels," Trueblood said. He treated Jonah and Mike to friendly pats on the backs.

Trueblood and Albrecht wore their royal blue tunics today, and Rex was in his long, black Reaper's coat.

However, Kevin, who leaned against the back of the sofa, was still dressed like any other sixteen-year-old wearing a hoodie, jeans, and sneakers. No long coat in sight.

Jonah crossed to the sofa to sit beside the young Fallen Reaper while Mike retreated to the old editor's desk in the back corner. Jonah couldn't resist grinning when Mike let out a disgusted yelp at the messy desk and began to hastily straighten up the notebooks and loose paper. He stopped when Albrecht approached.

"Ahh, the translation of the coded text," the mage gushed. He and Mike began a spirited, quiet discussion of his progress.

Kevin whispered, "I thought we cured Mike."

Jonah elbowed him. "Be quiet!"

The attic door slammed. Lynn, Robert, and Wick bounded up the steps.

Rex let out a loud grunt when he saw Robert's hand and went over to inspect the finger brace. "Too bad your folks already know about this," he said, turning over Robert's hand. "I expect a healer may have been able to do something with it."

Robert gaped at the man. "Seriously? I could get it healed?"

Lynn stepped in. "Dad would go crazy if he saw you healed so soon."

Robert's sudden enthusiasm wilted. "Oh, yeah."

"Well, now wasn't a good time anyway," Rex concluded. He glanced at Trueblood, who nodded in confirmation.

The mage clapped his hands. "Everyone, this is Mage Albrecht." He gestured to the shorter mage, who seemed reluctant to break off his conversation with Mike. "He's also a member of the Alliance Council."

After Albrecht nodded to everyone, Robert raised his good hand. "Huh, we never really met you," he said, pointing at Trueblood.

The mage looked stunned. "Oh, I'm Eleanor's brother, Mage Trueblood."

"He's also on the Council," Rex supplied.

Robert whistled. "Really? How many people are on the Council?"

"Nine," Jonah and Mike said at the same time.

Jonah laughed and gestured for his friend to continue.

Mike stood up straighter like he was about to answer a teacher in class. "There are three mages, three Fallen Reapers, and three mortals."

"Correct." Albrecht gave Mike an encouraging nod. "We can talk about that later. Right now, we have more pressing matters." He motioned to Lynn. "I understand your intuition is being blocked?"

"Yes," Lynn answered, although she seemed guarded. Jonah could sense her deeper hope that the mage would have an answer.

Albrecht adjusted his glasses while scanning her but didn't move closer.

It was Trueblood who raised his hand with the palm toward Lynn. "May I scan you?"

"You're not a Memory Charmer," Jonah blurted out.

"No, I'm not." Trueblood smiled at Jonah over his shoulder. "I'm not scanning her mind for a compulsion. I'm looking for signs of a hex or maybe a potion."

"A hex?" Lynn looked appalled at the idea. She dropped her arms to her side and didn't move. "Do it."

Trueblood faced her again and muttered a complex spell under his breath. A soft, golden light engulfed Lynn's entire body. Sections of the glowing aura, particularly around her head, turned a dark green color, like a virus.

Wick ruffled his twists while gawking at the display. "Is that what I think it is?"

"If you mean a magical block, you're right." Trueblood lowered his hand but stopped because a dense, dark green haze surrounded the water bottle Lynn held.

When Lynn noticed, she dropped the bottle and backed away from it. "No way!"

Trueblood lifted the bottle and held it at arm's length. "It would seem your water's infected." He peered at Lynn. "Where did you get this?"

Lynn placed a hand over her mouth while staring at the bottle. She shook as she answered, "I have a large container of it at home, in the refrigerator. It's a mixture…"

Robert looked as sick as his sister. "That's wicked! Who would do that?" He glanced at the others. "I know. The mole. But how?"

"Robert has a point," Kevin said. "They couldn't get into their house. It's protected from that."

"It is?" Jonah asked, pulling his gaze away from Lynn's contaminated bottle.

Kevin nudged him. "Keeping you from phasing wasn't the only reason to protect your house."

Mike let out a shocked sound from the back desk. "That's why you had to phase to my backyard?" he asked Kevin. "The Alliance protected my house."

"Given what's happened," Trueblood said, "I think we should also protect the young mage's house."

Wick raised a hand in a hesitant manner. "I've already done that." When the adult mages all looked at him, he wilted a little. "Sorry."

"In this case, your actions proved correct," Albrecht said. He turned to Lynn. "It's obvious they infected one of the ingredients to your mixture before you got home."

Lynn covered her mouth again and her eyes went wide. "Oh, no! That huge guy rammed into me at the store and I dropped everything. I remember feeling that something was wrong, but I thought…"

"What?" Robert pressed her.

"I thought the feeling was about my fight with Rico. I should have known better."

"Don't you start blaming yourself," Robert warned his sister. "This isn't our fault."

"Yeah," Jonah seconded his cousin. "That guy was a Wraith."

"It seems they've been watching you and planning this for a long time," Rex agreed.

"The mole and his people are behind all of this!?" Lynn shouted.

Jonah knew the look in his cousin's eyes. She wanted to hit something. And he agreed with her. But he had another target. "I bet it was the Alliance guy. He told the mole everything about us. Can we do something about him now?"

Jonah was gratified when Lynn seconded the idea.

But Trueblood frowned and Albrecht remained quiet.

Jonah turned to Rex in desperation. "You could do a Reaper's stare on him, couldn't you?" Like Trueblood, Rex didn't seem open to that idea, causing Jonah's irritation to flare. He didn't get why the Alliance adults thought they had to leave this guy alone.

Kevin tapped his shoulder. "Jonah, Alastor isn't a fool."

"So what?"

"He probably didn't know anything about this side of the plan."

Jonah spread his hands. "What difference does that make?"

"Plausible deniability," Albrecht explained. "He could honestly say he didn't know and pass a Reaper's Stare, even if we could manage to get the Council to agree to one."

Unable to respond, Jonah settled on exchanging an infuriated glance with Lynn, who looked just as angry.

Trueblood broke the silent tension first. "Jonah, I know you're frustrated with us, and believe me, no one hates hiding and subterfuge more than I do. I'm a what-you-see-is-what-you-get type of person." He placed a hand on Jonah's shoulder. "It's why your dad sponsored me for the Council, but even I had to learn to be more… subtle. The mole may just be the tip of an iceberg. Like any undercover operation when the goal is to ferret out everyone involved, the best way to accomplish it is to pretend you haven't uncovered their activities."

"Symon," Albrecht warned.

"I'm not telling them any Council secrets." Trueblood gestured at Jonah and the others. "They're all intelligent young people, and we should treat them like that and not like little kids."

In that moment, Jonah didn't care what his uncle thought of Trueblood. He liked the mage.

Trueblood met each young person's gaze in turn, as if making a silent pledge to them. "You all understand? We're not doing nothing. We're building a case and trying to catch everyone that's involved. But that's dangerous and takes time. I'm trusting you all to keep that among yourselves."

Everyone nodded.

"Good!" He turned to Wick, who was unusually quiet. "Now, I understand you've come a long way?"

Wick's response surprised Jonah and interrupted his brooding thoughts about Alastor. Normally, the young mage was ecstatic at any chance to talk with an adult mage. But today, Wick fidgeted in a subdued, quiet manner. "I'm sorry about what happened."

"It wasn't your fault," Trueblood assured him. "Albrecht and I agree it was sorcery that caused your harmless flames to go astray."

Wick's posture straightened as he listened.

"You're a talented, young mage," Trueblood continued. "I assured the Council that you didn't lose control of your magic."

"You did?" Wick's eyes widened. "I mean, thanks."

Albrecht squared his shoulders. "That being the case, you've shown a lack of wisdom in so openly using your powers. On behalf of the Alliance Council, we're here to warn you."

"I understand."

"Don't look so glum," Trueblood said. "I'm staying behind in Mount Vernon for a few days to observe and coach you."

Robert leaned on his buddy's shoulder. "See? They aren't locking you up."

Albrecht approached Wick, peering at him through his big glasses. "A proper mage-trainee would have been able to stop the attack at once. If you had been in one of my classes, you would have done so."

"He should get formal training," Trueblood agreed, rubbing his chin and nodding, "like any other young mage."

Wick perked up.

Albrecht motioned to him. "Show me a flame."

Wick glanced at his buddy and hesitated, another response he had never done before.

Trueblood clapped his hands. "Don't be shy now. Show us your stuff."

Wick's frown twisted into his lopsided grin. He held out his hand and a ball of purple flame flared to life.

Albrecht made a disapproving sound but Trueblood was nicer. He raised his own hand and, with a quiet puff sound, a ball of purple flame appeared. Jonah could see the difference at once. Wick's flame, through impressive and pretty in a way, appeared weak and less distinct around the edges.

Trueblood's ball of flame was solid and almost perfectly round. Then the mage did something Jonah had never seen Wick do: He made his ball of flame smaller and smaller until it was almost a pinpoint of light.

"You're a natural, and I sense very powerful," the mage said. "No doubt it runs in your family, just like mine. But you need to learn finer control." He snuffed out his flame with a flick of his hand. "Don't sweat it. We'll turn you into a proper mage."

Wick's normal enthusiasm for magic returned and he grinned from ear-to-ear. Once again, Jonah felt a rush a gratitude toward Trueblood, this time, for alleviating Wick's dour mood.

Meanwhile, Trueblood turned to Robert. "Are your parents at home?"

"No."

"We should throw out that contaminated mix." He motioned to Rex. "Give us a lift?"

Rex held out a pair of keys. "You should learn to drive."

Trueblood grinned as he took the car keys and ushered Lynn to the attic stairs. "We'll be back," he said to Jonah in a perfect *Terminator* imitation. Rex laughed and followed.

"I think now is a good time to discuss some rules of conduct for mages-in-training." Albrecht pointed Wick toward the clubhouse section.

Wick gulped and said, "Yes, sir." He slouched to the sofa and sat down. Robert trailed behind and, when Albrecht didn't object, sat beside his buddy.

Jonah was happy for Lynn, Mike, and Wick. Despite solving the individual attacks, they still were in the dark about the mole and the sorceress. In effect, the club had reached a dead end.

Mike came over. "We should go."

"Where?" Jonah asked, distracted.

"Your house." Mike held up the pieces of the triptych. "I can tell you about my conversation with Patrick on the way."

"Who's Patrick?" Kevin asked.

Jonah motioned for him to keep his voice low. "We'll tell you on the ride to my house."

Kevin snorted. "Pass. I'll just meet you there."

Jonah grabbed the older boy before he could phase. "No. Ride with us."

"I don't have a bike. Smart guy."

"You can use Lynn's," Jonah explained. "It's outside and I know the lock code." He hefted his book bag on a shoulder. "Let's go."

CHAPTER TWENTY-FOUR
ANKH OF LIFE

A gust of strong, autumn wind blew fallen leaves across the street. Jonah's tires crunched them constantly as he, Mike, and Kevin rode to the Hightowers' house.

Releasing a loud yelp as a large acorn bounced off his head, Mike exclaimed, "Hey!" He paused in his story about Patrick to glare at the offending oak tree.

Kevin snorted, but Jonah prodded his buddy. "So, Patrick overheard Niqab Girl talking about love potions?"

"Not love potions, just potions in general," Mike answered, rubbing the sore spot on his head. "He checked out Mystic Worlds."

"Tell me that clerk didn't help him," Jonah interrupted.

"No, he didn't. When Patrick left the store, he ran into a woman in a cloak. She offered to sell him a potion."

Patrick's stupidity stunned Jonah. "That idiot didn't think that was dangerous? And he poured it in your soda? What if it had been poison?" His voice climbed to a near shout by the end.

Mike shrugged. "I know. But it shows how much he really liked me." Jonah glared at him and Mike didn't say anything else until they pulled into Jonah's neighborhood. "He meant well," Mike finally added.

Jonah opened his mouth to argue about that when Kevin veered close enough to shove him. "Stick to the point. Did Patrick see the woman's face?"

Mike shook his head. "She remained hidden under the cloak's hood."

"We should get Robert to scan Patrick's pea-brain, anyway," Jonah suggested. And then he remembered Robert's injured hand. "Dang! Another useless clue."

"Maybe not," Mike countered. "She was wearing a strange amulet featuring a woman with a lion's head. Those can't be too common."

Jonah let out a sigh of disappointment. "Robert picked that out of the jewelry store owner's memory."

They reached the Hightowers' house and Jonah noted the rental car parked at the curb. *Good,* he thought. *At least Trueblood and Rex were still there.* The boys rolled their bikes into the backyard to lean them against the shed before hurrying inside.

Rex sat at the kitchen table, reading one of Uncle James's magazines. Lynn's empty sports mix container lay on the counter, drained of all its contents. Trueblood stood near the sofa, holding one of Mage Albrecht's small vials in his hand and watching Lynn.

Lynn sat on the sofa, leaning her head back with her eyes closed.

Trueblood searched Jonah's face as he held a finger to his mouth. "Not too loud. We're trying to encourage her to rest to let the potion work."

"What potion?" Jonah asked. "You made one?"

Trueblood chuckled. "Albrecht said there are only so many ways to block her power, and he came prepared with an antidote to neutralize the effects of them all."

Rex rose from his chair, which creaked in response. "We should go, Symon. Me and Albrecht need to get back to HQ."

Trueblood slipped the vial into his pocket and whispered to Lynn, "Remember, get some rest."

She nodded.

"Take care of them, Kevin. We'll talk later." Trueblood waved to Jonah and Mike, then he and Rex left the house like normal people.

As soon as the Alliance men were gone, Lynn's eyes popped open. "Okay. What's going on?"

Jonah motioned to Mike. "You explain while I get the box." He also listened to Mike who told a modified version of the Patrick story, making the boy out to be a girl.

Ducking into his room, Jonah snagged his mom's locked box from his memento shelf and returned to the family room. Mike went quiet while avoiding Lynn's thoughtful gaze.

"That *girl* gave you this love potion?" she asked. When Mike didn't answer, she let out a huff. "What's his name?"

Mike's face reddened.

"I already know about you, Mike."

"You do?" Mike's eyes widened. "I mean, how?"

"Doesn't matter." She raised an eyebrow.

"Patrick."

Lynn tapped her bottom lip, thinking. "Don't recognize the name." She looked up at Jonah. "Why didn't you tell us about this?"

Jonah shrugged.

Kevin intervened and offered to hold the box. He turned it around with the lock facing Jonah so he could activate it.

Lynn's eyebrow arched when she saw that. "Now you have a secret box? Where's mine?" Jonah heard the mock-outrage, a healthy sign that his cousin was feeling better.

Mike, who was clutching the triptych, disconnected the pieces and held them out. But as Jonah reached for them, the thought that kept bugging him finally crystalized. The first time he saw the amulet that Robert drew, Jonah thought it looked familiar.

Now, with his mom's box open and the photo album in sight, he knew where he first saw the amulet. Jonah dug under the photo album and pulled out the envelope with the pictures of Aunt Ruby and her family.

He could feel everyone's eyes on him as he slid the pictures free and searched through them. When he found it, Jonah's hand began to shake so badly that the other pictures slipped from his grasp.

"Jonah? What's wrong?" Lynn asked as she scooped up the dropped photos.

He ignored the question, his full attention remaining on the picture of Aunt Ruby and Uncle Amos. Around her neck was the woman-with-the-lion's-head amulet! It was exactly the same as the one in Robert's picture. That meant the woman was his Aunt Ruby all along!

Lynn peeked over his shoulder. He held up the picture. "It can't be!" Lynn hissed in disbelief. "She's in Titusville. Maybe the sorceress just has the same bad taste in jewelry."

"It's her, Lynn."

Kevin frowned at them. "You mean, your aunt?" Jonah and Lynn nodded in unison. "Here." Kevin thrust the box into Jonah's hands. He pulled out his phone and walked into the kitchen while talking in rapid tones with someone on the other end.

Mike peeked at the picture and his face paled. Then he let out a gasp and plucked a different picture from Lynn's hand. "Look!"

Holding the picture of the Ankh of Life bookstore, he pointed at the store's front window. "See the statuettes on the windowsill?"

Jonah's insides froze. Among the row of little figurines and statuettes was a free-standing replica of the amulet.

Mike and Jonah glanced at each other.

Lynn's face showed abject denial. "We should wait until we know if she's in Titusville or not."

"Well, you can stop wondering," Kevin said, coming over. "Trueblood and Rex went there and found the woman your aunt was supposed to be staying with. They're still talking to her, but the woman appears to have been hexed. Your aunt's been using her as a cover longer than a week."

"That settles it," Jonah announced.

Lynn shook her head. "But how? Our aunt never had any powers?"

"What if the mole's helping her?" Mike asked.

"He's a Fallen Reaper," Jonah said, "not a mage." He showed Kevin the picture. "We should check it out."

"That could be dangerous. I'm supposed to keep watch over you."

"You can watch over me there." Jonah jabbed a finger at the photo. "Besides, I'll be with Lynn and Mike."

"Yeah, the Mount Vernon Social Club," Mike added with a smirk.

Jonah grimaced. "Maybe we should change the name."

Kevin gave them both a deadpan look, not amused.

Jonah imagined that the older boy recalled what happened the last time he went along with one of their harebrained plans. It was the reason he was currently in hot water with Mandara. Even so, Jonah met Kevin's gaze and silently pleaded with him.

The older boy's resistance wilted and he eventually nodded. "Fine, but we only stay until dark. Then we leave. If anyone's there, we leave. If you irritate me," Kevin added, leaning closer to Jonah's face, "we leave."

*

The Ankh of Life bookstore must have seen better days, although Jonah doubted the store had looked any different when it was open. He estimated that couldn't have been for several years.

Copious cobwebs hung from the corners of dirty windows. The peeled paint and multiple years' worth of dead leaves had accumulated all along the front edge of the store to contribute to its obvious abandonment and neglect. The few other businesses on the shabby, narrow side street also looked long deserted and vacant, imbuing an uncomfortable eeriness into the location.

This tiny town was long past its heyday, Jonah decided. Gazing at the store, he could not stop thinking how much smaller it seemed in person.

Mike leaned against him. "Is it just me or is this place always spooky this time of year?"

"I bet it's creepy all the time," Jonah replied as he stepped to the front window. Most of the figurines, including the amulet, were gone. The few remaining items were toppled onto their sides. There was a clear circle on the otherwise dust-coated inner window ledge where the replica should have been. "I think someone's already been here."

"Yeah." Lynn pointed at the door. Loose cobwebs hung in the corners, as if someone had hastily yanked them away to reach the door handle.

Kevin pulled out his blades, glancing up and down the street to make sure no one was around. Only then did he activate them. "You remember what I said?"

Jonah nodded.

Lynn tried the handle but the door was locked. "Break in?"

"Better idea." Kevin held out his arms for everyone to grab hold, but waited for Lynn to activate one of her own blades. When she did and everyone was securely touching him, Kevin phased them inside.

Immediately, Jonah sneezed at the dust they dislodged by their arrival. Clear footprints on the filthy floor were further evidence that someone had been here. Not to mention, how everything was thrown around.

Mike pointed past the front sitting room toward a half-torn set of velvet curtains. "That way?"

Kevin took the lead, Mike and Jonah followed next, and Lynn covered the back. The arrangement was at once familiar and comforting to Jonah, especially since he had no powers as long as he wore the bands.

On the other side of the curtain, off to one side, was an office. The door was wide open and the contents of the shelves and the old desk were thrown across the floor. On the opposite side of the hallway was a room with a table and a large crystal ball. Covered in cobwebs, Jonah found it strange that it appeared untouched by the intruders.

Lynn's voice was hushed when she spoke. "My great-auntie owned the store until she died. I wondered if she left a will."

"I bet she did. Probably as a trust fund or something like that," Mike said. "You know, from what you told me, I bet your mom was supposed to take over, Jonah."

Mike nodded as if agreeing with his own assessment. "She would have passed it on to Lynn. I surmise the gift only appears in one heir each generation. I mean, that's how these things normally work."

Kevin poked Mike in the arm. "You sure Albrecht cured you?"

Mike flashed a silvery, embarrassed grin.

Lynn pointed into a side alcove and a heavily dented, metal door. "I guess our aunt couldn't get inside."

"More likely, her huge friend," Jonah said. He peered closer and added, "And that's why they couldn't get inside!" Dead center on the door was a genetic lock. Unlike the simple button on his birthday present cylinder or Robert's archive box, this lock was larger and round with strange symbols etched into the metal surface: three rows of symbols, one within the other, and all slightly raised.

Jonah suspected it was Angel script. He stepped forward and touched the lock, but nothing happened except for a mild tingle that he felt along the tip of his finger. Jonah tried again. Still nothing.

Mike peered at the lock and then Lynn inspected it. "I wonder…"

Lynn returned his gaze. "You wonder what?"

"Try it," Mike suggested.

"Why would it work for me?"

Jonah got it. "My mom managed to get my DNA. No reason she couldn't do the same to you when she visited."

"We're wasting time," Kevin prompted.

"Oh, all right," Lynn huffed. She pressed her finger to the lock and said, "Oh!" as the Angel script lit up. The symbols spun around, each circle turning at different speeds. When they stopped, there was a symbol in each row, all in a line, and the lock glowed a vibrant yellow.

With a hollow click! the rows of symbols retreated into the surface and the door swung open to reveal a workroom beyond. "No way," Lynn whispered in awe.

Jonah nudged his stunned cousin through first. He wasn't being chivalrous as much as betting her presence would diffuse any magical traps. The door had been keyed for her, after all. He relaxed when he didn't feel the buzz of magic, but then again, he might not have with the bands on.

Ancient texts, drawings, and more modern maps covered the surface of a large desk that was positioned against the wall adjacent to the door. The room's shelves were lined with ancient-looking books.

Kevin walked around the perimeter, inspecting everything. Mike perused the desktop with Jonah.

Lynn gazed at a large mural on the wall above the desk. "This reminds me of something Robert would draw." She brushed her fingers over the artwork.

Everyone jumped when Lynn's phone rang. She yanked it out. "Yeah, hold on." She changed it to speaker and said, "We are all here."

"Where?" Robert's tinny voice asked.

"Yeah," Wick chimed in. "You're on a fun trip and didn't invite us? Hold on. We'll call right back." Lynn held up the phone in exasperation at the same time it rang again. She propped her phone against a couple of thick books when Robert and Wick made a video call this time. Their faces crowded into view on the small screen.

Mike flicked a switch near the desk. Not only did light flood the work area, but recessed lighting in the ceiling also came on and illuminated the wall.

"Whoa!" Robert said.

"That is wicked," agreed Wick.

"Jonah, it's just like the triptych." Mike pointed out the seven stars and typography of the wall map.

Robert glared at them on the phone's screen. "What triptych?"

"Long story," Jonah told his cousin. Mike was right. It was the same, only this had…

"Those are compass codes," Mike said before Jonah could. "And there're two sets." His eyes went out of focus for a moment. "They are mortal and Underworld coordinates."

Jonah nodded, growing excited at the news. "Hey, that means you can use the dialer in the Deliverer's cave to go to the other side!"

"Oh!" Mike exclaimed. "Like we did when we traveled to the Afterworld." He grinned. "We should try it. But not now, of course." He gestured around them.

Jonah was about to agree when he noticed the thin, hardcover, black books on the desk were actually journals. He opened one and recognized his mom's handwriting. Kevin came over and opened another.

Soon everyone was doing the same until Mike said, "I have the last one." He proceeded to flip through the pages at a brisk pace. When he finished, he took the other journals from Kevin, Lynn, and Jonah. In quick succession, he read through all of them. Jonah marveled at his ability to soak up the information so rapidly.

When Mike finished, he stared at the large map on the wall. "Your mom figured out what was happening."

"Mike, my mom's…" Jonah stopped

"I know, but she figured out what the map means." Mike pressed his hand to the open page of the journal as if he were trying to absorb the words through his skin. "Every seven years, on Halloween, those seven mortal nexus points align with the ones in the Underworld. When that happens, the nexus points become huge doorways, letting a lot of powerful Wraiths through all at once if…"

"A ritual isn't performed," Lynn said. She, too, gazed at the mural in rapt fascination.

Mike stood beside her as if they were the only two people in the room. "The person requires the amulet of Pakhet."

Lynn bobbed her head in agreement. "Pakhet. She's the goddess of the night and the hunt. If they have her amulet, they can call forth her full essence to lead an army of Phantoms and other Underworld creatures on a rampage across the mortal world."

Lynn sucked in a startled breath. "I remember now." She turned to Jonah. "Your mom used to tell me that story all the time when I was little. And… she had the amulet back then! Or a copy of it." Her eyes widened. "This must have been what my aunt ranted and raved about when they locked her up."

"Yeah, seven years ago," Robert said. His voice sounded even more hollow over the phone's speaker.

"But Aunt Ruby has the amulet now," Jonah pointed out. "So why break into the store?"

"Because she doesn't have the *real* amulet." Mike snapped the journal closed that he had been holding. "Your mom returned it to your great-auntie. She hid it to keep anyone from opening the nexus points." He glanced around the room. "I'm starting to think your aunts were the guardians of the amulet."

Lynn laughed while also staring around the chamber. "Maybe so. It's clear our dear, old Aunt Ruby thought the real amulet was locked in here."

"Then we better close it up and go." Kevin glanced at his watch. "Time's up anyway."

Mike shook his head. "You don't get it, Kevin. The amulet's not here."

Jonah had a more pressing concern. "Ah, Mike? When do the points line up?"

Wick was the one to answer. "Isn't it obvious? It happens at midnight on Halloween. That's when the barrier between the mortal and Underworld is at its weakest point. *The Witching Hour!*"

CHAPTER TWENTY-FIVE
ALASTOR TRAPPED

Alliance personnel, including a couple of the huge Council Guards, flooded the old Ankh of Life bookstore. Lynn and Mike, who had never seen the guards before, reacted with shock to their impressive size as well as when the captain greeted Jonah by name.

But Jonah's attention was on Trueblood's demeanor. The mage looked as if someone had sucked all the joy out of his life. When he touched one of the black journals, Trueblood closed his eyes, and the pain was instantly evident on his face.

Jonah understood the reaction because he felt the same way when he opened his mom's lockbox. He expected to experience the same dull ache when he finally examined the rest of her things from her office.

Once the Alliance adults arrived, they ushered the young people out of the map room and into the crystal ball parlor. Mike poked the ball with a slender finger, carefully avoiding the cobwebs lest they cling to his hand. Lynn positioned herself at the doorway, straining to hear the conversations happening down the hall.

She moved away from the door just before Kevin stepped into view "We can go."

"What about the store?" Lynn asked. "I should lock the back room."

"No. They want to leave it open just in case Ruby comes back."

"Why?" Mike asked.

"Because they want to catch her!" Kevin said. He held out his arms for everyone to grab hold of him and then phased them all back to the clubhouse.

Robert and Wick were eagerly waiting for their return. The boys hustled Lynn, Jonah, and Mike to the club area while Kevin returned to the bookstore.

Mike held back. "I have to go."

Jonah wondered if he were meeting with Patrick but he kept that to himself. As Robert and Wick proceeded to pepper them with questions about the old bookstore, Jonah let Lynn talk.

The gang knew all about the big plan and had already confirmed his aunt was working with the mole. But something else nagged Jonah. Why come after his friends and family but not him? There had to be more to the whole thing.

He said as much to the group.

"We need to dig deeper and unearth more of the puzzle," Lynn agreed.

"But how?" Robert asked, looking around. "We don't know where to find the mole's group."

Except for Alastor, Jonah thought.

"Can I borrow your blades?" Jonah inquired, breaking the tense quiet.

Lynn raised a questioning eyebrow, waiting for the explanation.

"I asked Rex to show me the deflection spell," Jonah lied. "I want to try it on my own."

Lynn shrugged and handed over the blades. She went back to describing the interior of the Ankh of Life shop to Robert, who already had his sketchpad out and seemed determined to manage despite his injured fingers.

Jonah used their distraction to head for the door. While the Alliance sent their trap for his elusive aunt, Jonah decided to pay the overly friendly Alastor a visit. With any luck, he'd get some answers.

*

Jonah almost faltered in his plan when he entered Hackett's and saw Mike working the register. But it was too late to change course.

"Hey, Jonah." Mike waved. "You came to talk about Pakhet's amulet?"

Jonah glanced around the store. "Actually, I came to see Alastor."

Mike frowned. "Does Kevin know you're here to see–"

"Mr. Blackstone." Alastor appeared at the end of the History aisle, his brown eyes darting between the boys. "Did someone mention my name?"

Jonah gave his buddy a slight shake of the head. Mike's frown deepened as he grabbed a pile of discount paperbacks off the counter and disappeared down the Romance aisle.

"Well," Alastor said, watching Mike a moment before turning to Jonah. "How can I help you, Mr. Blackstone?"

"I need to talk with you."

Alastor raised an eyebrow. "We can talk in the office." He led the way.

The last time Jonah had seen Hackett's crowded office was two summers ago, when Mr. Hackett asked him and Mike inside. Not only did he discover the bookstore owner was a talented fantasy artist, but the man's immense wealth of information about Fallen Reapers and the Protector's Ring had more than shocked them.

Only now did Jonah attach more significance to Alastor running the store while Hackett was away. He began to wonder if Alastor were the Fallen Reaper that Mr. Hackett claimed to know. That would make Mike's uncle part of the plot too.

That thought troubled Jonah as he sat on the grey folding chair and faced the cluttered desk. Alastor closed the door and leaned against the side of the desk. Jonah scooted his chair back, giving himself more room.

Alastor didn't appear to notice the move but clapped his hands together like they were old friends. "Well, what can I do for you?"

The sound of the man's false cheeriness goaded Jonah. He stood, pushing aside the chair, and activated one of Lynn's Reaper blades. He was dimly aware of the chair knocking over one of Hackett's numerous paintings but he didn't have time to worry about that. Alastor was his exclusive focus.

The little man pressed against the closed door, keeping his eyes on the shiny weapon. "Careful with that, Mr. Blackstone. It's not a toy."

"I know how to use it." Jonah whirled the blade in his hand.

"So I hear."

"Yeah, I bet you did. I know who you are too."

"Really?"

"I heard about the Alliance Council and how you came to Mount Vernon to talk me into doing something stupid."

Alastor smiled. It didn't convey any happiness, just a sickening deceitfulness. "I didn't have to talk you into anything. I watched you scouting those houses on your own."

Jonah lost the effort to hide his surprise, causing Alastor to grin as he continued.

"The plan was already seeded in your devious, little mind. I merely helped it along."

Jonah's hand shook with anger and he had to concentrate to steady it. "You work for the Hardliners." With conscious effort, he refrained from shouting that Alastor also worked for the mole. That wasn't an option anymore, not after promising Trueblood he'd keep quiet.

"I see you've been talking with someone. Marcus?" Alastor gave him a questioning look. "No. He's too fond of keeping you in the dark. Perhaps Trueblood?"

Jonah wouldn't let the man distract him. The problem was that he couldn't accuse Alastor of working with his aunt or Niqab Girl, either. That would also indicate how much information the Alliance had on the man. But that didn't mean Jonah couldn't ask him about certain other things though.

"Why were you at the funeral? Why'd you really help me at Latrell's house?"

"I merely wanted to facilitate the development of your skills."

"Liar!"

Alastor raised his hands and grinned at Jonah again. "Why would I lie to you?" He tapped a dirtied fingernail against his forehead. "You can sense if my answer is the truth."

The more Alastor said, the more thankful Jonah was that his godfather was a Fallen Reaper as well as a lawyer. Marcus could make a statement that was true while excluding a whole bunch of damaging information. Jonah found it interesting that Alastor did the same thing now.

He was also reminded of what Albrecht said: Plausible deniability. Alastor was deliberately excluded from some parts of the plan so he could pass a Reaper's Stare.

"I'm not a weapon."

"I never said you were," Alastor agreed. "Now, put that Reaper's blade away."

Jonah wavered for a moment before he complied.

Alastor watched Jonah slipping the blade into his pocket. He leaned under the harsh light from the lacquered lampshade right above the desk. "That isn't yours."

"Yes, it is," Jonah lied.

"No, it isn't. First of all, you haven't chosen your own blades yet. Second, that one clearly doesn't fit you, although it did hum in your hand." Alastor slipped behind the desk and sat down. "Ah, yes. It must belong to your cousin, Lynn. Sometimes families tend to share an affinity toward particular blades."

The man's knowledgeable comments about blades ignited a flurry of questions in Jonah. And just as quickly, he realized this devious man was only doing it to distract him. Jonah couldn't let that happen because he feared Kevin would return to the clubhouse at any moment and discover he had slipped away. The young Fallen Reaper knew Jonah well enough to search here first.

Jonah reined in his natural curiosity and remembered his reason for confronting Alastor. "Why are you here?"

Alastor stared back in what Jonah thought was real surprise. "You honestly don't know? You were the first person in two thousand years to use a Protector's Ring. You defeated a Hunter by draining him of power." Alastor leaned forward with his hands pressed flat on the desk. "We're still curious how you managed to do that."

"We?" Jonah asked. "You mean, the Hardliners?"

Alastor seemed disappointed when he nodded. "Apparently, you're destined to be The One. The Seers have prophesied your emergence." Alastor tilted his head to the side as he watched Jonah's expression. "And then there's your friend, Mr. Littleton. The first true Seeker in two thousand years."

"Leave him alone." Jonah's hands tightened around the blade cylinders.

"Of course, we also read about your Afterworld adventure with your best friend. It's nothing less than remarkable."

Jonah suspected the man of lying, hoping he'd reveal more details. But he had no intention of discussing his time in the Afterworld with Alastor. "I don't trust you."

Alastor spread his little hands. "It can't be helped."

That small gesture caused Jonah's temper to flare. Getting answers from Alastor was frustrating. One minute, he gave a real answer, then he'd hold back the details or explanation. Jonah had no doubt Alastor was still trying to goad him into doing something he preferred not to do. He returned the man's gaze, searching for a new approach.

Wait! If Alastor claimed he wanted to help, why not give him the chance?

Jonah sat up in his chair, acting like an eager student. "Why are they messing with me? You've seen everything. What do you think?"

Alastor's eyes widened. "That's an interesting angle, Mr. Blackstone."

"I really want to hear what you think." Jonah funneled all of his sincerity into the statement. It wasn't hard because he was genuinely interested in hearing what the guy would tell him.

After a moment, Alastor let out a nervous laugh. "I believe you, but there are some things you and your cousins need to discover for yourselves."

"That's what you want us to do. You're still using me, and seeing what I can do." Jonah nodded with the certainty of it.

"Of course."

"You're evil," Jonah said, unable to hide his pent-up frustration any longer.

A hardened look replaced Alastor's mocking amusement. The little man sat forward, hands folded but shaking with repressed emotion. "I am not evil. The people who used you are the evil ones, young Blackstone. They killed your parents."

"Don't talk about my mom and dad!" Jonah activated the blades.

This time, Alastor didn't appear afraid at all. In fact, he seemed satisfied at Jonah's reaction. "You have a right to be angry with the Alliance. You didn't ask for this burden, but it's been placed on your shoulders all the same."

Jonah struggled to put the man's words into perspective. He had to remember that Alastor worked with the mole and wasn't any ally.

"You can decide to do whatever you want," Alastor continued.

"That's what you want: A weapon."

Alastor shot to his feet, nearly banging his head on the low-hanging lampshade. "Be yourself. Embrace your power, no matter what the Alliance, the Grim Reaper, or the Grand Oracle say."

"You're just trying to push me into—"

"I know what happened to Agent Hunter," Alastor hissed, his voice more urgent and pressing. "Tell me, young Blackstone, how did Marcus and Kevin react to you?"

Jonah stared into the man's eyes. "What do you mean?"

"They were afraid of you, weren't they? Everyone is afraid of you. None of them will ever truly trust you. Not even the so-called Hardliners."

Jonah felt the pressure of the man's will on his own. Though frightened at first, something inside him automatically pushed back. The pressure relented and disappeared.

As a movie quote entered his mind, Jonah surprised himself and laughed. "Turn to the dark side? My hate will make me powerful?"

Alastor frowned at him, though Jonah didn't know if it were because of his statement or because he diminished the pressure. But the man quickly overcame his initial shock. "You are too powerful and too dangerous."

Just as Alastor reached inside his coat pocket to withdraw his own blades, the office door banged open and Kevin charged in. His blades were already out and he brandished them at Alastor.

The little man leapt sideways and smacked into the wall, sending a pile of stacked books tumbling to the floor and knocking over several finished paintings. At the last minute, however, he seemed to come to his senses and left his own blades concealed.

"How dare you threaten me! I work for the Alliance Council!"

"So do I," Kevin snapped without lowering his blades.

"Mandara will find out about this!"

Kevin snorted. "Tell him. I don't care." He deactivated one blade and slipped it into his pocket so he could grab Jonah's arm.

Just before they phased, Jonah caught a glimpse of motion at the opened office door. He turned and saw a confused and wide-eyed Mike staring at him.

CHAPTER TWENTY-SIX
DANITA'S EXCLUSIVE

"Have you lost your mind?" Kevin yelled, not bothering to keep his cool.

Jonah hunched his shoulders and kicked at the loose brick in the hideaway's courtyard. "I wanted to get some answers."

Kevin gaped at him. "Do you know why you didn't get anything from him? Because Alastor isn't stupid, Jonah." The older boy stalked around the hideaway, visibly agitated.

"I'm sorry."

"You keep saying that, but then you go and do something stupid."

"You sound like Marcus."

Kevin's nostrils flared and he stormed right up to Jonah, standing over him. "If you think this is funny, let's go see what Marcus has to say about it."

"No. I don't. And I already said I'm sorry."

"Then mean it, and use your brain the next time."

Jonah shrank away from Kevin's anger. He had never seen the boy so worked up. As they locked gazes, Jonah could sense his deep concern. "Okay." His voice wavered.

The effect on Kevin was immediate. His expression softened as he gripped Jonah's hands, pulled him close, and kissed him.

Jonah didn't know how long they kissed. He lost track of time until a chill ran down his back. He thought it was just the wind or maybe the same jolt he and Kevin had experienced the last time they kissed.

Kevin was the first one to pull away and in an instant, his Reaper blades were out and ready.

Jonah turned to find Latrell standing behind him. "What are you doing here?"

When Kevin moved toward the ghostly boy, blades raised, Jonah shouted, "Don't!" He grabbed the Fallen Reaper's arm to stop him, but Latrell had already disappeared.

"How is he still following you around?" Kevin asked. When Jonah shrugged, he let out a low grunt of anger and began to pat Jonah's coat and then his pants. That's when he touched the ankh. "What's this?"

"Well, we were kissing…"

"Don't even go there," Kevin growled.

Jonah dug the ankh out of his jeans pocket.

Kevin snatched it and held it up to Jonah's face. "Latrell can follow you around when you wear this. That's bad, Jonah, because he's a Wraith."

"We can't be sure about that."

"He's working with the mole. He gave you the clue about the ankh." Kevin shoved the ankh in his own pocket.

"I know you feel sorry for him, but you have to face the truth." He checked his watch. "We need to go."

"Not yet." Jonah grabbed the boy's hand and held on.

"We have to. Mandara ordered me to check in every evening."

"Do you think Alastor told him already?"

Kevin frowned. "Yeah. Like I said, I don't care. I'll fight to stay here. Someone needs to make sure you don't do anything else stupid."

Jonah ignored the dig because he sensed Kevin's real concern and the deep desire not to leave him again. "Will you come back tonight?"

"No. I'll have to stay at the Guest House in Atlanta."

"Oh." Jonah gulped. "Say hello to Mabel for me."

Kevin sucked in a deep breath, forcing himself to calm down. "Jonah, you have to start listening to us."

"I know." He leaned against Kevin and wrapped his arms around the older boy's waist. The Fallen Reaper's higher body temperature felt wonderful to him on a chilly evening.

Kevin stared across the courtyard, his face a mask of worry. "This is serious. You can't let your emotions take over, not now. It's exactly what they want."

*

Jonah had never experienced such a mix of opposing emotions and sensations in his life. On the bad side, he had to wear the power-nullifying bands, and he'd made

Kevin furious with him. On the plus side, Kevin kissed him again.

As he and Kevin entered the attic, he was brought back down to Earth with a rude bump.

Mike, Robert, Lynn, and Wick turned to face them, all with matching serious expressions.

"What's up, guys?" Jonah asked even though he suspected Mike must have rushed there to tell everyone else what he witnessed. "Hey, Mike. Why aren't you working?"

"Why did Kevin burst into my uncle's store?"

"We'd like to hear the answer, too." Lynn's voice was tight. "But first…" She strode up to Jonah and held out a sheet of paper she'd been holding when he arrived.

Jonah took it. "What's this?"

"That is Danita's latest piece. She just emailed it to me." Lynn leaned against the back of the sofa. "You should read it." She folded her arms.

Jonah held the paper up to avoid her gaze. Mike crowded in to read over his shoulder.

THE GHOST OF VICTIMS PAST

None of us will forget the tragic news about the death of Latrell Mitchell. Despite your personal leanings, the premature death of a young person is always a shock and sad. The case of Latrell Mitchell took an unusual turn this week when Drew Edwards confessed to having bullied the boy before his suicide.

Drew made this confession to the school principal, his parents, and most surprisingly, to Latrell's parents. The Edwardses have promised that their son will receive some much-needed anger management therapy.

Jonah paused and lowered the page. He also tried to keep his face blank because everyone was watching him very carefully.

"This is great," he said. "Latrell's bully finally confessed. I thought Danita was writing about the black cat."

Lynn's eyes narrowed. "She was. You'll see; just keep reading."

Jonah didn't want to because he feared where the piece would go. But he did.

Many of you may know about my piece on black cats and superstitious beliefs. After reports of the black cat being spotted in Drew's neighborhood and discovering he saw it, I decided to question him for the next installment of my series. I've known Drew since the first grade, and while telling me about the night of the black cat sighting, he revealed something really unbelievable to me.

I found myself conducting an exclusive, impromptu interview with the troubled teen, being privy to the shocking nature of his confession. With some encouragement, Drew told me that he confessed to bullying Latrell because the boy's ghost visited him. That's right, reader!

In an encounter comparable to Charles Dickens's Scrooge, Latrell's ghost supposedly took the boy to various locales, including the high school hallway, Latrell's home, and finally, to the cemetery. According to Drew, as he lay sobbing in front of Latrell's grave, the ghost demanded that he confess his involvement in the matter.

Whether you believe in ghosts—I don't—or just think Drew ate some bad pizza before bed, one thing is for sure: The experience totally freaked out the kid. I don't endorse bullying of any kind, but should we thank Latrell's ghost for showing Drew the error of his ways?

Of course, I surmise this ghost was simply someone pretending to be the spirit of Latrell to scare Drew into doing what was right. But if any of you insist on believing in the supernatural, then I'll warn all the other bullies out there. Be careful or one night the victim's ghost might show up in your bedroom next!

Jonah flashed his cousins a nervous smile as he lowered the article. "That's really good. I like the bit about the ghost." His shaking hand betrayed his futile attempt to appear calm.

Behind Jonah, Kevin snorted.

Mike clamped a hand over his own mouth and backed away, his eyes showing dawning awareness.

Before Jonah could say anything to his friend, Robert hooked an arm around his shoulders. "Is there anything you want to tell us, little cousin?"

"Me? No."

"You sure, Jonah?"

"Yeah. I'm glad Drew confessed. He sounds like he needs mental help."

"Don't play dumb," Lynn warned, glaring at him. "Danita was more accurate than even she could appreciate."

"I don't…"

"Don't lie to us," Lynn warned.

"Jonah, Jonah, Jonah," Robert said. "Who do we know that can grab hold of someone and phase them from one location to another?"

"That's not what the article claims. Drew said it was a ghost."

"Drew explained everything to Danita," Lynn said, "including how it felt to phase. I asked her. You're just lucky she discounted it as utter nonsense, otherwise it would have been printed in bold there. That being said, what Drew described matched how we felt when Kevin phased all of us." She stood right in front of Jonah. "We all know it had to be you."

Jonah's shoulders slumped. He couldn't get out of this. It never occurred to him that Danita would interview Drew. "Fine. I did it." Jonah waved his arms in surrender.

Wick darted forward and gripped Jonah by the forearm, staring at his wrist. "What the…"

"Let him talk first," Robert said.

"But you don't understand, Bobby. This is a stun band." He gripped Jonah's other forearm and forced it up so the others could see the second band. "They're like stun cuffs."

Momentary surprise flitted across Robert's face when he heard that.

Jonah couldn't avoid it any longer and everything had to come out now. If he cooperated, maybe it wouldn't be too painful.

Robert peered at the bands. "Why does he have these on? Where'd you get them?"

Lynn tapped his arm. "Robert, don't you get it?" She turned to Jonah. "That's why Marcus came to see you, isn't it?"

Again, Jonah nodded, taking a deep breath before he confessed everything. And despite the imminent collective beat-down, confessing was a great relief until Lynn pulled him into a real headlock.

She ruffled Jonah's bushy hair. "Let's see if I have this straight. You didn't tell us that you went after Drew the first time." Lynn jerked her arms, tightening the hold.

"Ow! Yeah."

"Then," Lynn continued, tightening her hold again.

"Lynn!" Jonah squirmed in her grip.

"Quiet. Let's see, you go after the second bully. Only that time, Kevin must have interfered and you got into trouble for trying to be a vigilante superhero." Lynn twisted her arms a third time.

"Yeah. Okay, ow!"

"Anything else you're," she tightened the hold again, "forgetting to tell us?"

"No. I promise."

Lynn released Jonah, who took three staggering steps over to the sofa. The others huddled around him as he recited the highlights of his talk with Alastor.

Kevin stirred when Lynn glanced his way. "Hey," he said, "I've already yelled at him about it."

"Good," Lynn said.

Jonah braced himself for more, but Lynn and the others started discussing their next step.

Kevin tapped Jonah's shoulder and whispered, "I'm out of here."

Jonah hopped to his feet and trailed Kevin to the spot in front of the large attic window. The boys stared at each other, both knowing they couldn't hug or do anything else affectionate in front of the others.

"Bye," Jonah said.

After Kevin left, he started to rejoin the discussion but heard footsteps descending the attic stairs. Lynn, Wick, and Robert were still gathered around the steamer trunk, but...

Mike! Jonah hurried after his buddy and caught up to him just outside the Summit door. He grabbed Mike's arm.

His friend shrugged free. "Leave me alone!" His face darkened with real anger and he punched Jonah in the chest.

"Ow! Stop! Mike, I'm–"

"What if someone had seen you? What if you actually hurt Drew?"

"I didn't hurt him, and he deserved it. He bullied Latrell."

"You can't turn into a bully just to get even. That's wrong and it goes against everything we do in the club, the club which you started."

"I'm sorry I scared Drew. Okay?"

Mike pressed his hands flat against the second-floor railing, his breathing now heavy and fast. "You were totally wrong, Jonah." He turned his face away when Jonah stood beside him.

"I'm sorry. Really, I am."

Mike whirled on him and Jonah stepped back. "The worst part is: You lied to me. You already had plans to go after Brandon even though you promised me otherwise."

"Technically, I didn't promise and I didn't think it was wrong." Jonah realized too late that he said the wrong thing.

Mike's eyes flared with anger. "If it were right, then why did you find it necessary to lie to everyone?" He worked his jaw to keep from yelling further. "You knew we'd try to stop you! Just like Marcus had to do."

Mike moved away as Jonah reached out. "I can't get over you lying to me." He turned for the spiral stairway.

"Wait. Where are you going?"

Mike's angry expression shifted for a second and became guarded. "I'm going to the movies with Patrick."

"After what he did to you?"

"I talked to him. Well, I shouted," Mike said, adding, "he just wanted me to like him."

"Yeah, but there was the slight problem that he was being used by my aunt." Jonah slid closer to Mike. "Besides, Patrick just wanted to go all the way with you. He thought that potion would do the trick."

Mike grimaced. "I know that. And I can deal with him." When Jonah opened his mouth to argue the point, Mike grew testy. "We promised we'd help each other as Deliverer and Seeker. I guess you forgot about that." He hurried down the steps.

As Jonah watched his buddy stride across the atrium below before exiting through the front doors, he didn't know how things could get any worse than they were now.

CHAPTER TWENTY-SEVEN
BRANDON'S REVENGE

Every student read Danita's story about Drew on their mobile devices the next day. Jonah guessed that was a positive for the Summit's popularity, but he wasn't proud of what he'd done.

The muted, stinging sensation of the wristbands was an ever-present reminder of the price. He supposed that was the reason his godfather made him wear the wretched things. As bad as he felt about the *null-cuffs*, his private name for them, Mike's continued cold shoulder stung him even deeper.

He stubbornly refused to say a word to Jonah during their first joint anti-bullying patrol. By the end of the patrol, Jonah couldn't take it anymore.

Mike had already closed his locker and started to leave when Jonah tapped his shoulder. "Hey?"

Mike tensed at the touch and turned, clutching his notebook in one hand. His other hand was in his pocket. "What?" He refused to look at Jonah.

"I wanted to tell you something."

"You mean apologize?"

Jonah blinked in surprise, his own irritation rushing forward. "I already did that."

Mike's jaw tightened as he ground his teeth. "I'm helping the new club member on the last patrol today, so you'll be with someone else." With that, Mike turned and slipped through the students that were clogging the hallway.

*

Because Mike was a wizard at organizing things, Jonah let him handle all the patrol assignments for the Tolerance Club. When Mike handed Jonah his new assignment, and Jonah saw the location, he knew his buddy was simply getting even. Mike not only broke up their team by pairing Jonah with Anthony, but he also sent them to the opposite end of the school from himself.

Mike crossed his arms as if waiting for Jonah to complain further or assert his role as the club leader. Instead, Jonah snatched the slip of paper with the assignment on it and beckoned Anthony to come over before heading off to the secluded stairway.

The custodians used the area at the top of the steps to store extra supplies, broken touch boards, and the like. The doors to the roof stood at the far side of the space and behind a pile of old supplies.

Some student had evidently discovered the access door and created a narrow path between the boxes. The club had heard scattered rumors of students using it to catch a smoke on the roof. Occasionally, bullies took smaller kids in there for beat-downs.

He and Anthony posted themselves at the top of the stairs and spent the time talking about the upcoming Halloween Bonfire. Things were fine until Brandon showed up. The bully grinned up at them as he mounted the stairs before rudely shoving his way between Jonah and Anthony.

He pulled out a cigarette and a crooked smile appeared on his face. "What are you doing here, DC?"

Jonah stood his ground. "You're not supposed to be smoking in the school or on the roof." Anthony nodded in agreement.

Brandon made a show of lighting and taking a puff of the cigarette. "I thought you were just anti-bullying?" He held out the cigarette to Jonah. "Wanna try one?"

Jonah waved a hand in front of his face, trying to dispel the smoke. "Put it out!"

"Or what?" When Jonah didn't respond, Brandon laughed and glanced at his expensive watch. With a final snort, he threaded his way between the boxes and out the roof access door.

"Think we should report him?" Anthony asked.

Jonah shook his head. "His dad will make too much of a fuss. Leave it."

Anthony's phone pinged and he checked it. "Hey. I need to meet someone. Mind if I head off a little early?"

"Nah. Go ahead."

Anthony took the first few steps and paused, turning back. "You sure about Brandon?"

"He's fine as long as he's alone."

With that, Anthony nodded and hurried away.

Jonah turned to peer at the sunlight streaming through the crack between the roof doors. He also caught the acrid whiff of cigarette smoke on the cool air current. Maybe he should have reported Brandon…

The door opened, cutting off that silent debate. Brandon stepped inside and threaded his way back through the box path. He stepped free and squared off with Jonah.

"You still here, DC? I'm starting to think you like me or something."

At that moment, Jonah realized all at once that Brandon was acting braver and calmer than usual, considering he was alone and without his usual admiring crowd. As soon as that thought crossed Jonah's mind, he sensed the person behind him. His assessment was rudely corrected when two people firmly grabbed his arms and legs.

Brandon wasn't alone after all. At the same time, a horrible realization occurred to Jonah. Not only did the wristbands nullify his phasing ability, they also muffled his Death Sense.

Jonah struggled, but he couldn't use any of the defensive moves that he'd mastered in Practice Club. Brandon dropped his cigarette on the ground and snubbed it out with a foot.

"Right on time, guys." He laughed as he loomed closer. "Hold the freak tight."

Jonah saw Brandon tensing up just before the boy threw the first punch to the face. A stinging pain exploded across Jonah's upper lip and nose before the sensation of wetness splatted on the top of his mouth and dribbled down onto his chin. He sucked in a startled breath, accompanied by fresh pain in other places.

One of Brandon's buddies called out to him, "Watch it, Brandon. You don't want to leave obvious marks on him or we'll get into trouble."

A look of frustration transformed Brandon's face, like he didn't want to be told what to do. His expression subsequently turned thoughtful as he scrutinized Jonah's struggling form.

"You're right."

This time, Brandon delivered three solid punches to Jonah's midsection, causing him to gasp in pain as he struggled to breathe.

Brandon pulled back and smirked at Jonah. "Those were for Drew." He punched Jonah again in the stomach. "That one was for Antwan." Another punch. "And that one was because I don't like you."

Despite the excruciating pain, Jonah prepared to twist his body when Brandon reared back to deliver another punch.

"This is because I hate your stupid club." Brandon swung, and Jonah twisted. The result was having the bully's fist impact the side of Jonah's chest, hitting him squarely in the ribs.

That pain was even worse. Jonah's only satisfaction was Brandon's grunt of anguish. The boy cursed and shoved Jonah's head back, producing a sharp jab in his neck. "Let him go."

The guys did and Jonah sagged to the ground, still clutching his midsection. The blood from his nose ran down his cheek and pooled onto the cold floor. He listened to the boys laughing as they descended the stairs.

Jonah lay there, struggling to catch his breath while trying to ignore his injuries. In an odd way, he was reminded of his fight with Agent Hunter in the Afterworld. Before now, that was the last time he hurt so much. He touched his nose and winced. It wasn't broken, just bloodied.

He broke it two summers ago when he and Brandon had their first-ever duel. But this time was different. The continued dull, throbbing pain indicated that his healing factor wasn't working either.

Jonah struggled to his feet and made his way to the nearest bathroom. The tissues he used to staunch the bleeding came away scarlet red. He started to lift his sweater and winced. When he finally exposed his abdomen, he couldn't believe all the bruises.

Brandon's friend was right. The nose and busted lip were the only clear signs of the attack. Still, he worried that his relatives would notice even those. With his healing factor blocked, he would have to fully endure the pain of the attack just like any other regular kid. For all Jonah's desires to be normal, today, he wanted his powers back more than ever before.

*

His nose eventually stopped bleeding, but Aunt Imma noticed his constant wincing and the busted lip as soon as she came home from work.

"What on Earth?" She lifted Jonah's chin and inspected the bruise.

"It's nothing. Just a rough game of basketball."

Aunt Imma made a disapproving sound. "First Robert and now you."

She went off to her room to change out of her work clothes. Although his answer quieted anymore questions, he hated lying to his aunt. But he also couldn't tell anybody the truth. How would it look for the leader of the anti-bullying club to be victimized?

All the other kids would quit, Jonah decided. Then again, the work of the club was to get kids to report any bullying. Yet here he was now, refusing to do that too. Either way Jonah considered the situation, he felt like a fraud.

To ease his burning shame over the whole sorry ordeal, Jonah tried to concentrate on his homework. With his books spread all over the kitchen table, he worked there because it was less painful than moving the short distance it took to get to his room. His phone buzzed and vibrated, disrupting his attempt to study.

When Mike's ID flashed, Jonah dropped the phone on the table and returned to his homework. He didn't want to talk to Mike, not when he still blamed his friend for what happened.

The phone buzzed again with Mike's second attempt to reach him. Jonah glared at it, hoping his buddy would hang up. This time, Mike included a text message before he called the third time.

By then, Aunt Imma had returned to the kitchen and started pulling out items for dinner. "Why don't you answer your phone?"

"Yes, ma'am." *Dang it.* "What?" He hissed into the phone as his aunt clanked around in the pot cupboard.

The silence on Mike's end told Jonah he wasn't scoring any points. But right now, he didn't care.

Mike let out a huff like he was counting to ten to calm himself. Then he said, "It's all your fault."

Jonah's stomach tightened. He had no clue what he did wrong this time and frankly, he was sick of people jumping on him. Before he answered, he rose slowly to his feet and lumbered outside to the patio. "What are you talking about? What did I do wrong this time?"

"Alastor! After you talked to him, he closed up the store and left town. I found a note saying I'd have to keep it open until he comes back."

"That wasn't my fault."

"Yes, it was. You and Kevin scared him off."

Jonah snorted and grimaced, clutching his stomach. "Alastor wasn't afraid of us."

"Well, you busted his cover. Either way, he packed up and left."

"He's probably just reporting to his boss. I'm sure he'll be back."

"No, he won't."

Jonah wanted to say *too bad*, but even in his sour mood, he knew that would set Mike off. "When's your uncle coming back?"

"My dad called him today, and he won't be back for two months. We have to work the store until then."

"So what's the problem?"

"I have to keep the store open, every day, after school. My dad thinks it'll build character!"

Despite his friend's anxiety, Jonah found the circumstances a little humorous. He fought to keep the amusement out of his voice. "I'm sorry, Mike, but I know you can handle it."

"I won't be able to do the things I want to do or see the people I want to see."

Jonah couldn't believe his friend. "Mike, how can you still see Patrick?"

"You should have to help me," Mike said, ignoring the question.

"What? Why?"

"Because I need your help."

The unexpected plea for help stopped Jonah's mounting anger in its tracks. "Well… ah, what about Patrick?"

"He's not a big reader. You know the store better and…"

"And?"

"And I may forgive you for lying to me."

Jonah rubbed his forehead, wincing at the start of a headache. If he did that, it could help patch things up with Mike. "When?"

"Get over here now."

"Now? But–"

Mike ended the call.

After clearing it with his aunt, Jonah slowly put his books away. He didn't look forward to the painful bike ride, but knew it would also be worth it.

CHAPTER TWENTY-EIGHT

FIRST DATE

One unfortunate effect of Alastor's departure was the reduced operating hours. This forced the usual daily customers to mingle with the evening crowd. Jonah had never seen so many people in the store at one time.

He crossed slowly to the sales counter and waved. "I'm here."

Mike was all business. "Cover the register," he barked before moving off briskly to help a little woman find a rare book.

Reminding himself that it was worth it, Jonah eased behind the counter and spent the next two hours ringing up purchases. In no time, he had his own routine down. In between waiting on customers, he helped shelve the traded-in, used books, which they kept on the lower shelves only.

He experienced a pang of regret when he realized how much fun he and Mike could have had at the store, if he hadn't been such a jerk by lying. Things remained civil between the boys until an hour before closing.

Patrick came into the store. "What'sup?"

Jonah waved to the sullen boy just as Mike appeared from a side aisle with an arm full of paperbacks for the customer who was following him.

He hesitated when he saw Patrick and dropped the books on the counter. "Jonah, you handle this."

"Sure thing."

Jonah gave the customer a cheery smile, but did not fail to notice Mike motioning to Patrick to go to the back of the store and the office. Jonah rang up the customer as quickly as he could. After that, he moved from behind the counter, ignoring the prickles of pain, and approached the back of the store.

Patrick's angry voice carried out to him. "This sucks, Mike! I want us to go."

"It's my job to watch the store and close out everything afterward."

"Why can't Jonah do it?"

"Jonah has his own plans for tonight," Mike answered.

"Really? Admit it. You like hanging out in the books with your old boyfriend."

Jonah recoiled at that statement, grimaced, and shuffled backward. It was fortunate that he did because Patrick stomped away from the back office and barely glanced at Jonah while storming by. Mike came out and started straightening the books with agitated movements.

Part of Jonah was thrilled to see Patrick and Mike having problems. However, he didn't want to see his friend in pain, either. "Mike?"

"What?" Mike scanned the store. "Is something wrong?"

"No."

"Well, did you finish the used books?"

"Yeah, I did." *While you and your boyfriend were fighting.* Jonah took a deep breath as Mike began stacking magazines. "If you need me to cover for you tonight, I can. I'm not doing anything else later on."

Mike's mouth worked as if he repeated Jonah's words. "Seriously? I mean, thanks."

They faced each other in awkward silence. Jonah started to apologize when Mike sprinted for the front door.

Once again, Jonah reined in his mixed feelings. He'd only made the offer because he hoped Mike would accept his apology, not so he could chase after Patrick. He groaned as he reached the front door and peeked through the multi-colored glass. Mike and Patrick stood outside in the gravel parking lot, talking.

Remembering to be happy for his best friend, Jonah turned back to his work. His aching mid-section aside, he discovered he liked working the store alone. For one thing, he didn't have to hide his pain from anyone. In addition to that, the lower number of customers near closing time made it easy to help each patron individually.

Mike showed him how to close out the register and put things away in the safe that was located in the back office. *It was strange*, Jonah reflected. He loved bookstores, but never imagined working in one before, much less, owning one someday. He rang up a customer, who saw his happy expression and smiled back.

"Thanks for coming," Jonah said. He was about to turn and put away a stack of trade-ins when the door opened and Kevin strode inside. The tall boy stopped to take in the cramped store before crossing to the counter, all the while watching Jonah's expression with a neutral look.

"What are you doing here?"

Kevin hooked a thumb over his shoulder. "You're not supposed to be out on your own after dark, remember?"

"But I thought you had to check in regularly and were staying in Atlanta."

"I did check in and I'll head back to Atlanta. First, I have some news for you."

"Oh. How did you find me?"

Kevin grinned. "It wasn't hard. You're a boring kid, you know that?"

Jonah didn't bristle at the taunt. Instead, he smiled because he liked Kevin playfully sparring with him.

The final customer came to the register. Kevin moved aside and pulled a magazine from a nearby rack. Jonah finished with the customer and caught Kevin watching him out of the corner of his eye. Once the patron exited the store, Jonah took the trade-ins and eased around the counter.

He began shelving books in the Military Science Fiction section while Kevin watched his every move. "Didn't you have something to tell me?" Jonah asked.

"Oh, yeah." Kevin leaned against the bookshelves.

"We had Alliance Guards watching your aunt's old shop. Well, someone busted in."

"Was it my aunt?" Jonah asked, his hopes rising. "Did they catch her?"

"No, it wasn't her. And the person got away by busting out the wall in the back of the store to escape." Kevin rubbed his chin, looking thoughtful. "Almost like they expected the guards to bust in."

Jonah was disappointed, but at least Lynn had been right. "Aunt Ruby doesn't have the real amulet. That's good. It means she doesn't know where it is either."

"True," Kevin agreed, "but it also indicates she'll have to start looking in other places."

An unpleasant alternative occurred to Jonah. "Maybe she'll think I have it."

Kevin's gaze turned intense. "Well, she'd have to get through me first."

The comment thrilled Jonah so much, he made the mistake of reaching too high and had to suck in a painful breath.

Kevin was at his side in a second. "What's wrong with you?"

"Nothing." Jonah couldn't hide the fact he didn't want to reach up again.

Kevin took the book and slid it onto the shelf.

"Thanks," Jonah said. He tried to select the next book but Kevin took the stack and set them on the floor. He gripped the bottom of Jonah's sweater, but Jonah stopped him. "Kevin, don't."

"Be quiet." Kevin pushed Jonah's hands aside and lifted the sweater. The cool air on his bare skin slightly eased the pain.

Kevin hissed in anger as he examined Jonah's bruises. The boy's super warm hand felt wonderful.

"Who did this?" Kevin's voice was tight with suppressed anger.

"Brandon and his guys ambushed me."

"I'm gonna put my fist through his arrogant face!"

Jonah gulped at the raw fury in Kevin's tone. "You can't do that. I'm wearing these bands because I went Batman on him."

"I don't care. You could have a broken rib or two! Those stun cuffs must be interfering with your healing factor too."

Jonah winced at Kevin's continuing examination. "Is it broken?"

"No. Just bruised," Kevin answered. He let Jonah's sweater drop but his hand lingered underneath it and against Jonah's abdomen for a moment. "Why didn't you let the school nurse check you out?"

"Are you crazy? She'd have reported it and then, everyone would know what happened."

"Brandon would have gotten in trouble that way," Kevin shot back.

"Yeah, and totally embarrass me in the process. The head of the Tolerance Club getting bullied!"

"Shouldn't you set the example by reporting it?"

Jonah gaped at him. "You really want me to do that?"

The young Fallen Reaper shrugged, his jaw clenching.

"Kevin?" Jonah waited for the boy to meet his gaze. "Don't do anything to him. Please. I don't want you sent away forever."

Kevin nodded, but Jonah knew he needed to distract the boy so he nudged the books with his foot. "Help me put those away."

Kevin obliged, slipping the books into the slots where directed. "Where's Mike?"

"Out with Patrick." Jonah didn't bother to hide his disappointment.

Kevin turned on him. "After what he did?"

"Tell me about it." Jonah was relieved to have Kevin agree with him. "I tried to talk to Mike, but he wouldn't listen. I don't get it."

"Well, I don't get either of you geeks," Kevin said with a laugh.

Jonah shoved him and regretted it when his bruises throbbed. Maybe he should have let Kevin pound Brandon into a pulp anyway.

Kevin slipped an arm around Jonah's waist and helped him walk to the front. Jonah didn't need the help but he loved the contact. "Hey, lock the door and turn the sign around."

"Lock the door?" Kevin smirked at him.

"You know what I mean," Jonah could feel his own face warming.

When Kevin returned, he glanced around the store. "What else do you have to do?"

"Why?" Jonah asked, curious.

"I can get us dinner and bring it back here."

Jonah began to mention that Aunt Imma had probably cooked something before he nearly kicked himself. Dinner in the bookstore with Kevin sounded wonderful! Plus, it presented an opportunity to be alone with him longer. The more Jonah considered it, the more he liked it. Besides, his aunt knew he was working at the store anyway. "Yeah, that's cool. I can close up things while you go and get it."

Kevin brightened at the idea and left.

Jonah went about his duties closing out the store and putting everything away. He had just finished dumping the trash out the back and was washing his hands when Kevin knocked on the door.

Jonah grinned. "You knocked?"

"This place is protected against phasing." Kevin held up the take-out boxes from a nearby restaurant. The enticing aroma of the hot food made Jonah's stomach grumble with anticipation. But Kevin also had a regular convenience store bag in the other hand.

He withdrew a cold compress from the bag and shook the packet as he pulled up Jonah's sweater. When the ice-cold compress touched his skin, Jonah sighed in relief.

Kevin stared into his eyes while he held the bag in place. Jonah could almost read the boy's thoughts.

"You promised."

"I'm not gonna touch the punk," Kevin said. "Come on."

Jonah held the compress in place as he followed Kevin to the Occult section, where Hackett kept a small table and some fold-out chairs. Kevin placed the dinners on the table and pulled out Jonah's chair for him.

They began to eat and soon Jonah asked Kevin about his time away from Mount Vernon. He was relieved when Kevin relaxed and told him about the missions. Jonah listened as the older boy's confident voice filled the quiet store. It was the longest Kevin had ever talked to him without pausing and Jonah loved it.

Eventually, the Fallen Reaper finished discussing his assignment and gazed at him. "I need to get back soon."

Jonah swallowed. "Okay." All at once, he realized that sitting there in the darkened store, under the soft lamp light, he was having his first real date with Kevin. Well, with anyone! "Do you have to leave right now?"

"No," Kevin said, his voice tight. "I have a few minutes."

"What do you want to do?" Jonah's voice shook. But his anticipation spiked and his heart thudded in his chest when the older boy rose, leaned across the table, and kissed him.

CHAPTER TWENTY-NINE
GARAGE ATTACK

Jonah stretched and yawned, feeling refreshed. It was Saturday morning, and the night before, he'd had his first real date with Kevin. He rolled over, reliving the wonderful experience, and his mind suddenly registered there wasn't much pain. Sitting up, he threw back the cover and raised his t-shirt. The bruises on his abdomen were fainter, almost gone. He tentatively pressed his rib and received a very minor ache.

Yes! His healing ability had kicked in during the night. Relieved that at least one of his powers still worked, Jonah rose from the bed and got up. He took an extra-long shower and dressed for the day in a much better spirit. He even pulled on a light-colored sweater that Mike once told him looked nice against his skin color.

Even thoughts of his Aunt Ruby couldn't dampen his mood because he had an idea blossoming about how to find her. There was one person around who might have known his aunt's whereabouts: The store clerk Wraith. As weird as it was, the man had been honest after all. With a start, Jonah realized Deyanira had also tried to help him.

Beware, young Blackstone.

Jonah knew better than to think the evil Reaper did it out of any real affection for him. She simply hated the mole. Is the enemy of my enemy my friend?

Yeah, he would go and talk with the store clerk, but he couldn't go alone. The problem was Lynn already made plans to help Uncle James and Kevin was off doing Alliance work. Jonah's next best choice was Wick. After a quick bowl of cereal, he fetched his bike and rode to the Teen Center.

Jonah entered the center and spotted Mike at once in the café. He crossed the atrium and sat at the table.

Mike was wearing one of the pullovers his big brother had sent him from college. He also seemed in a good mood this morning. "Thanks for closing the store."

"No problem." Jonah meant it. His night had turned out great. He smiled a little to himself.

Mike noticed. "Wow, you must be in a good mood."

"Why do you say that?"

"You're wearing that sweater I like on you and smiling. What happened?"

Jonah whispered, "Kevin stopped by last night."

Mike's eyes grew comically wide, then his grin turned wicked. "I see." He scanned Jonah's face. "What did you two do?"

Jonah smiled. "Nothing." Then, mimicking Mike when he had asked about Trevor, he mumbled, "We just talked." Mike reached across the table and punched Jonah's arm. Feeling better about his life, despite the predicted doom at midnight on Halloween, Jonah decided to clear the air. "I'm sorry I lied to you, Mike. You're my best friend and I promise–"

"Jonah, don't…" Mike's protest trailed off as his eyes flashed.

Jonah experienced an intense wave of goosebumps along his skin and pushed up his sleeve to examine his arm. "What the…"

"Be careful with your promises," Mike said, his voice serious. "We're part supernatural, so all promises carry extra weight. They told me that at Alliance HQ."

"You mean…"

Mike nodded. "You'll have to keep that promise."

"Oh, well. That's no problem. I was promising not to keep you out of the loop again." Jonah lowered his sleeve back into place. "By the way, your eyes flashed just then."

"So did yours. I think it's because you're the Deliverer and I'm your Seeker."

As a shocked silence slowly ensued, Jonah tapped the table. "Hey, I was thinking of going to Mystic Worlds and asking the Wraith what he knows."

Mike's jaw dropped. "Are you sure that's a good idea?"

"He's not dangerous. He helped me before. And he tried to tell me about the potions, remember?"

"Still." Mike pointed at Jonah's wrists. "You have those bands."

"Yeah. I was gonna ask Wick to go with me."

"He's upstairs practicing his spell casting."

"Cool. He's always complaining about not going on any of the good trips." Jonah rose but paused because he had forgotten something obvious. "You want to come along?"

"Thanks, but I don't think so." Mike leaned back in his chair, crossing his thin arms. "I want to make more headway on the translations. Tell me what happens when you get back."

*

"Let's be clear about this." Wick stopped Jonah just outside the former Mystic Worlds bookstore. "If Lynn finds out, this was your idea, okay?"

"Chicken," Jonah teased. He opened the door and entered.

Wick sucked in a breath when he crossed the threshold. "Whoa!"

"What?"

"I forgot they rearranged this place to dispel the magical energy." Wick scanned the store while ruffling his hair twists. "Yep. Look at the bookshelves. They're scattered like that on purpose. I bet there are sigils on all of them. Slick."

The store clerk approached and eyed Wick for a moment. "Mage?" His voice was low because there were other customers browsing among the aisles.

"Yeah, I am." Wick puffed out his chest, acting his usual confident self. That reassured Jonah. "I know why you have the bookshelves arranged like this."

The clerk nodded, visibly impressed. "You can't be too careful." He spread his hands in an inviting way and focused on Jonah. "How may I help you today?"

Jonah heard the genuine willingness in the man's voice. "Thanks for the potion warnings."

The clerk's eyebrow rose. "You neutralized that threat?"

"Yeah. And we know about the Pakhet legend and the amulet."

"Then you should recognize the great danger threatening this whole town," the Wraith added. "Be forewarned, young Blackstone. You must find the amulet."

"Sure thing," Wick said, "as soon as you tell us where it is."

"I have no information regarding the amulet's whereabouts."

Jonah thought the surprise on the clerk's face was sincere. He wasn't worried because he had another idea. "Does Latrell know?"

The clerk shook his head. "I doubt it. If he did, the Wraiths working with your aunt would also know." His eyes narrowed. "You do realize that the shadow of Pakhet still rests upon your aunt? She may no longer be herself."

"She's still a bad person–" Jonah stopped. The clerk held up a hand as a customer approached the back counter before moving away to help her.

Wick whispered in Jonah's ear, "Is he lying?"

"I can't tell," Jonah admitted. "The bands are messing with my Reaper's Stare."

The front door opened, cutting off their hushed conversation. Bright morning sunlight streamed through the entrance, casting an eerie glow around Niqab Girl.

She stepped aside while the clerk ushered the remaining customer out the front door. Her eyes, the only thing visible through her face mask, never left Jonah's face. "I'm looking for some books on powerful amulets."

The clerk closed the door and scowled at her while fingering an amulet hanging around his neck. It was in the shape of a flattened pyramid. He directed his attention to Jonah and Wick. "Is there anything else I can do for you gentlemen?" He flicked his eyes to Antwan's cousin briefly before opening the door.

"Nope," Jonah answered as he tried to pull Wick toward the exit. "Come on."

But Wick wore an uncharacteristic, enraged expression. "You're the one who messed with my magic at the show!" He raised his hand, calling on his magic.

Niqab Girl reacted in kind, stretching her right hand out. But she frowned and glared at the clerk.

Wick blinked and stared at his own hand as he tried several times to perfect a throwing motion but nothing except a brief spark appeared before it faded.

The clerk positioned himself between them. "There're no magic duels allowed in this store. It's neutral ground." He motioned to Wick and Jonah. "Please go."

Jonah had to shove Wick out the door. All the while, Antwan's cousin grinned at him.

Once they were outside, Wick tried to pull free of Jonah's grip, but Jonah succeeded in getting the young mage across the street and onto the opposite sidewalk.

Wick glared at the store. "Get out of the way, Jonah."

"That's not too smart." Jonah held up his wrist and showed off the band. "You want Trueblood and Albrecht to do the same thing to you?"

"She's gloating about the whole thing," Wick protested. Then he went still.

That scared Jonah. He followed Wick's gaze and spotted Antwan's cousin exiting the bookstore. She made a point of glancing at them before walking down the opposite sidewalk at a brisk pace. Wick set off down their sidewalk, keeping up with her.

Jonah followed. "Where are you going?"

"I need to find out what she knows."

"Following Antwan's cousin is pretty risky. The store clerk told us to beware."

"He said *be forewarned*." Wick continued down the sidewalk.

"Whatever. We should still be careful," Jonah said. He didn't know what to do. Wick was bigger than him and strong enough to push him out of the way and keep pursuing Niqab Girl. For a moment, Jonah considered calling Lynn or Robert even though that would only have made things worse.

"What are you gonna do when you catch up to her?" Jonah asked.

"Just have a nice talk with her." Wick flexed his hands.

Even with the effects of the bands, Jonah could sense the magic gathering around the boy.

Wick pointed at the retreating girl, who was now a block away. "We need to see where she goes. Come on."

"We already know she's hiding out at Antwan's."

"Maybe she's on the way to report to your aunt?" Wick countered. "You ever think of that?"

Jonah let out an exasperated sigh. "Lynn and Kevin would skin us alive if anything happens."

"Then we won't tell them. I have to do something," Wick pleaded. "We can't wait around until they find the amulet." He turned to Jonah. "I thought you would understand?"

"Excuse me." Jonah raised his wrists again. "No powers."

Wick ruffled his twists in irritation. "I have enough for both of us."

They crossed to the other side of the street and hurried to close the gap with Antwan's cousin. Wick fingered a shield bracelet on his right wrist, catching Jonah's attention. He noticed now that his friend had also given up his trademark unlaced, black boots for black high-tops that didn't make any noise on the sidewalk. Jonah wondered if Wick expected something like this to happen.

Up ahead, Antwan's cousin turned onto a side street between the shopping strip and a parking garage. Wick and Jonah broke into a run. They reached the corner just in time to see the young girl ducking into the parking structure.

A sudden thought struck Jonah and he glanced sideways at Wick. "She knows we're following her."

"Yep…" Wick pointed. Antwan's cousin sprinted to the far corner of the first level and into a stairwell. He led the way, weaving around rows of cars, and slipped inside the same stairwell. The girl's running feet made a huge racket, convincing Jonah she wanted them to follow.

The boys sprinted up the stairs. As they passed the fourth level, the exit door on the fifth level opened and closed with a loud bang!

Wick motioned Jonah to stop. "She may have just opened the door to fool us and then gone up to the sixth level."

When they didn't hear more footsteps, they continued their ascent and rounded the last few stairs to the fifth floor. Wick opened the access door as quietly as he could, poked his head out, and looked around.

"Okay, let's go," he said.

Jonah's Death Sense gave the mildest of twinges, almost imperceptible, as Antwan's cousin stepped into view, her arms crossed.

Wick frowned. "She's up to something." He fingered the bracelet again. A loud bang! came from behind them. Jonah and Wick whirled around to see a cargo van with the back raised off the ground. The huge man stood there using one hand to lift the whole rear of the vehicle. He wasn't wearing a nice suit today. Instead, he wore mechanic's coveralls. And his silhouette, outlined by the sun at his back, resembled a gorilla's. Once he had their attention, he let the van drop and it rocked back and forth.

Jonah recalled this was clearly the hulking man from Robert's drawing. As if to leave no doubt, the man's eyes flashed a solid milky white.

The girl spoke, and her voice filtered through her black mesh face wrap. "Why are you following me, Son of Isaiah?"

"I'm the one following you, evil witch," Wick said before Jonah could stop him.

"Wick," Jonah whispered. "Don't make her mad. The *Hulk* is a good friend of hers."

The Wraith sneered at them and spittle flew from his mouth as he shouted, "I should grind you two pathetic mortals into dust for what you did."

"I think we should leave now," Jonah suggested. He felt naked without his normal powers.

Wick shrugged off Jonah's grip, refusing to move. For some reason, he wasn't afraid; in fact, he appeared strangely confident about challenging the Wraith.

Oh, well, Jonah decided. He stood his ground. "Where's my Aunt Ruby?" When they didn't answer, Jonah added, "You'll never get the amulet if you don't tell me."

The Wraith's eyes widened. "I told them you were too dangerous! It's better that I kill you now before you ruin everything."

In one quick motion, he grabbed hold of a nearby ticket box and ripped it from the concrete. Wick muttered a spell under his breath. The hairs on the back of Jonah's neck prickled just as light flashed in front of them and the two spells collided. Almost at the same time, the Wraith flung the ticket box toward them.

Wick jumped directly in front of Jonah. As he did so, the young mage turned his right side to the oncoming ticket box and held up the arm with the bracelet. A popping sensation washed over Jonah and a faint blue circle of distortion appeared around him and Wick. An instant later, the ticket box slammed into Wick's shield.

Even with the added protection, Wick fell backward into Jonah, sending them both to the ground. The box itself arched back through the air and hit the shocked Wraith squarely in the face. The huge guy stumbled backward and right over the edge of the parking garage, the ruined ticket box close behind.

An echoing thud reached them, followed by the lesser bang of the ticket box hitting the ground.

Wick got to his feet and helped Jonah up. "Sorry about that, Padawan. The shield stopped the ticket box, but it couldn't stop the kinetic energy." He glanced in the girl's direction, but Antwan's cousin was gone. "She attacked at the same time, but I don't think she expected me to deflect the hex."

Jonah's jaw dropped. "You've been practicing?"

"Yeah," Wick said, peeking over the concrete barrier that formed the edge of the parking garage.

Jonah joined him. Five stories below, the broken body of the man lay on large spools of industrial grade cabling that filled the narrow space between the parking garage and the next building. The tangled debris of the busted ticket box covered portions of the man's twisted arms and legs.

Jonah sucked in a breath. "He's dead."

"You didn't do it." Wick's voice shook, but that didn't make Jonah feel any better.

"If we hadn't followed her," Jonah began, "he wouldn't have tried to kill us, and…"

Movement below caught Jonah's attention. He pointed. "Look!"

The man's head twitched suddenly and he sat up. His left arm was bent at an unnatural angle under his body, so he took a moment to pop the arm back into the socket. Jonah and Wick winced when the crack of the realignment reached up to all five levels. If the mortal were still alive inside with the Wraith, that had to have hurt.

The Wraith glared up at them, got to his feet, and scrambled over the high fence. When he dropped onto the ground on the other side, he paused to gaze up at them before hobbling down the street and disappearing around the corner.

Wick let out a low breath. "I don't know if that's very cool, or very sick."

*

Jonah and Wick took turns retelling the parking garage adventure for Lynn, Robert, and Mike. Lynn congratulated Wick on saving Jonah's life. Mike remained quiet. Jonah suspected his buddy would say "I told you so" later.

But Robert got incensed with Wick for leaving him wondering where they were.

"Sorry, Bobby. You couldn't have gone with your busted hand."

Robert's face reddened in anger.

"He's right about that, Robert, but," Lynn speared Jonah and Wick with a steely glare, "they were both stupid to follow the girl."

Wick puffed up with anger. "She wrecked my show and hurt a lot of kids, Lynn. We can't let them get away with that."

"You're the older one," Lynn countered, waving Wick silent. "If you had waited, I would have told you that I discovered where to look for the amulet." She punctuated her words by plopping into a chair in the clubhouse section of the attic. The others hurried over to join her.

She had her hands steepled like she was deep in thought. "I've given Mike's comments about my great-auntie a lot of thought." She smiled at him. "The Sight ability appears in only one woman in each generation of my family. I did some checking into the family records. All the women with the gift were buried in a family crypt."

"Whoa!" Wick said. "That is so…"

"Wicked," Robert finished. The two boys glanced at each other, and Jonah could see the eagerness on their faces.

He sat forward. "You know where, don't you?"

Lynn nodded. "Yes, I do."

CHAPTER THIRTY
FAMILY CRYPT

Jonah had ominous thoughts about visiting his second graveyard in as many weeks. This one was ancient, far older than the Oak Hill cemetery. The gravestones here were a dingy, dark grey from all the dirt and pollution that had accumulated over the decades. In some cases, it had been over a century since the person's death.

He, Lynn, Mike, and Kevin appeared in what they hoped was a remote corner of the cemetery. Lynn had anticipated the trip and done plenty of research to find pictures of the place, but unfortunately, they couldn't match the pictures with a map.

Kevin adjusted the hang of his Reaper long coat as soon as they arrived. The older boy acted perturbed, but Jonah thought he looked cool in it. Mike agreed, and of course, having two geeks admire the coat only made Kevin want to change it even more.

Jonah finally told him, "Take it off."

"Can't." Kevin ruffled the coat. "Mandara thinks it best to have the extra protection until things settle down. Trueblood agreed." He scanned the surrounding tombstones.

Mike held out the map he downloaded off the cemetery's website. Lynn shook her head and closed her eyes. After a moment, she pointed up the sloping hillside. Near the top were mature trees and rows of above-ground family crypts.

"It's up there," she announced.

Lynn never faltered, leading them straight to an ancient crypt at the very apex of the hill. The angled roof was higher than the rest, and given its aged appearance, Jonah concluded it pre-dated all the others.

The oldest of the surrounding trees had huge branches that extended out and over the crypt, shrouding it perpetually in shadows. This morning, an eerie wind blew across the hilltop and Jonah huddled in his light jacket as Lynn walked right up to the building.

Impressive marble columns that framed the door and a wrought-iron security gate created a porch-like structure. Lynn pulled open the security gate and leaned in to examine the ornate metal door. Like the room in their great-auntie's old shop, this door also had a circular, genetic lock. Its status light blinked at them, waiting for the right person to touch it.

"I'm starting to think your mom must've owned stock in the company who makes these things," Mike quipped.

"You've got to admit, at least they work." Lynn positioned her finger over the lock. "Ruby and her Hulk friend weren't able to get through the door at the palm shop." She glanced at Kevin. "Think we should open this?"

"We're here. Plus, I have this." Kevin pulled a compass-like, golden disc from his pocket. About five inches in diameter, it had symbols evenly spaced around the outer edge of the surface and a large center button.

"What's that?" Jonah pointed at the device. "It looks like a flatter Seeker's compass."

Kevin exchanged a glance with Mike. "It's called a codex. Mike helped the Alliance create them."

Jonah gaped at his friend and knew this must be one of the top-secret things his friend couldn't mention.

Mike shrugged. "Sorry. I took an oath."

Lynn eyed the device. "So it's not a bomb?"

Kevin laughed. "No! It's an emergency transporter. It's like the compass except it only goes to one location, and anyone can use it. All you have to do is press the button and it takes you to a safe room."

"Really?" Jonah avoided pressing the center button and instead brushed his fingers around the outer edge. The device felt like it was made of the same metal as the Seeker's compass. He was instantly intrigued. "How did you make it?"

Mike opened his mouth, but Lynn interrupted. "Let's talk about that later. Okay?" She pressed her finger against the genetic lock and it lit up, followed by loud clicks from the vault door.

Kevin took that as his cue, put away the codex, and gripped the door's vertical handle. When he pulled the heavy door outward, a low moan escaped, sending a chill down Jonah's back. *It's just the wind*, he thought. Then the stale air, carrying the stench of death, emanated from the vault.

Lynn shivered and, with a quick backward glance at the others, she entered. Jonah screwed up his nerves and followed. The place felt larger inside than it looked from the outside. There were six crypts stacked lengthwise, three on either side of the structure. And in the very center stood a large, marble coffin. The name chiseled into the side facing the door was FOLAMI.

Jonah didn't recognize the name. He was expecting something like their great-aunt's given name, which he learned was Victoria.

Mike ran his fingers over the letters. "It's a West African name that means *Respect me*."

"I knew that because I looked her up," Lynn said to him, slightly shocked. "But how did you know?"

"The mind boost," Mike answered.

"He can translate any language, spoken or written," Jonah added. "It's pretty awesome."

Mike shrugged at the comment and strictly focused on the name. "She must have been the first in the line. My guess is she was a freed slave."

"Yeah." Lynn nodded. "I read she was freed from slavery after the Civil War. Even before then, she was known to possess a lot of power. The story goes her owner wanted a prediction to help him escape the Union soldiers. Flame told him a lie and he was subsequently caught and shot."

"Wow," Jonah said. He touched the tomb–which was cold against his fingertips–thinking everything must've started with her. Moving around his ancestors' tomb, he gazed thoughtfully at the line of ornamental plaques along the right wall. Each identified it descendants and their specialty.

All of these women were powerful mediums, psychics, and, in the one case, a Seer. Jonah found that interesting. The place exuded an intriguing sense of history. What boggled his mind even more was that he never even knew about this, and he adored history.

Since the bodies were arranged in chronological order according to their death dates, it was easy to find their great-aunt Victoria, the last one to run the Ankh of Life shop. But Jonah froze when he noted the next space below her crypt had a blank bronze plaque.

That slot was empty because his mom had been buried beside his dad back in D.C. In addition to his mom's empty slot, there was one more open niche. Jonah glanced at his cousin, Lynn, to see her expression. She met his gaze for a moment before focusing on Great-Aunt Victoria's crypt.

Mike pointed out the obvious. "It's sealed."

Kevin pulled a short crowbar out from the inner pocket of his long coat. He raised it and ordered the others to stand back before jamming it into the mortared edge of the covering stone. With a grunt, he shoved the tool clear through.

In quick order, he proceeded to knock away enough of the mortar to slip his hands into the opening. With a little effort, he ripped the cover stone away and revealed the black coffin within.

Lynn darted forward to help him pull it out far enough to rest one end on top of Folami's tomb. Kevin met her determined gaze and, on the count of three, they pried open the lid. Everyone gagged and covered their noses.

Their great-auntie was nothing more than a skeleton covered in a faded, long dress and purple cape that had a royal look to it. Her white hair was amazingly well preserved around her desiccated skull. That only added to the horror and oddity of the macabre sight.

Lynn, one hand covering her nose, pointed at a box in the woman's death grip. Kevin pried the skeletal fingers from around the box and handed it to Lynn. She, Mike, and Jonah retreated to the other side of the space while Kevin closed the lid and shoved the coffin back into the receptacle.

Jonah tapped the box, getting surprised by how thick it sounded. "Is it heavy?"

"Yes." Lynn hefted it.

Mike rubbed a finger over the engraved sigils covering the lid. "It's warded to keep supernaturals from detecting it." He pointed out the separate designs. "These are really powerful and complex."

"In that case, we'll keep it closed," Lynn said.

"And hand it over to the Alliance," Kevin added, joining them.

Lynn's objection was stopped before she could utter it because her face paled.

A minor tremor in his Death Sense alerted Jonah, but it was still too muted. Yet, if he felt that…

Something huge suddenly charged through the door and power-dived into Kevin, knocking him clear across the crypt and against the back wall with a solid bump. Jonah heard the codex and Kevin's blades clatter to the ground, but in the dimness, he couldn't spot them.

Kevin rebounded and grappled with the huge Wraith. He managed to gasp out to Jonah, "Get it out of here!"

Jonah realized that Kevin meant the codex. Mike was ahead of him and had already knelt to search the ground for it.

While Jonah hesitated, Lynn shoved the box into his hands and pulled out her own blades. Just as she moved to help, Niqab Girl stepped into the crypt and shot a hex at her. Lynn spun around just in time to deflect the first one. But her timing was slightly off and a second hex caught her in the side and sent her tumbling to the ground.

As the young sorceress turned on Jonah, he grabbed Mike and dived behind the center tomb. The hex hit with a loud bang! and shattered a corner. Heavy pieces of the tomb's lid crashed to the floor within inches of Mike's leg.

He managed to roll aside, letting out a painful grunt, and reached underneath himself, holding up Kevin's deactivated blades. Without warning, he shoved them into Jonah's back pocket.

"Mike, don't. Toss them to Kev–"

The side of the tomb took another direct hit, right above Jonah's head. Niqab Girl had shifted to the side to get a clean shot. Jonah and Mike hustled around in the opposite direction to keep the tomb between her and them. He realized their mistake too late. In focusing all of his attention on her, he failed to see the second Wraith–

possessed goon who had entered the mausoleum before he rushed their position.

Jonah's first concern was to protect Mike by placing himself in front of his buddy. That proved a second mistake since the Wraith only wanted him. The large man pinned Jonah in a painful bear hug and started pulling him toward the door. Jonah tried to toss the box to Mike or just release it. The problem was the Wraith's hold was crushing the box against Jonah's chest.

Niqab Girl weaved her hands toward the ceiling of the crypt and shouted, "Kufanya!" Sigils that prevented any phasing instantly appeared all over the ceiling and walls.

At that moment, Ruby entered the crypt. She laughed at Lynn, who had struggled to her feet, looking murderous. "Thank you for opening the crypt, my niece! I could never have gotten in otherwise." She shifted her gaze to Kevin and the huge Wraith, still grappling with each other. "Leave him be, my pet."

The Wraith growled and hurled Kevin into the back wall. The Fallen Reaper used his hands to lessen the impact. He spun around, ready to keep fighting, but Lynn stopped him. In the quick lull, Mike darted from behind the damaged tomb and joined them.

Kevin took one of Lynn's activated blades and pointed it at the Wraith holding Jonah. "Let him go."

Aunt Ruby sneered, "He's coming with me. I have special plans for my nephew."

Kevin's arm moved in a blur and the blade zipped through the air at the Wraith. Less than a foot away, the weapon smacked into a barrier and ricocheted into one of the crypts. Niqab Girl, however, had erected a ward to guard their retreat.

Kevin let out a growl of frustration.

Jonah's insides burned with shame as the Wraith yanked him through the door and outside. He struggled, but it was useless without any powers. Aunt Ruby came next and Antwan's cousin last, her hands poised to cast a hex at the others. Once they were clear of the crypt, the hulking Wraith slammed the door and blocked it with two heavy, metal beams.

Jonah was getting a bad feeling about what was happening as he listened to Kevin's repeated pounding on the door. It actually bucked with each of his anger-fueled blows.

Ignoring the pounding, Ruby held up the amulet box and smiled. "I should have known. The old bat hid the amulet in a warded box to keep me from detecting it." She nodded to the huge Wraith.

The man made a show of holding up a remote. Two more Wraith goons scrambled away from the crypt. One dropped down from the roof and hustled over to the others. Jonah noted small square blocks of what looked like clay attached to the roof. They were just below the overhang.

Oh, no. "Don't do it."

"Watch your friends and family die, young Blackstone."

The Wraith holding him gripped Jonah's chin to force him to look.

"It'll be a tragedy to kill my niece," Ruby continued, "but you need to experience this emotional pain. You need to see their broken bodies."

"Don't, please, Aunt Ruby!"

Ruby leered at him and signaled the big Wraith to press the remote's button. When the charges went off, the crypt's roof seemed to jump half a foot into the air before slamming down onto the rest of the crypt. The entire structure collapsed in on itself in a tremendous crash of stone and debris.

CHAPTER THIRTY-ONE
ALLIANCE GUARDIANS

Pieces of stone and marble slid loose and fell to the ground before the dust finally settled around the shattered mausoleum.

Jonah's voice was raw from shouting and tears streamed down his face. His friends and cousin had been cruelly crushed to death. How could his aunt be so evil that she would kill her own niece? He hated the woman now more than anything, even more than the Grim Reaper.

Ruby was ecstatic. "They all treated me like an outcast, even your mom did. Well, to hell with all those witches! I got the last laugh." And she did laugh. It sounded demented and totally devoid of any compassion.

"Shut up, witch!" Jonah screamed, even though it tortured his throat.

Ruby glared at him for a moment before taking a deep breath and her gloating expression returned. "You need to feel this pain, nephew." She motioned to the hulking Wraith. "Dig their bodies out. I want him to see."

The eagerness in the Wraith-possessed man sickened Jonah. His horror mounted as Ruby's obedient servant lumbered toward the heap of stone, plunging his huge fists into the rubble, and heaving off the first slab of marble. The brute flung it aside, careless of where it landed. In this case, it knocked off the top of a nearby obelisk headstone.

His obvious disregard for the dead and his willing depravity produced a deep desire inside Jonah to act. A silent growl worked its way up from his stomach and climbed into his chest. It was like a tidal wave of heat and energy. The Wraith holding him suddenly let out a scream of pain. And to Jonah's surprise, the goon's grip also slackened.

Somehow, despite the bands, a surge of power rippled through him. Calling on his training, Jonah bucked his entire body and broke loose from the Wraith. *Yes!* He sprinted for the closest tombstones, determined to put as much distance as possible between himself and these lunatics. Most of all, he intended to survive.

Jonah thought he'd make it but the Wraith recovered faster than he anticipated. The man lunged and, wham! He hit Jonah between the shoulder blades. The blow lifted him off his feet and sent him tumbling over a row of tombstones. Jonah tried to tuck and roll but he landed too hard and slammed into the base of a large statue.

No, I won't let them win!

Fear and the primal need to survive drove all thoughts of pain out of his mind. Even as the heavy footfalls of the Wraith approached, Jonah again scrambled to his feet and pelted down the row of graves.

There, to his right! A dark shape leapt at him, and Jonah dodged to the left and into the next row over. Just as fast, he changed his direction, perhaps gaining a precious few more seconds because the larger man wasn't quite as agile.

The entire time, Ruby screamed in the background at the top of her lungs for her henchmen to catch him.

"Ah!" Jonah grunted in pain when something hot exploded against a nearby headstone; some of the flying pieces nicked his face. A hex. Jonah dodged into the next row to avoid another missile from Niqab Girl.

"Ruby!" Antwan's cousin shouted, sounding frustrated. "You've used up all your power. We should leave."

"I want the boy!" Ruby roared.

"We need to get the amulet to safety."

Jonah zigzagged through the gravesides, using the downhill slope to gain more momentum. One of the Wraiths leapt in front of him, forcing Jonah to double back up the hill.

Antwan's cousin created a vortex so she and Ruby could leave. Jonah made the mistake of staring at it for too long. The hulking Wraith charged in from the left and landed a solid punch into his shoulder. Pain paralyzed Jonah's left side, like he'd dislocated it.

His body spun into a large, stone angel, the breath as well as the fight knocked out of him. The hulking Wraith grabbed his arm and twisted it, causing excruciating pain. But the man seemed overly interested in Jonah's sleeve. Too late, Jonah realized that the Wraith had already figured out why he couldn't phase away.

Sure enough, the Wraith yanked up Jonah's sleeve to expose the band around his wrist, letting out an evil laugh as his eyes narrowed in malicious glee.

"We were ordered to bring you back alive, but no one said in one piece."

He lifted Jonah off his feet and threw him hard. Jonah landed at the base of a broken obelisk. The scattered pieces of it pressed into his back harshly. Though dazed by the anguish and pain, at the same time, he heard clicking sounds in his back pocket and felt something hard there. *Kevin's blades!*

Jonah pulled out the deactivated weapons. Just holding the blades brought up horrid images of Kevin lying dead in the rubble. Another surge of fury rushed through Jonah and the cylinders began to hum in his hands.

The large Wraith took his time stalking Jonah. "You're gonna pay for sending my fellow Wraiths back to the Underworld, you filthy abomination!"

Confident that he finally had a plan and a way out, Jonah activated the blades but kept them hidden behind his back as he leaned against the broken headstone. When the Wraith loomed over him, sneering, Jonah readied himself. He would have one chance only to surprise it.

"Let's see how you like enduring multiple broken bones," the Wraith taunted.

He reached down to snatch Jonah, and that's when Jonah acted by swiping the blades across the Wraith's chest. He was shocked at how easily the blades cut through the coat and shirt, like a hot knife through butter. Without any resistance, the blades sliced into the mortal's flesh beneath, scoring a deep wound in the man's chest.

As always happened, the cut sparked and bled. The Wraith inside the mortal screamed out in agony and pain.

Jonah experienced a savage rush of satisfaction as the huge mortal stumbled away from him, seeking a safer distance.

The second Wraith paused in fear while staring between his wounded buddy and the sizzling, bloody Reaper's blades still in Jonah's hands.

Grateful for the man's fearful hesitation, Jonah regained his balance and jumped onto his feet. He was pissed and ready to make both Wraiths pay for what they had done. At that moment, he didn't care if the mortals lived or not. They were equally to blame for allowing the evil spirits to possess them.

Before Jonah could exact his vengeance, a Reaper blade whistled through the air and embedded itself into the second Wraith's shoulder.

Jonah blinked in surprise and whirled around to see Kevin! The boy's hair and his Reaper coat were covered with dust, but he was still alive!

Kevin's eyes radiated pure fury that matched Jonah's as he grabbed the injured, hulking Wraith and landed several consecutive punches. Kevin ended his barrage and hurled the man into the waiting SUV. The impact was so hard, all the windows shattered and the vehicle almost tipped over on its side. When Kevin moved in to finish off the man, the mortal opened his mouth in a silent scream.

The Wraith inside exited the mortal's body as a dark, gaseous stream of evil. Seeing this, the second mortal threw back his head and opened his mouth. The second Wraith exited its host body too. Suddenly drained of the Wraiths' power, the mortals sank to their knees.

With a high leap into the air, Kevin sliced at the escaping Wraiths but missed. The evil spirits fled off over the gravestones, heading down the hill and clean over the cemetery wall. Jonah had no clue where the Wraiths would find other host bodies. But he had the horrible certainty there were fools ready and willing to harbor them for the sick honor of it.

Kevin stalked over and gathered Jonah into a tight hug. All the tragic despair, hatred, and willingness to get revenge suddenly left Jonah's body. The embrace felt almost like the nullifying bands, except in this case, it nullified all his pain.

"Lynn and Mike are okay too," Kevin whispered, holding him tight.

A vortex opened and Kevin released him. Jonah tensed, expecting his aunt to return. He was ready, but he should have paid more attention to Kevin's relaxed pose. Instead of trouble, two Alliance Guards rushed out to subdue the mortal hosts.

Only then did Jonah let out a breath as he also registered what a mass of pain his body was in again. He shook as the adrenaline of the fight began to evaporate.

Kevin slipped off his Reaper's coat and wrapped it around Jonah. "You okay?"

"I'm fine." He huddled in the surprisingly warm coat. "I'm sorry I didn't stop Ruby. She has the amulet and now she can work the spell."

Kevin tweaked Jonah's nose. "It's not your fault, crumb snatcher."

Jonah couldn't believe it. Kevin hadn't called him that in almost two years. The last time was the night his family's house in Virginia burned down, the night before he was sent here to Mount Vernon. The old nickname filled Jonah's body with warmth the same way it had the night Kevin made the first promise to him.

Now that Jonah understood what promises meant between two supernaturals, he grinned.

"Feel any better?" Kevin asked.

"Yeah." He did too, with Kevin standing beside him. The boys watched as more Alliance people arrived and inspected the now destroyed mausoleum. After a while, Jonah asked. "Where are Mike and Lynn?"

"They're both alive and well," Trueblood answered, walking over to them. He took in the situation a moment, frowning. "I think you should escort Jonah to the safe room." He handed Kevin a new codex.

*

The safe room wasn't exactly what Jonah imagined. It was a room, sure, but it was huge and circular, at least a hundred feet in diameter.

The first thing Jonah noticed when he arrived was the rather large sigil covering the center portion of the floor. Then he studied the glowing designation stone he saw on one side. That was as far as his amazement took him because Lynn and Mike tackled him a moment later.

"We thought they took you away with them!" Mike shouted as he pounded Jonah on the back.

Lynn gave him a genuine hug. "I'm glad you're okay, geek boy."

Jonah's throat tightened when she released him.

"Now that you're here," Kevin said, "I need to get back. Don't break anything while I'm gone." With that, he phased.

Jonah didn't want Kevin to leave him. Aware that the others were watching him, and waiting, he glumly hid is disappointment. "How did you guys get away?"

Lynn's face broke into an impressed grin as she gripped Mike's shoulder. "Show him."

Mike pulled out his Seeker's compass. "I used this to get us here."

"How? And why didn't you use Kevin's codex?" Jonah asked.

"A huge slab of that big tomb landed on it," Mike answered. "Smashed the center button." He glanced at Lynn. "And then she went crazy, saying we had to get out of there while Kevin was banging on the door."

"I didn't go crazy, Mike." Lynn nudged the side of his head. Then she shrugged and added, "I guess it took a while for my ability to truly come back, or maybe it was due to the situation. Like a flood, I suddenly got all kinds of impressions of danger." She shook Mike by the shoulder. "But your buddy used his quick thinking and managed to activate his compass."

She frowned and glanced around them. "You'd think this place would prevent anyone from getting inside without a codex device."

Amulet of the Goddess   327

Mike held up the Seeker's compass, smiling. "I made the codex, and my compass has the coordinates inside."

It seemed odd to Jonah that his parents had given him the compass as a belated birthday gift, yet the device belonged to his friend now.

"How did you get away?" Mike asked, getting Jonah's attention. "Did Kevin save you?"

"I had his blades. Remember? You put them in my pocket? I attacked the Wraiths just before Kevin showed up. He was so awesome."

"Wow," Mike said.

Jonah turned on the spot, taking in the rest of the place. High overhead was a vent and a whirling fan. The faint air current it provided felt refreshing and cool. Around the edges of the space were a desk and chair, two comfortable-looking cots, a set of lockers, and stacked boxes marked as food.

Mike stood beside Jonah and explained all the features of the safe room. "And it even has a satellite hookup for internet and computer access to the outside world." He nodded to a large, wall-mounted screen. "You could stay here for a long time and be comfortable."

"Really?"

"Yes. There's a bathroom through that door and on the other side is a small place to heat up your food."

"It's cool," Jonah said, audibly impressed. "But it also reminds me of a jail, you know? Someplace to keep a person fully confined." Jonah caught the uneasy look on Mike's face and wondered at it. "Is this for Council Members?"

Mike crossed his arms, hugging himself. "Yeah, it can be. Or for anyone else who needs a safe place to crash."

"You mean, me?" Jonah waited. Mike finally nodded. "So, they built this just for me?" That worried him even more than the recent fight. "The Alliance expects something will happen to me?"

"I don't know, Jonah," Mike confessed. "They didn't tell me everything."

Jonah believed Mike, but he suddenly knew why the room felt so much like a cell. "There's no door to the outside," he observed. "How do I get out if I want to?"

"You wait until someone comes and gets you." Mike glanced at Lynn like he needed help. "Kevin has a talisman. I've seen one before. It's made of bronze-colored beads."

Jonah nodded, taking in that small detail. "And that's the only way out?"

"Yes. You hold onto someone else with the talisman."

"Can you use the compass to get us out of here?" Jonah touched the Seeker's compass with a finger. He hadn't held the thing in a while.

Mike hesitated, as if trying to figure out the meaning behind his questions. "Only if I have a talisman or I'm holding onto someone who does, yes, I can."

Jonah gave his friend a knowing smile. "Do you have a talisman?"

"No, I don't." Mike held up his hands when Jonah's eyes narrowed. "Honest. I wouldn't lie to you, Jonah."

"I suppose the Alliance made you take an oath not to tell me."

Mike's voice grew a bit testy. "Well, they didn't. And if they had, I'd just tell you that I can't talk about it, okay?"

Lynn finally spoke up. "What's your problem, hero?"

Jonah gestured around the place. "They built this specifically to lock me in."

"They designed it for your protection," Lynn said, narrowing her eyes at him.

Mike nodded in agreement.

Jonah disagreed. All this time, he assumed everyone was worried for him, but Alastor had a point. Marcus and Kevin were afraid of him. When he took Agent Hunter's power in anger, they stood frozen in place, unable to hide their own fear.

And the Grand Oracle called him an *abomination*. Had he also misread Trueblood's fear? Being here in this safe room made that seem more of a possibility.

To Lynn and Mike, he said, "Sometimes I wonder if everyone's afraid of me and what I'll do."

Lynn huffed and crossed her arms. "Stop feeling so sorry for yourself."

"I'm not," Jonah protested, but he secretly suspected he was doing that.

Mike at least seemed to understand his reference to their adventure in the Afterworld. He slid an arm around Jonah's shoulders. "I told you before. I'm not afraid of you."

"Neither am I, so get over it," Lynn said. She glanced up at a blinking light, high on the curved wall.

Mike jumped and pulled Jonah away from the center of the room. "Someone's coming," he explained.

A moment later, Kevin appeared. Jonah, Lynn, and Mike crowded around the young Fallen Reaper for an update.

"The two mortal hosts are being questioned at HQ," Kevin began.

"Aren't we at HQ?" Jonah asked.

"Ha ha. Nice try." Kevin smirked at him. "The Alliance is covering up the true cause of the explosion and dealing with any eyewitnesses."

Jonah acknowledged that last piece of news with a nod, but he wanted to remain on track. "You're not gonna tell me where we are?"

"Nope. Security precaution." Kevin held up a hand to stop Jonah's next question. "And before you argue with me, I don't even know where we are."

Lynn pulled on Jonah's sleeve. "Give it a rest. Can we at least go home now?"

Kevin let out a long breath. "Nope, you can't."

Mike, Jonah, and Lynn chorused, "Why not?" at the same time.

Kevin backed away from their combined outrage. "Whoa, don't bite my head off! Marcus wants to see all of you in his office."

Jonah exchanged a glance with Lynn and Mike, knowing they were all thinking the same thing. *They were in trouble— again.*

CHAPTER THIRTY-TWO

Even before Kevin finished the phase, Jonah knew they weren't headed to Marcus's office. He could almost sense the extra protections they passed through, which Marcus's office didn't have. Sure enough, when the mortal world appeared around them, they stood on the rooftop of the Alliance HQ.

Mike let out a startled "Wow!" as he gazed out at the northern Atlanta suburbs, which were all visible from their vantage point.

Lynn remained quiet as she too scanned their surroundings. "Where are we?"

"Alliance HQ," Jonah answered. He motioned for his cousin to follow.

Lynn's eyes widened with heightened awareness before she gripped Mike's elbow and pulled him along.

Kevin had already moved toward the portico where Marcus stood, at the top of a short flight of marble steps. Jonah's godfather wore his Reaper's long coat and looked rather intimidating this evening.

Marcus wasn't alone. Omar and Symon Trueblood stepped into view. All three men wore similarly serious expressions.

Omar at least managed a warm smile once Jonah and the others reached the top of the stairs and entered the portico. "Good to see you again, Jonah. My God, you've sprouted over the past few months."

Jonah shrugged, feeling a little embarrassed at the unexpected attention. "I guess so."

Omar grinned. "You'll be as tall as Isaiah soon."

A pit formed in Jonah's stomach at the mention of his dad. Omar didn't seem to notice because he moved on to greet Lynn and Mike.

But Marcus watched Jonah's expression. He wondered if his godfather regretted putting him in the bands, given what had just happened.

Marcus adopted a shrewd look. "You can relax, Jonah. I'm not angry about the cemetery. You had no way of predicting Ruby would show up. And Kevin informed Symon of your plan beforehand."

Jonah caught the way Trueblood avoided looking directly at Marcus. He could see the slight tension between the men. "Then what were you arguing about?"

Trueblood cracked a smile.

Marcus frowned. "We were talking about Alastor."

"What about him?" Jonah felt his anger toward the devious man surfacing, but he didn't care. "He left Mount Vernon. I had to help Mike keep his uncle's store open."

"Yeah," Mike agreed. "Is he here?"

"I'm sure he is," Marcus said. "But being here is a preferred change from Mount Vernon."

"That may be," Omar said. "But hasn't Alastor tipped his hand? Goading Jonah gives us more evidence against him. Perhaps Cedric will listen to reason now."

Kevin let out a loud, derisive snort.

"Who's Cedric?" Jonah asked, watching his godfather for the answer.

Marcus sighed. "Cedric Mandara. He's the leader of the Hardline Council members. That's a moot point for now."

He's not telling the whole truth, Jonah thought. There was something about Cedric, something that caused Marcus to dread any discussions about the man. It had to be more than the Council member just being a Hardliner, or sending Alastor to Mount Vernon.

"I called you here because it's time that you knew about your mom," Marcus announced.

"My mom?" Jonah's jaw dropped in astonishment. Lynn and Mike moved to stand on either side of him. He welcomed their support. "What about my mom?"

Marcus motioned for them to sit down on the large center cushion. Kevin hovered nearby.

Jonah waited for his godfather to continue, but it was Trueblood who began to pace with his hands clasped behind his back.

"It's nothing ominous, Jonah," the mage began. "It simply pertains to what's happening now." When Omar nodded encouragingly, Trueblood took a deep breath and continued.

"I've already told you how Omar, your mom, and I met. We joined the Alliance at the same time. What I failed to mention were the little adventures we enjoyed during the summers and our off-time. The room you found in the old palm reading shop is where we used to hang out."

"Really?" Jonah sat up straighter. Trueblood had confirmed his suspicions about the mage's earlier reaction at the Ankh of Life shop. "You recognized her journals?"

"I did. Me and Omar were there when your mom wrote most of them. You see, we had a project that we called The Phantom's Path. Those seven locations on the mural were part of it." Trueblood stopped his pacing and leaned against a column. "Your mom wanted to learn all she could about her power as well as the supernatural world. And me? Well, I became arrogant in my abilities. It didn't matter the subject nor how dangerous, I was supremely confident I could master it."

"And I was ready and willing to go along," Omar said. "They took me into their group like I was an old friend."

"What did you do?" Lynn asked the adults in general.

Jonah wondered if she used her intuition or her normal skill to sniff out a confession. She had done it to him enough times.

Trueblood clasped his hands together, twisting them in a nervous way that Jonah had never seen before. "It was really your great-aunt's prodding that piqued our interest in the Underworld. But once me and Janice were hooked, we went full tilt. As the youngest from a long line of shamans, spirit quests were second nature to me. You see, you have to get the right drugs and mix them in the right proportions–"

"Symon, that's too much information," Marcus said.

Trueblood ruffled his dreads, looking as if he were trying to regain his train of thought. "Oh, yeah. I guess that's not important. Anyway, all we wanted was to journey into the Underworld on a modified spirit quest."

The knot in Jonah's stomach began to grow. He gritted his teeth, preparing himself for what the mage might reveal.

"I met a Seer. Although the human host was,... older, the Seer herself had died at a young age. I...*flattered* her until she helped us."

Kevin covered the smirk that twisted his mouth.

Lynn frowned at the mage. "Seriously? You sound worse than my brother."

"Like I said, I was young and full of myself, okay?" A little of Trueblood's humorous nature returned as he smiled. But the mage quickly sobered and continued. "So, after, ah, convincing the Seer to help us, we began to go on a spirit quest into the Underworld. We only had two rules: Don't take anything and don't hurt anything. That was fine. Janice recorded our journeys, and Omar used his artistic skills to make the triptych and the mural."

Everyone turned to stare at Omar, who ran a hand over his bald head and down the back of his neck. It struck Jonah that he was stalling before he chose his next words.

"The trips were unlike anything I'd ever experienced," Omar began. "The Seer told us a lot of things and eventually showed us the areas of the Underworld called the Phantom's Path. Each location had a connected nexus point on the mortal side."

"And they also have designation codes," Jonah added. "Mike and I noticed that." He hesitated, reconsidering mentioning his desire to travel to the Underworld. With everything the adults were saying, Jonah was sure his godfather would nix the idea anyway.

"Yes, they do," Omar said, watching Jonah's expression. "Seven nexus points connected by an eighth location."

"But there were only seven locations on the map," Mike pointed out. "Where's the eighth?"

"We never found out," Trueblood answered. "When your Great-Aunt Victoria discovered what we were doing, she pressured Janice into taking something from the Underworld. Like I said, she was the one who turned us on to the plan anyway."

"What did you steal?"

"Pakhet's amulet," Trueblood admitted, looking a bit embarrassed. "And we may have hurt some of the guardian creatures around it called *Felines*."

"The Seer banned us from the Underworld," Omar added. "We gave Janice our pieces of the triptych and never returned. We thought she gave up researching the Phantom's Path. But it seems she continued gathering information on her own for a while. I guess she thought the goddess was the key to the eighth location."

"So," Jonah began, "what about our Aunt Ruby?"

Trueblood raised an eyebrow. "You've seen what a Seer can do, right?"

"Yeah, they read the future and make prophecies," Jonah said.

"Or warnings," Mike added.

"That's correct." Trueblood looked like he wanted to be somewhere else now, but he continued. "The Seer was more than a little angry with us and pronounced a curse on us. She said we had to forfeit our firstborn."

Lynn seemed the most spooked by that statement. She stared at Trueblood in concern. "Did that really happen to you?"

Trueblood blinked in surprise. "Who me? No, I'm a confirmed bachelor. And Omar," he glanced at Marcus, "well, he wasn't exactly worried about any actual firstborn." Trueblood's expression turned thoughtful. "Unless you were to use a surrogate–"

"Symon," Marcus cautioned him, looking uncomfortable with the subject.

"Fine. Anyway, Janice married your dad and everyone said it would be impossible for them to have kids. So we counted ourselves lucky and never discussed the curse."

"Then your mom got pregnant with you a few years later," Omar said. "We talked to her, but in the end, we convinced ourselves nothing would happen. For seven years, nothing did happen until the Wraiths contacted your Aunt Ruby."

"Your mom explained the Sight to us," Trueblood took up the story, "when she revealed she had it." Trueblood pointed to Lynn. "And now, you have it."

Lynn nodded. "And my Aunt Ruby never had any real ability. That made her furious."

"Yes, it did." Trueblood stroked his jaw, watching Lynn. "I met old Victoria. She wasn't a tolerant woman when it came to people without abilities. She fawned over Janice while all but ignoring Ruby."

"When old Victoria died," Omar added, "Janice locked everything away. She wasn't interested in running the old shop and didn't want anyone else getting into it."

"Except me," Lynn raised her hand. "Jonah's mom coded the room specifically for me."

All the news left Jonah dumbfounded. He knew bits and pieces, but he never imagined that his demented aunt may have been a victim herself and that his mom and her friends had done something so reckless and cruel. He wanted to run away to have time to deal with it all.

Perhaps Omar sensed his thoughts or maybe he noticed the look in his face. He came over and stood close. "Don't feel sorry for Ruby. She made her own decisions. No one forced her down a dark path."

Jonah met Omar's serious gaze. He gulped, unsure if he wanted to know the thing he'd asked about before. "What happened to me, seven years ago?"

Omar's brow furrowed and he paused for a long time, his breathing audibly slow and even.

"Can you tell me?" Jonah pressed. "If my aunt is gonna hurt people, I want to know why."

Omar shook his bald head. "I agree with Marcus. Now is not the time to unblock those memories. But I can tell you what happened that night."

"I don't understand."

Mike nodded in agreement.

Lynn said, "I don't either. If you can tell him, why not unblock the memories so he can remember them, himself?"

Omar pressed his fingertips together, tapping them against his bottom lip while thinking. "Having the actual memories versus being told what happened can be a world of difference." He raised an eyebrow, prompting Jonah.

But Jonah still didn't get it.

"Consider this," Omar tried again. "When the Wraiths contacted your Aunt Ruby seven years ago, she was more than willing to put you through a traumatic experience in exchange for power. She subjected you to a forced Wraith possession, Jonah. Your mother found out and arrived just in time to stop it." Omar sucked in a shaky breath. "She called me to block your memories. Do you understand now?"

"No. I mean..." Jonah frowned. "Not really."

Marcus stirred. "In the Afterworld, when you took Trevor's power, you told us you gained some of his memories. That's because you touched his soul and transferred the memories into your own mind."

"When a Wraith possesses a mortal, it also touches the mortal's soul," Omar said, drawing Jonah's attention. "That person's memories and knowledge are open to the Wraith. But the reverse also occurs. The mortal has access to everything the Wraith has done."

Jonah's jaw dropped as he began to see the true significance of what Omar was trying to tell him. "You mean I saw the Wraith's memories?"

Omar gave Jonah's shoulder a reassuring squeeze. "I'm afraid you did. Can you imagine a seven-year-old boy seeing all that horror? Your mother wanted me to protect you from the ordeal of that vile Wraith's memories as much as from the pain of the possession."

"Your Aunt Ruby's up to her old game again, Jonah." Marcus stepped closer, towering over him. "We suspect she intends to subject you to a powerful Wraith again. It would explain why she tried to take you."

Kevin cursed under his breath. "That's why she needs him to be emotional."

"The attacks on your family and friends were meant to worry you as well as pull away their support." Trueblood explained. "Alastor goaded you into a fury over the bullies, and there's also his conversation with you before leaving."

Jonah glanced at Kevin, recalling how enraged the boy had been about his confrontation with Alastor.

"Trueblood's correct," Omar agreed. "And the most obvious way to turn you into an emotional and mental wreck would be to open your block and allow all those horrible memories and images to flood your mind." He gestured at Jonah's head. "Someday, when you're older and stronger, maybe you *should* unlock those experiences. But right now, I'm afraid we'd just be playing into their hands."

Jonah sensed the utter sincerity in Omar's words. But the man's comments reignited his concern about the safe room. A ringing began in his ears. He paid distant attention to the conversation, tuning into his own, troubling thoughts.

"Isn't this convenient?" Lynn asked. "Ruby gets out just in time for the Witching Hour?"

"It's no coincidence, Lynn," Marcus answered. "It's part of a plan. We think Ruby went crazy because of a Wraith possessing her. As the time drew closer, her condition began to improve at an accelerated rate."

"It kept her crazy for seven years?"

"Time isn't the same for humans as it is for supernaturals," Trueblood added.

Marcus nodded in agreement. "The Grim Reaper and Grand Oracle have been working on their plan for over two thousand years. Only now are we glimpsing their end game."

Mention of the Rulers of the Afterworld only added to Jonah's feeling of betrayal. Unexpressed anger welled up inside him.

"Jonah?" Mike's voice seemed to reach him from inside his head as well as through his voice. "What's wrong?"

He's my Seeker. He can always find me. Jonah responded to the call and came back to the present awareness. Everyone stared at him, causing the ringing in his ears to return. "You don't trust me. You're all afraid of me."

"Jonah..." Marcus began.

"That's why you have the safe room." Jonah let all the bitterness and self-doubt he harbored inside spill out. "If my memory block fails, you can lock me away."

Lynn slid an arm around his shoulders to comfort him, but he was on a roll. "And now you say my mom did something she wasn't supposed to do and ultimately got a curse placed on me? And my aunt was bullied, which eventually sent her over the edge? What am I supposed to do when I face her? Tell me that!"

"Jonah..." Lynn tightened her grip, rocking him.

Trueblood came over. "That's Alastor talking. Forget whatever he's told you." He pressed his palm to Jonah's chest. "Remember what I said? Whatever your mom and dad were, so are you."

"Did she know? Did she laugh at my aunt?"

"No, Jonah." Trueblood's shoulders slumped. "Your mom loved her sister. That night, she..." He hesitated. "She tried to protect your aunt. Do you believe me?"

"Yeah, I guess so."

"Your parents were honorable, strong people, and you're even stronger. As far as Omar and I being afraid of you, we're not! You know why? Because inside, we know you're a good person."

Mike leaned against Jonah and whispered, "Told you."

Marcus met Jonah's gaze. "You shocked us, Jonah. That's all."

Kevin nodded. "And I'm not afraid of you either, little man."

Jonah's face warmed with embarrassment. Alastor, the mole, and his aunt were the ones manipulating his feelings and emotions, just as Omar said.

"If you ever face Ruby, I know you'll do the right thing," Trueblood continued. "Everyone has a past. Some people with ideal experiences and backgrounds turn out to be monsters. Others with wretched pasts become kind angels. It's not the experiences we endure, but how we allow them to shape us that determine who we are."

Jonah met his godfather's gaze. *I decided to be a vigilante.* In that moment, he understood why his godfather worried about him so much.

"It's okay, Jonah." Trueblood's voice was reassuring and understanding. "Everything that's happened was all about you. That's a lot to deal with."

Marcus came over. "It's been a long day for all of you. Time to go home."

CHAPTER THIRTY-THREE
BANDS OFF

Jonah awoke refreshed. The bruises from Brandon's ambush were gone and the nicks from the battle in the cemetery were even fainter. Once again, his beleaguered healing factor had snapped into action. Better yet, his sleep hadn't been disturbed by nightmares or dream-walks. The net effect was that he felt prepared to go to school and fully ready to face whatever Monday would throw at him.

Due to the reworked club assignments, Mike and Jonah were patrol partners again. Jonah's pride in his group increased because they handled every situation that day without incident. The only thing to impact his good mood was Brandon's superior swagger around the hallways.

The boy was smart and didn't openly gloat about their run-in. But that didn't stop the bully and his friends from snickering at Jonah every chance they got.

Brandon, being Brandon, couldn't resist taking things further. During lunch, he passed by Jonah in the cafeteria and deliberately bumped into him. He grinned and in a voice full of false concern said, "I'm sorry. Didn't mean to hurt you!" Then he laughed and walked off with his friends.

Jonah glared at him with the tray shaking in his furious hands.

"Don't fall for it," Mike warned.

Jonah sucked in a deep breath to calm himself. Keeping his head down and letting his body heal was proving more difficult than he expected. He could sympathize with Lynn and the frustration she experienced over losing her Sight.

He had taken his power for granted. It was a vital part of himself, like his hands, arms, and legs. To go without it was not only humbling, but also infuriating.

He doubted he'd ever complain about not being normal again.

*

In addition to staying away from trouble while he healed, Jonah's desire to know what happened to him seven years ago was no longer so urgent. In a rare moment, Jonah actually agreed with his godfather. He didn't want to remove the block if it meant he had to relive the Wraith's memories.

The new information about his mom, Trueblood, and Omar just added to all the other concerns swirling in his head. By Tuesday afternoon, Jonah opted to finish his homework at home, alone. He still valued those moments away from others and guessed he always would.

But he wasn't trying to be anti-social. He intended to finish his homework early so he could go by Hackett's and hang out with Mike. Notebook and textbooks scattered across the kitchen table, Jonah bowed to his mountain of homework. He made good progress until Kevin arrived.

"Am I interrupting?" Kevin asked as he entered through the kitchen door and pulled out a chair.

"No." Jonah rubbed his tired eyes and pushed aside the book he was reading. He experienced a pang of doubt, wondering if Kevin had bad news or not.

"Don't worry about Ruby," Kevin assured him. "The Alliance is searching for her."

"I'm not worried about her." Jonah opened and closed the cover of his textbook. "I just hate waiting for something else to happen. If we can't find my aunt, we need to find the eighth nexus point."

Kevin slid his hand inside the book to stop Jonah's repetitive movement. "I asked Trueblood about it. He doesn't think the site is a nexus point."

Jonah nodded. "Mike said the same thing." Reminded of his plans to meet his buddy, Jonah glanced at his watch. "I need to finish my work."

Kevin laid his hand on top of the textbook, palm upward.

Jonah brushed his own fingers across Kevin's and intertwined their fingers. "I really have to study."

"I know." Kevin's eyes remained fixed on their clasped hands. "I guess you want to be ready for tonight?"

Jonah gazed at him, confused and a little excited. Did Kevin have something planned for them? This was the first time, since their impromptu date a couple nights ago, that they had been alone together.

"I was gonna go and see Mike at his uncle's bookstore," Jonah said. "Why?"

Kevin paused and his brow furrowed as if he didn't believe Jonah. He pushed up the sleeve of Jonah's shirt to expose the band. "This comes off tonight. Did you forget?"

"What? No," Jonah lied, because he *had* forgotten about the deactivation of the bands. It wasn't his fault. So much had happened to him, it was hard to keep all the events straight.

"Wow!" Kevin fingered the band. "I thought you'd have that marked on your calendar. You geeks like your schedules and appointments so much."

"Funny." A smile spread across Jonah's face. "Are you gonna be here?"

"Yep. I have to return the bands to HQ."

"I mean…" Jonah trailed off as he hesitated to ask what he really meant. "We can… do something."

Kevin smirked. "Like what?"

"Maybe phase around."

"To where?"

"*Around*," Jonah repeated. "Maybe we'll end up at the hideaway." His face warmed.

Kevin frowned. "There's nothing there. Plus, it'll be pitch black. What are we–" His eyes widened for a comical moment.

It heartened Jonah to see him really considering the idea.

But Kevin shook his head. "It's too dangerous with Ruby on the loose."

"The mole doesn't know about the hideaway," Jonah pleaded.

"Can't you cover for Mike tonight?" Kevin suggested.

"Oh, yeah." The idea hadn't occurred to Jonah. On the plus side, he wouldn't have to hide anything from Mike. "Yeah. I'll ask him."

"Cool." Kevin reached over to ruffle Jonah's hair. "We can do dinner again."

Jonah heard the eagerness in Kevin's voice. They were thinking the same thing. *Make out.*

As if he couldn't wait, Kevin leaned clean across the table, his face nose-to-nose with Jonah, and kissed him. When he pulled back, Jonah let out a frustrated huff.

Kevin stood up and slid the chair back in place. "Call me and tell me what you decide later. All right?"

Jonah nodded, afraid he couldn't speak. After Kevin left, he slumped back in the kitchen chair and stared at the door. It took an act of supreme will to refocus his mind on the homework. Even then, Jonah couldn't remember anything he read or wrote.

*

Jonah flopped on his bed after dinner. He called Mike, enduring his jokes and innuendoes, but set up everything for the evening. As the time drew close for the bands to deactivate, Jonah began to worry about Kevin. The Fallen Reaper was a no-show so far.

"Kevin will be here," Lynn said as she, Wick, and Robert crowded into Jonah's room. "He has to take them back, right?"

"Yeah." Jonah squirmed under the combined attention. They watched him as though they expected him to drop dead, sprout wings, or grow a second head.

"Be still," Lynn ordered.

"You want to trade places?"

"I didn't act like a vigilante. You did." Lynn leaned against the closed door.

Wick sat at Jonah's small desk while Robert crossed over to the window, splitting his attention between what was outside and Jonah. As the bedside clock changed to read *five fifty-nine*, everyone stared at Jonah in hushed silence.

Lynn walked over and pushed his head. "Come on."

"Fine." He sat up and stretched his arms out on the bed in front of himself, palms up so they could see the magical bands. Six o'clock came and still, nothing happened.

Lynn sighed. "He said six?"

"Yeah. That's when they first got activated."

"Maybe," Wick started, "his clock was slightly off–"

Jonah sucked in a startled breath just as the bands flared before popping loose from his wrists and becoming three sizes too big in an instant. The feelings that suddenly surged back into him were staggering. He took long, deep breaths, welcoming the part of himself that was sorely missed. All at once, he was whole again.

Wick grabbed a band as soon as Jonah slid them off his wrists and held it up to inspect it.

Lynn took the other. "We should lock these up in Robert's box, just in case."

"Lynn, please." Wick reached for the second band. "I won't do anything bad with them."

Jonah tuned out the argument for the time being. With his powers regained, he could phase around whenever he chose to. And his Death Sense would also be working again.

"Take my side, Bobby." Wick waved his friend forward. Lynn crossed her arms, ready to argue both boys down, when a knock came at the front door.

Lynn slipped out of Jonah's room while calling out to Aunt Imma, "I'll get it!"

Jonah recognized Kevin's low voice as he greeted Aunt Imma. Moments later, he followed Lynn into the already crowded bedroom.

As soon as Jonah saw Kevin wearing the Reaper's coat, he knew their plans were a bust. "What happened?"

"Work. Sorry." Kevin withdrew the slender box from his coat pocket and opened it.

Wick's face fell. He held up the bands, a pleading look in his eyes as he turned to Kevin. "Can I hold onto one?"

"Sorry. Albrecht's orders."

Wick took his time placing the bands in the box. He ran a finger along the edge of one, like it was a long-lost possession.

Kevin snapped the box closed and met Jonah's disappointed gaze. "It's not my fault."

"Whatever," Jonah mumbled, not bothering to conceal the dissatisfaction in his voice.

Lynn watched them. "What's not your fault?"

Kevin slid the box in his coat pocket before answering. "Jonah wanted to celebrate by phasing around Mount Vernon tonight. But he can't do that now. It would be too dangerous."

Lynn narrowed her eyes, "Weren't you gonna help Mike at the store for a couple of hours?"

"Yeah. Me and Kevin were gonna phase around afterward, you know, before I came home." Jonah pouted for Kevin's benefit. He wanted the boy to feel as bad as possible for messing up their plans.

"Well," Kevin added, avoiding Jonah's direct gaze, "since I can't stay tonight, an Alliance Guard will watch you."

That news excited Wick and Robert, who exited the room. Jonah listened to their footsteps retreating toward the front door. Lynn gave Jonah and Kevin one last suspicious look and then left the room.

Kevin threw up his arms. "I'm sorry. Mandara says he needs me for something important." Kevin made air quotes on the last word.

"He's purposely keeping us apart!" Jonah plopped back on his stacked pillows when another thought occurred to him. He sat up again. "You think he knows?"

"What? That you're a horny, little teenager?" Kevin grinned.

Jonah hurled a pillow at him. "About us."

"There is no *us*, yet. I guess." Kevin sat on the edge of the bed. Jonah leaned against his back, resting his chin on Kevin's shoulder. His skin tingled where it touched the enchanted coat.

"This sucks."

"Yeah," Kevin agreed. "But I have to get back. He's probably watching the clock." Kevin stood up.

"I hate him," Jonah said. Kevin frowned at the comment and Jonah noticed. "What is it about Mandara that gets everyone so worried whenever I mention him?"

"Nothing."

"But–"

Kevin kissed him, cutting off the mild protest.

"Wow," Kevin said when they stopped kissing. "I'll remember that whenever I need to shut you up." He slipped out the door, narrowly avoiding Jonah's second thrown pillow.

CHAPTER THIRTY-FOUR
MIDNIGHT READING

Mike stayed on and kept Jonah company at the store. He and Patrick weren't doing so well after all. Or so Jonah hoped. Mike said he was done messing around with someone who was not good for him. Jonah considered asking why but dropped the sensitive subject.

The boys sat on stools behind the counter and talked about any and everything, including Kevin and what Jonah did and didn't know about the boy. Once again, he was reminded of Kevin's promise to tell him about his First Death. All Fallen Reapers had original lives before joining the Undead.

"Trevor told you about himself," Jonah reminded Mike.

"Yeah, he did." Mike folded his arms, thinking. "I got the impression he needed to tell his story. Maybe he sensed something would happen to him."

Jonah thought about that. "You're just better at this than I am."

Mike leaned into him. "No, I'm not. Trevor didn't hesitate to do anything."

Jonah raised a questioning eyebrow and Mike scowled at him.

"I don't mean that, Jonah."

"I still don't believe you two just talked," Jonah laughed.

Jonah sobered as he thought about Kevin. How would he handle anything Kevin revealed to him? The Fallen Reaper hinted more than once that not everyone died a noble death. Those thoughts invaded Jonah's mind as he and Mike finished closing up the store.

The Alliance Guard escorted both boys home, stopping by Mike's house first. Once Jonah returned to his house, he peeked out the bay window in the den. The Alliance Guard's black SUV remained parked outside for nearly fifteen minutes before driving off. They were probably waiting to see if he went anywhere, Jonah decided.

He was about to move away from the window when he saw two red eyes across the street, staring back at him. His heart leapt into his throat. But unlike two years ago, now he had a lot of experience with Grim Hounds. And, with the bands gone, his Death Sense was working as normal. He didn't sense any danger from the beast.

It must have been the same one that chased off the cat outside Drew's house. Throwing caution to the wind, he opened the front door and stepped out onto the front walkway. The eyes continued to watch him but the Grim Hound remained in the shadows.

Jonah moved away from the house, his senses on alert as he stopped near the end of the driveway. Come on, he urged the beast.

It responded instantly, emerging from its cover beneath the neighbors' overgrown bushes. The Grim Hound was huge. Jonah concentrated on it and sensed its familiar tug. It was Deyanira's Grim Hound.

The beast padded across the street, eerily silent, considering its size. It was like a black, moving shadow and would have struck fear in anyone else. But Jonah wasn't afraid. As the beast drew closer and extended its snout, Jonah stretched out his hand. The Grim Hound sniffed his hand before moving closer to nuzzle him, like a fond pet.

Jonah patted its large head and received a low, satisfied rumble from the creature in response. "What are you doing here?"

The Grim Hound stared at him with its red-in-red pupils.

"Did Deyanira send you?"

The Hound bobbed its head in the affirmative.

That intrigued Jonah. He scratched it behind the ears. The creature let out more low rumbles and bumped against him. Jonah was imagining he could have the strangest pet of anyone in the neighborhood when his Death Sense suddenly spiked. The Grim Hound's body went rigid too and it turned its ears toward the west, pointing up the quiet street.

Jonah peered into the darkness, but he couldn't see what had alerted him. He wondered if it were the black cat or someone who was working with his aunt. The Alliance's warning became very real.

The Grim Hound growled at what Jonah couldn't see. Within seconds, the presence receded and disappeared. The Grim Hound relaxed as it released a low, mournful sound.

"I should get inside." He petted the creature once more and turned toward the house. The Grim Hound followed. Jonah paused on the front porch, genuinely amused. "I can't take you inside. You're too large."

The Grim Hound nuzzled him again before it set off around the side of the house. For some crazy reason, Jonah knew where it was heading. He re-entered the house and hurried into his bedroom. Even before he reached his window, he saw the red eyes staring through the window at him.

He pressed his face to the window and watched the Grim Hound circle on-the-spot three times right outside his window before it finally settled down, like it intended to stand guard.

As weird as it seemed, the creature's presence reassured Jonah, even if the Grim Hound actually belonged to Deyanira.

He changed and climbed into bed, hoping for a nice dream about the date he should have had with Kevin. Instead, he endured a nightmare of sorts. It wasn't a dream-walk, although it contained extremely real visions, like Jonah was actually living through them.

In one horrible dream, he was an ancient Berserker, a crazed and powerful warrior, cutting down enemy after enemy. The sounds of the blade hitting another blade and slicing through flesh and bone were authentic. The screams as the smaller warriors died were too real. Even the horrid and unbelievable smells were so vivid and vile to Jonah that he didn't know what to make of them.

The Berserker reveled in the gory nightmare, enjoying every moment of it. Then the dream changed in the way dreams often do.

Next, Jonah was a medieval High Church official, an Inquisitor, pronouncing judgment over a group of male witches. At their feet lay their royal blue cloaks, and on each man's forehead was branded the Alliance symbol. The wounds had long since healed over, suggesting the men had done this to themselves as a sacrificial badge of honor.

But to the crowd of filthy peasants shouting, spitting, and even urinating on the condemned, the symbols only signified their evil allegiance to Satan.

Jonah knew better, both as himself and as the Grand Inquisitor. These men represented a threat to the Grand Oracle's plans. That was why he had to burn them alive. Jonah marveled at the man's knowledge and nefarious intent, now laid bare to his own perusal.

"Burn them!"

Men with torches set the piles of wood and brush ablaze. The condemned, all mages, muttered silent incantations before turning the flames into the harmless blue variety. Jonah—or rather, the Inquisitor—raised his hand and changed the flames back to angry red fire. The peasants didn't even consider a religious man using an incantation as anything suspicious.

They all focused on the real, bone-chilling screams of the mages. Jonah couldn't look away because the Inquisitor's eyes were also riveted on the spectacle.

The mages' skin blistered, blackened, and burned before splitting open to reveal the crimson, angry flesh beneath. Their final, agonized screams echoed in Jonah's mind as the scene changed again.

This time, something was very different. It wasn't the past, but the present, or maybe even the future. Downtown Mount Vernon was on fire and he could see it in the distance. Jonah, or whomever he currently inhabited, stood in his own neighborhood. Large, black cats and Grim Hounds roamed the streets, attacking innocent mortals and ripping them apart in an orgy of violence.

With the wave of a hand, a circular window opened in the air near him. Scenes from all over Mount Vernon appeared there. Angry Phantoms and super-powerful Wraiths, zooming through the streets, cutting down anyone they caught outside.

At Jonah's feet, he saw his relatives' destroyed house. It looked like a bomb had gone off dead center and ripped it wide open. Uncle James, Aunt Imma, Robert, and Lynn's broken bodies lay sprawled among the other debris that buried the front lawn.

Mike and Wick were among them. Jonah tilted back his head and laughed, but the sound was not his own voice at all. It was the mixed voices of his aunt and the goddess, Pakhet.

Kevin ran up to him, his Reaper's coat ripped and cut. He pleaded, "Jonah, stop this! You have to resist!"

Jonah laughed again, raising his hand, and blasted Kevin with a powerful hex. He watched in smug satisfaction as the Fallen Reaper sailed clear into the next yard, where he landed and didn't move again.

Trapped inside his aunt's head, Jonah's soul screamed out in horror and protest. Everyone he loved was dead at his feet and it was all his fault.

The scene changed yet again, surrounding Jonah in total darkness. For the first time, he wasn't witnessing events from being inside someone else's mind.

"Will you resist, young Blackstone?" a voice asked out of the darkness.

Jonah whirled around, but he couldn't see the speaker. "Who are you?"

"Will you do all in your power to fulfill your destiny and stop what you've just seen?"

"Yes." Jonah meant it with all his soul. He didn't want to kill his family and friends. He wasn't like Aunt Ruby, nor was he a killer.

"Do you swear?"

"Yes, I do."

A pale hand reached out of the darkness and gripped Jonah's forehead.

He awoke in his own bed, and his own room. Sitting up, he pressed a hesitant hand to his forehead and then hugged himself, rocking back and forth. That was the most terrifying dream yet. So much of it seemed real. He threw off his covers and looked out his window, but the Grim Hound was gone.

Not ready to close his eyes again yet, Jonah stumbled out of his room and into the kitchen. With shaky hands, he poured himself a glass of cool water and plopped down at the kitchen table to sip it.

Whenever one of the scenes from the dream popped back into his mind, he pressed his eyes closed tightly and willed it to go away. He flooded his mind with only nice and beautiful memories. Eventually, he imagined being with Kevin, which seemed to work the best.

He glanced at the clock and groaned. He didn't want to go back to sleep now and raised the glass to sip more water just as the kitchen doorknob twisted.

Fear gripped Jonah and he sloshed water down his chin and chest. "Dang it!" He jumped up to grab a paper towel and dry the front of his pajamas.

Lynn entered the house and paused when she saw him. "What are you doing still up?"

"Not waiting for you to come home," Jonah snapped back. He took a deep breath and said, "Sorry," when Lynn raised an eyebrow at his curt tone.

She stepped into the kitchen and set her purse on the table. "What's up? Another dream-walk?"

Jonah shook his head and sat down. "No. A nightmare." He paused, not knowing if Lynn would understand, but felt he needed to tell someone or he'd go crazy. The first thing that came to mind was the last part of the dream. He swallowed and said, "I have the feeling that whatever happens next, it's gonna be up to me to end it. Me alone."

"How do you know that?"

"It's just a feeling. I can't explain it."

Lynn moved her purse aside and sat opposite him. She stared at Jonah with an indeterminate look before placing her hands on the table, palms up. "Give me your hands."

"Why?"

Lynn tilted her head to the side, willing him to get it.

Jonah did. "You want to read me?"

"I practiced a little, back before Aunt Ruby interfered with my powers." She wiggled her fingers. "Come on, before I change my mind."

Jonah slid his hands into hers. She tightened her grip, but not too tight, and closed her eyes. Jonah didn't know what to do. The last time a Seer read his future, she merely touched him.

He was wondering if Lynn would have a similar reaction when she bucked in the chair. Her eyes flew open to reveal slightly clouded pupils, but not as bad as an actual Seer.

Jonah recoiled and leaned as far away as their clasped hands would allow. "Lynn? Are you okay?"

"I'm fine, Jonah." Her voice was hollow and deeper than normal but her eyes remained wide open. The little jerks of her head to the left and right unnerved Jonah. It was if she were watching a movie on the insides of her eyelids.

Jonah's stomach churned because he suspected she was seeing what he dreamt. He didn't want her to see that last part, not where they were all dead.

A startled moan escaped Lynn's mouth. She released his hands and lowered her head to the table. The kitchen was eerily quiet as he waited for her to say something.

"Well?" he prodded.

Lynn raised her head and met his worried gaze. Her eyes had gone back to normal but her brow furrowed. "You're right. It will be up to you alone."

"What did you see?"

She shook her head and rose. "I can't be sure. Mostly just rapid jumbles of images from other times. It must have been…" She let her voice trail off as she grabbed her purse.

"Lynn?" Jonah wanted to ask her so much more about her power and what she thought it all meant, but he could tell she didn't want to talk about it. At least, not tonight.

She paused by the breakfast bar. "When the time comes, I'll fully endorse your decision to face your destiny alone." With that, she hurried off to her bedroom.

My destiny? Jonah knew she had seen everything then, including his promise to the voice in the darkness. And he recalled something else that happened. When he made that promise in the so-called dream, he experienced the familiar goosebumps along his arms.

Jonah didn't know how, but he clearly sensed he'd made a real promise to a supernatural being.

CHAPTER THIRTY-FIVE
WRAITH IN THE ATTIC

Lynn was back to her normal self at breakfast. Jonah played along and never mentioned their late-night reading session. He had something else to worry about now, besides an evil aunt on the loose. Wick had come by before school and sat at the kitchen table beside Robert.

Jonah learned that he, Robert, and Lynn wanted to summon Latrell. "He has to know something," Wick insisted as he ended his little speech.

Frankly, Jonah never once considered the idea, partly because he pitied the boy. "I don't know."

"He admitted he was part of the plan. They even gave him an amulet," Robert pointed out. Wick nodded.

When Jonah frowned, Lynn nudged his chair with her foot. "Why are you stalling? I thought you wanted to find the eighth location?"

"I do." Jonah couldn't meet her eyes because he thought Latrell had suffered enough while a mortal. And besides, he wasn't sure what the boy might reveal. Latrell had seen him and Kevin together. "It's not fair to him."

"Jonah..." Lynn blew out an exasperated breath. "He's a Wraith! He will go crazy eventually and probably haunt his sister or something."

"You can't be sure of that."

"I agree with Jonah on that point," Wick interjected before raising his hands to hold off Lynn when she whirled on him. "We should summon Latrell, but the boy may not go crazy. Not all Wraiths are crazy."

"Yeah," Robert jumped in. "Some are mad, evil, and homicidal. Take your pick."

"The Seers aren't like that." As soon as Jonah said it, he blushed. Seers weren't exactly normal people either. "Well, that bookstore Wraith warned me about the danger. He's all right."

A haunted look came over Lynn's face when Jonah mentioned Seers. "We'll do it this evening, and no more stalling. Halloween's in two days and we haven't found the eighth location yet."

Wick glanced at her. "Four sound okay? That should give us enough time to ask our questions."

"That's the plan." Lynn poked Jonah in the shoulder. "You be ready to do your thing. No excuses."

"Yes, ma'am." Jonah saluted her. He half-feared she would pull him into a headlock, but she left the house without a second comment.

*

Mike and Jonah sat in the clubhouse side of the attic, at the old card table. Their books and notebooks were spread across the surface as they did their homework. The old sofa and armchairs had been pushed apart and the steamer trunk was moved aside to make room for Wick's spirit trap.

Despite all attempts to distract himself, Jonah grew more apprehensive as the time to summon Latrell drew closer.

"It'll be all right, Jonah." Mike reached over and tapped his hand. "You'll see. They won't hurt him."

"I'm not worried about that. It's something else." Jonah closed his book and slid it inside his book bag. "I'm scared of what Latrell might say when he shows up."

Mike's eyes narrowed. "What do you mean?"

"The last time he appeared, I was with Kevin." Jonah raised an eyebrow until Mike's own eyes widened.

"Oh." He leaned closer. "Latrell saw you two kissing?" Jonah nodded. "Wow. And you're worried he'll tell your cousins?"

"Yeah. Wouldn't you be worried?"

"No." Mike bit his lower lip as he sat back in his chair, thinking. "I doubt Latrell would do that to you, Jonah. Maybe you should tell them though, just to be safe."

Jonah didn't get a chance to voice his thoughts about that idea because he suddenly felt the telltale shift in air pressure.

Mike sucked in a breath as he, too, noticed.

Kevin appeared near the large window. He spotted them at the card table and strolled over. "Thanks for calling me."

He paused as he maneuvered around the spirit trap. "It sounds like a good plan."

"Yeah," Jonah said without any real enthusiasm.

"What's wrong with you?" Kevin asked.

"Nothing."

Mike gave him a disapproving glare and said, "Jonah's worried because Latrell caught you two kissing."

Kevin had just grabbed a chair and he paused in mid-motion, watching Jonah. After a moment, he shrugged and sat down at the table.

Jonah shoved him. "You don't care if he mentions it?"

"Honestly? I don't know. It's not like I have to worry about any relatives knowing about me, remember?"

Jonah couldn't tell for sure, but he detected a little bitterness in Kevin's tone and he suspected why. Not only had Kevin been the youngest Fallen Reaper, but unlike Jonah's dad and godfather, who'd been Reapers for decades, Kevin had only been one for a short time.

The older boy told him about a family–a mom, dad, and little brother–still living in Chicago. In that moment, he wondered if that was why Kevin was so willing to tag along with them, even if he got into trouble with Mandara and the Alliance.

"I'm sorry," Jonah said, not knowing what else to add.

"Don't sweat it. Go ahead and summon Latrell early."

"How did you–"

Kevin playfully tapped Jonah's forehead. "I know your wicked, little mind."

Mike stood. "You better hurry if we want to hide it from the others."

"We're not hiding it from them," Jonah said, realizing the hypocrisy of the statement. "We'll just talk to Latrell first…"

Mike glanced at the candle stands visible between the sofa and chairs. "What if we can't do it?"

"I can."

"You don't have the amulet."

"He doesn't need it." Kevin eyed Jonah. "He can summon Latrell to him whenever he chooses to."

Jonah nodded in agreement as he held up a hand with the pinky finger extended. "You in? I'm being up front with you."

Mike finally nodded and locked his own pinky finger around Jonah's. Kevin smirked at them. With fifteen minutes left before Wick and the others were due to arrive, Jonah hurried to turn off the overhead lights before closing the dark blue curtain over the attic window. The desk lamps and floor lamp near the sofa would remain on.

Jonah stepped between the candle stands and positioned himself at the edge of the sigil design. He wanted to leave plenty of space for Latrell.

Mike lifted the final link of chain off the trunk and stood close, his expression determined. "You ready?"

Jonah took a deep breath and closed his eyes. He pictured Latrell and reached out with his Reaper power, mentally calling to the Wraith. Then his lips parted and he said, "Latrell, come to me. We need to talk."

Mike gasped at the same time a fog of coldness hit Jonah. He opened his eyes and found Latrell standing right in front of him. The extreme nearness of the spectral boy caused Jonah to stumble backward, almost tripping over the chains. He had to make an awkward leap to avoid pulling everything down.

Mike overcame his own shock and clicked the final length of chain in place.

Latrell reached out for Jonah. *What's wrong?*

The spirit took a step and bumped into an invisible wall. His eyes widened in fear when he noticed the sigil below his ghostly feet.

What's this, Jonah? Let me out!

"It's okay," Jonah said. "I wanted to talk to you." He turned to translate for Mike and Kevin. "He said–"

"I heard him," Mike assured Jonah.

"Me too," Kevin added.

"Really?"

Kevin sounded impatient as he explained, "Fallen Reapers can hear ghosts, Jonah."

Mike shrugged. "I'm changed, remember?"

Latrell watched their conversation. Once it ended, he turned on Jonah. *Why trap me?*

"We need answers," Mike said as he moved to stand beside Jonah.

Latrell stared at Mike for a quiet moment before turning back to Jonah. *Let me out!*

"If you answer my questions, I will."

"Why are you here?" Mike fired at the boy. "Why did you give Jonah that amulet?"

I wanted him to have it, Latrell said.

"Why?" Jonah asked, his voice beginning to rise. "Are you part of my aunt's plan to open the nexus points?"

Latrell's face showed signs of shock. *You know about that?*

"Yeah, I do. And the Phantom's Path."

As soon as Jonah uttered those words, the attic door opened.

"We got company," Kevin announced.

The ghost boy went crazy, blurring into motion as he repetitively hit the invisible barrier over and over.

"Latrell, it's okay. They're just my cousins."

Latrell stopped whirling around, but he continued to tremble with fright as Lynn, Robert, and Wick stepped into the attic.

Lynn ran over. "Jonah! Why didn't you wait for us?"

"I wanted to talk to him on my own."

"How did you summon him?" Robert asked as he hastily crossed to the filing cabinet.

Wick called out to him, "No use looking in the Seeker's box, Bobby." He walked around the circle, peering at Latrell. "Jonah can summon Wraiths because of who he is—a Reaper."

Lynn tossed her braids with an angry flick of her head and glared at Kevin. "You let him do it?"

Kevin grinned. "Alliance override."

Lynn huffed and focused her attention on Latrell with a fascinated expression. "What did you learn?"

Jonah shrugged. "Nothing, yet."

I don't know anything. Latrell rotated his vaporous body, trying to keep everyone within sight while Mike translated for Lynn, Wick, and Robert.

Lynn shook her head. "I'm not buying that. We know you distracted Jonah."

Jonah gave his cousin a sharp look. Kevin had been the only one to suggest that so far. He had the growing suspicion that Robert, Wick, and Lynn were holding frequent, private discussions about him.

"Where's the eighth location?" Lynn asked.

Latrell gave a sudden, violent shake of his head. *I don't know! It's secret and they guard it. The goddess of the hunt would hurt me if I tried to find out.*

After waiting for Mike's translation, Lynn narrowed her eyes at the ghost. "Did you even try?"

Latrell lowered his head. *Yes. Her Felines are worse than Grim Hounds. They can tear a Wraith or mortal apart.*

"Felines?" Lynn asked. "You mean the creatures that guarded the amulet in the Underworld?"

Yes. Latrell looked between Jonah and Kevin. *Reapers like to call on Grim Hounds, but the Felines are just as bad. The goddess also uses them as her symbol and harbinger. At least, that's what I was told.*

"Of course!" Wick pulled out his lighter, flicking it open and closed so fast, his hand shook. "The black cat everyone's been seeing around town is a Feline. I bet you!"

Jonah had seen one outside Drew's house and several in his nightmare about Mount Vernon on fire. And, if he weren't mistaken, there must have been one outside his house the night Deyanira's Grim Hound came to him.

Latrell confirmed Jonah's sinking feeling when he said, *That one wasn't a harbinger. It was her shadow transforming into the cat and roaming around.*

"That's impossible!" Lynn shouted. "My aunt–"

It's not your aunt doing it! Latrell became more agitated by the second. *Whenever her shadow falls on a mortal, she gains limited power. But they have to be careful not to drain themselves. If the person is magical or special, Pakhet can bestow more abilities on them. It's why she possesses special people.*

"But in our aunt's case…," Lynn began.

"She keeps draining herself," Jonah finished. "That's what Niqab Girl said to her in the cemetery."

"Okay," Robert said, "but transforming into a cat has to use up a lot of her limited power."

Lynn poked Latrell with her finger, then quickly pulled it back. "That's what she's doing, isn't it? Our aunt is so power hungry that she would stoop to doing stupid tricks, just to show off."

The finger poke startled Latrell but didn't seem to hurt him. *Yes. She is.*

"Danita!" Mike shouted.

"What about Danita?" Jonah didn't like Mike's horrified expression.

"She wants to prove someone's using that cat purely to exacerbate people's superstitious fears."

Lynn's eyes widened. "I may have encouraged her when she turned in the piece about Drew." She stepped closer to Mike. "What has she done?"

Mike gulped. "She knows where the cat has been appearing most often. She went there this evening, hoping to take pictures or a video…"

Lynn swore under her breath and rushed to her computer. "I'm guessing you and Kevin have never been there?" She flicked her eyes toward Jonah and then back to the monitor.

"No, I haven't." He turned to Kevin, who shrugged and crossed to Lynn's side.

"Latrell?" Jonah faced the boy. "She'll hurt Danita, won't she?"

The ghostly boy nodded. Jonah motioned to Wick. "Let him go."

"But what about the eighth site?"

"He's telling the truth. I can sense it on Wraiths too," Jonah said.

"Oh." Wick unhooked one chain, then used a knife to scrape away a portion of the sigil.

Latrell waved to Jonah. *I'm sorry.*

The apology sounded genuine. "It's okay. We're all being used."

Latrell nodded before he disappeared.

As Robert and Wick joined Lynn and Kevin at the computer, Jonah hurried to the curtain, pulled it aside, and opened the attic window. Cool air rushed across his face.

He closed his eyes and quested out using his Reaper powers. Just like with Latrell, Jonah concentrated on his connection to the Grim Hound. He pictured the beast in his mind and within a second, he connected. *Come to me. Now.*

"Jonah? What are you doing?" Mike whispered from right behind him.

"Wait."

A loud, deep bark sounded from below the window. Kevin exclaimed a curse in the background.

Jonah leaned out the window. The huge Grim Hound was below, peering up at the window with its red-in-red eyes. "Find Danita," Jonah said. He knew he didn't have to yell for the creature to hear him. "She's in the north park. Protect her. Understand?"

The Grim Hound bobbed its head in acknowledgment before it streaked off like a rocket. The speed of the hounds always amazed Jonah, but he had no clue if it would reach Danita in time.

Mike gripped Jonah's shoulder. "That was a Grim Hound."

"You—you could see it?"

Mike nodded, his eyes wide. "When did you get a pet Grim Hound?"

"Shhhh," Jonah warned his friend, but it was too late.

Lynn and Kevin had already stepped away from the computer.

Kevin looked the angriest with him. "Jonah, what was a Grim Hound doing here?"

"A Grim Hound?" Wick called out. "Where?" He hurried over to peek out the window.

"I doubt it's there now," Kevin replied, crossing his arms.

Jonah knew he had to explain part of it. "I think Deyanira sent her Grim Hound to watch out for me."

No one said a word for several shocked moments.

"We can talk about it later," Jonah announced. "Right now, we need to save Danita, right?" He raised his eyebrows.

"Oh, we're gonna talk later," Lynn warned.

Kevin shook his head, grabbed Jonah's arm, and said, "We'll be back."

CHAPTER THIRTY-SIX

PAKHET'S SHADOW

Kevin and Jonah's first stop was the Hightowers' house.

"Get your Reaper's coat," Kevin told a confused Jonah.

"Why?"

"It'll protect you from a Feline's claws. Hurry."

Jonah did, ducking inside the house and returning in record time. The last stop was inside Kevin's hotel room. The young Fallen Reaper's coat lay across one of the double beds. He snatched it up while Jonah slipped into his own coat.

"Follow me," Kevin said before he phased.

Without hesitating, Jonah dived into the aether after the boy. Seconds later, he reappeared in a clearing in the middle of a deep forest of pines. He glanced around without seeing any sign of a park.

Kevin turned and pointed off to the north. "The park borders the national forest here. Lynn thought this was a good place to avoid any people."

"She's right," Jonah agreed, but he worried they wouldn't find his friend in time. "Danita could be anywhere."

"Think, Jonah. I know you're probably connected to the Grim Hound. Where is it?"

"Oh, yeah." Jonah closed his eyes and concentrated. He felt the beast's presence at once. "It's…"

"Phase. I'll follow."

Jonah obeyed Kevin and phased. They reappeared not far from a jogging trail. Nearby, two huge, dark shapes slashed and fought with each other. The deep, angry growl of the Grim Hound countered the higher-pitched snarl of the Feline.

Danita wasn't far away, sprawled on the ground and holding her injured arm. Her slashed jacket sported a red stain. Danita stared in shock as the supernatural creatures tumbled and tussled with each other.

Her attention was so focused, she didn't hear Antwan's cousin stalking toward her from the opposite direction, her hand raised and ready to hex.

Jonah phased right in front of his friend and used his Reaper's coat to protect them both from the attack. Danita screamed and struggled, but Jonah held her tight as an unpleasant tingle shot up his back. Thankfully, nothing else happened and the enchantments on the Reaper's coat worked their magic.

Kevin appeared next to them, using his own body as a shield. He deflected a second hex into the trees with the swish of his blades. The thwarted attack splintered a trunk. "I have a bandage in my left coat pocket," he said.

Jonah fumbled, pulling the bandages free, and huddled next to Danita. He met her terrified gaze. "You're okay now."

He helped her stand and she clung to him, whimpering in pain as they moved away from the fighting beasts. Kevin covered their backs until they reached a safe distance. Jonah checked Danita's wound and discovered three deep, bleeding cuts on her forearm.

He did his best at cleaning the cuts and putting the bandages on. All the while, he winced at the sounds of the fighting creatures and Kevin's continued blocking of hexes.

Danita moaned at his clumsy results.

"Sorry," he whispered.

As Jonah completed his work, a vortex appeared in front of them. Antwan's cousin stepped out and hurled a hex, but Kevin moved in a blur and blocked the renewed attack.

Frustrated, the girl turned on the Grim Hound and caught it with a hex. The beast yelped and let go of the large cat. But the Grim Hound recovered quickly and growled in defiance at the young sorceress and the Feline. Instead of charging, the hound drew even with Kevin as they faced off with the girl.

The Feline's outline shimmered before it transformed into Aunt Ruby. The evil woman didn't appear weakened from the injuries she suffered, made evident by her torn clothes. With her eerie, glowing, orange eyes, she looked even more powerful.

When she spoke, it was Pakhet's tones intertwined with her own, just like in his nightmare. "So, my sister's son is The One? The Deliverer? Release all the limitations the Alliance has imposed on you. Embrace your true power and destiny, something your dear, old mom never could."

"Leave my mom out of this!" Jonah screamed. He moved forward, but Danita clutched his arm for dear life, pulling him back. Unwilling to leave his friend, Jonah settled on making sure that Danita remained behind him. "You don't know anything about my mom."

Ruby laughed. "Poor child, you fail to understand that she's responsible for all this. Refuse me now, young one, but when I release the true goddess of the hunt, your friends and family will be the first to suffer from her wrath. At the Witching Hour, the beginning of their end will be at hand."

When she whirled her arms, Jonah and Kevin tensed, expecting a renewed attack. But Aunt Ruby produced an outpouring of supernatural power that obscured her and Niqab Girl's escape.

The Grim Hound let out a whine of frustration and bumped against Kevin, who hesitated before he patted the beast on the head.

Danita stared at the creature in mounting shock.

"You can see it?" Jonah asked.

She nodded, as if afraid to speak. And then she fainted. Jonah caught her and lowered her to the ground. He knelt, cradling her head in his arms. His own body trembled with the prolonged release of pent-up, nervous tension.

The Grim Hound moved closer to sniff her. Jonah reached up and scratched the hound behind the ears. "Thanks for saving Danita." The beast growled in a strangely modulated fashion.

Kevin stepped closer. "We need to get her to safety."

"Well, it's good she fainted," Jonah pointed out. "We can phase her to the clubhouse without her ever knowing."

"That doesn't matter," Kevin said, frowning.

His meaning became clear to Jonah. "Don't let them take her memories away."

"Those are the rules. And Danita's not cool with supernatural things anyway."

"She could see the Grim Hound. That has to mean something."

Kevin deactivated his blades and shoved them into his pocket. "It means Danita's seen someone die, in person."

Jonah stared at the Grim Hound and then into Danita's face, wondering whom that person could have been. After a moment, he met Kevin's gaze. "I know what it's like to have your memory blocked. I don't want her to go through that."

"You're not the only one having to deal with a memory block," Kevin snapped before he stopped himself.

"What?" Jonah's eyes widened. "You've been–"

"You didn't feel this way about Brandon and Antwan," Kevin interrupted him.

"They deserved it," Jonah shouted. He couldn't believe Kevin would go there. "Plus, we had to hide what they saw. I phased Antwan and…" Jonah trailed off at Kevin's raised eyebrows.

The young Fallen Reaper reached down and lifted Danita into his own arms. "I'm just telling you what Marcus's argument will be."

"Do you think it's right?" Jonah wanted Kevin to agree with him.

After a moment, Kevin let out a low breath. "I trust you, Jonah. If you say she'll be okay, I'm with you."

Jonah relaxed when he heard that. "You'll tell that to Marcus and the others?"

"Yeah, I will. But it's not our decision."

*

Kevin's prediction was right on target. No sooner did the Alliance members arrive to inspect Danita, than they took over the situation. Jonah and the others stood aside and watched as a Healer repaired the gash on her arm.

Trueblood opened a vortex. "Back to the clearing."

An Alliance Guard held Danita in his massive arms and turned for the opening.

"Wait," Jonah protested. Kevin pulled him back, but Jonah struggled. "Why take her back there? That's dangerous."

Trueblood's posture relaxed for a moment as he met Jonah's concerned gaze. He stepped away from the vortex. "We have people in place. It'll look like an animal attacked Danita, and a passerby scared off whatever it was."

"But–"

"Let us do our work." The mage motioned the Alliance Guard through the magical doorway.

But Jonah couldn't let Trueblood go without at least trying to do something for Danita. "I don't think it's fair to extract her memory. Kevin agrees with me."

Kevin, who looked like he wanted to stay out of this argument, nodded when Trueblood glanced in his direction.

"It's the standard policy for a reason," Trueblood stated. "No special treatment."

"But it doesn't work all the time," Jonah countered. "It didn't work with Brandon and Antwan. They just became more suspicious of me." He stopped himself from mentioning the recent fight. "What good is that? There have to be other ways to do this. Or just talk to the person instead of yanking their memories clean away." Jonah's voice rang off the attic rafters when he finished.

For a moment, he thought Trueblood would be angry with him, but the mage watched with a bemused smile on his face.

That bothered Jonah. "It's not funny."

"I'm not laughing at you, Jonah. It's just that you are so much like your dad," Trueblood assured him. "Isaiah always saw through the pretensions of the Alliance and their efforts to make people uncomfortable by clinging to outdated rules."

"He–he did?"

"Oh, yeah. It's why we became good friends." Trueblood gestured to his dreadlocks.

"I was a rebel from birth and drove the elders of my tribe crazy." A thoughtful gleam entered his eyes. "You make a good point. We do have other options available besides memory charms and blocks. There's no reason to continue using this all-encompassing approach."

Jonah never accepted the possibility he'd actually win the argument. "So, you'll give Danita a chance?"

Now Trueblood frowned. "I'll mention it to the Council, but I'm afraid for tonight, it's just the status quo for Danita. I'm sorry." He nodded to Kevin and stepped through the vortex.

Robert, Wick, and Mike all congratulated Jonah on his convincing argument.

Even Lynn couldn't avoid grinning as she congratulated him. "Not bad, hero."

"And don't worry about Danita," Kevin added. "Alliance people will stay around to protect her. She'll be fine."

*

Jonah grew concerned when Danita didn't show up by lunch period. "Did you see her this morning?" he asked Mike.

"No, I haven't. I'm sure–"

"She's okay," Jonah finished. A little irritation entered his voice. "Everyone keeps saying that." He rose and threw away his half-eaten lunch. "I'll check with you later."

Jonah knew Danita liked books as much as he did. So he went to the school's library and that's where he found her, squashed in a back corner, hunched over a stack of books.

She glanced up at his approach and smiled. "Hi, Jonah."

"How are you?" Jonah dropped into a seat across from her.

"What? Oh, I'm fine." She narrowed her eyes, growing curious. "How did you find out?"

Jonah never expected her to ask that question. "Ah, Mike told me."

Danita frowned for a second, then her face smoothed. "I probably mentioned it to him. Anyway, it was scary."

"What do you remember?"

"Well, I was searching the woods for the cat when it suddenly showed up and attacked me."

"And…" Jonah prodded, wondering what the Alliance could have taken from her.

She frowned. "It hurt my arm." She pulled up her sleeve to show him the large bandage.

Seeing the injury produced an involuntary, sympathetic ache in Jonah's own body.

"I fell, but, after that, I remember nothing," Danita continued. "I blanked out. Someone heard my scream and came to help." She nodded more to herself than Jonah. "They spotted something running off when they approached." Her hands shook a little. "I guess I was pretty lucky."

"At least you're all right." Jonah's relief was genuine, but it was chilling to see a Memory Charm at work on someone he cared about. Brandon and Antwan didn't matter to him. Danita, however, was his friend, and that made the whole thing more frightening.

"You were right," Danita said as she reached across the table to grip his hand. "It was dangerous to go there alone.

I'm sorry I didn't listen to you."

"That's okay."

"No, it isn't. Now I don't have the last part of my story. I wanted to get it finished today because Halloween's tomorrow."

"You still want to prove people are just being superstitious?"

"Of course." The fire in her eyes reassured Jonah.

Still, he couldn't let it go. "But what about the cat?"

"It was just a black cat, Jonah."

"It hurt your–"

"There you are!" Anthony Freeman interrupted, popping up on the other side of the bookshelf. He froze when he saw their clasped hands.

Jonah and Danita jerked their hands apart.

"I was just checking on her." Jonah stood.

Anthony worked his jaw, clearly wanting to say something or maybe even fight.

Thankfully, Danita reached out and pulled him into a chair beside her. "We're just friends, Anthony. You know that."

"Yeah, whatever," the boy groused.

Jonah hurried off when Danita puffed up, ready to argue. He hoped to be spared having to witness any of that conversation.

CHAPTER THIRTY-SEVEN

GRIM ATTIRE

Saturday morning dawned with a grey, overcast sky. *Just perfect*, Jonah thought, glancing out his window. Today was the day–or rather, tonight was *the night*. Aunt Ruby would open the nexus, although the Alliance still hadn't located the eighth site. And there was also the inevitable awareness that his moment of decision was soon coming.

Jonah expected Lynn to mirror his growing anxiety, but she seemed in high spirits when she met his curious gaze at the breakfast table.

"Glad you're happy about tonight," Jonah grumbled, pulling out the cereal box.

"We're making the right decision–or you will be."

He was pouring milk in his bowl but tilted the carton upright just enough to stop the flow. "But what if things go wrong?"

"Then they're meant to go wrong. But I doubt that."

Jonah set the milk carton down rather hard. "When I make my decision?"

Robert exited his room and Lynn shushed Jonah. She made a show of focusing on the folded newspaper in front of her.

After breakfast, Jonah and his cousins rode their bikes to the Practice Club clearing, where transformations were already underway. Bags of decorations and other items lined the edge of the clearing while long tables had been set up for the massive spread of food from local restaurants.

Local firefighters stacked wood for the bonfire near the center of the field. They lived in the neighborhood and volunteered to make sure everything went off without any problems.

Jonah, Robert, and Lynn joined the other kids decorating the surrounding trees with Halloween-inspired items. They hung orange and black streamers and set out the real, miniature jack-o'-lanterns from their church pumpkin sale. Tonight, they would all be lit up with small candles. Copious amounts of skeletons, pumpkin heads, and bats soon could be seen dangling from overhead branches.

On the paths from the nearby school and the makeshift parking area, fake pumpkins were neatly arranged that would light the way. The temperature was expected to be a cool fifty degrees. *Not too bad*, Jonah concluded.

And it would be cloudless too, something Rodney appreciated for his band. He worked with the group erecting the portable stage at the north end of the field.

The preparations brightened Jonah's mood. He could almost forget that somewhere out there, his deranged aunt wanted to unleash a goddess and her Phantoms on the town.

He had just helped another club member hang a streamer of miniature paper skeletons when Mike poked him in the back. Jonah turned. "Hey."

"I wanted to ask you something." When Jonah nodded, Mike asked, "Can I borrow your coat?"

Jonah glanced at Mike, who looked warm enough in his own light coat. "Uh, what's wrong with yours?"

"Not this one." Mike laughed and then leaned closer. "I meant, your Reaper's coat."

The request surprised Jonah, but he didn't mind. "Sure, no problem."

"Cool. It should hang just right."

Although Mike was correct and they were within an inch of each other's heights, Jonah had already noticed an added benefit of the enchanted coat. Before school started, he wore it once, on the same night his godfather gave it to him as a birthday present.

The incident with Danita was his second time wearing the coat, and in between those two occasions, he had grown taller. Only when he took it off to hang in his closet did he notice the enchanted garment had actually lengthened to compensate for his recent growth spurt.

"Yeah," Jonah agreed. "We can go by my house when we leave here."

Mike flashed a thumbs up and ran off to finish hanging the remaining decorations. As Jonah surveyed the clearing, he thought Kevin had a point when he opted out of helping. With all they knew about the supernatural world, it seemed odd to celebrate Halloween like this. Still, Jonah wished the Fallen Reaper had hung out all the same. Not only did he feel safer with Kevin near, he was also craving some alone time.

It occurred to Jonah that he and Kevin could have worn their matching Reaper coats. He imagined everyone would have assumed the coats were from some fantasy film, but that didn't bother him.

By late afternoon, and with everything done, Mike followed Jonah home. He gushed over the feel of the coat as soon as Jonah handed it to him. "It's lighter than I expected." He slipped it on his own thin frame. "Oh." His eyes widened.

"What? Did it hurt you?"

"No. I…" Mike shook his head. "Light jolt, but it's okay now."

Jonah grinned. "It was adjusting to your height."

"Really? Cool!" Mike admired himself in Jonah's mirror. "This is really nice. Why don't you wear it more often? It looks so good on you."

Jonah shrugged. He could get away with putting it on during the winter. But it looked so formal and dark. Maybe he could wear it to church sometime. A dress shirt and tie would fit well. "I'd look too goth in it."

"Hmmm." Mike turned his profile to the mirror. "That's precisely the look I want tonight."

"What about Patrick?"

"He's too image-conscious to wear more than a mask."

Jonah had a sudden thought. "Does he know what you have planned?"

"No, and he also doesn't dictate what I can wear." Mike sounded confident, but Jonah knew the signs in his friend. Mike bit his lower lip when he was unsure about something, and he worried that lip right now.

The conversation reminded Jonah that, aside from his idea that he and Kevin could have dressed in their long coats, he didn't have a costume. Even though he never said it out loud, he just planned to go as himself and keep busy working. Now that seemed like a really lame option.

He sat on the edge of his bed, regretting his choice not to have put more thought into the matter. "My mask would have been perfect to wear."

"You can't." Mike whirled on him. "What if Drew or Brandon shows up? They'll recognize it in an instant."

"I said it *would have been* perfect." Jonah threw up his hands. "I'll think of something else."

Mike took off the coat, slipped the hanger in, and gently folded it over his arm. "You only have a few hours left." He checked his watch. "Well, I have to go. And thanks for letting me wear this."

"Big date." Jonah tried to keep the envy out of his voice. He didn't think he succeeded, judging by Mike's expression.

"Jonah, we can't do anything about your aunt. The Alliance is watching all seven locations. They'll be ready to handle anything that comes through."

"Yeah, I guess so," Jonah muttered.

"That's not the real issue, is it?" Mike said while running his fingers over the fabric of the coat.

"I just know it'll come down to me. It always does."

"We'll be right there with you." Mike's confident tone made Jonah feel even worse. "Don't forget, we have the safe room to protect you, although I know you don't like it."

Jonah forced a smile. "Actually, it's pretty cool."

Mike seemed to relax and he motioned to the door. "Walk me out."

Jonah rose and followed his friend. "See you tonight," he said when they reached the front door.

Mike waved and left. As his friend walked up the street, Jonah tried to see the bright side of things.

*

Jonah still hadn't thought of a costume to wear by the time Robert came home. His cousin paused to get a carton of juice from the kitchen before turning for his room. He had a long case slung over his left shoulder.

Jonah pointed. "What's that?"

"You'll see." Robert beamed at him as he marched into his room and shut the door.

Jonah would have guessed it was the bow, but the case was different, and more expensive looking. He tried to imagine what his cousin planned to wear and concluded he'd find out soon enough.

Lynn pranced out of her room and into the kitchen. She wore dark green tights under a full-sleeved, earth-green jacket, the perfect image of a fantasy elf.

She tugged on two fabric sheaths tied to her emerald green sash. "I can store my blades inside these and leave them activated. Just in case."

"That's cool," Jonah said, admiring his cousin's clever costume.

Instead of the usual white-blond hair the movies favored, Lynn kept her hair in braids, plaited tightly to her head. The hairstyle highlighted her grey eyes and thin face.

She spun on her heels and called out, "Robert!"

Robert exited his room, wearing similar green tights and a short green cloak studded with glittering, stuck-on gems. He also carried an authentic-looking, African long bow over his left shoulder.

As Jonah watched, Lynn used makeup to accent Robert's already angular eyebrows even more so. Together, they were stunning to see.

"Wow, guys."

Robert tilted his chin upward. "You dare speak to me, mortal?!"

Lynn shoved him while Jonah laughed. Despite the fun, he began to feel out of place with everyone else. Even Mike had a plan, and a date. Jonah frowned, hating that he wasted his great mask to play the vigilante. Now he couldn't wear it.

He slumped into the kitchen chair, his earlier excitement over the bonfire rapidly waning. Robert and Lynn exchanged a glance.

Jonah caught it. "What?"

"Something told me," Lynn said as she winked at him, "that you didn't have a chance to come up with a costume for yourself. So, I already took care of that."

"You did?" Jonah sat forward. "What did you get for me to wear?"

Lynn held up a finger. "Just wait." She busied herself sprinkling glitter on Robert's tunic. Several minutes later, someone knocked on the back door. Robert opened it and a wizard entered.

Jonah couldn't believe it. Wick was dressed as a typical fantasy wizard, complete with a long, scraggly beard, a crooked, pointed hat, and a tall, knobby staff. What didn't go with the theme was the heavy, black robe he had draped over his arm.

Wick greeted him with a dramatic voice. "Greetings, Padawan."

"I'm surprised you didn't come as a Jedi," Jonah said.

"I thought about it, but this seemed more on the mark."

"Yeah, right." Jonah laughed. "Trueblood and Albrecht don't look like that."

Wick shrugged and pulled a large, plastic bag from under the heavy robe and held it out to Jonah. "This is for you."

Jonah took it and peeked inside. A full-face skull mask and a foldable, fake scythe were inside it. He pulled out the mask for a closer look and discovered it wasn't a cheap one from the superstore. It was well crafted and substantial, gleaming a metallic white even under the pale kitchen light.

Wick held out the black robe to him and Jonah's stomach knotted. "You're kidding, right? I can't go as a Grim Guard." He experienced a quiet moment of panic as he recalled the real Grim Guards from his dream-walk.

"Why not?" Wick asked, failing to perceive his momentary shock. "It's perfect!"

"But…"

Robert draped the robe over Jonah's shoulder as he promptly propelled him toward his bedroom. "Go change. We have to get there in time to greet the first guests."

Jonah experienced an unpleasant pit in his stomach when he changed and looked at himself in the mirror. A Grim Guard stared back at him. The skull mask was even more form-fitting then the Komainu mask and downright spooky to see. Given the quality of the mask, Jonah wondered where Wick could have gotten it.

This is so weird, he thought. He started to smile behind the mask when a sudden image from his recent nightmare popped into his head. The power of it was so real that Jonah stumbled backward, his legs bumping against his bed. He yanked off the mask and struggled to calm his breathing.

He was shocked at his own expression in the mirror. Worse, his legs began to shake, forcing him to grip the edge of his chest just to remain on his feet. He hated this moment of weakness. Yet the urgency of the onrushing decision couldn't be denied. He had a path to take, and Lynn agreed.

For a moment, he wanted to rush out into the family room and demand that she tell him exactly what she had seen. *No, I can't do that.* He pushed away the panic by calling up the memory of his parents. Even at the end, he witnessed the resolve on his dad's face and his mom's acceptance.

We did everything out of love for you.

Jonah sucked in a ragged breath as something unusual happened. Strength of purpose filled his chest. His breathing slowed and he stood taller as Trueblood's fortifying words came back to him. *Everything your parents were, so are you.*

His parents were brave, and so was he. Jonah wiped a tear away with a rock-steady hand. He decided to walk forward, bravely meeting whatever challenge he had to face. After slipping on the mask, he gazed at himself again in the mirror and thought, *I'm ready.*

CHAPTER THIRTY-EIGHT

HALLOWEEN BONFIRE

Two huge, sci-fi troopers stood at the entrance of the practice field. Given their size, Jonah had no doubt they were Alliance Guards. The men augmented their regular uniforms with fake armor plates on their chests, legs, and arms. But their stun weapons were clearly evident.

As Jonah approached, he recognized the guard on the right. It was the captain who fetched him the night he chased after Aunt Ruby.

The captain smiled and gestured to himself, showing off the armor pieces. "What do you think?"

"That is so cool," Jonah said as he came to stand beside the man. He held out his right forearm, giving Jonah a closer look and tapped the surface of the fake armor piece. It looked real, but was actually no more than hardened plastic that was painted to simulate battle damage. "Did you make the armor?"

"Oh, no. My son did these for us. He's rather gifted at product fabrication."

"Your son? Is he here?" Jonah scanned the area, eager to meet any kid who could create something as realistic as the armor. He also wondered if the captain's son would be as huge as his gigantic dad.

"I'm afraid he doesn't want to hang around his old man." The captain's voice did not even try to mask his weariness. "I think the only reason he did these was because he loves being creative."

Jonah nodded while trying to hide the sudden sadness he felt at knowing he would never get a chance to be in the same place with his own dad. Right then, he'd have given just about anything to see his father one last time.

The captain patted Jonah's shoulder and his expression revealed a knowing compassion. "Sorry."

"It's okay," Jonah said, anxious to switch to another subject. "How well can you move in the armor?"

The captain adjusted his stun weapon and suddenly shocked Jonah by whirling it around before snapping it back into place. "The design is practical enough, but we can detach the pieces in seconds if the need arises."

Jonah nodded and adjusted his robe. Despite the heaviness of the garment, he could also move around quite freely with it. Only now did he consider the necessity and advantage of being able to do that.

He was fidgeting with his mask when Anthony marched up, dressed as a X-Wing pilot. He seemed a little aloof, more so than normal, with Jonah.

"We're working the entrance with…" Anthony nodded to the Guard Captain.

"Cool."

Anthony crossed to the other side and took his post without another word. Jonah made a note to talk to Danita again. Or maybe he should have just had it out with Anthony? Thinking of her, he scanned the small number of club members and their friends already positioned on the field.

He spotted Danita, dressed as an Amazon warrior. Jonah blinked several times, and glanced over at Anthony. The boy was watching him. *Yeah, we'll have to talk.*

More kids began arriving and soon occupied Jonah's full attention. Many people had gone all-out with their costumes. Others were cheesy and cheap. Still others were obviously quite thoughtful, like a girl who was walking around in a cloth-covered, wire-framed coffin with her face painted a sickly green.

Several of the kids hovered around the huge Alliance Guards, arguing over which video game the costumes came from.

Jonah snickered when the captain waved the gawking kids through the entrance, urging them to hurry with the constant phrase, "Move along!"

Mike, having chosen to dress as a traditional vampire, looked sleek and handsome in Jonah's long coat. Jonah didn't even recognize him at first. As expected, Patrick wore a simple half-faced mask, the least you could do and still be allowed inside.

Jonah decided to have some fun. He stepped in front of the boys and turned his scythe horizontal just to block their way.

Patrick looked defensive but Mike peered into Jonah's mask, and nodded.

Jonah pointed the scythe at Patrick without speaking.

The boy puffed out his chest. "A half-mask is okay."

People behind them got restless or shifted to the other line, bypassing Anthony.

Deciding he had played it out long enough, Jonah said, "It's too lame, Patrick. That's why you can't come in."

Mike laughed and said, "That's a good costume."

Patrick didn't find it funny at all.

After receiving an annoyed glance from Anthony, Jonah waved them forward. That's when he saw Brandon and Antwan approaching with their dates. The boys both wore expensive, store-bought pirate costumes. Their dates were clad in period dresses. *Gee whiz,* Jonah thought. He searched the crowd for Drew, but didn't see the boy anywhere.

His senses tingled when he spotted a girl in a bone-white mask that covered her face. It had the merest suggestion of a mouth and vertical, cat-like slits for the eyes. Jonah was certain it was Antwan's cousin. She wore a dark nun's habit, but the girl's tall frame and signature movement were unmistakable. Plus, it didn't hurt that he easily sensed the magic in her.

She shifted to his line, intending to enter right past him. When she drew even, she paused with her mask only inches from his. "Interesting choice in costume, Son of Isaiah." Jonah heard the amusement in her voice. "See you later."

The mysterious girl slipped by and instantly seemed to evaporate into the gathering press of kids. Jonah pulled out his phone and typed a quick text message with one hand while waving people through with the other. *She's here.*

He and the others had previously set up a texting group.

White Mask.

Jonah's phone buzzed with a response from Lynn.

I see her.

Jonah exchanged duties with another Practice Club member as soon as he could, and then entered the open-air party to find Lynn. She nodded toward the far side of the stage, where Rodney's band was already well into their first song. Antwan's cousin stood near Brandon and Antwan but she remained aloof, watching the surrounding crowd.

Jonah, Lynn, and Robert traded off watching her, but the girl remained tethered to her cousin for most of the evening. When Wick took over the task, Jonah could finally relax. He pushed up his face mask, leaned the scythe against a tree, and eagerly enjoyed the party. Lorraine grabbed him for a dance to make Rodney angry, or so he suspected. They danced for two songs.

He was grateful for Danita's interference when Lorraine tried to rope him into the third straight song. She pulled Jonah away while smiling, "He promised we'd dance."

"Fine." Lorraine whirled around before she stormed off.

"I think she and Rodney are at it again," Jonah said.

"Of course," Danita agreed while she hooked her shield to a catch on her back, freeing her hands. She and Jonah danced to a slow song. She gazed into his eyes and Jonah had to admit the contacts really set off her large, brown eyes.

"Thanks, anyway," he said.

Danita smiled. "You looked like you wanted to get away."

"I did," Jonah whispered while glancing around. "But I don't want Anthony mad at me again."

"Don't worry. He's helping his dad bring in more drinks from his truck."

"Oh. Nice costume, by the way. It's so eerie." Jonah meant it. He had always considered her a bookworm and geek, just like him and Mike. He never even noticed that she had a female body.

Danita beamed at him. "Jonah Blackstone, was that a real compliment?"

"Ha ha. Everyone jokes." He produced a mock frown.

Danita laughed and then jiggled his hand, her expression conspiratorial. "What's going on? I saw you doing a lot of texting."

Jonah gulped, trying to come up with a valid excuse. "Nothing. Just keeping in touch with the rest of the club members."

Danita's eyebrows drew together as she leaned against him. "This feels familiar somehow. We've never danced before, have we?"

Oh boy, Jonah thought, fearing her memory block wasn't working.

His phone buzzed with a message and he tried to shield it from her view as he read. Wick wanted to change up. "Look, I have to take care of something with the party. See you later?"

Danita nodded, giving him a curious look. Then she folded her arms, striking an unintentional pose that matched the warrior theme of her costume. Unable to resist the urge, Jonah snapped a quick picture with his phone before he slipped through the crowd.

He found Wick near the base of the short hill on the east side of the gathering. "What's up?"

Wick pointed to the side of the clearing where Brandon was holding court. "She's stuck with them all evening. Seems pretty strange to me."

"Tell me about it."

"Well, I need a break." Wick motioned to his girlfriend, Tamara, who was dressed as an Egyptian priestess. Jonah gaped at her when the duo disappeared into the throng of dancing and laughing kids.

A motion at the top of the hill caught Jonah's attention and he turned to find two red eyes peering at him from the shelter of the trees. Jonah hurried up the hill and the Grim Hound bounded forward to nuzzle against him. It let out a low, satisfied growl when Jonah petted its head.

"You can't keep that as a pet," Kevin said. He stepped into view, wearing his Reaper's coat.

The Grim Hound sniffed him and nudged Kevin's hand until he consented to pet it.

Jonah smiled. "I thought you weren't coming."

"I have to keep an eye on you, especially tonight." Kevin motioned with his chin to the surrounding trees.

Jonah peered into the darkness and made out several more Alliance Guards, complete with the added fake armor. They stood at intervals around the clearing. "I didn't know they were here."

"We're trying to maintain a low profile."

Jonah pointed in Brandon's direction. "Niqab Girl is here too. That can't be good."

Kevin raised a small device to his mouth and spoke in quiet tones. One of the Alliance Guards motioned to another, who descended the hill and moved into the activity on the field.

Without thinking about it, Jonah stood beside Kevin with the Grim Hound between them. They were like two silent sentinels outside the flow of normal activity while still being on the lookout for trouble.

At eleven, the bonfire was lit and everything become louder and much more raucous. Jonah glanced at Kevin. "You wanna dance?"

"Not with you," he deadpanned.

"Oh? Whom do you prefer to dance with?"

Kevin shoved him and whispered, "Maybe later."

The Grim Hound went rigid. Its ears twitched as if it could hear something they couldn't. Then it took off through the woods and trotted around the outskirts of the gathering. Its heavy footfalls dwindled as it went further away.

Jonah gazed at Kevin. "What was that–"

A loud squeaking came from Kevin's device. Movement around Jonah alerted him to the presumption that all the Alliance Guards must have gotten the same call.

Kevin listened, his face growing more somber by the second.

"What happened?" Jonah moved right up against him, trying to overhear, but he couldn't make out the words.

Kevin lowered the device. "Wraiths are streaming out of the nexus points."

"But it's not even midnight!" Jonah pointed out.

"I know. But the nexus is opening." For more than a few minutes, Kevin listened to more messages, and his voice grew hard. "They're all opening! Wraiths, Phantoms, black cats, and even Grim Hounds are coming through and causing trouble for mortals."

Jonah experienced a flash of fear. It was the dream happening all over again, except this was real. "The Alliance is handling them, right?"

Kevin balled his hands into fists as he shook his head. "Grimnions have begun showing up in places, adding to the chaos. The Alliance is stretched thin, trying to keep all the mortals out of harm's way while taking on the Wraiths."

A voice streamed out of the device in Kevin's hand. Jonah recognized it as the Guard Captain. "Kevin! Several Phantoms have penetrated the Crossroads. They're headed this way."

Before Kevin could respond, a light flashed inside the gathering of kids. It was Antwan's cousin. When she had

Jonah's attention, she nodded, whirled, and fled through the crowd.

Jonah's legs moved automatically as he sprinted down the hill and into the bonfire party, giving chase.

"Jonah, wait!" Kevin called.

But Jonah couldn't respond. The flickering heat from the bonfire and the incessant yells of the kids became an annoying distraction as he strictly concentrated on following the girl. She was quick and seemed to disappear and reappear among the other kids.

A rowdy football player stepped right in front of Antwan's cousin. Without missing a beat, she held up a glowing hand and knocked the player sideways, straight into his friends. The display of lights shocked some of the kids but most laughed and clapped like it was part of an act.

Jonah wasn't far behind, pushing his way through the clueless kids. Another flash of light only produced more yells. People noticed him running and sidestepped out of his way. That allowed him to glimpse the girl as she slipped past the rope barrier before dashing into the darkened trees.

He plunged ahead into the gloom and ran through the stand of trees that surrounded the clearing. Just as he got into the vast expanse, he managed to make out her dark silhouette waiting for him.

Something's wrong.

He skidded to a stop at the same moment his Death Sense spiked. Light flared and the girl cast a spell at him. But Jonah had no intention of standing still and making himself an easy target. He charged forward and phased before the spell could hit him. For a split-second inside the aether, he managed to keep his focus and come out of the phase, landing almost on top of her.

Antwan's cousin stumbled back before somersaulting away. Using that moment of awkwardness to her fullest advantage, she sprinted toward the ravine. In the dead of night, all that appeared was a large, black chasm. The girl turned at the last minute to cast another spell. And Jonah prepared to phase again when Kevin unexpectedly appeared in front of him and deflected the attack.

A group of Alliance Guards caught up with them. And that's when the eerie howls reached his ears. Phantoms—glowing, ghostly apparitions as terrifying as the Grim Guards—zeroed in from all directions. Unlike the Grim Reaper's personal minions, these beings wore ragged but flowing, white robes covering what looked like ancient, decayed knight's armor.

Each carried a shield and a long sword. Though their bodies glowed with ethereal light, their faces remained hidden in the pitch black of their battle helmets. All that was visible to their enemies were the tiny, bright specks of light that represented their eyes. Their howls were worse than a Grim Hound's bark in their shrillness, which nearly froze Jonah's blood.

The Alliance Guards were unaffected. They snapped into motion, using their stun weapons to defend themselves and Jonah from the Phantoms' swords. The clanking of weapons colliding with other weapons was so deafening that Jonah was thankful the bonfire music muffled the raging battle. None of the mortal kids had a clue that a primal struggle between two opposing forces raged around them in the darkness.

Kevin stuck close, blurring into motion to hold off Phantoms with his Reaper blades. He scored some hits, but the armor the Phantoms wore prevented him from easily dispatching the creatures back to the Underworld.

Jonah welcomed the protection, but he also wanted to fight. He had his chance when a Phantom came for him. With his power humming in his ears, Jonah extended his hand before Kevin could intervene. He swiftly opened the rip to the Underworld. The Phantom didn't have time to stop and it tumbled straight into the opening.

When the other Phantoms swerved away, giving him and Kevin a break, Jonah thought it was because they feared begin consumed by the rip he had just opened. Then his Death Sense flared and he knew better.

The mole appeared, along with several milky-eyed Grimnions carrying their signature, handheld scythes. The Alliance traitor pointed right at Jonah. "Kill the boy now!"

That ignited a firestorm of activity as every Alliance Member moved to protect Jonah. He didn't want that, of course, but what could he do? For the first time, he wished he had his own blades, or even the Protector's Ring. He vowed to take that up with his godfather if they all survived.

A roar greeted his ear as Deyanira's Grim Hound took down a Grimnion that had broken away and was headed toward the gathering. *They're trying to split us up.*

He patted the Grim Hound. "Go. Protect Danita and Mike." The beast barked and streaked off, taking out another Grimnion on its way.

The Guard Captain finally made it to Kevin's side and yelled, "Get Jonah to the safe room so we can protect the other kids. Go!"

Kevin pulled out the codex, gripped Jonah's arm, and activated the device. The clearing instantly disappeared, and the next second, they found themselves in the safe room. A group of milky-eyed men stood in a loose circle around them.

The mole had compromised the so-called security. And now, he and Kevin had inadvertently transferred themselves right into the enemy's hands.

CHAPTER THIRTY-NINE
CENTRE POINT

"Watch out," Kevin shouted. Pushing Jonah to the side, he drove a blurred fist into the face of an attacker at their immediate right. By doing so, Kevin and Jonah success-fully avoided the first volley of stun shots from the other Grimnions.

Kevin and the bad guy smashed into the lockers, but it was Kevin who whirled back and pushed Jonah to the floor. He used his own long coat to cover them both, just as the Grimnions fired again.

Jonah's nerves were frayed as tendrils of power played over Kevin's enchanted coat. The Fallen Reaper grunted in pain, taking the brunt of the assault that somehow managed to leak through the protections.

The mole's order for his men to attack finally made sense. The Alliance traitor knew the Guard Captain would have sent Jonah here, since it was the only way to get him alone. And the mole must have given those guys a working codex. The traitor's level of access to top Alliance secrets scared Jonah.

Just when he thought Kevin couldn't take anymore, there was a change in the air pressure and the assault came to an abrupt halt. Loud grunts and the dull thuds of delivered punches filled the room. Kevin stood up and Jonah could see what was happening.

Five Alliance Guards that appeared in the room were taking on the Grimnions. One of the guards was down, his blood pooling on the floor from a vicious slash across the upper arm.

The Guard Captain had another Grimnion in a two-handed, overhead grip. He brought the struggling guy down on one knee, cracking the henchman's back.

Jonah stared in shock as the dead man sprawled out on the floor.

The captain noticed his reaction. "No time for the niceties."

In short, brutal exchanges, the bodies of all five Grimnions soon littered the safe room floor. All of them appeared dead. Without intending to, Jonah reached out with his Reaper side and gulped. Their mortal spirits or souls were already gone. He shivered as he stood up to survey the scene.

The Guard Captain checked on his injured teammate and pulled out his communications unit. "Team one to Marcus." He waited. Static and the clamor of fighting filtered out of the speaker.

"Marcus here."

Relief flooded Jonah when he heard his godfather's voice.

"We secured the safe room for now, but its location has been compromised."

"Acknowledged. Sending a second package."

Kevin pulled Jonah away from the center of the room. A second later, Mike, Robert, Lynn, and Wick appeared. Excluding Mike, who held his Seeker's compass in his hands, all the others looked stunned and ruffled.

"Jonah!" Mike, rushed forward along with Lynn and Robert to hug him.

"What about the bonfire and the other kids?" Jonah inquired. He wanted to ask a million other questions but midnight–*the Witching Hour*–drew ever closer.

"They're fine," Lynn said, waving Danita's fake warrior shield. "The Alliance people who stayed behind broke up the party and sent everyone home. The Phantoms were only interested in you, and they ran off once you left."

"Oh," Jonah said. He pointed at the shield in Lynn's hands. "What are you doing with that?"

"Trueblood enchanted it to deflect their spells."

The mage's fast thinking impressed Jonah. He also suspected that Lynn suggested the change. Instead of asking, he glanced at Mike. "Was Danita okay?"

"That Grim Hound protected her."

"All right, everyone!" The captain signaled his team. "We have to move. The mole will know something has gone wrong and eventually send more people."

He snapped his fingers and the guards moved as a unit, surrounding the kids, with Jonah and Mike at the center. A teammate helped the injured guard to his feet.

With everyone in place, the Guard Captain nodded to Mike.

Looking more composed than Jonah would have expected, Mike held up his Seeker's compass. It hummed with power and Mike's eyes glowed. Jonah and the others shot worried glances at the floor when it started vibrating beneath their feet. Loud clicks came next before a space appeared around the edge of the sigil design.

Jonah had to shift aside when a thin pole extended from the center of the floor and stopped at waist height. Mike clicked his compass into an opening at the top and the device instantly lit up.

The whole setup awed Jonah. It was a modified version of the travel platform they had used before. He only had a moment, however, to marvel at the newer design when Mike chose a location and activated his compass.

*

"The entire sigil is an emergency transport option," Mike explained as the group reappeared at the hideaway.

The concept intrigued Jonah too much to be angry with his buddy for not telling him about the modification. "How long did you work with the Alliance on the room?"

Mike shrugged. "Ever since we returned from the Afterworld."

Robert and Wick examined the platform, uttering quiet comments about adding the device to their video game as a way to move between levels.

Lynn stood beside Kevin. Both watched the Alliance Guards fan out around the small clearing, setting up a perimeter.

"Are we going up to the courtyard?" Kevin asked.

Lynn shook her head as she met Jonah's gaze. The time for his decision rushed forward.

He turned to get the captain's attention. "How do we know the mole hasn't already found out about this place? I mean, he ruined the safe room."

"This is safe, Jonah," Kevin said, sounding irritated. "Marcus never shared that information with the Alliance, not even the Council."

"But what about Trueblood and Albrecht? They're on the Council."

"Yes, but they're also part of Marcus's inner circle."

"As am I," the captain added, "and my team. We're all determined to find the mole."

Jonah relaxed at hearing that news but a knot developed in his stomach when he glanced at his watch. It was already eleven forty-five. The Witching Hour was only fifteen minutes away and they still hadn't found his aunt. How could he face her and do what he had to do? Maybe it would have been better to let the goons just take him.

But that couldn't be right. It didn't feel like the correct decision somehow. He glanced at Lynn who merely stared back. At a loss for what to do next, Jonah turned to the others and asked, "What are we gonna do about Aunt Ruby?"

No one had an answer, which further irritated Jonah, making him grow impatient. He prepared himself before he suggested they return to the safe room alone when Mike yelped and pointed at the device in Kevin's hand.

"What's that?"

"It's a codex," Kevin answered in confusion. "What else would it be?"

Releasing an exasperated huff, Mike took the device and examined the surface. "It's not the same as the ones we use."

"How can that be?" Jonah crowded closer. "You had to make them, right?"

"Yeah, but…" Mike trailed off. "None of the prototypes were designed for the safe room. We did tests first. Once they perfected the process, the Alliance Council picked a location for the safe room in secrecy. I guess that backfired though, huh?"

Jonah agreed, but something else worried him. "Are you saying you don't know where this one goes?"

"No, I'm just saying they made me use different locations during the tests. The Alliance chose the destinations. The mole could have easily used his contacts to pass along his own destination, claiming it was just another test."

Kevin swore under his breath. "I took that from a Wraith back in the safe room. I bet they planned to use it to take Jonah to Ruby."

"If that's true," Lynn began as she came over to examine the device, "can you tell where this one goes?"

In answer, Mike closed his eyes. The symbols on the enemy codex glowed and pulsated with light. When Mike reopened his eyes, they had turned a rich amber color. Given his unblinking stare, Jonah doubted his friend even saw the present. It was if he were peering through space and time.

"It's for a place called Centre Pointe," Mike announced. After blinking his eyes several more times, they returned to their normal color. "That's in central Georgia."

"Yeah," Jonah agreed. "It's an ancient monolith site, like the Georgia Guide Stones but much bigger."

He glanced around at the confused faces. Mike and Wick were the only ones who nodded.

"My grandmother told me about Centre Pointe," Wick began. "Old rumors circulated for decades that spirits haunted the place, particularly during this time of year."

"But what is its significance?" Robert asked.

Wick shrugged. "No one knows, nor who built it and why."

"Well, that's clear now," Lynn said. "It has to be the focal point for Ruby's ritual."

Jonah did not fail to note the resigned tone in his cousin's voice and the way she kept meeting his gaze. He swallowed hard because the time had come, and he was sure of it. Now, at the actual moment of decision, Jonah wasn't afraid.

"Centre Pointe is the eighth location!" he said. "The one that controls them all."

Kevin frowned at him. "How do you know that?"

"It just makes sense," Wick answered, earning a warning glare from Kevin. "Think about it. Wraiths and spirits haunt the place."

"In that case, we need to tell Marcus," Kevin said to the Guard Captain.

The captain tossed his communication device aside. "No go. We have to assume they already compromised our communications channels."

"Then I'll phase to his location and–"

"That won't matter," Jonah interrupted. In his mind, he was already walking on the path he had to take. *Will you sacrifice yourself for the sake of others?* He said yes in the dream. Now he was primed to face the real decision.

"Jonah, we have to do something," Kevin insisted.

Every pair of eyes turned to Jonah who shook his head. "My aunt's already opening the nexus points. We won't have enough time to break through a ward." He hoped Kevin would accept his coming decision, but knew the Fallen Reaper wouldn't. "The Alliance is busy fighting Wraiths and keeping mortals safe. That was the plan all along. Keep them busy so the mole could get to me." Jonah's voice grew more confident as he spoke.

"We have to try." Kevin turned to the captain for support.

Jonah gripped the boy's forearm and turned him back. "No, Kevin. My Aunt Ruby will finish the ritual and unleash Pakhet before the Alliance can stop her. The only way to end this is if I go alone."

Everyone objected to that idea, everyone except Lynn that is, as Jonah expected. He pressed on. "It's about me. Wraiths always need a mortal host to do the most damage in this realm. My aunt's body is limiting Pakhet's power. But if she had me…"

"You're the Deliverer," Mike said, an expression of horror consuming his face at the idea.

Kevin remained defiant. "How can you get through? Huh?"

"She wants me. She'll undo whatever protection she has."

"No. You can't do that!" Kevin made an imploring gesture to Lynn. "Back me up on this."

But Lynn shook her head, causing Robert to gape at his sister.

"You can't agree with him!"

"I do, Robert." Lynn took a deep breath and drew herself up. Jonah always thought his cousin possessed a regal bearing in those unguarded moments. But tonight, she carried an air of supreme power about her. Lynn raised her chin as she surveyed the expectant faces around her. "I've seen it already with my Sight. Jonah has to embark on this part alone."

Robert looked like he might puke. He shook his head, but his shoulders slumped in glum acceptance. Wick couldn't hide his own grim expression.

The captain gazed at Jonah with a determined look in his eyes before gracing him with a curt nod. "Your orders, sir?"

"Watch over everybody. And listen to my cousin."

The captain grinned. "I already have. She was the one who told us to follow you to the safe room."

The guard's words only deepened Jonah's reverence for Lynn's gift.

Kevin's knuckles cracked in the sudden silence as he worked his fist. "I'm coming with you."

"You can't. Either my aunt will conduct the ritual while you fight or…" Jonah couldn't finish the sentence.

"They'll kill you and take Jonah anyway," the captain said.

"I don't care!" Kevin's voice echoed through the clearing.

"Kevin," the captain moved beside him, "You're a member of the Alliance. We must make hard decisions sometimes. The young man–" he gestured to Jonah, "the Deliverer is right."

"Plus," Wick said, holding up his watch, "we're nearly out of time. The Witching Hour will occur in less than ten minutes."

Kevin whirled around, glaring at everyone. "What are we supposed to do while Jonah sacrifices himself?" He turned on Jonah, his emotions washing over Jonah like a tidal wave. "What if you're wrong? What if you …"

"I won't be," Jonah replied, finding it odd to suddenly be the secure and calm one. "I resisted them when I was seven, and I'm much stronger now. Besides, I'm ready."

Kevin reached out and stopped himself for a fraction of a second before going ahead. He pulled Jonah into a tight hug and only released him when the captain gripped his shoulder and pulled him back.

Lynn stared up into Kevin's anguished face. "Don't worry. We have a part to fulfill too, just not with Jonah yet. Trust me."

Jonah used her distraction to wipe his own eyes. He reached out for the counterfeit codex and Mike gave it over before he slipped out of Jonah's coat.

"You should wear this too." Mike's voice quivered.

Jonah smiled. "Trust Lynn. It'll turn out okay." Mike nodded but he didn't look convinced. All at once, the certainty that Mike had a bigger role to play overcame Jonah. A voice rang in his ears and his mind. He didn't know if it were the revolutionary spirit of the Deliverer inside him or not. But his own voice was steady and sure as he added, "You're my Seeker, my Pathmaker. Open the way when the time comes."

Mike blinked and his posture straightened. This time, when he nodded, all doubt was gone from his face.

Jonah threw aside his heavy, black cloak and donned his Reaper's coat, savoring the unique but familiar feeling of having it adjust to his body. He stood tall, taking one last moment to meet everyone's gaze with his own and reached Kevin's intense eyes last.

"I'll be okay," he said. "I promise." With that, Jonah pressed the activation button on the codex and left his friends and family behind.

CHAPTER FORTY
RUBY'S STORY

Jonah instantly experienced a horrible moment of déjà vu. The codex had deposited him at the bottom of a shallow hill and just below the impressive stone site called Centre Pointe, the eighth location, which was just as it appeared in his dream-walk.

Seven tall, stone pillars rose high above him. All were spaced around a large, seven-sided raised platform or stage made of granite. Even from where he stood, he could see incomprehensible words etched on the pitted, marble sides of the pillars. At the center of that was a large table of stone.

His aunt was standing there, her body glowing with a shimmering, yellow outline. Her arms reached toward the sky and she tilted her head back, uttering words that Jonah couldn't hear because of the constantly billowing wind. The clouds overhead churned and roiled as if they would soon spawn a tornado.

A dome of magical energy protected the entire ancient site, just as Jonah had predicted. Debris, kicked up by the wind, slammed hard against the barrier and flared, illustrating the danger to anyone who dared try to get through.

As soon as Jonah appeared, he had to dodge and duck the Phantoms that patrolled the outside of the dome. Even now, Felines and Grim Hounds loped from the surrounding darkness toward him. But Jonah wasn't afraid. As one Phantom zoomed close enough to harass him, Jonah raised his hand and ripped an opening to the Underworld.

The Phantom let out an inhuman screech before it reversed course. After that display of power, the others were wary and kept their distance. But that didn't stop them from brandishing ghostly swords at him.

Grim Hounds and Felines continued to stalk him, matching his progress up the hillside, snarling and hissing.

Jonah moved right up to the barrier until its magic pulled on his skin. His aunt sensed his presence. She lowered her arms and gazed at him with orange, cat-like eyes that were definitely non-human. Waving a hand, she produced an opening in the barrier, that was just big enough for him to enter.

No going back once I step through, Jonah warned himself. Summoning all of his courage, he cautiously entered.

Antwan's cousin hurried toward him from one side, but she stopped short. She also scanned the hillside, no doubt, looking for Alliance people.

"I'm alone," Jonah told his aunt but not the others.

Ruby motioned and a Grimnion patted down his long coat and pockets. He quickly found the fake codex and took that. Once he moved away, Ruby finally spoke.

"So, you are your father's son after all." Her voice was deeper and strongly accented now. "He, too, would have come on his own in order to save the others. It would have been a useless gesture, of course, just as your attempt will prove to be." She shouted to her minions, "Take him!"

Jonah didn't resist when two Grimnions darted forward to grab hold of him. The stronger than normal humans had no problem lifting him and carrying him to the stone slab. They laid him on top of it, spreading out his arms but keeping his legs together. *Almost crucifixion style*, Jonah thought.

For the first time, Jonah experienced real fear. His heart rate increased even faster when a different Wraith-possessed goon approached, carrying several long, cement nails and a huge mallet in his hands.

Jonah's dread spiked because he recognized the Wraith. He also sensed its unique hatred for him. This was the same hulking Wraith that he previously cut and whom Kevin kicked around. The mortal wore an expression of savage fury.

Struggling proved futile because the Grimnions held him fast. The man dropped the nails on the slab and they clattered against the hard surface. He grinned in triumph while taking his time to choose the first nail. Positioning the tip right over Jonah's palm, he forcibly pressed the sharp end into the flesh.

It took all of his effort but Jonah restrained his urge to respond violently and refused to utter a sound as the pain mounted. The Wraith frowned, visibly disappointed. He positioned the mallet over the nail's head next and with a malicious grin, raised the mallet, ready to strike the nail and plunge it through Jonah's hand, thereby nailing him to the slab.

Jonah couldn't move, nor could he call upon his power, owing to the effect of the barrier. He tried to mentally prepare himself for the agony he was about to endure. As the Wraith brought the mallet down, a hex fortunately hit the man's mallet arm, causing him to miss the nail altogether. The mallet splintered the stone slab where it impacted, sending stone shards and slivers flying. One nicked Jonah's cheek, drawing blood.

The Wraith whirled around, his eyes blazing with fury as he shouted at Ruby, "Why? You told me I could do it!"

Ruby smirked. "I lied."

The Wraith growled, raising the mallet again.

Ruby hit him with another hex, but this time, it froze him in place. Jonah marveled at his aunt's growing power.

"I said no! I don't want to inhabit a broken body, fool!" She twisted her hand and the Wraith let out a scream of pain. "Obey me or I'll send you straight to the Underworld myself."

The Wraith managed to nod before he dropped the mallet. When Ruby released her hold, he slumped to the ground.

A rustling of cloth came from Jonah's left, accompanied by the quiet crunch of shoes walking softly on grains of sand or dirt.

"Are you going to thank me, nephew?" His aunt waved her hand and magical bonds appeared to hold his feet and hands in place. The Grimnions that previously gripped him backed off.

In a fit of stubbornness, Jonah refused to shift his head or look at her. The soft hiss of fabric and quiet footsteps grew louder. Jonah could feel the heat of his aunt's body leaning over him. When he felt her exhaling a deep breath on his face, Jonah jerked his head to the side.

His aunt laughed. "So defiant! And so much like my sister. You have her features."

"Don't talk about my mom." Despite his personal intent to not respond, he turned to look into his aunt's lean face.

She, too, resembled his mother, except for the crazed look in her wildly dilated pupils. Her cheeks lifted in amusement, reducing her eyes to mere slits.

"Why shouldn't I talk about her? She was my baby sister. I knew her long before you arrived, child." Aunt Ruby nodded. "Yes, I wiped her bottom when she was just a baby. I raised her as much as our parents did. So," she gripped Jonah's face by his cheeks and squeezed. "I have every right to discuss Dear Sister."

She gave his face a little shove and released him.

When she laughed, Jonah yelled, "I know what you're gonna try. It won't work." Before Jonah could restrain himself, he blurted out, "It didn't work the last time because you're only a palm reader!"

Antwan's cousin gasped, turning her masked face to watch Aunt Ruby.

Jonah charged on. "I heard they laughed at you and jeered, calling you a palm reader because you didn't have any real power."

Aunt Ruby's reaction baffled Jonah. He expected her to yell back or hit him. Worse still, she could have let the Wraith come back to nail him to the slab after all.

Instead, she remained unmoving for a second before crossing her arms. "Yes, you're so much like your mother. Arrogant in your abilities. Disdainful of others whom you don't think measure up."

"I'm not–"

"Silence!" Ruby's voice rolled across the hillside. She paused to collect herself again. "You're right. I wasn't able to do it last time. You were more powerful than anyone thought. This time, you're an emotional wreck. I can see all the anger and pain over everything that's happened."

Aunt Ruby drew closer, the gleam in her cat eyes unnerving Jonah. "And when the Witching Hour comes, and the barrier between the mortal and supernatural world is at its weakest, the goddess will take you. And this time, you won't be able to resist."

Ruby glanced off to Jonah's left. He turned his head and saw an hourglass floating in the air. He didn't know the exact amount of time remaining, but judging by the minuscule amount of sand in the top portion, he knew the Witching Hour couldn't be more than five minutes away. Ruby leaned over him, running her soft hands over his face. Jonah shuddered and jerked as much as the restraints would allow.

"Don't touch me!"

"I'm your aunt. Family."

"I don't care." He swallowed and tried to calm himself. Ruby was correct. His emotions were raw. One moment, he'd think about the doomed Latrell, or Lynn's pained demeanor when her power was blocked, and the ensuing sadness he felt threatened to overtake him. And the next moment, he would remember Robert and Danita's wounds, or all the kids that were injured at the magic show, and he got furious. The incessant jerks that pulled him in different emotional directions were mentally exhausting.

In an attempt to get his mind off that, he spoke to his aunt. "Why?"

Her eyes widened. "Why? Because I was always the one that had to make sacrifices. I raised your mother and uncle. I had to find a job at an early age to help the family out. When they were old enough, they all got to go off to college and earn their fancy degrees."

Ruby leaned against the slab, fingering the beaded necklace that hung low on her bosom. "You don't know about the women in our family, do you? Only one lucky female from each generation got the *Sight*. They became famous or wealthy in their time. After all I sacrificed for my family, did I get the gift? No! Your mother was the chosen one! As an added insult, my brother, James, even got a trace of the *Sight*. I was nothing more than a *palm reader*."

Ruby spat out the phrase while glaring at Antwan's cousin. "I became the pariah of the magical community, especially by those women who were gifted as sorceresses. I was nothing to them, and brusquely pushed to the side like a fallen leaf."

She whirled around to face Jonah again. "Then, the Wraiths approached me seven years ago with an offer. If I could give you to them, they promised to make all my life's dreams come true. They said they would grant me the spirit of a Seer!"

"A Seer?" Jonah asked before he could stop himself. "You want to become a human priestess?" All this trouble and death simply because she wanted to be a Seer?

"Yes!" Ruby's eyes grew wide and wild. "They can call on the Wraith prophets to possess their bodies. When that happens, whole vistas of time and knowledge open up: the ultimate *Sight*. I would become a true prophetess and legitimately take my rightful place among my peers."

Jonah thought about the Seer he met before his world turned upside-down. She was a frail, old woman, almost entirely unnoticed. She wasn't flashy like his aunt, nor did she try to show everyone her ability. Jonah began to wonder if the Wraiths would honor their promise and actually give his aunt that privilege.

"My dreams were within reach," Ruby continued, "until you happened." She peered into his eyes. "Little Jonah Blackstone resisted the Wraith. Then your mother came and rescued you." Ruby gave a sad, little laugh. "Your father wanted to hunt me down, but Janice prevented that. Even so, my own family ostracized me. My husband and kids shunned me. And they locked me away in that awful place for seven long years. But the shadow of Pakhet came to visit me."

Jonah's aunt thrust her hands into the air, like she had just received the Holy Spirit in church. "I kept the faith!" she shouted. Then she lowered her hands and stared at him. "Eventually, they came back to me and renewed their promise. All they wanted," she poked Jonah's cheek with a finger, "was you!"

That statement unstopped his tongue. "You can't trust them."

Ruby laughed. "The Wraith King will keep his promise to me."

"Ruby?" Antwan's cousin said. "What are you talking about? You're supposed to deliver Jonah to the mole when this is over, not to the Wraith King."

"And what can the mole or Deyanira offer me?" Ruby asked, whirling to face the girl. "She's wholly concerned about you, her precious sorceress-in-training. Neither she nor the mole care about me! Only the Wraith King can offer me what I truly desire."

The girl moved quickly and raised her hands to cast a spell. Jonah sensed the magic gathering, but the girl didn't expect to find betrayal from another source. The Wraith Ruby had embarrassed instantly came to her aid. He knocked Antwan's cousin in the shoulder, causing her spell to miss Ruby before it flashed against a pillar with a loud crack!

The Wraith followed up with a solid blow to the girl's face. Jonah winced at the sound of her mask splintering. The lower half flew through the air and smashed against another pillar like a porcelain cup. Antwan's cousin dropped and didn't move. For a moment, Jonah worried she might be dead.

Ruby snapped her fingers. "Chain her! The cuffs will nullify her power."

The Wraith picked up the girl in one arm like she weighed nothing and dropped her at the base of the pillar where her broken mask lay. He chained her hands at the wrists and then wrapped the chain around the pillar. The girl's head lolled to the side. The upper portion of her face was hidden by the remaining half of her mask.

Ruby leaned over Jonah. "You see, I never had to worry about them betraying me. I was in control all along. Even that treacherous Alastor didn't suspect my true plan." Ruby cackled like a madwoman. "They have no idea. The Wraith King wants this to happen right this time. After Pakhet has her ride tonight, leaving a wake of chaos and destruction, she will reward me."

"What about the mole?" the Wraith who tied up Antwan's cousin asked. "He may also come."

"I'm not stupid." Ruby gestured around her at the pillars. "This place is protected against that kind of meddling by Reapers. And besides, he only had two codex devices."

She leaned close over Jonah and hissed in his ear, "That's right. You can't fight it this time. No mother or father to save you now. Give in to the despair and fear. It'll only hurt if you try to resist. I tell you that merely as a kindness, nephew."

Ruby stood and held the real amulet aloft. "Prepare yourself." With that, she slipped the amulet's chain around Jonah's neck and let it settle on his chest. "The Witching Hour is upon us."

CHAPTER FORTY-ONE
WITCHING HOUR

The air above Jonah stirred and twisted in waves on itself. Aunt Ruby resumed her incantation, and her modulated voice rose to a fever pitch. Jonah struggled but accomplished little more than violently turning his head from side-to-side. Despite his attempts to shift his gaze from the gathering magical energy in the air high above the slab, he couldn't resist for long.

His aunt may have been a simple palm reader, but her strident voice filled the site, and even seemed to mix with the shifting air. She stumbled while uttering the strange sounds, as if she had memorized or was recently taught the spell a short time ago.

Jonah suspected that must have been the case. He heard the nervous stammering in his aunt's delivery. What she lacked in finesse, she made up for with her growing intensity. And the spell worked. The pull of the magic on his skin increased before a painful jolt to his mind occurred. For a horrible minute, something awful flashed through his head and he sucked in a startled breath.

As his aunt continued, another flash of unrecognizable memory appeared in his mind, accompanied by a relentless, stabbing pain. He grunted and his head jerked, but his eyes remained wide open, staring into the contorting air. Jonah heard himself panting and fear seized him. *Were those the blocked memories?* The brief images produced so much shock and pain that it horrified Jonah.

Despair threatened to overwhelm him. He felt helpless, unable to even look away from what was coming next. As if in answer to his pain, the air ripped apart and a brilliant light enveloped the entire stone slab. Jonah blinked into the blinding light until his eyes adjusted—or, rather, something moved around on the other side, thereby blocking the light. He caught glimpses of blurred shapes that reminded him of buildings.

The rip widened and Jonah saw a glowing, amber eye. Fear choked him and he wanted to yell, but his throat was dry and nearly collapsed. The shape moved and its other eye peered through the rip, narrowing in clear malice. Waves of hate boiled through the opening, buffeting Jonah with their intense force and power.

Somewhere off in the distance, as if magically magnified, the soft dong of a church bell penetrated the growing roar from the rip and extreme elements. Jonah noted the continued strikes of the bell. Four, five, six… His whole body trembled. Seven, eight, nine… This was it. Pakhet was due to come through and possess him and he couldn't save himself nor could he fight back.

Ten, eleven, twelve… The rip burst open, instantly forming into a ragged circle above his head. Jonah had a full view of Pakhet. Just like the amulet, her body was that of a woman but she had the head of a lioness. She was sitting on a glowing throne. The angry, orange eyes flared and she wailed a bone-chilling battle cry before she launched herself toward Jonah. Ruby's chanting stopped and she scrambled away from the slab and hunkered between two pillars, watching.

Pakhet roared loudly as she rushed out of the rip and engulfed Jonah. Every inch of his inflamed body ached. He screamed in helpless anguish and bucked when the goddess's essence flowed into his open mouth, nose, eyes, and ears. Once that ordeal ended, his head exploded with severe pain. Then something deep inside Jonah resisted.

No!

A new source of strength flowed into him and he reacted to the pain and the flagrant violation of this body. Pakhet's hold was unmitigated and felt like a million arms wrapped about him, smothering him. Jonah called on his Reaper power and yelled in his mind, *Get out!* When he let up, the pain only increased as Pakhet pulled him deeper and deeper toward darkness. Jonah knew he'd be lost forever if that happened.

He imagined grinding his teeth and pushing back with all of his strength while screaming in his mind, *I command you to get out!*

All at once, he experienced a wrenching sensation of motion. He seemed to tumble forward, which was odd, considering he still lay on the table. But in his mind's eye, he saw himself being propelled upward before flying through the rip in the air. As he crossed over, the goddess was torn away from him. But Jonah thought she must have hooked her tendrils into him because it felt like he was being cut. Searing pain flared all over his body, as if she were scraping his skin raw.

The forward motion changed and he fell faster and faster until he hit the dirt-covered ground. A wave of nausea came next and he rolled over, gasping for breath, and barely managing not to vomit. That's when he registered he wasn't at Centre Point anymore. He was somewhere else. He saw a crowd of people and a group of bound witches in the foreground.

Jonah shook his head. Unlike his recent nightmares and the Wraith's memory fragments, this time, he wasn't stuck inside the Inquisitor's mind. He was free to move around the medieval setting. Jonah rose slowly to his feet and shifted through the crowd of poor, dirty peasants as his nausea faded.

He stalked around the witches, all of whom were tightly bound to stakes. The uneven noise of the crowd grew in volume and cheers. A space opened and the Wraith, disguised as an olive-skinned priest this time, marched out.

Like the Inquisitor in the previous nightmare, this high priest clutched a Bible to his chest and his eyes glowed milky white. Jonah wondered how all the people failed to notice that. *Maybe only I can see it because it's his memory.* It didn't matter though and Jonah resisted the urge to back away and hide.

As the priest took his place at the head of the crowd, Jonah fastened his gaze on the man's face. Eventually, the Wraith turned to stare back at him. Pain sliced through Jonah's head again. He winced, but managed to maintain his eye contact and even moved closer. All that mattered anymore was the Wraith. He could sense the events playing out around him and any eye contact rushed along the flood of memories. When the pain became unbearable and his legs faltered, the scene shifted again.

It stabilized, and Jonah blinked in surprise because he found himself alone in the attic clubhouse. Everything inside the space was the same as the mortal realm, except for his colorless vision. It wasn't black and white, however, just a muted wash of blue, like he was strictly an observer of the place.

"Hello?" Jonah's voice sounded hollow and alone in the empty space.

That unnerved him even more. He scrambled to his feet and hurried up the attic steps, bursting onto the second floor of the Teen Center, where he stopped because no one was around. What about downstairs? After searching the entire Center, Jonah gave up and returned to the attic.

I must be all alone in this weird version of the mortal world, he thought before he dropped into a desk chair. Only now did he register that he could even sit in it. *Was this a dream-walk or a nightmare?* There were strange elements that defied both.

More importantly, where am I?

"Prepare yourself, young Blackstone." The accented voice came from behind him. He shot to his feet and whirled around to find the Egyptian Wraith standing near the steamer trunk.

The Wraith's Egyptian attire and ancient breastplate looked entirely out of place in the clubhouse. He watched Jonah, the amulet around his neck shining like a bright star.

Jonah couldn't believe his eyes. "What are you doing here?"

"I came to warn you."

"Too late. Pakhet already tried to possess me."

The Egyptian nodded, folding his hands behind his back as he strolled from his spot behind the sofa over to the attic window. He looked out. "She may yet succeed."

"How?"

"Look around. Where do you think you are?" When Jonah didn't answer, the Wraith continued, "What do you remember happening at the Witching Hour?"

"I…" Jonah paused, rubbing his still-throbbing head. "I saw Pakhet. She lunged out of a rip above me and… and she flowed into my mouth and eyes and…" Jonah shuddered.

"Pain?"

"Yes."

"And then what? Think and remember."

"I felt like I was falling, going back through the rip."

The Egyptian held up a finger. "You didn't fall through the rip when you resisted the possession. In her fury, Pakhet yanked you through the doorway."

"Why?"

"It's simple. Even in your present emotional state, as long as your soul remained intact, you were too powerful and could still resist. But if your soul was forced out of your physical vessel, as it is when you take your dream-walks…"

"My body…" Jonah's jaw dropped.

"… is still lying on the stone slab at Centre Point, free of your soul and wide open." The Egyptian watched Jonah. "All is not lost, young one. Both you and Pakhet have entered this realm."

Again, the Wraith went silent while watching Jonah's reaction. "Here's one bit of fortunate news. As long as you wear the amulet…" He pointed to the amulet around Jonah's neck and finished, "no other Wraith can take over your body. It connects your soul to hers."

Jonah didn't think that was good news at all. "What about her?"

"She landed in the furthest reaches of the Underworld. She must find her way back. Make no mistake: She will. There's a doorway that leads back to your body, young man. You must cross through it before she does. Otherwise, the goddess will trap you here forever."

"But I don't understand this place."

The Egyptian nodded. "It's a modified form of dream-walking. Your unique nature will allow you to shape this portion of the Underworld according to your memories."

Jonah's eyes widened. "My memories?"

The Wraith inclined his head. "Now you begin to understand. The block is dissolving. Your aunt was right about trauma breaking through it. As it dissolves, you'll recover the memories from seven years ago, including–"

"The memories from the Wraith who attacked me," Jonah finished. "Omar told me about that."

The Egyptian leaned forward. "He's a wise Memory Charmer. That is why you must prepare, young Blackstone. You must experience these memories before you can find your way back. My advice: Don't fight them, despite all the pain or what you see. Accept it and move forward."

"I did that in the last memory, just before coming here."

"Good. Your instincts have served you well."

"Wait a minute," Jonah said. He rubbed his head, thinking. "Three nights ago, I had a terrible nightmare. It was about places and people I'd never seen–"

"Those were also the Wraith's memories. Your previous block was fractured, which was your aunt's plan."

Jonah's upper lip trembled, recalling the fragments of memories. "They were bad scenes. All the fighting, killing, and death…" Jonah shook his head. "I was seeing things through his eyes and feeling what he felt."

The man nodded. "I'm sorry. He was a Wraith. You may experience the memories in the same way here, or not. The Underworld works differently. You may even be an objective observer, as a way to protect your mind."

"It did!" Jonah said. "I was outside the Wraith's mind, almost like a dream-walk."

"Then remember," the Wraith admonished, "the quicker you accept, the faster you'll get through the pain." His mouth opened, but he said nothing else. Instead, his eyes narrowed. "I'm sorry."

Before Jonah could ask why, pain exploded in his head again as the next memory yanked him away from the attic clubhouse.

CHAPTER FORTY-TWO
HELL ON EARTH

This new memory was of a colonial village near the sea. The tall masts of sailing ships could be glimpsed over the tops of the shabby buildings surrounding the clearing. Occupying the dead center was an enslaved male, stripped naked. Blood oozed from angry welts, which covered every inch of his glistening, ebony body. Still, the punisher was only resting.

He abandoned the wooden peg he'd been using as a seat and took a drink of water from a ladle. Satisfied, he unfurled his long whip and tested it, producing a sharp snap! that caused the watchers to stir uncomfortably. When he was ready, he started the brutality again.

Each lash of the whip produced a spray of blood that splattered across the ground and the crossbeam holding the poor man. Jonah averted his gaze, but something caught his eye. He looked, wincing with each blood-spilling blow of the whip, willing himself not to get sick.

Blood and open wounds on the poor man's lower torso obscured a symbol. At first glance, it resembled a tribal tattoo or marking. Jonah suspected the slavers probably thought the same thing, but he recognized it. It was the

Alliance Symbol, branded on the man's body, just like the mages did in that awful dream-memory.

This man had been singled out because he was part of the Alliance! But if he were African and the symbol was used as a tribal marking, that meant a much larger Alliance, with members from many cultures and many peoples.

The whip sliced into the slave's already puckered and damaged flesh. Jonah finally averted his eyes. He didn't have to watch this horrible scene to follow the Egyptian Wraith's admonition.

Spotting the offending Wraith was easy. Tall and dressed as a ship's captain, he motioned for two servants to bring horses forward. A third servant attached the condemned man's wrists and legs to ropes and then to the horses. The animals were moved apart until the unfortunate man was suspended in the air, his leg and arms straightened painfully out.

Jonah knew what would happen. He read about this form of torture in one of his parents' books. His sense of revulsion and horror propelled him forward. He stood close, gazing into the Wraith's eyes until the captain turned and looked at him. The constant throbbing pain increased as the whole memory passed between them. Jonah saw the horrible thing to come, but he gritted his teeth without breaking contact.

Once again, the pain mounted and he stumbled until the scene changed. Jonah fell back and hit solid ground. The world around him came back into focus, indicating he had returned to the clubhouse.

He collapsed on the solid-feeling floor and sucked in breaths as his excruciating headache subsided.

"What did you see?" The Egyptian's voice was soft, but urgent.

Jonah rolled on his side, resting his head on the floor. He let his breathing slow considerably before he answered. "The Wraith was having a man flogged and…" His voice faltered.

The Egyptian nodded in understanding and moved closer. "Did you resist?"

"I don't know how to resist what I'm seeing." Jonah swallowed. Memories of the last headache caused him to feel a bit nauseous again. "How long will this last?"

"Until you've integrated all the memories."

"I don't want to integrate them!"

Jonah got the point even though the Wraith remained quiet. If he thought that way, the pain would only get worse. And he could never return to his body. "I saw the Alliance symbol on the slave's body, just like the forehead of the medieval mages. How long has the Alliance been around?"

"From the moment the Grand Oracle and Grim Reaper took over, others have fought and tried to resist them. The Alliance, as a group, is almost as old as the Rulers of the Afterworld. Their rise to power has never been stronger than it is today. You are their most prized possession."

Jonah lifted his head, staring at the Wraith in disbelief. "I'm not a weapon."

"Don't be so naïve, young one. Why do you think the Wraiths have tried twice now to possess you? You successfully escaped the clutches of the Grim Reaper and the Grand Oracle."

"That still doesn't make me a weapon," Jonah said while hauling himself into a seated position.

"You really don't know what the Alliance has planned for you? It's not surprising, I guess."

"What does that mean? What are you saying?"

"Time grows short. You must work your way through the memories and return to your body. I can only help you so much."

Jonah rose to his feet, glaring at the Wraith. "But you're not helping me!" He aimed a kick at the back of the sofa and flipped it over. The solidness of the furniture was reassuring, however, in its own way.

The Wraith was unmoved. "I'm trying to help you–"

"Then do it!" Jonah raised his fists. "Stop lying to me. How are you even here?"

The Egyptian stood tall. "You summoned me."

"No, I didn't."

"Yes, you did. When you first came to this way station, your soul called out for help. I came through at the Witching Hour when the drain on myself was at its minimum. Your summons led me here."

Jonah gaped at the Egyptian, not fully trusting him. "Why do you call it a way station?"

"Because, out there beyond these walls, our realm, the Underworld, exists. But you created this bubble to hide from the truth."

"I don't understand."

"Each time you resist a memory, your weakened block strengthens, and you come here." The Wraith paced around Jonah. "A memory block says as much about the recipient as it does about the Memory Charmer. Do you know why they tell the receiver to *let go*, young Blackstone? Without the subject's willing participation, the block could never completely work."

Jonah thought about the time he spent with the Alliance members. He'd seen Omar tell Antwan to let go of the memories.

The Egyptian nodded. "A sufficiently powerful intellect could never succumb to a Memory Charm."

"So, each time I return here…" Jonah began.

"You're allowing the block to solidify and wall off the memories." The Egyptian gestured around him. "This is a place of great importance to you. Your friends, family, and allies all travel through this location. It's only natural that you would choose it now as a place of refuge."

That was true, Jonah thought. The attic clubhouse was a central part of his life. But he could tell there was more than that. He scanned the Wraith while summoning his Reaper sense. "You're not telling me everything." An air of deception or half-truth permeated the ghostly warrior. Jonah grabbed the Wraith by his breastplate and shoved him across the room.

The man was agile and turned the backward motion into a controlled tumble. Even so, he looked irritated by Jonah's unexpected response.

Jonah stepped toward him. "If I summoned you here, I can just as easily send you away."

Fear touched the Wraith's face. "If you do that, who'll help you?"

"You're not helping me now." Jonah raised his hand, fingers spread. "Talk, or you go back to wherever a Wraith belongs. Tell me now!"

The clubhouse shook with Jonah's power. The walls creaked and bits of ceiling fell around them.

Despite glaring at Jonah, the Wraith answered. "Hell on Earth. That's the Grim Reaper's ultimate plan. He's creating more Wraiths than normal because he's managed to block untold numbers of mortals from moving on. He would prefer to make himself a god in his own right, granting and denying rites of passage to all mortal souls."

Jonah's anger cooled as he considered the Wraith's words. "Okay, I get that, maybe, but what about you? Why don't you support him?"

"Because he would deny all of us passage, keeping us in this realm forever. He promised full access to the Afterworld for the Wraith King and all faithful Wraiths. But our King doesn't trust the Grim Reaper. He wants to use you as a weapon against the Rulers of the Afterworld."

"But…" Jonah raised his hands to his head as he turned on the spot. "I still don't know why you're fighting your own people."

"Some of us believe our king would be as bad or worse than the Grim Reaper," the ancient warrior explained, "if he had ultimate power to grant or deny passage to the final destination. We refuse to exchange one tyrant for another." The Egyptian moved close enough to touch Jonah's shoulder. "You are The One who's destined to restore the balance."

"You mean, bring balance to the Force?" Jonah asked. He couldn't resist the quip and needed the brief respite from all the building tension and worry.

The Wraith frowned at him as if seriously considering his comment. "Essentially, yes. The Seers and I have invested our faith in you."

That sobered Jonah again. "But why do you trust me so much?"

The Wraith hesitated and sighed. It was strange to see the ghost do that. "Because you are my descendent."

"What?! You're *my* ancestor?" Jonah's eyes widened.

"It's why I could hear you and respond to your summons." He raised a finger. "Stay focused on the task at hand."

Jonah gulped and nodded. "So you want me to take control of my body and…"

"Be yourself, young Blackstone. Merely fulfill your destiny and set things right."

Jonah gazed at the man, sensing total honesty from him this time. "What if I do the wrong thing?"

"There's good in your heart, young one. That is the quality inside you that prevented the Wraiths from possessing you." He cocked his head to the side. "I'm certain your memories confirm the evil of most Wraiths that are still stuck in between."

"Yeah," Jonah agreed. "What do you mean by *in between?*"

"Simple. Why do you think I'm not a raving ghost?" He gestured around them. "Those demented Wraiths are the ones who don't fully cross over to our realm. They're left *in between*; they can see and hear mortals but are unable to touch or interfere, except in rare occasions. The futility of their ambiguous position drives them crazy."

"Latrell said he was trapped in between."

"It's our king's own form of punishment." The Wraith frowned.

"Why doesn't he stop Wraiths like you?"

"He would, if I were not so careful. Once granted access, a Wraith can go and come, at times. Unless the king decides otherwise and withdraws the privilege from us."

Jonah narrowed his eyes. "You're hiding out in here, aren't you?"

The Wraith didn't move for a few seconds. Then he nodded. "You are perceptive, young one. You are also accepting the truth. I can feel the block fading again."

At his words, another memory yanked Jonah away.

CHAPTER FORTY-THREE
PAKHET'S SPAWN

Jonah groaned and dropped to his knees. The transitions were taking a heavy toll on him. When he was sure he wouldn't vomit, Jonah raised his head and froze. He was fully expecting yet another horrible memory from the Wraith but instead, he found himself facing a large, old-style, four-poster bed against the wall opposite him. At least two people moved back and forth in the darkened bedroom.

One was a skinny, black man with glowing, milky white eyes. The other looked like his mom. Jonah gaped at the woman. It was his aunt, albeit a younger, leaner version. She muttered under her breath, waving her hands back and forth over a young boy strapped down to the bed.

Jonah stood up for a better look and stiffened. A pallid, younger version of his own face lay among the damp pillows. Jonah pressed his back against the wall in horror as his mind caught up to the situation. This was the time his aunt sadistically subjected him to a forced Wraith possession.

When his younger self bucked and twisted, Jonah knew with horrific certainty that the Wraith was already lodged inside him. Writhing in anguish, younger Jonah cried out in severe pain. His aunt's eager expression sickened Jonah. The woman showed no compassion for the torture he suffered. Anger and rage made his blood boil.

Younger Jonah's hands slipped free of the restraints and he flailed around. Aunt Ruby leaned over the boy, pressing her weight on top of him to keep him down. Older Jonah tried to strike her, but his attack went through Ruby's shoulder without any adverse effects.

No longer able to contain himself, Jonah roared in frustration as his younger self released a piercing scream. At that moment, the bedroom door burst open to reveal his mom. She drew her Reaper blades but faltered at the threshold, visibly torn between her struggling son who was pinned under Ruby's weight, and the helper Wraith, which swiftly pulled out a scythe.

His mom snapped into conditioned motion, diving forward and coming in low under the Wraith's swing. She cut him across the chest with one blade and stabbed him with the other by thrusting up through the base of the man's jaw. The eyes flared as the Wraith and the human died.

Ruby leapt from the bed, her arms raised.

Jonah's mom pointed one blade at her. "What've you done to Jonah?"

"Only what I had to do…"

Jonah's mom let out a growl and used her blade to cut the amulet from around her son's neck. She dropped the object to the ground and drove the blade through it. When the amulet flashed and popped, the Wraith's form instantly detached from younger Jonah's body.

His mom whirled and cut the Wraith's head from its body before it could escape. The spirit dissolved into more fragments.

Ruby had bolted around the bed, heading for the dresser. She grabbed a shotgun, leveled it at his mom, and fired. The explosive sound of the gun startled Jonah. However, his mom's deflection spell created an invisible barrier in front of her, causing the bullet to ricochet before it punched a huge hole in the bedroom wall.

Janice Blackstone leapt over the bed, almost coming down on Ruby, who tried to raise the gun and fire again. His mom sliced upward with one blade, severing the barrel. The other blade cut into Ruby's hand, splattering a spray of blood across the wall.

Ruby gasped in pain, dropped the gun, and cradled her injured hand. She darted to the window and plowed through, shattering the glass and taking half the curtains along with her.

Jonah's mom halted at the window and turned to check on her son. He could see the warring emotions on her face. At last, her shoulders relaxed and she dropped her blades on the bedside table. Sinking onto the edge of the bed, she warmly gathered younger Jonah into her arms.

She hummed an old hymn as she rocked her son. A creak came from the hallway and two people loomed in the darkened doorway. Jonah recognized Symon Trueblood's silhouette from the dreads. The other was Omar.

"Where is she, Janice?" Symon stepped inside, wearing his blue mage tunic.

Janice nodded toward the window. "Gone."

"I'll catch her."

"Ruby knows all the hideouts in the back woods."

Symon pointed at the dark stains on the floor and wall. "You hurt?"

"No. I cut her."

"That'll make it easier. And she used magic tonight. It should leave a trace." With that, Symon nodded and hopped through the broken window before fleeing into the night.

Jonah's mom beckoned Omar to the bed. "Help me. He's trembling." As Omar leaned on the opposite side of the bed, young Jonah grunted, then began a series of spastic jerks.

Omar's brow furrowed in worry. He leaned closer, rubbing his hands together. "Are you sure?"

"He's suffering, Omar."

"That Wraith must have left wicked memories behind. He'll have nightmares if..."

"Do it." When Omar hesitated, she gripped his hand. "I appreciate what it means to you, but he's my son. And this is our fault."

A look of guilt and sadness crossed Omar's features. He nodded, placing his hands on little Jonah's head. She had to restrain her son because he continued to jerk at odd moments.

"Jonah?" Omar's rich, deep, African voice was soothing. "Jonah, let them go. Let go of the memories. Those aren't yours. I know you're scared." Omar's arms and shoulders jerked and his head tilted back as he grimaced.

Young Jonah shouted out, his voice clear and frantic. "I have to warn him. He's in danger." Then he went limp, shuddering again.

"No, Jonah." Omar lowered his chin and said, "Let it go. Don't hold on."

Again, Jonah spoke in a clear voice. "Dad! You have to get out of here. He's coming!"

Omar, brows drawn together and hands shaking, kept his eyes closed as he spoke in an urgent tone. "Say something, Janice. Maybe your voice will get him to relax. I've never seen anyone hang on so relentlessly."

"Jonah, it's me. Let go, sweetheart. Please." Younger Jonah's body seemed to relax and the trembling subsided. "That's it. Let it all go."

"That's it," Omar echoed. "Let it all go, Jonah."

A soft glow appeared over Omar's hands and settled on little Jonah's forehead. After a long moment, Omar removed his hands and sat back. He hunched his muscular shoulders and hugged himself. "It's done," he said, closing his eyes. "That Wraith was horrible. Your sister should be…" His voice faded softly.

Jonah's mom peered into Omar's saddened face. "How long will the block last?"

"It should last until he's an adult." Omar opened his eyes and met her gaze. "Unless you choose to remove it."

She shook her head. "I'll never tell him what happened here."

"I understand, Janice, but it's part of who he is. If Jonah's anything like Isaiah, he'll find out one way or the other."

"Omar…" She faltered and focused on stroking her son's wet forehead. "What was that about Isaiah?"

"Janice…"

"I'm his mother."

Omar frowned. "I only got bits and pieces, but Isaiah and Marcus were in a restaurant and everyone died, except them."

The horror in his mother's eyes mirrored Jonah's own. He remembered that strange dream. Omar had been performing the Memory Charm on Brandon and Antwan when the procedure managed to trigger one of Jonah's blocked memories.

The Alliance adults convinced Jonah it was part of the general block. Now, however, he knew better. That memory predated this event in his life.

"That's all I could see," Omar continued. "How could the Wraith have that memory? It's almost like it was Jonah's, except long forgotten." Omar raised an eyebrow. "He's never been to a Memory Charmer before, has he?"

"No." She met Omar's gaze. "He hasn't. And don't tell Isaiah about this."

"Janice, it's his right as a father."

"He'll kill her."

Omar shrugged while Janice rocked her son back and forth. Little Jonah's breathing was even and unlabored now. In fact, Jonah thought his younger self might have even dozed.

"She's my sister, my family. I fear what would happen to Isaiah if he killed her. He may be angry now, but someday, he'll regret it. I won't add that burden on him."

"Things will be worse if you don't tell him," Omar warned. "He's a fair man, Janice, but he and his brother are too much alike when they get angry."

My dad's brother? How would he know my dad's brother? Omar was magical, but still lived a normal lifespan. Jonah's dad had been a Reaper for decades, and his mortal family were all dead.

Jonah only just now realized his mom had remained quiet while gazing at his younger self and stroking his damp forehead. "Fine, but I'll tell Marcus and the others first. If we're all there, Isaiah will listen."

Omar peered into her eyes. "You sense that?"

"It's a narrow possibility. But if I tell him alone, he'll run off and kill Ruby."

"I trust you. But..." Omar squeezed one of her hands and his expression grew somber. "Why couldn't you sense this?"

"It's always hardest dealing with family. It's a blind spot that we all have."

"I see." He nodded in understanding, but his expression remained sad. "What's wrong?"

"Now that I've experienced this…" Her voice trailed off as she slid her fingers through young Jonah's short afro. "I'll never be able to bring him back here to Georgia."

Omar's jaw dropped. "You're that sure of it?"

She nodded. "Jonah won't be able to grow up with his cousins, not like we wanted." She wiped away a tear. "I may have a way to bring them together, eventually." The sadness in her voice was painful for Jonah. Did his mom predict that something would happen?

Jonah moved closer until he leaned over his mom and his younger self. He knelt down while gazing into her tear-streaked face. *Mom.* He hadn't seen her in two years. He reached out a ghostly hand to touch her own.

Janice shuddered and looked around. "Who's there?"

Her reaction and the question startled Jonah so much that he leapt back before he could stop himself and fell through the wall.

Intense pain split his skull, causing him to cry out as he stumbled and sprawled on his butt. But he forgot the pain when he gazed around at the new memory. He was in a throne room, straight out of a dark fantasy movie. Or maybe a horror movie, he corrected himself.

The ground on which he sat had a patchwork of deep brown, black, and burning red rocks. The red portion shot through the other stones, like veins or blood, Jonah decided. Overhead, the ceiling was a shiny, black material that reflected the color from the lit torches lining the walls. The place was in a word, oppressive.

A Wraith knelt on the ground several feet away. Jonah wasn't sure if it was the Wraith from his memories or not, but he suspected it could have been. Not far from the kneeling figure, curved, black steps led up to a glowing, red throne. On the throne sat a figure, his features hidden in the shadows.

Jonah could see the outline of a crown on the being's head, perched above two angry red eyes. *The Wraith King?*

A motion to the left of the king's shoulder drew Jonah's attention. An image wavered on the flat section of the wall. Jonah sucked in an angry breath as the Grim Reaper's visage came into view. He had the hood of his robe pulled forward, obscuring his face. Like the Wraith King, all that was visible was the glow from his angry eyes.

The Grim Reaper spoke, his gravelly voice making Jonah's nerves stand on end. "What news do you have for me?"

The Wraith King motioned to the Wraith on the floor. "My servant failed in his attempt to take over Jonah Blackstone."

"I know of your failure," the Grim Reaper said. His voice carried danger in it. "Why haven't you sent this spirit to everlasting oblivion?"

The Wraith King nodded. "I understand your anger, Master, but this fool has important information." He gestured. "Speak."

The Wraith kept his head bowed, not daring to look at either being. "When I tried to take the boy's soul, I discovered something unexpected."

"And what was that?" The Grim Reaper asked.

"His impossible birth only became possible because of Pakhet's essence."

"What's this?"

The Wraith King stirred. "Master, Pakhet's amulet enhances the fertility of the one who wears it."

When the Grim Reaper nodded, the kneeling Wraith hurried on, "The mother possessed it before she conceived. The boy's body…"

"Would make a suitable host for the war goddess's essence," the Grim Reaper finished. "His body could contain the full power and achieve the first part of my plan."

"That is so, Master." The Wraith King inclined his head. "We should wait until the next alignment."

"That's seven years away! What about the aunt? We'll need her again."

"One of my minions still possesses her. We can control what she does until then."

"I want her separated from any influence by her family. Perhaps locked away for the duration would be best?"

"It will be done, Master." The Wraith King bowed.

As the Grim Reaper's image disappeared, the Wraith King rose from his throne.

He raised a glowing hand toward the Wraith on the floor. "As for you…"

Jonah ran forward and peered into the doomed Wraith's terrified eyes. A second before the Wraith King tortured or killed his servant, the memory shattered.

Instead of returning to the attic, he landed in a field of war in some far country of the distant past. Jonah suppressed a wave of panic and willed himself to accept the new memory without resistance.

Quicker than before, he found the Wraith, an arrogant captain this time, and made eye contact with the spirit-possessed person. The scene shifted. In the new scene, he discovered the Wraith taking possession of a foreign soldier who was in the process of beating and shooting a group of protestors.

Jonah was glad to turn his back on that. He preferred not to see the bullet-riddled bodies hugging the wall. After making eye contact, the scene changed again; and when it did, something amazing happened. A part of Jonah opened up, a part that didn't flinch away from what he saw, and the pain suddenly began to recede.

The process of moving from memory to memory sped up until the scenes were little more than a blur. An entire vista of memories stretched out before him. Even though he couldn't consciously see all the details, he had each one. That strange, strong part of him accepted it, propelling him forward. Each new scene flashed by with little more than an irritating bump against his soul's body.

Up ahead, Jonah sensed as much as he saw the approaching darkness. Fear returned because a frightening sense of finality loomed ahead. Jonah wrapped his mortal fears in the shielding calm of his Reaper side. Memory after memory flashed by until the darkness was upon him. All sense of forward movement ceased as he stumbled and fell in the total absolute nothingness of this scene.

With the darkness came the undeniable sense of Death, with a capital D.

CHAPTER FORTY-FOUR
YOU CAN'T CHEAT DEATH

The ticking of a clock echoed through the darkness. *No, not a clock*, Jonah realized. *It's a tap. Yeah, it's actually a tapping.* He focused on the muffled sound of a cane hitting a concrete sidewalk. It was important.

A grouping of blinking lights appeared, drawing Jonah's attention. He thought they were far away, but it was difficult to tell without any reference points. Slowly, a nighttime sky dissolved into the blackness and around the lights. Then, more sounds came: Cars, the dull, sliding thumps of many people walking, and music.

In the background, the tapping continued, punctuating all of the other noises. *Strange*, Jonah thought, *it reminds me of a ticking clock.* Time was slipping away rapidly. What could he do, all alone in the darkness? There were no Wraith's eyes to stare into that might possibly end this memory.

Out of the darkness, a hazy scene coalesced into shapes that grew sharper and clearer, soon revealing the bustling activity of city life. Jonah stood on a street corner, his eyes darting here and there, taking it all in. In the distance, the flurry of twinkling lights morphed into the illuminated upper portion of the Eiffel Tower.

Of course! This was the full memory he remembered glimpsing earlier in the summer. It had to be the same one that Omar referred to in the previous scene while talking to his mom. He would finally know the truth of the experience. But why Paris? What happened here?

All around him, Parisians hurried along. Some even walked right through his immaterial body. Although it didn't hurt, Jonah was unnerved by the sheer number of collisions. He whirled around, trying to find a clear spot on which to stand, and that's when he saw a younger version of himself. He was only a few feet away in his pajamas, his eyes wide with wonder.

I don't understand about the dream-walks yet.

It was odd to see himself again in a memory. This version of himself was younger than the last by a year. Jonah ignored the people walking through him as he moved closer to the younger Jonah. Then he heard the tapping again, only stronger, more methodical, and more insistent.

He and his younger self looked around, mirroring each other as they peered into the nighttime crowds. But Jonah remembered the sound came from a pale man. That's when he spotted the source.

A thin, pale man wearing a long, black overcoat, stark white shirt, black tie, and black top hat strolled through the crowds. Parisians moved out of his way as if he were a skiff, cutting through living waves. The man carried a long, black cane with a large, silver handle and silver tip. The tip made the tapping noise. With his top hat tilted back, his eyes never wandered from his destination.

Jonah's dread and fear grew exponentially. One glance at his younger self and he realized the feelings weren't his own. Even though this was just a memory, he was experiencing a sympathetic reaction inside himself.

The pale man reached them and nodded his head in greeting to little Jonah. And then he looked squarely into older Jonah's face as he continued past, never breaking his stride. Jonah shuddered and rubbed his arms just as little Jonah did the same thing.

They turned, watching the pale man proceed toward a restaurant. The dread from his younger self threatened to overwhelm him. It was right at that point when Omar's voice had intruded the last time. He and Jonah's mom lured him away from the memory. But they weren't here now.

Jonah knew he had to get inside that restaurant. He nudged himself into a phase and a moment later, stood at the front doors of the upscale Parisian locale.

Little Jonah appeared right next to him. The younger boy didn't hesitate to dart through the doors, literally, and go into the restaurant. Jonah followed. It was dark inside, elegant and full of hushed conversations in a variety of languages, but French dominated most of them. Little Jonah seemed to know where he was going as he weaved around the crowded tables and toward a back section.

Jonah followed and soon heard a familiar voice that caused his heart to jump into his throat. His dad sat at a table with three other people, two of whom Jonah didn't know, but the third was Marcus! A stab of fear hit Jonah and he glanced at his younger self. They had to warn his father. The strange man was coming for him.

"Dad!" they yelled at the top of their lungs, their voices mixing, younger and older, in a weird chorus of sound. But no one in the restaurant paid any attention to them, just as Jonah expected. The younger Jonah didn't understand so he yelled again.

"Dad! You have to leave! Get out! He's coming!"

Jonah's dad paused and glanced around. After a brief, puzzled look, he went back to his conversation. Marcus gave him a curious rise of the eyebrow, but his dad shrugged it off.

"Dad!" Little Jonah shouted yet again. His voice sounded so fragile and fear-stricken. Jonah wanted to tell his younger self that their dad couldn't hear him. At least, not yet. Maybe if he joined in, using his own voice, they could get his dad's attention.

Jonah opened his mouth to call out when a piercing scream filled the restaurant. More yells followed before the sound of dishes crashing to the floor and heavy thuds filled the room. Every person in the restaurant turned toward the commotion.

The pale man had entered the restaurant. His cane never stopped its incessant tapping. Behind him, bodies littered the floor. Like a wave, people in front of him also collapsed. Some suffered horrible spasms while others sprouted lesions and scars on their faces. All succumbed to horrible, painful deaths.

The carnage spread across the restaurant as waiters, the maître d', and customers perished wherever they stood or sat. Distant crashes and thuds even came from the kitchen. *Death*. The man was Death, personified.

Jonah turned back to his dad, but Death suddenly stood in front of him, peering down at younger Jonah. The coldness that emanated off the being chilled the young boy and Jonah, despite his long, insulated coat.

The effects of Death continued to spread around the restaurant until it reached his dad's table. Two of the diners fell immediately. Only Jonah's dad and Marcus remained on their feet. When Marcus pulled out his Reaper blade, Jonah's dad grabbed his arm and forced it down.

"Dad, run!" young Jonah shouted. Death smiled at him and raised a boney finger to his lips.

"Shhh. Your daddy can't sense you here, but Death can. One day, you'll be able to call out to him, when you're stronger." He met older Jonah's gaze. "You understand what I mean."

Little Jonah didn't, but older Jonah did. He gulped, loath to relive that memory of his parents' last stand.

"Now be a good boy and stay here while I have a talk with your daddy." Death raised his eyes from little Jonah to look at Jonah once more. "Both of you." He flicked his boney hand and rooted Jonah's body to the spot. Only his eyes could move, following the being's progress to the table. He suspected the same thing probably happened to his younger self.

Isaiah Blackstone turned to face Death, but the being flicked his hand, causing the chair to bump into Jonah's dad's legs and forcing him to sit down. The same thing happened to Marcus. Both men sat rigidly in their seats.

Walking around to other side of the table, Death waved his hand and sent the dead dinner companions flying across the room. They knocked over tables on the way to the far wall, which they hit with sickening thuds.

Death dusted off a chair, sat down, and leaned his cane against the table. After spending a minute to examine the unfinished meals, he pulled two half-finished plates toward himself and began to eat. "Exquisite."

Jonah's dad talked through a clenched jaw. "You can't take me now. You promised."

"I don't want you yet." Death ate another bite of food and took his time chewing it.

"Why are you here?"

Death put the fork down. "I'm here because of you, Isaiah Blackstone. When I told you how to rebel and to demand the ancient trial, you made an oath to me. And your wife also accepted the terms when you married her. Now that you have a son, you seem somewhat inclined to forget your vow."

He poured wine into a glass, then lifted it to his nose to sniff before taking a sip. "I don't care who's on top in the Afterworld. Nor do I care what the Grand Oracle hides in his pathetic repositories. In the end, everyone comes to me." Death lowered the glass and took another bite of food.

He swallowed, pointing his knife at Jonah's dad. "Even the Grim Reaper will face the ultimate harvest. It is the way of the universe. I will devour the souls of you and your wife."

Marcus struggled to move. "Did you have to kill all those innocent people?"

Death seemed perturbed by the question. "I assure you that unlike the Grim Reaper, I never take mortal souls except at their appointed time." He put down his fork and seemed in no hurry while sipping more wine. "All these people were destined to perish tonight in a terrorist gas attack."

"That's the way you'll play it?" Isaiah asked.

"Like you really care." Death smiled. "The only reason you're still alive is because of the Reaper blood in your veins. Don't worry; you'll still have your allotted thirteen years with your son. But mark my words, if you don't stick to the agreement for him, I will have you and your wife sooner than you can appreciate. The cosmic balance rests on the boy's future."

Death stood up, took his cane, and walked around the table until he was directly beside Jonah's dad. "You, of all people, should know that you can't cheat Death."

With a wave of his hand, the dead people disappeared from the restaurant. Then the tables faded, followed by the walls. Nighttime Paris also dissolved into the blackness until only Jonah's dad, Marcus, Death, and of course, Jonah and his younger self were left.

Everyone remained immobile, including young Jonah, even though Death had removed the invisible force holding them. Jonah moved closer to his dad, taking in his features. It had been two years since Jonah last saw him and tears welled up, threatening to spill.

When Jonah reached out to touch his dad, his dad inexplicably began to fade. Jonah thrust his arms out, trying to wrap them around his dad and hold on, even for a moment longer.

"No!" It was too late. His dad and Marcus were gone, along with younger Jonah. He was alone again in the darkness.

Except this time, the pale man stood nearby, his cane in hand. He ticked it against the ground as he strolled closer. The light followed him until both he and Jonah were perfectly lit.

"You understand about your father's fall?" Death's slightly Southern accent carried a note of curiosity.

Jonah nodded. "He went through a test. That was different from other Fallen Reapers."

"Precisely. His mission was to produce you." Death pointed his cane at Jonah. "The vessel of the Deliverer's spirit and power. Only a special birth could produce someone like you, half supernatural and mortal, both sides gifted, in their own ways."

Despite the fear, Jonah's anger flared. "Then why did you kill my mom and dad?"

"We all must play our parts. Your father accepted his role, despite the consequences and all."

Jonah's eyes blurred with tears. He remembered the way his mom and dad stood so tall in that chamber when they sensed him watching, like they… like they fully accepted what would happen. Jonah wiped the tears. "What about the Grim Reaper? How's it fair that he can screw things up?"

Death laughed and moved around Jonah, studying him. "Why do you think you're here, young man? If more powerful supernaturals were to interfere, that would further upset the balance. The Grim Reaper was mortal once. It's only cosmic justice that a mortal must overcome him."

Jonah's heart ached with the knowledge that his parents had to sacrifice their lives in order for him to survive. He shook his head, trying to deny his parents' final words. *Everything we've done is because we love you.*

Death peered into his eyes. "Accept the truth along with the burden. You are what you are, young man." He pointed his boney finger at Jonah's forehead. "You took in the Wraith's memories. Your Reaper half did that, dulling the pain and shock from your mortal side. It was the instinctive thing to do and something you would have learned years ago if your mother hadn't interfered."

"My mom saved me."

"Did she? Because of her love and fear, she held you back from fully developing. Then your parents tried to hide from the truth of your birthright, sheltering you in secrecy for years. They wanted to have a normal son, but you, young man, are so much more."

Everything we've done is because we love you. Jonah couldn't ignore the words.

Death nodded. "Yes, even then, as misguided as they were, they acted primarily out of love." He waved his cane and below them, a scene wavered into view. It was like standing on a glass walkway high above an empty street. Jonah didn't recognize the shabby rows of mom-and-pop businesses.

Then his eyes came to the blinking, lavender palm in the window of the old Ankh of Life store halfway down the dingy side street. "That's my great-aunt's store!"

"And also the doorway back to your body." Death inclined his head toward the scene.

Jonah noticed a gathering darkness at the far end of the main street, perhaps ten blocks away.

"What's that?"

"The goddess has made her way to the doorway. She's gathered the Wraith King's Phantoms to fight with her." Then Death pointed toward the storefront. Streams of vapor whirled around the shining door. "Your aunt has also summoned Wraiths to bar your way."

Jonah gaped at the vision because the faces of Wraiths appeared in the vapors. Ice water flowed through his veins. So much wasted time! He had to get back, yet he didn't know how. In desperation, he turned to Death.

"Can you help me?"

Death raised an eyebrow. Jonah realized he must have sounded foolish for asking. Yet, for a second, he thought the being might refuse.

"If I were to render aid," Death finally said, "you would have to make an oath to me, here and now."

Like my dad did. "I'll do it." Jonah glanced at the advancing darkness of Pakhet's spirit.

"Do you understand the nature of oaths to us?"

"Yes, I do." Jonah said, his fear growing as the darkness moved another block closer to his aunt's store.

"Very well." Death leaned closer. "Remember, you can't cheat Death." The being placed his cane on Jonah's right shoulder. "Do you swear to fully accept your destiny and do all in your power to correct the imbalance, even if it means sacrificing your own life in the future?"

Jonah gulped, finally understanding what Death meant about the oath. But he also experienced a moment of déjà vu. It was the line from his dream. This was the moment! He glanced below. The Darkness rolled down the next block, picking up speed. Jonah met Death's intense gaze and repeated the words from his dream. "Yes. I swear."

Thunder shook the floor as Death lifted the cane. "Then I will help you."

Before Jonah could ask what he planned to do, Death disappeared, leaving him behind. "Huh, hello? What about me?"

Jonah turned on the spot while below him, on the street, the cloud of darkness dissolved into multiple Wraiths, their bodies like thunderclouds and now only a few blocks from his aunt's store. Behind them loomed the larger evil of the goddess essence that wanted his body. Jonah was about to call out again when Death reappeared.

"It's done."

"What did you do?"

Death gave him a severe look. "I fulfilled my part of the bargain." He moved so fast, he seemed to phase before he stood right in front of Jonah. "Now, perform your duty, Deliverer." With that, he touched Jonah's forehead with two boney fingers and light flared around them.

The next second, Jonah stood in the Underworld version of the attic clubhouse. The Egyptian Wraith hurried over to him. "You've done it!"

Jonah nodded. "I have to get to my great-aunt's store. That's the way back to my body."

"Then do what you would in the mortal world. Phase." The Wraith reached out a hand to stop Jonah. "Remember that you can also shape this realm around you."

Jonah didn't understand but he didn't have time to figure it out. He pictured the street in his mind and phased. He reappeared on this realm's version of his aunt's side street, just outside her business. The cloud of angry Wraiths, Phantoms, and Felines rounded the corner and bore down on him.

CHAPTER FORTY-FIVE
THROUGH THE DOORWAY

Several regular Wraiths streaked toward Jonah as soon as he appeared. He raised his hands to defend himself when green fire shot overhead, effectively slamming into two of the gaseous beings. They screamed in agony as the flames consumed them. The others scattered, diving to either side. Jonah ducked and heard a brief swish before the solid thunk! of an arrow finding its mark. More death screams followed.

"Jonah! Get your butt in gear!" Lynn's strained voice came from behind him. He turned and his jaw dropped. Not only was Lynn's spirit here, clad in elf garb and holding gleaming Reaper blades, but Wick was also present, his glowing hands conjuring fire with ease. And Robert had also come. He held a bow in his hands and was firing off dozens of glowing arrows like a cool version of Legolas. Happily, Robert's spirit version of himself didn't have any broken fingers.

Behind the group stood Mike, his eyes ablaze, holding his hands aloft. Jonah wanted to shout for joy as Kevin and four Alliance Guards charged from the Deliverer's cave and into the Underworld. Mike had to use the Deliverer's seal to open a pathway to this location.

Of course, Jonah realized. *The designation stones!* He and Mike both noticed each location on the triptych had assigned codes. In the mortal world, each designation stone had six symbols etched into the surface. *Why wouldn't the same apply to the Underworld version of the stones?* Jonah thought as he searched the ground at his feet.

What he saw shocked him. Instead of a single designation stone, the individual symbols formed a huge circle. His Death Sense spiked, interrupting his moment of discovery, and alerting him that he had temporarily lost focus. Dodging to the side on instinct, he avoided the swipe of a sword from a Phantom that streamed right over his head.

The Egyptian's advice crystalized in his mind and he knew what to imagine. In a split second, he held two gleaming Reaper blades of his own. The weight of the familiar weapons reassured Jonah and he snapped into action, whirling and slicing as he backed toward his cousins and Wick.

"How did you guys get here?" Even as he shouted the question, the answer came to him instantly. *Death.*

Robert was skewering another Wraith with an arrow through its open mouth when he replied, "A strange guy dressed in all black showed up and said he could take us to you."

"Lynn didn't trust the dude," Wick said, nailing a Wraith of his own with green fire. "At least, she didn't until Kevin vouched for him."

"That's when Mike knew what to do and opened the portal to this place," Lynn answered, her blades never pausing for a second.

Jonah nodded toward the glowing, T-shaped door that led into this version of his great-aunt's store. He noticed the large, digital clock situated above the entrance and considered asking about it when the advancing vanguard of Pakhet reached the side street.

"We can handle this," Kevin announced. He blurred into motion and cut down a Phantom with two upward slices of his blades.

The Alliance Guards had spread out and were battling the undulating feline shapes that leapt at them from all sides. The guards' sizzling weapons flashed and slashed through the air as the men bravely fought. As valiant as they were, Jonah couldn't help but worry; for every creature they smacked down, it seemed two more charged in to replace it.

Wick turned and fired off a shot at the advancing darkness itself, which now rolled across the sky above them like an all-consuming storm cloud. But all that did was anger the goddess. Tendrils shot out in all directions, morphing into the forms of individual Phantoms as they swiftly approached.

Wick held his left wrist aloft, and a shield sprang up around him. The closest Phantoms collided with the barrier, howling in fury when they tumbled past. Others swooped in to hack away at the shield with their swords but thankfully, all failed to break through.

Meanwhile, Robert and Lynn were holding their own against the swarm of regular Wraiths charging down on them from the store roof. Jonah worried for Robert when he noticed his quiver only had one arrow left. But as soon as his cousin took that one, the quiver instantly refilled.

From Jonah's perspective, Wick seemed to be in the most peril. Minions of the goddess continually dived and battered the young mage's shield, besetting him from all sides. Jonah sprang forward into the thick of the assault and sliced away. Like angry wasps, the Phantoms turned and swarmed over him.

But Jonah anticipated their reaction and he phased all around the street, keeping the Phantoms frustrated. Plus, each time he reappeared, he'd take down another before phasing away again.

Kevin appeared beside him and they moved in sync with each other. Jonah could feel the older boy's presence for the split second he entered the aether, and he respectively adjusted. With Kevin instinctively doing the same, they became a blur of lethal blades that the Phantoms couldn't penetrate.

The distraction worked. Wick lowered his shield and attacked the Phantoms from behind. He fried at least four of them with green fire before they realized their imminent danger. When they tried to refocus, Kevin and Jonah moved in and overwhelmed them.

Freed to adjust his attack on the regular Wraiths, Wick combined a shield explosion and green fire to decimate most of the group that was hampering Lynn and Robert.

"Hah!" he shouted.

With the Alliance Guard holding back the Grim Hounds and Felines, the makeshift strategy seemed to be working well. At least, it was until a bellowing tendril of energy streaked down at Wick from behind. Colliding with him, it knocked him several feet down the street. The cloud spiraled up before diving for Robert and Lynn next.

The twins stood their ground. Robert shot several arrows straight into the cloud. Pakhet let out angry, disembodied screams of fury as each one hit its target. If a tendril drew close enough, Lynn sliced it and cut it with her Reaper's blades.

The goddess circled overhead, *giving up that plan*, Jonah thought. Then the cloudy substance hit the ground and solidified into feet, legs, a torso, and finally, the head.

Jonah stared in amazement at the giant, beautiful Egyptian goddess that stood at least thirty feet tall.

She wore a short, red-and-white skirt, cinched in the front with a golden ring and white fabric tie. Golden sandals adorned her feet and segmented, sleek, gold armor encased her legs. Armored bracelets covered her forearms and her fingers ended in long, lethal-looking nails. In her left hand was a short, curved, Egyptian khopesh sword, and with her right hand, she held a long staff with a curved handle featuring a cobra's head at the end.

Her face was Aunt Ruby's instead of that of a lioness. She wore a battle helmet with fringes that dropped down and barely managed to cover the tips of her exposed breasts.

"Whoa!" Robert gushed, his mouth hanging open. Sinking his bow even lower, he and every other guy stared in openmouthed awe at the goddess.

Lynn smacked her brother across the back of his head. "Get a grip, Robert!"

Robert gestured at the giantess's voluptuous chest. "But they're huge!"

"Must I remind you? You're ogling *your aunt!*"

The reality of the situation apparently dawned on Robert all at once because he responded with gagging sounds. "Agh! I'm gonna be blind for the rest of my life!"

Jonah noticed Kevin staring and elbowed him. "What are you looking at?"

Kevin smirked. "I'm not blind."

Jonah didn't think it helped that this representation of the goddess seemed to be striking a pose.

When Pakhet pointed her cobra scepter at Lynn, Jonah's cousin raised her enchanted shield instinctively and braced herself.

But Pakhet spoke in their aunt's voice. The power of it rolled across the scene. "You should serve me."

"No way!" Lynn shouted back.

Pakhet turned her eyes on Jonah next. "You're a child of my power. Serve me! Ignore your bargain with Death. I'll show you the true nature of the Deliverer's spirit. Together, we'll rule this mortal world."

"Sorry. But I can't help you." Jonah was proud that his voice sounded so calm and sure. He was also aware of the others giving him curious glances.

"Very well. Then prepare to die." She waved her hand and hordes of Phantoms instantly appeared both in front and behind Jonah and the others. Phantoms outnumbered them by a thousand to one. This was the main army, which she planned to rampage across the mortal world, starting with Mount Vernon.

Jonah's group backed up, moving toward each other, and forming a loose circle. They would fight as best they could, but Jonah couldn't figure out how to manage so many spirits on their own. As if in answer to his unspoken plea, a shiver ran down his spine and the Egyptian Wraith appeared beside him. The man nodded to Jonah as he pulled out two long, black poles with curved khopesh blades on both of the ends.

Lifting his eyes to Ruby's towering figure, he shook his head. In a flash, his ebony features transformed. The nose elongated into a snout with extensive, sharp teeth and his head also became longer and more angular. Jonah gaped at the man because his head soon changed into the black dog's head of Anubis.

Anubis raised his sword.

Around Jonah's group, more apparitions began to appear. All were women, clad in glistening, shining armor that barely covered their attractive bodies. Golden shield pieces were artfully wrapped around their forearms and lower legs and they all wore golden sandals. Long, thin, intricate braids fell to their shoulders. The most prominent weapons were the slender, sharp knives located at the end of the gauntlets they all wore.

Each one had glowing, narrowed eyes and they crouched, facing the Phantom army, ready to strike.

"Who are they?" Jonah asked in a quiet voice.

"The daughters of Pakhet, warriors who normally serve the goddess," Anubis answered.

Jonah found it odd to see the dog's mouth move as regular words tumbled out. He also noticed the Egyptian Wraith's normal cadence had taken on a barking, guttural quality.

"So they're on our side, right?" Jonah asked.

Anubis nodded. "They disapprove of the negative aspect of the goddess being used by the Wraith King and your aunt." He turned his snout toward Jonah. "Normally, the user of the amulet can choose or dictate which aspect of the goddess comes forth, be it positive or negative. But the Grim Reaper and Wraith King have used their powers to summon the huntress and they fuel her with a blinding rage."

Jonah's eyes widened because he recognized the larger meaning for himself. He could use the Deliverer spirit for good or evil too.

"Traitors!" Aunt Ruby yelled. She raised her armored right foot to stomp on Lynn and Robert.

Jonah's blades glowed brighter in his hands and he leapt to his cousins' defense. "Leave them alone!" He didn't bother to run but micro-phased right under the huge foot, scoring two deep gouges in the metal. He hoped he managed to penetrate into the flesh beneath.

The goddess wailed in agony and staggered back, giving Jonah a chance to plant himself between his cousins and the hostile being.

That's when he saw Wick, who was entirely cut off from help. Jonah ran for the goddess and phased on top of her left shoulder. Jabbing a blade at the ornamented collar she wore, he intended for it to be more of a distraction than any real attempt to cut her. The shock of the attack, however, caused the goddess to rear back and swing at him. Jonah had already phased to the street below. In a moment of unbridled fury, she pointed her huge scepter at him and fired. The blast took out half the structure beside this version of his great-aunt's store.

The explosion also acted as a signal, alerting the rest of Pakhet's Phantom army to commence their attack. But the warrior women moved like ghosts themselves. They shifted in and out of sight while also gathering in groups to help each member of Jonah's team. They sliced away at the enemy, racking up a heavy kill ratio in seconds.

Jonah dodged a second blast from the goddess and phased again. This time, he reappeared beside her left leg. He caught Kevin doing the same thing on the giantess's right. But Pakhet was quick. She swiped at them with her khopesh sword. Kevin used his blades to block, but the raw power of the goddess sent him tumbling along the street and right into a tree.

The blade caught Jonah's coat just before he phased away, causing his body to spin. That motion continued as he appeared on the other side of the street. He rolled into the wall, banging his head.

He couldn't focus long enough to move as Pakhet leveled the scepter at him and fired. But Wick dived in front of Jonah and activated a protective shield. The power of the shot pressed them both against the wall, but the shield held—for the moment.

"You have to do something," Wick said, his voice tightening with the effort to keep the shield in place.

"What? Change myself into a giant mummy or something?"

Wick gritted his teeth, strictly confining his attention to protecting them.

Around them, Pakhet's minions cornered the rest of their group. Eventually, she would stomp them to death, if nothing else. That's when he noticed the sparkling amulet she wore. Jonah stared down at the replica around his neck.

That was the connection! His mortal body still wore the actual amulet. He tapped Wick's shoulder. "As soon as I'm gone, help Lynn and Robert."

"Gone?"

"Just do it, Wick."

Jonah readied himself as the goddess prepared to fire on them again and shouted, "Now!" As soon as the shield disappeared with a popping sound, he charged forward, waving his arms as a distraction and trying to draw her aim. When the goddess shifted her weapon, Jonah phased.

He reappeared on her left arm and jammed his right blade into the hand holding the scepter. He didn't wait to see if she dropped the weapon, but ran up her arm and dove right for the amulet. Clutching his remaining blade with both hands, he plunged it into the outer metal of the amulet and mentally urged the weapon on, willing the metal to melt like butter so he could drive his blade further inside.

And he succeeded. A gaseous darkness swallowed him up instead of real flesh, blood, and innards, which would have ensued if the goddess had actually possessed a physical body. Around him, the substance that made up Pakhet convulsed into spasms. Jonah could also feel the vibrations from her continued stomping.

He hoped that Wick had time to raise a shield over his cousins; otherwise, this would have been for nothing. And it would also be futile if he didn't get moving with his hasty plan. Jonah curled himself into a ball and opened his Reaper self to the goddess.

"You want me? You got me."

As expected, once he connected to her soul, memories from her experiences through the ages flooded Jonah's mind. He protected his mortal self from the sudden surge by allowing his Reaper side to fully engage in the experiences. Like before, he surfed the memories without being affected or traumatized.

The goddess's essence reacted to his invasion by causing tendrils to coalesce around him, entangling and holding him in what she thought was a death grip. Jonah welcomed it, even wanted it. Only when he called on his power to vanquish her did the goddess realize her mistake.

But Jonah held on doggedly, refusing to let go. *No! you won't get away!* He summoned all the command he had, relishing the sureness of his Reaper heritage inside.

He also manipulated his long coat. It writhed and the ends shot outward, intertwining with the spirit's essence and grasping it tightly.

Pakhet's struggle intensified, trying to expel him, but Jonah's coat clung to her. That's when the cracks appeared. Memory after memory, going back for thousands of years, shattered like glass and immediately disintegrated. Pakhet screamed again.

Jonah concentrated and imagined his power rushing through the being. She may have been powerful and old, but he was the Deliverer, a spirit that was just as old and powerful. As the tendrils were extricated from his coat, the true amulet came into view, shining like a familiar beacon in the larger darkness.

With a thought, his blades activated and he used the Reaper's coat to propel himself forward, like a squid thrusts itself through the ocean. As he neared the glistening amulet, Jonah reared back before driving his blade straight into the heart of the jewel.

Fractures raced across the amulet and it shattered at the same time the blackness around Jonah also exploded into a million flaming fragments. That proved unfortunate because he found himself over thirty feet up in the air. Too stunned and weary to phase, Jonah plummeted toward the ground. Before he hit, however, Kevin appeared and caught him, phasing both of them safely to the street below.

The Fallen Reaper lowered him to his feet. Before Jonah could thank him, the goddess exploded with an outpouring of supernatural energy that rushed away from them in a shock wave.

"That was *wikid* cool," Wick whispered, plainly awed.

Jonah nodded his agreement, only now taking note that Robert, Lynn, and the four Alliance Guards had also survived.

The Phantoms ended their attacks at Pakhet's demise and now, they were all wailing in their final death throes. The women warriors waded into their midst and cut them down like saplings. Only the regular Wraiths remained behind.

Wick called, "I've been waiting all night to do this."

The staff in his hands glowed as Wick twirled it overhead and shouted in a perfect Gandalf-like voice, "You shall not pass!"

When he brought the staff down, a wave of forcible energy shot out, knocking all the regular Wraiths back and away. Broken and defeated, most scattered or disappeared.

Above them, the clouds still churned impatiently.

"You dissipated Pakhet's energy," the Egyptian observed, still in Anubis form. "But you must take care of the remnant still residing inside your aunt. Free the goddess from her control."

"He's right," Lynn agreed. "You need to get back and stop Ruby."

Kevin gripped Jonah's shoulder and pushed him toward the door. "Go. We'll cross over after you leave." He nodded with his chin.

Mike had already reopened the doorway to the Deliverer's cave. When a few remaining Wraiths zeroed in on him, Mike raised his hands and opened other doorways in the air, right in front of the spirits. That caused them to slip into other locations before they could reach him.

"Wow," Jonah said, clearly impressed.

In the lull of action, Kevin lifted him up. "Get going now, little man." Heaving Jonah through the glowing doorway, he swiftly shoved him back into his real body.

CHAPTER FORTY-SIX
WRAITH TO THE RESCUE

Jonah sucked in a ragged breath and opened his eyes. At once, he knew something was horribly wrong. Although he had returned to his physical body, he sensed he wasn't alone. Someone or something else pressed against his consciousness.

For a horrid moment, he feared the remnant of Pakhet had inhabited his body anyway. As he summoned his Reaper power to expel the invasive spirit, he heard the familiar voice of the Egyptian Wraith in his mind.

Calm yourself, young one. I will leave your body now.

And Anubis did, but it was unpleasant. Jonah's muscles locked, rendering him helpless as the Wraith streamed from his body. The most shocking part was when it exited through his mouth and eyes. The sensation was excruciating, causing Jonah to pity mortals who willingly opted for this.

As soon as the Wraith was free, all sensation and control returned. His body and rigidly contorted muscles relaxed even though he was still held fast to the slab by Ruby's spell.

His Aunt Ruby stumbled from her hiding place between the stone pillars. The Egyptian Wraith, now merely a tendril of billowing smoke with the Anubis head, snarled and attacked her, driving her back.

Then he changed directions and dived at Aunt Ruby's Wraith-possessed henchman. When the Wraith impacted the man, he disappeared inside the mortal's body, causing the man to collapse to the ground while bucking with spasms. Seconds later, both Wraiths emerged from the mortal's body and whirled around the site, locked in mortal battle.

They collided with the pillar that Antwan's cousin was chained to before barreling right over Jonah, causing him to shudder when they swept by.

Jonah glimpsed the enemy Wraith's true form. He was some kind of serpent, with a head that looked like a fabled dragon. Whenever the Wraith's reptilian body was visible in the vapor, Jonah could see it wrapping itself around the Anubis Wraith.

Several times, the battling Wraiths forced Ruby to duck as they smashed against the pillars. Jonah, who silently urged on his ancestor, thought the impacts were entirely random until the Wraiths whizzed by him again and hit a different pillar. The stone fractured and bits fell away, breaking the restrictive sigils Ruby had skillfully emblazoned on the surfaces.

Power surged into Jonah and he pulled himself free of Ruby's magical locks. With her own abilities diminished, Ruby let out a frustrated yell and charged him, clutching a knife in her hands. Jonah twisted just in time and the knife scraped against the stone. The tip broke and would have cut him in the back if not for his Reaper's coat.

He swung his left hand, catching Ruby in her chest. The woman only staggered a step before stopping. She was much stronger than he expected. Her enraged eyes changed to the bright orange of a lioness.

She held out her hand and produced one of the strange, purplish vortices. "Attack!" she shouted to the remaining Phantoms on this side. With that, she leapt through the vortex and disappeared.

Jonah rolled off the slab and prepared to fight, but the Phantoms disappeared instead of attacking him. To his surprise, the Felines and Grim Hounds also turned and bounded away at inhuman speed into the surrounding darkness.

Behind him, the reptilian Wraith expelled a death shriek as Anubis ripped out its ghostly throat. The enemy Wraith exploded into fragments, leaving a battered Anubis behind. The canine eyes met Jonah's before he nodded and disappeared.

Kevin, Lynn, Robert, and Wick arrived a moment later. Jonah turned to them, unable to hide his mounting fear. "They're going for the others."

Lynn's own face paled. "Dad!"

"What?" Robert asked.

"She hates him as much as Jonah and his mom."

Robert's jaw dropped. "We have to get there."

"A little help this time," Kevin said to Jonah. "Phase to the street in front of your house. Don't try the backyard."

Jonah nodded as he grabbed Wick's forearm and phased home.

*

"Oh, my God," Lynn exhaled as soon as they reappeared.

The reason for Kevin's orders became clear in an instant. The Hightowers' home was now a raging battlefront. Marcus, Rex, Eleanor, and Symon Trueblood were all outside on the front lawn, fighting off Phantoms, Felines, and Grim Hounds. Behind them, a dome of protection covered the entire house and backyard.

Inside that bubble of protection stood Anthony, Rico, Tamara, Danita, and Uncle James. The kids huddled together, gazing in shock at the combat going on all around them, while Uncle James stood with them.

Deyanira's Grim Hound fought alongside Marcus and the others, taking on any other Grim Hound that attacked. Marcus finally noted their arrival and motioned them closer.

Kevin and Lynn held their blades out and fended off anything that came their way. Overhead, a stream of Phantoms dive-bombed the shield, hitting it in one spot and sacrificing themselves to weaken it.

"Our barrier won't last much longer," Symon called out to Marcus. He waved his hands and conjured a huge, black bear that lumbered around, making the ground tremble like an earthquake as it took down random Felines and Grim Hounds.

His sister, Eleanor, had her wand out to conjure her fiery phoenix. The huge, flaming red bird soared into the air, emitting an ear-splitting screech. It intercepted the Phantoms, but many managed to make it through before they swooped down to plow into the shield.

"It's our aunt," Jonah told Marcus. "She still has power."

Despite Trueblood's phoenix, the Phantoms blasted a hole through the barrier, which caused the entire protective dome to collapse. A flash of purple vapor bloomed in the backyard as Aunt Ruby stepped through, right in front of Uncle James.

"No!" Lynn shouted. She grabbed Jonah's hand. He didn't need any explanation before he phased them.

Aunt Ruby raised her hand and fired a hex at her own brother. But Lynn was there in an instant, raising an enchanted shield. She knocked the hex away and brandished her blades at her aunt. "Stay away from my dad!"

"Yeah," Robert shouted. He joined his sister a second later with his bow and arrow in hand.

Jonah, Kevin, and the Alliance adults crowded around the kids to protect them as they fought off the dwindling numbers of Phantoms. The ghostly knights seemed more interested in preventing Jonah and the others from interfering. His group couldn't interfere anyway because their aunt had erected a protective barrier around herself, Lynn, Robert, and Uncle James.

Ruby cackled like a mad woman. "Watch your son and daughter perish just to save you, James!" She attacked her own niece and nephew. When Robert and Lynn rebuffed her, the tricky woman tried to hide her surprise by summoning her remaining power from the goddess's essence to slip in and out of the aether. Jonah's jaw dropped as his aunt used a technique similar to the one Kevin taught him.

But Robert and Lynn acted as one. Witnessing their coordination convinced Jonah, more than ever, that the twins communicated with each other without talking. Or maybe Robert shared his sister's intuition. As Ruby ducked and dodged, appearing at random around them, attempting to reach their dad, Robert and Lynn never failed to meet her either with a blade or bow.

"Whoa!" Wick said. "Who knew Robert had it in him?"

Ruby scored a hit to Lynn's shoulder and followed that up with a swipe of her hand. The enchanted shield soared away and landed off to the side. Ruby shoved her niece away. Robert faltered for a second over his sister's condition.

Recovering quickly, Robert whirled around to face Ruby each time she appeared in a different location. Even with Lynn down, he seemed even more capable of tracking their aunt and protecting his dad. He pulled back on his bow, ready to let an arrow fly when the mole appeared inside the barrier.

The Alliance traitor moved in a blur and knocked Robert's arrow aside before it could hit Ruby. The traitor continued his movement, grabbing Robert's right arm and deftly slicing off his hand with a Reaper's blade.

Everyone screamed at the same time and rushed forward. The mole threw down some shiny objects. They sparked and a barrier sprang up around him, Ruby, and Jonah's cousins. It meshed with and fortified the shield Jonah's aunt had already erected.

Inside, Robert's shock displaced his own ability to make any sound as he dropped to his knees beside his sister. The mole yanked the bow free and broke it in two. He gripped Robert by the afro, pulling his head back and exposing his neck. Jonah's cousin cried out in pain while cradling the bloody stump where his hand had formerly been.

Ruby raised her hands, ready to hex her own brother, when the mole shouted at her.

"We don't have time for revenge. Do it now and let's get out of here!"

Marcus and the other Alliance adults attacked the mole's barrier with everything they had, but it stubbornly held.

The shocking turn of events stunned Jonah, as did the fear at having to watch his cousins and uncle die in front of his eyes. But he was wrong. They all were wrong.

Ruby whirled in his direction and her magical power spiked, something he didn't think she could accomplish. Before Jonah could move away from the barrier, she hurled a hex that penetrated the shield and hit him squarely in the chest.

Marcus screamed his name, but the hex had already engulfed his body. The pain was unbelievable but thankfully, only lasted seconds.

One moment, he cried out; and the next, he was high above the scene, looking down on his physical body as it dropped to the ground, spread-eagled. A large, dark stain marred his chest.

Kevin reached his side first and dropped to his knees, cradling the limp body. Marcus whirled to attack the mole but the traitor and Aunt Ruby had already fled the scene.

Ruby killed him! Jonah screamed for someone to spot him floating above. *Mike! Marcus! Kevin!* But no one heard him.

That realization accompanied a sudden lurch before he spiraled downward into total darkness, screaming for help that would never come. He was dead, and his soul was hastily being sucked into the Underworld.

CHAPTER FORTY-SEVEN
SEER'S BLOOD

Jonah was alone, in total darkness, and terrified. He called for help until his voice was hoarse from the effort. "Mike, hear me!" he tried one, last time. "You're my Pathmaker!"

Nothing except absolute, nerve-wracking silence. He huddled on his knees, his entire body shaking with sobs and complete incredulity over what had happened. His aunt had been the one to kill him! It wasn't supposed to happen that way.

He would never see his friend, Mike, again. He could never argue and poke fun at his cousins. The memory of Robert losing his hand made him feel even worse. And he didn't even know if Lynn were still alive.

Marcus was gone, and Kevin could never hold him again. Jonah swiftly descended into total despair. Is this what Death meant by that promise? Had he been tricked? He didn't know how long he remained huddled and sobbing, consumed by the horror of being alone for all eternity.

A quiet voice punctuated the silence, calling his name. Jonah ignored it. When he heard the voice again, he thought it was a trick concocted by his addled mind until the Egyptian Wraith's voice spoke again, only much stronger.

"Young Blackstone? Are you all right?"

Jonah raised his head and wiped his eyes. Slowly at first, the attic clubhouse materialized around him. The Egyptian Wraith stood nearby with a worried look on his noble face. But that didn't abate Jonah's fears. "Is this Hell? Am I doomed to repeat the same thing over and over forever, and always return here?"

"First of all, it's the Underworld, not Hell." The Wraith arched an eyebrow. "That's a fiction produced by the Grand Oracle and Grim—"

"Why're you here and not Anubis?"

The Wraith was shocked. "How do you know about that?"

Jonah thought the Wraith was joking with him. "What do you mean? You changed into Anubis when we fought Pakhet. I went back and stopped her but… but… my cousin… my aunt killed me," Jonah finally said. "And I came here to the Underworld."

A mixture of emotions played across the Wraith's face before settling on unmasked awe. He darted forward. "You've seen the future. What happened?"

Jonah stared at the Egyptian in disbelief. How could he see the future? "I… I died. My aunt killed me."

The Wraith drew back. "That's a possibility that hasn't happened yet."

"I don't understand," Jonah shot back while rising to his feet. "I lived through it all. It was real!"

"I warned you, this realm can do strange things," the Wraith insisted. "And your power could have made it possible to view the future as if it had already happened."

For the first time, Jonah's abysmal shock and despair began to recede. "You mean it really was a vision?"

"Have you ever experienced a vision before?"

Jonah thought back and nodded. "Yeah. I had one of Pakhet using my body to destroy Mount Vernon and all my friends and family. That was a nightmare. This was… real."

"Of course it felt that way. You made it real."

"So, it won't happen?" When the Wraith didn't answer at once, Jonah's fear returned but he wouldn't give in. "I'm gonna stop it from happening."

"It's difficult to alter what you've already seen. Most often, the very actions you take become the ones that combine to ensure the future you saw."

Jonah shook his head. "You said it was just a possibility. Now you're saying it's gonna happen? Make up your mind!"

"I'm sorry. The future is always fluid."

But Jonah was thinking from another angle about what he experienced. It wasn't just a vision about the final fight. He also saw everything that led up to it. He pointed at the Wraith. "Look at me now. In the vision, you knew that I'd recovered the memories. My Reaper side did it." Jonah spread his hands. "Well? Did I do it or not?"

The Wraith narrowed his eyes. A second later, he said, "You have."

Jonah nodded. "I need to stop what happened next, and I will."

"How?"

"I know where to start. The Underworld version of my aunt's store is the doorway to my body."

"If what you say is accurate, then you must do what you would do…"

"…in the mortal world. I know. I have to phase there," Jonah finished. He lifted his chin. "Let's go, and bring your swords."

*

Several regular Wraiths streaked toward Jonah and the Egyptian Wraith as soon as they appeared outside the Underworld version of his great-aunt's store. He raised his hands and imagined two flaming Reaper blades like he did the last time, instantly conjuring a pair.

"How did you…?" the Egyptian Wraith asked, even as he brandished his swords. "Oh, of course."

They proceeded to defend themselves. All the while, Pakhet and her army drew closer.

"I need to pass through the doorway and stop my aunt."

"What about Pakhet's essence?"

Jonah dodged a Wraith but another immediately appeared, blocking his way. "I fought her. You said I dissipated her essence."

"Then you must do the same thing again." He sliced a Wraith in two and the ghost screamed as it flared before it died. "To go over now would be useless. Your aunt would draw a steady power stream from Pakhet."

Jonah's frustration mounted. He wanted to get straight to his aunt so he could end this. If things went the normal way, Robert and Lynn would suffer. As he thought about that, green fire shot overhead, slamming hard into two of the gaseous Wraiths. They screamed in agony as the flames consumed them.

A welcome swish and the thunk! of Robert's arrow finding its mark came next.

"Jonah!" Lynn arrived still clad in the elf garb. She was holding her gleaming Reaper blades. Wick was there too, conjuring fire, and Robert held his bow in his hands, firing off glowing arrows.

Behind them stood Mike, his eyes ablaze and his hands held aloft as Kevin and four Alliance Guards charged from the Deliverer's cave. Just like before.

Jonah took command and called out to the Guard Captain, "Put one of your people with Robert, Lynn, and Wick. You're with me and Kevin."

"Jonah?" Kevin asked.

The Guard Captain snapped into motion, arranging his people. That done, Jonah said to Wick, "Watch your back."

Just then, the bellowing dark cloud that was actually Pakhet streaked overhead. When she dived at Jonah's friends, they held her off now that they were better coordinated and expecting her.

Pakhet circled overhead, giving up that plan. The cloudy substance hit the ground and solidified into feet, legs, a torso, and finally, the head. She was a gigantic, beautiful

Egyptian goddess, at least thirty feet tall, fully clad in protective armor.

"Don't forget that's our aunt, Robert. No gawking," Jonah taunted his cousin.

"What…? I…" Robert sputtered and his face reddened.

"That goes for you too," Jonah said to Kevin as he elbowed him. He raised his face to look Pakhet in the eyes. Even as she lifted her huge sword, Jonah called out, "Lynn's not gonna join you and neither am I, so kill the speech, Auntie."

Pakhet glared down at him. "Insolent."

"Yeah, my godfather hates that about me."

"Very well. Prepare to die." She waved her hand and hordes of Phantoms appeared both in front and behind Jonah and the others. They were outnumbered by a thousand to one, just like before.

But Jonah stood tall, although his friends and family shifted nervously. "Don't worry," he told them. "We have help."

"I like your spirit, son, but these are bad odds," the Alliance Guard Captain said.

Jonah ignored the comment and turned on the Egyptian Wraith. "I need Anubis and the daughters of Pakhet. Now!"

The Wraith arched an eyebrow but didn't bother to ask any questions.

He lifted his eyes to Ruby's towering figure and shook his head. In a flash, his ebony features transformed into a black dog's head.

Anubis raised his right hand and sword while, around Jonah's team, a new group of apparitions appeared. All were women in glistening, golden armor, and they crouched, fully poised to strike the Phantom army.

"Protect my friends and family," Jonah ordered the women. Then, not waiting for Pakhet to smash them all, he yelled, "Attack!"

The women warriors and the Alliance Guards snapped into action, so swiftly that Pakhet's army was caught entirely off guard. *Good*, Jonah thought. He needed that surprise to last a moment longer.

Phasing atop Pakhet's shoulder, now that he knew what to do, he dived right for the amulet. He willed the metal of the amulet to melt like butter under his blades so he could plunge his weapon inside.

As soon as he did, Jonah curled into a ball and opened his Reaper self to the goddess. "You want me? You got me."

The goddess's essence reacted to his invasion and her tendrils flowed around him, entangling him. Jonah responded by manipulating his coat to do the same. The garment intertwined with the spirit's essence and held fast.

With the knowledge of what happened before, Jonah called on his power to vanquish the goddess. He waited for the reaction, and sure enough, the tendrils released his coat and in the process, revealed the true amulet. Once that happened, he used his Reaper's coat to propel himself forward, reared back with his right arm, and jabbed his blade into the very heart of the jewel.

Cracks and fractures raced across the amulet before it shattered. The blackness around Jonah also exploded into a million flaming fragments. Prepared this time, he phased to the street below as the giant body began to dissolve with the outpouring of disseminated energy. The last bits of the powerful goddess essence rushed away from them in a shock wave.

Like before, the Phantoms broke off their attacks and wailed their final death throes as the women warriors cut them down.

"That was wikid cool, Padawan," Wick whispered, still visibly awed.

"I know," Jonah agreed. He pointed at the regular Wraiths that remained behind. "Now do your Gandalf move."

After giving Jonah a puzzled look, Wick twirled his glowing staff overhead and shouted in a perfect Gandalf impersonation, "You shall not pass!"

When he brought the staff down, a wave of energy and powerful force shot out, knocking all the Wraiths back and away.

Jonah turned to Kevin. "I need to get through the door to deal with Ruby. You leave after I'm gone."

"Wait!" Kevin called out.

"Come on, Anubis." Jonah motioned to the Egyptian Wraith. With that, he ran for the door and dived through.

*

Happily returned to his physical body, Jonah didn't resist this time when Anubis left him but attacked his aunt and the other Wraith. While they fought, Jonah tried to think of a way to change what would happen. He managed to take down Pakhet's essence in the Underworld, but he still had to stop the events from occurring at his house–or at least, alter them.

Anubis broke the final restrictive sigil and a flood of renewed power surged into Jonah. He pulled himself free of Ruby's magical locks and went through a kind of strange replay as he combated his aunt. He was acting strictly on auto-pilot now.

Eventually, she held out her hand and produced one of the strange, purplish vortices. "Attack!" she shouted to the remaining Phantoms on this side. With that, she leapt through the vortex and disappeared.

Once again, the Phantoms vanished instead of attacking him, and the Felines and Grim Hounds bounded away at inhuman speed before fading into the surrounding forest.

Just then, the reptilian Wraith let out a death shriek and Anubis ripped out its ghostly throat. The enemy Wraith exploded into fragments, leaving a battered Anubis behind. The canine eyes met Jonah's, who nodded and promptly disappeared.

Jonah was ready when Kevin, Lynn, Robert, and Wick showed up. He told them, "Aunt Ruby's going for Uncle James and the others."

"A little help this time?" Kevin said to him.

"Yeah, I know: Phase to the street in front of my house. Don't even try the backyard."

Kevin shook his head.

Jonah was about to grab Wick's forearm when he noticed Antwan's cousin was still chained to a pillar. With the sigils gone, she should have gotten her powers back, unless the chains themselves were enchanted. He hadn't paid attention to the girl the last time. Now, he saw a way to do something different.

"Give me your blade," he told Kevin, the plan only now forming in his head. They deliberately left her chained, but if he could free her and convince her to stop the mole, maybe that would be enough to alter the final outcome.

Kevin scowled but handed over a blade. Jonah rushed to the girl and cut her chains with two swipes of the weapon. Like throwing a switch, she leapt to her feet, hands raised and ready to hex.

Jonah held up the blade to protect himself. Wick, Lynn, and Kevin were at his side in an instant, ready to back him up.

"Cool it," Jonah told the girl. "Can you get to the mole?"

She smirked. "I'm not telling you."

"I didn't ask you to. Tell him what Ruby did."

The girl lowered her hands a fraction. The frown on the visible portion of her face told it all. "Why do you want me to do that?"

"Because we both have a problem with my aunt. I'm guessing the mole does too." At the last moment, Jonah remembered someone else who wouldn't have approved of Aunt Ruby's betrayal. "And Deyanira won't like it either. She sent me her Grim Hound, after all."

The girl stared at him for a long time. Too long in Jonah's opinion because they needed to get home. Finally, she nodded. "One day, we'll have you on our side."

With that, she produced a vortex and stepped through.

"Why'd you let her go?" Wick asked, pointing toward the spot where the girl once stood.

"I had to. It's the only way to change things."

Kevin frowned at him. "Change what?"

Jonah met Lynn's gaze, but didn't answer. Instead, he gripped Wick's arm and phased home.

CHAPTER FORTY-EIGHT

HOME FRONT

Before they could even arrive, Ruby's Phantoms had already breached the Alliance's ward around the Hightower house.

"No!" Lynn shouted. She grabbed Jonah's hand and he phased them into the backyard.

To make up for lost time, Jonah reappeared right in front of Uncle James. Lynn raised the enchanted shield to block Ruby's hex. Then she brandished her blades at her aunt. "Stay away from my dad!"

"Yeah!" Robert shouted, joining his sister a second later with his bow and arrow in hand.

Jonah moved back with Kevin as the Alliance adults crowded around the kids to protect them as well as to fight off the dwindling numbers of Phantoms.

Like before, the ghostly knights seemed more interested in keeping Jonah and the others from interfering, and he knew why.

Jonah stayed clear as the familiar events played themselves out again. If the mole appeared, he had to be ready.

Ruby ducked and dodged, appearing at random around the twins, attempting to reach their dad. Robert and Lynn met her either with a blade or a bow.

"Whoa!" Wick said. "Who knew Robert had it in him?"

Ruby scored a hit to Lynn's left arm and followed up with a swipe of her hand. The enchanted shield soared off and landed on the side. Ruby shoved her niece out of the way, causing Robert to falter for a second.

But he recovered, whirling to face Ruby and forcing her to evade once more as he protected his dad. Jonah's insides squirmed. It was right about now that the mole should have appeared to change the course of things. As the seconds ticked by and the traitor still hadn't arrived, Jonah knew his plan had succeeded.

Because he was thinking about that, he failed to notice that Ruby also realized something was off. She pulled away from Robert and turned toward Jonah. That's when Jonah understood how stupid he'd been. Whether or not the mole showed up, Ruby still had every intention of killing him since she couldn't use him. He was not out of danger yet.

As his Death Sense spiked, Jonah dived for the shield and came up with it at the same time his aunt fired. The enchanted shield repelled her attack, but it still managed to stagger him. His swift tactic, however, shocked and distracted her. She was so focused on him that she ignored Robert who bared his teeth and narrowed his eyes. He released his arrow and it flew straight and true, hitting Ruby directly in the chest.

The shock on her face as she clutched the protruding arrow was priceless.

"How dare you shoot me?"

"You're lucky. I was aiming for your version of a heart," Robert spat out.

"Ungrateful…" She never finished her words because she crumbled to the ground.

The remaining Phantoms let out anguished cries. Jonah opened the rip between the realms and quickly dispatched all the Phantoms back to the Underworld.

The frightened looks his friends gave him would have stopped Jonah any other time. But he pushed that aside. He hurried over to Lynn, who, with the help of Robert and her dad, was sitting up and trying to shake off the negative effects of Ruby's hex.

Jonah shifted his attention to his aunt. Pressing his hand against her forehead, he summoned his Reaper power and felt it surging through him as the appropriate words popped into his head. "You are released from your bond. Come out!" he commanded.

His voice shook the ground, startling everyone. The goddess essence obeyed and withdrew from his aunt. Even in her pain, Ruby struggled and her grasping hands strained to hold onto the essence, as if she wanted to draw it back into her body.

The woman's feeble attempts disgusted Jonah. In the end, however, she was too weak and limply slumped to the ground, unconscious.

The goddess essence, now free of his aunt's evil influence, transformed back into its natural form: A regal female with large, expressive, dark eyes. Judging from the muttered comments he heard around him, Jonah suspected everyone else could also see her true form.

The goddess peered into his face, looking deeply into his soul. "Well played, Deliverer."

Her gaze shifted to something over his shoulder and she bowed.

Jonah turned to find the Egyptian Wraith floating there. His fight with the reptilian Wraith left his ghostly garments ripped. But he returned the nod with a regal bow of his own.

The women warriors soon joined the entire gathering and ministered to their goddess.

Jonah watched, relieved at the demonstrative change in Pakhet's demeanor. The Egyptian Wraith must have sensed his thoughts because the being stepped closer and spoke to him in a quiet voice.

You wonder at her change, young one?

"Yeah," Jonah admitted. "I mean, you told me every spirit of power has a negative and positive aspect."

The Wraith blinked in surprise. *Yes, that's correct.*

"And the Grim Reaper and the Wraith King brought out her negative aspect."

Again, correct. He gestured at Ruby. *Your aunt was a willing vessel to them. But once you freed Pakhet…*

"She reverted back." Jonah's eyes widened.

The goddess isn't just the huntress. She also bestows fertility, as well as other kind blessings. He peered at Jonah. *Power is always neutral. It's how you use it, whether for good or evil, that reveals what resides in your own heart. Understand?*

Jonah did now. He had inadvertently allowed his anger over Latrell's suicide to turn him into a bully. He winced at the memory and checked to make sure Marcus wasn't listening. "Have you been talking to my godfather?" Jonah grinned at the Wraith's perplexed look.

Pakhet's form began to glow, drawing their attention. "Come, sisters." She raised her arms and, along with her warrior women, disappeared in a flash of light.

After a stunned moment of silence, Marcus gestured to Rex. "Get Ruby to the healer. Fast."

Rex complied, picking up Aunt Ruby's limp body and phasing away.

"Don't help her!" Robert screamed. His voice sounded raw with anger.

Symon Trueblood gripped his arm. "You don't mean that, Robert. She's your aunt and you won't want her death on your conscience."

Robert stared at the mage in defiance.

"He's right," Jonah agreed, entering the argument. "The Wraith inside her drove her crazy. It was only following orders to do it. I saw it all in a dream-walk."

"Jonah, she was already evil," Lynn countered. She was on her feet but a little unsteady. Rico held on to her.

"I know that, but..." Jonah couldn't believe he was defending his aunt, the woman who had tortured him seven years ago and tried to kill him just now.

He was glad when Uncle James stepped forward. "Lynn," he said, placing his hands on her shoulders, "no one can be pure evil and good at the same time."

"It's the Grim Reaper's fault." Jonah's voice had risen. "He's behind all of this."

His uncle nodded and pulled Robert and Lynn into a tight hug. Jonah hesitated until Uncle James grabbed his arm and pulled him into the hug too.

"Thank God you're all right," he said in a voice choked with emotion.

When he released them, Lynn nodded to her father with a knowing look on her face. "This is why you talked Mom into visiting her friend in Savannah."

Uncle James smiled. "You're not the only one with uncanny ability." His smile faltered when he met Symon's gaze. Lynn whispered something to her dad. He nodded before walking over and offering to shake the mage's hand. "Thank you for protecting my family."

Symon grinned. "That's just part of the job."

Jonah whispered to Lynn, "What did you say to him?"

"It's a secret." She glanced sideways at him. "I knew you'd fix things."

Jonah gaped at his cousin. "You knew?"

Lynn refused to answer. Instead, she held out a hand to Rico and he came over and wrapped his arms around her.

Jonah realized his cousin had seen everything that night she held his hands. That's why she got so spooked. Yet, she still trusted him to figure it out. That thought sobered him.

While Jonah slowly registered the idea, the other kids rushed forward to surround them. Tamara was already hugging Wick and talking in hushed, urgent tones with him.

Anthony patted Robert on the back, congratulating him, while Danita rushed to Lynn's side. "That was so amazing! I never saw anything like that." She took the shield and turned it over in her hands.

Mike tapped Jonah's shoulder and leaned close. "I told you."

Jonah whispered to his friend, "You told me what?"

In answer, Mike nodded at Danita, Anthony, Rico, and Tamara.

Jonah noted the other kids revealed their nervousness by a slight shakiness to their voices, or the not-so-hidden trembling of their hands. But they were excited rather than terrified.

He got it. Mike insisted the other kids joined his Tolerance Club because they liked or admired him. And Rico already knew Lynn had abilities. No doubt the others had followed Rico here, into the danger, instead of running home.

"Maybe," Mike whispered. "It's time for the Mount Vernon Social Club to expand its membership."

By now, Rico had already extricated Lynn from the Danita fan club and they walked a little way off, leaving Wick to answer questions.

Robert watched his sister walk away, smirked, and said, "I bet Rico's trying to talk Lynn into wearing one of those warriors' outfits next Halloween."

Jonah would have laughed if not for Uncle James looming behind them, frowning. "That's not gonna happen. Your mom would kill all of us." He clapped Robert on the shoulder. "Not bad with the bow and arrow."

"Thanks." Robert grinned as he clutched the bow.

Uncle James tapped his son's right fist. "Do I want to know how you healed so fast?"

"Not really," Robert said.

"Well, in that case, I think you should wear the brace a little longer." Uncle James raised his hand to stop Robert from objecting. "At least two more weeks. We don't want people asking questions."

"But that'll suck!"

Uncle James squared his shoulders, looking stern.

Robert's shoulders slumped. "Yes, sir."

Jonah was about to tell his cousin of all the times his own mom made him wear bandages long after his bumps and cuts had healed. The intense curiosity of the other kids forced Jonah to reconsider mentioning that aspect of his abilities.

Robert must have sensed his thoughts because he whispered, "The guy in black fixed my hand so I could help out."

Jonah's eyes widened when he heard that. Death said he had helped, but at the time, Jonah had no clue what the strange being might have done. That only reminded Jonah of his oath to Death, something he didn't want to think about at the moment.

"What are they doing?" Danita asked, pointing at the Trueblood siblings.

The mages walked in a circle around the scene, waving their hands all around. For a moment, their spells undulated in the air, moving away from them and toward the surrounding neighboring houses.

"We're strengthening the deflection charms to keep prying eyes away," Symon explained after joining the group. "They should last until we clean up this mess."

"Still, I think we should move inside," Marcus suggested, motioning everyone toward the house.

Kevin and Jonah stood back, observing the activity.

Jonah wondered what would happen to his friends. "Memory charms?"

Kevin shrugged. "Most likely, unless they agree not to talk."

Even though Jonah had argued for Danita being given a chance, he never thought about this aspect of it. "Would the Alliance trust them?"

"They'd have to take an oath just in–" Kevin jerked and swore under his breath because the Grim Hound trotted over and licked his hand.

Jonah laughed and petted the beast. It nuzzled against him. "Thanks for protecting my friends and family." The Grim Hound bobbed its head. Then it looked away as if someone called it. Jonah understood. "You're gonna report to her, aren't you?" Again, it bobbed its head and made a strange, growling sound. This close, Jonah could feel and hear the subtle rhythm, and nature of the growl. It was a language.

He closed his eyes as the Grim Hound repeated the modulated growl. The vibrations stimulated his mind and slowly formed a mental image. In a moment of clarity, Jonah extended his hand and opened the rip to the Underworld.

The Grim Hound took a playful nip at his hand before it turned and leapt through the opening.

*

Marcus, Eleanor, and Symon had all the young people gathered together in the family room. The Guard Captain was the only one of his team to enter the house and he took up serious space. Uncle James provided people with something to drink, but everyone was restless and no one seemed thirsty.

Lynn and Robert excused themselves and headed to their rooms to change. Wick had yanked off his hat and wig before he sat with Tamara, who looked intensely interested in what Marcus would say.

Danita and Anthony clung to each other, looking scared and uncertain despite Mike whispering reassurances to them.

Rico leaned against the mantel, arms crossed and trying to look brave, but not succeeding.

Jonah stood in the kitchen because whenever someone looked at him, he saw the questions in their gaze. He thought Robert and Lynn had the right idea and headed for his own room.

Marcus stopped Jonah in the hallway and whispered, "Trueblood told me of your impassioned plea for a change of policy. So we'll talk to each person and offer them an option." He searched Jonah's expression. "That is what you wanted?"

"Yeah, it is. Thank you."

"You're welcome." Marcus straightened and scanned the quiet crowd of kids waiting for him. "Are you going to stay?"

Jonah glanced at his dirty, long coat. "No." While Marcus stepped back into the den to begin his comments, Jonah retreated to his room. He was about to close the door when Kevin slipped inside and closed it for him.

He had already taken off his long coat so he waited for Jonah to slip out of his own. Then Kevin wrapped his arms around Jonah's waist and hugged him for a long time, rocking him back and forth. They listened to the low voices coming from the den and didn't care at the moment.

Jonah welcomed the embrace, settling into it, along with his general sense of safety and closeness whenever he was with Kevin. Without warning, he began to shake as he came to terms with everything they managed to accomplish. It seemed impossible, but they were all still here and safe, for now.

Kevin rubbed Jonah's arms until he stopped shaking. The Fallen Reaper's higher body temperature enveloped Jonah, and he loved it. While they embraced, Kevin used his enhanced hearing to relay what Marcus said to the others. The kids weren't told everything, just enough for them to decide which way they should go.

Jonah knew there would be a lot of questions in the coming days if his friends chose the oath and not the

Memory Charm. After a long moment, Jonah leaned back and glanced into Kevin's eyes. The older boy looked down before brushing his lips against Jonah's. Just as they kissed, a knock came at the bedroom door. They released each other, though neither wanted to do so.

"Yeah?" Jonah called out.

Mike opened the door and peeked inside the room. Jonah saw someone moving past his buddy in the background and heard the sounds of people leaving the house.

"Sorry," Mike said as he closed the door behind him. "I didn't mean to interrupt."

Kevin waved off the apology. "I guess Marcus is finished?"

Mike nodded and his eyes sparkled with excitement. "Everyone's gonna take an oath instead of the Memory Charm."

Jonah pumped his hand in the air.

"Then I'll have to go." Kevin released a long breath. "We have a lot of cleanup work to finish before the morning." He gave Jonah a quick hug before leaving the room.

Mike looked stricken. "I'm really sorry." He sat on the edge of Jonah's bed.

"It's cool," Jonah assured him, pulling off his sweaty shirt. "What's up?"

"Two things. Are you gonna ask Danita and the others to join the club?"

The question caught Jonah off guard. "Well, not tonight."

"I know that. But they'll have a lot of questions for you."

"We'll deal with that later." Mike gave him a frosty look and Jonah added, "I promise," before he could stop himself. Right on cue, goosebumps raced up his arm. "Dang it."

Mike grinned while his eyes flashed, indicating a sealed promise. "That takes care of that."

Jonah eyed his friend, wondering if Mike had bluffed him into making the promise. "What's number two?" he asked.

"Oh, I wanted to know if I could sleep over here tonight."

Jonah paused after tossing his shirt in his dirty clothes bin. "Why? You afraid to stay at home alone?"

"No." Mike frowned. "All the action's here."

Jonah couldn't disagree with that. And it would be nice for a sleepover. "Yeah." He took a fresh shirt out of his drawer and pulled it on. "What about your parents?"

"I called them." Mike glanced at the door. "After okaying it with your uncle, they agreed. My mom's bringing over some clothes and other stuff for me."

The front doorbell rang right on cue. Jonah stepped out of his room just as Uncle James answered. After talking with Mike's mom, he closed the door and held up a small gym bag. "This is for Mike."

Mike ducked into the hallway and took the bag. "Thanks."

Uncle James proceeded into the family room and started picking up cups and stacking them in the dishwasher. He noticed Jonah standing at the entrance. "You and Mike okay?"

"Yes, sir."

"Well, if you use any dishes, put them in the dishwasher when you're done. I'll run the load in the morning." With that, he patted Jonah on the shoulder and headed off to his own room.

Jonah glanced at Robert and Lynn's closed doors and decided they must have turned in for the night. He fetched two juices for himself and Mike, who was stretched out on the bed and patting the empty space beside him.

Jonah obliged. They were both skinny but still pressed tightly together on the small bed.

Mike poked him in the side. "You need a bigger bed. Aren't you afraid Kevin will tumble off?"

Jonah flashed him a scandalized expression and shoved him back. But they settled down, side-by-side. Jonah turned on some music to help cover their voices and Mike rested his head on Jonah's shoulder as they talked about everything.

It was wonderful for Jonah, talking with his best friend again. Sometime later, Mike went silent before Jonah heard his buddy's soft snore. He slumped down into a more comfortable position, being careful not to awaken Mike.

After propping up a pillow, he leaned back and closed his eyes, falling quickly into a sound and dreamless sleep.

CHAPTER FORTY-NINE
THE DARK AVENGER RIDES AGAIN

Jonah and his cousins didn't have the luxury of sleeping in late the next day because of school. He at least got to enjoy the change of pace with Mike sitting at the kitchen table, eating breakfast and talking with them.

Once at school, Jonah was surprisingly alert as he and Mike walked through the halls. The activity of ninth grade seemed way too normal compared to what they had gone through the night before. Jonah, however, welcomed the normal and wanted to put some distance between himself and all the things he had discovered. He would never forget a bit of it, but that didn't mean he had to dwell on them either.

Perhaps Mike thought the same thing because he distracted Jonah by doing the Human Lie Detector gag again. This time, Jonah actually had fun. It also helped that the person in front of him today was telling the truth, a rare but welcomed change. There had been enough lies, secrets, and half-truths to last him a lifetime.

"That went well," Mike said as he threw away their lunch trays and gathered his things.

"Yeah, it did."

Mike paused, regarding him. "You aren't mad at me about the Human Lie Detector?"

"Nope. It took my mind off what happened."

Mike stopped fidgeting with his book bag and sat down. "Jonah, do you remember all those memories from the… Wraith?" Mike glanced around, but no one paid any attention to them.

"Yeah, I do."

"That's horrible."

Jonah shrugged. "Yes and no. Since they weren't my memories, I can treat them like scary movies I've seen. I remember them, sure, but they don't bother me as much. You know what I mean?"

Mike frowned. "I guess so. But what about your aunt and what she did seven years ago?"

"At least, now I know what happened. That's a good thing. I don't have to wonder about it anymore." He smiled at his buddy and gathered his book bag. "Seriously. It's cool." Jonah leaned closer and whispered, "My Reaper side can handle a lot."

He laughed at Mike's expression as they walked to the next class.

*

Jonah and Mike had their regular monitor duty that afternoon. Even before they arrived on post, they heard the laughter and catcalls. Above it all, Jonah recognized Brandon's snide voice.

They rounded the corner and found the boy and a few of his buddies. In the center of the group was a girl. Jonah recognized her as Heather, someone who once considered joining his club.

Mike also recognized her and let out a grunt of disbelief. He marched up to the boys just as Brandon pushed Heather.

"She's kissed more girls than you, Wayne," the bully taunted while tweaking Heather's long, single black braid.

Heather's eyes narrowed in anger as she clutched her books to her chest, trying to break through the hostile ring. Mike came to her rescue and shoved his way between the bigger boys, acting braver than Jonah expected.

"Back off, jerks."

Jonah joined him. "That's right."

"We were just talking, weren't we, Heather?" Brandon winked at the girl.

Jonah shoved one of the guys out of the way so Heather could leave. She sniffled as she hurried down the hall and out of sight.

Brandon and his buddies sneered at her.

Mike faced Brandon. "You know bullying isn't allowed."

"Whatever. Come on, guys," Brandon said. He looked straight at Jonah and mimed smoking a cigarette before walking off.

Mike huffed. "He's getting worse."

"I know," Jonah said, watching Brandon swagger down the hallway with his friends. "Hey, I'll catch up with you after class."

Mike gave him a searching look before shrugging as he left. Jonah waited a second and then turned in the opposite direction. If he hurried, he could still make it.

He burst into the nearest bathroom, aiming for the farthest stall, slamming the door, and locking it. Jonah took a deep breath and thought about the shaded spot next to his backyard shed. In a second, he'd left the bathroom stall behind and was standing beside the tree in his relatives' backyard.

Jonah hustled into the house and went into his bedroom, where he threw open the closet doors. His heart pounded in his chest from all the apprehension. He had already promised not to do the vigilante thing again. But as he pulled out the paper shopping bag with the mask, hoodie, and black pants inside, he suddenly didn't care if he had to spend another week in Marcus's magical wristbands.

After making sure everything was still inside, Jonah returned to the secluded spot beside the shed outside. He huddled in the shadow of the tree, thought about the bathroom stall, and phased.

When he burst out of the confined space seconds later, he startled a boy who hadn't been in the bathroom when he left.

"What the… " the boy's eyes widened. "I swear no one was in here."

Jonah wondered if he'd caught the boy smoking or doing something else that was forbidden. He glanced back at the stall he exited. "You were peeking in the stalls?"

The boy's face darkened with embarrassment. "No!" He hurried from the bathroom.

Jonah grinned until he realized he'd be late to class himself. He could endure the detention because there was something he needed to finish for Latrell as well as himself.

*

Coming up with an excuse to dodge a suspicious Mike after class wasn't easy. So Jonah told him what he had planned. Mike's light complexion darkened in anger.

"You wanted to know," Jonah reminded him. "Brandon deserves it anyway."

"What about your godfather?"

"I'll be more careful this time." Jonah raised his eyebrows, praying Mike would agree.

"Fine," Mike huffed. After a moment, he nodded and grinned. "Just don't get caught."

With that out of the way, Jonah ducked into a bathroom and changed his clothes. He kept the mask hidden until he reached the out-of-the-way staircase that led to the roof access door. He ascended halfway up before pulling the Komainu mask over his face and tugging the hoodie's top over his head.

That done, he climbed up the rest of the steps to the storage area. Jonah didn't have to wait long for Brandon and his buddies to enter. Whatever Brandon was saying to his friends died in his throat as soon as he noticed Jonah, whose face was hidden behind his mask.

The shock on the bully's face was worth all the risk. Brandon's buddies didn't notice his reaction at first because they were too busy moving around Jonah from either side to block his retreat.

Wayne was the first to realize that Brandon wasn't acting normal. "Hey, what's wrong? You look like you've seen a ghost."

Brandon regained some of his snide arrogance. "What do you want? Halloween's over."

Jonah pointed at the boy, whose face instantly drained of color.

"Brandon?" Wayne's voice betrayed his nervousness.

That seemed to snap Brandon out of his fear, and he motioned to Jonah. "Hold him."

Jonah expected that. As Wayne and the other boy closed in, reaching for him, Jonah stepped backward and phased. Wayne and the other boy grabbed empty air while Jonah's micro-phase put him about two feet behind the boys' grasping hands.

They couldn't stop their forward momentum and tumbled into each other, letting out surprised grunts. Wayne recovered first and took a swing. Jonah blocked it at the same time he sensed the second boy coming from behind. He phased and reappeared behind that boy in a crouch.

With a sweep of his leg, Jonah caught the boy by his ankle, causing him to lose balance and fall into Wayne. Both went down in a wild flurry of arms and legs. Jonah sprang to his feet and charged at Brandon. The bully let out a high-pitched scream but, despite his fear, Brandon stood his ground.

When Jonah came close enough, Brandon swung at him. Jonah blocked the first punch and used another micro-phase to dodge the second attack. He appeared behind Brandon and slapped the boy across the back of the head.

Brandon howled in frustration and turned, already swinging. Jonah ducked, phased again, and smacked Brandon on the head with the flat of his hand again. When Brandon whirled to face him, Jonah backed away.

Come on, run at me!

Brandon snarled and rushed forward, just as Jonah predicted. At the last second, he phased, allowing Brandon to plow into the metal shelves behind him. He heard a satisfying crack! followed by Brandon's muffled howl of pain. The boy fell backward onto the ground, blood seeping between the fingers he used to cover his nose.

Jonah resisted the urge to gloat or say anything at all.

"Brandon!" Wayne shouted as he charged at Jonah, who grabbed the boy and twisted him around. A surge of power augmented Jonah's strength as he moved. Wayne let out a startled yelp before his feet left the ground.

Jonah hurled the boy into his friend and both subsequently smashed into a stack of old monitor boxes. The boys slumped to the ground, dazed.

Brandon shrank away from Jonah, mumbling beneath the hand that still clutched his bloody nose. Jonah slipped behind the bully, pulling him to his feet, and phased, taking Brandon along.

*

Jonah told Mike everything as they walked to their bikes after school. And to his relief, Mike laughed before catching himself.

"You shouldn't have done that."

Jonah pulled a skeptical expression. "Really? You gonna tell on me?"

"Of course not."

Jonah unlocked his bike and hitched up his book bag. "Good. I'd hate to have to visit you one night in the mask." He faked a scowl at Mike.

"Don't try it," Mike replied, unconcerned. "I'm fantastic at opening portals. I'd hate to send you somewhere too strange."

Jonah shoved him. "You were freakin' cool!"

They set off for the Teen Center and Mike explained how he came up with the defensive move. The boys were still talking when they reached the door to the attic clubhouse where they found a wrapped package right outside.

"It has your name on it," Mike pointed out.

Jonah plucked the package off the ground. It was heavy and clearly held a long box inside. He took it up into the attic space before opening it. Inside were a pair of Egyptian swords.

"Wow," Mike gushed, running his hands along the dark, aged metal. "These are real."

"They are, and I bet they belonged to the Egyptian Wraith."

Mike gaped at him. "Why would he give them to you?"

Because I'm connected to them, the Wraith replied. He silently appeared behind them in the clubhouse area of the attic. And Latrell was with him, looking calm.

The adult Wraith bowed. *You can call on me, but if you take my swords, I can appear without you having to do that.*

Jonah walked over, Mike trailing behind him. "But why give them to me?" Even as he asked it, Jonah had the feeling the Wraith was going away. "What do you want me to do?"

Open the doorway to the Underworld. We'll both go through.

"No," Jonah protested. "You'll go to the farthest reaches of the place if I do that."

It's okay, Latrell answered. *He's gonna show me how to avoid going mad.*

"That's good, Latrell, but why can't he just take you over? He can go back and forth at will. Can't you?"

Only at certain times, the Egyptian Wraith explained. *I can't take another spirit with me and I want to help the boy.*

"Wait," Mike spoke up. "There's another option."

"You mean your defensive move? Won't that send them somewhere weird?" Jonah asked.

"I don't mean that way, Jonah." Mike pulled out his Seeker's compass. "I can open a portal to the Underworld and send you to one of the seven locations on the triptych."

The Egyptian Wraith gave him an impressed look. *You would do that for us?*

"I'm the Pathmaker, and Jonah's my Deliverer." Mike's voice was strong and sure. "And you helped us. I'm only returning the favor."

"We can't just pop into the Deliverer's cave, can we?" Jonah asked. He liked the idea but could they get away with it? "Aren't there any guards?"

"Jonah! I'm the Seeker. I have a special pass to use the portal whenever I want." His sureness wilted. "I'll just tell them I'm doing research for Alliance HQ."

Jonah's doubts faded as the idea took hold. "Okay. Let's do it." He turned to the Egyptian Wraith as Mike called up the Deliverer's cave code on the compass. "See you there?"

Yes. The Wraith nodded before he and Latrell disappeared.

Jonah remembered to grab the box and take it with him. Here he was, about to travel halfway around the world in the blink of an eye to help two spirits pass into the Underworld. *So much for a normal life*, he mused as Mike activated the compass.

CHAPTER FIFTY

DELIVERER NEXT TIME

Over the course of the week, Danita finished her series on the black cat, still advocating her insistence it was all superstition. Jonah found her position odd considering she'd made an oath with the Alliance and knew the supernatural existed. It was Mike who pointed out Danita was only denying it as a cover so people wouldn't notice her sudden change in attitude.

Jonah doubted it were that simple, but he didn't argue. Even weirder still, none of his friends asked him any questions. They reacted to him just the same, or tried to. Jonah also noticed a slight change in Anthony's demeanor: He was less cocky.

Local news reported a series of strange yet coordinated acts of violence on Halloween night. The common consensus was that a small group of individuals organized the violence using social media with the goal of disrupting and causing mayhem. Jonah knew the Alliance was pushing that narrative to obscure the real events.

When Marcus arrived at the Hightowers' house early Friday evening, Jonah feared his godfather had already found out about their unauthorized visit to the Deliverer's cave.

After talking with Uncle James and Aunt Imma, who had recently returned from Savannah, he stopped by Jonah's room and knocked on the door. "May I come in?"

Jonah was lounging on his bed, reading a book for his book club, and waiting for this moment. He set the book aside and leaned against his headboard. "Sure."

His godfather wore suit pants, a medium blue dress shirt, and a dark tie, like he just phased down after a day at work in the Alliance law offices.

"How are you?" Marcus asked, entering the room and resting an elbow on the dresser top. He must have seen Jonah's grimace because he laughed. "I realize everyone keeps asking you that question."

"Yeah, they do. But I'm fine. I found out my parents tried to protect me, but I'm stronger than everyone thinks, right?"

Marcus nodded. "You are. Perhaps keeping you away from the supernatural world wasn't the best thing to do, but you can't fault your parents for that."

"I don't." Jonah unclenched his hands now that his godfather hadn't mentioned the trip to the Deliverer's cave. Still trying to avoid it, he said something else. "What about the amulet?"

"It's safely tucked away at HQ. We've made repairs to the Centre Pointe columns, now that we understand its true significance."

"Do you know who built it?"

Marcus shook his head. "I hear Mike is looking into it with a few of our best historians."

Jonah nodded. He expected Mike to work for the Alliance as a lead historian one day. He already had access to more than Jonah did. But thinking about his buddy just now reminded Jonah of his other friends. "Danita and the others took oaths, but how does that work with them? They aren't even part supernatural."

"No, they aren't, but the oath is still binding. Of course, we explained what would happen if they ever tried to violate it."

That interested Jonah, but he wondered if his godfather would answer when he asked, "What would happen?"

Marcus shrugged. "Nothing bad. They would probably just get tongue-tied."

Jonah gaped at his godfather, trying to imagine how that would play out. *Was he being literal?*

His godfather narrowed his eyes. "What's really bothering you?"

Jonah should have known he couldn't hide his real concern. Ever since he recovered his memories, one thing remained at the forefront of his thoughts, even though he incessantly tried to avoid it. *Paris.*

"I saw a memory," Jonah began. "One that Omar thought a different Memory Charmer hid."

Marcus glanced out the open bedroom door. Jonah heard the TV along with his aunt and uncle, who were talking in the kitchen.

But Marcus lowered his voice anyway. "What was it?"

"When I was five, I had a dream-walk and saw you and my dad in Paris."

Marcus's face went slack.

"I saw Death too," Jonah continued. "He came into the restaurant and told my dad he would die. He talked about the way my dad fell and said he had to stick to their agreement about me. What did he mean? You never told me the whole story." Jonah paused to take a breath and calm down.

Marcus frowned. "I'm sorry, Jonah. The time never seemed right to explain everything."

"My parents knew they would die. Death said he gave them thirteen years to spend with me."

True pain and regret seemed to radiate off Jonah's godfather. "Yes, they did, but he did not say how or when. Well, perhaps your mother knew. That's why they ran on their own the night they died. We would have stayed with them and, well, possibly also died in an attempt to save them. Isaiah and Janice would never have allowed that."

Jonah experienced a fresh wave of pain and revelation that the dreams provided. It was a lot to take in, and he imagined it would require some time to sort out. Mike often suggested he write everything down. That way, he wouldn't have to worry about remembering and could go back later.

It was a good idea, Jonah eventually decided. And that reminded him of the other thing Mike suggested. Jonah hopped off his bed and unzipped the small pocket on his backpack. He pulled out a thumb drive and held it out to Marcus.

His godfather took it with a puzzled expression. "What's this?"

"My mission report. Mike thinks I should start writing them down." He felt a little guilty because he didn't mention his glimpse into the future in the final report. Except for telling Mike, Jonah decided not to reveal that aspect of the Underworld experience. Besides, it involved Lynn, and she already made it crystal clear she wasn't ready to have people gawking at her.

"That's very astute. This will help," Marcus said as he slipped the drive in a pocket. "I'll read it when I get back to my office."

Jonah hesitated to mention the last thing that bothered him. Of course, his godfather seemed to sense that. Before he could ask, Jonah blurted out, "There's something else I heard when my mom and Omar were talking after they saved me."

A serious expression settled on his godfather's face but he waited, listening.

"Omar insisted my mom tell my dad what happened, and he mentioned my dad's brother and–" Jonah paused when he caught the slight flinch in his godfather's eye, and he hopped off the bed. "You said my dad's family died a long time ago and he was also a Reaper for a long time. I looked it up. Omar wasn't even born when my dad was a mortal. So how could he know about my dad's mortal brother?"

"Jonah…" Marcus moved to the window.

Jonah suspected his godfather wanted to put more space between them. That thought spurred him on. "Did he tell Omar and you about his brother?" Jonah pressed. "Why?"

"Many members of your father's family died on that tragic day." Marcus steepled his fingers, staring at them as if coming to a decision. Finally, he met Jonah's eager gaze. "Your father wasn't the only one to become one of the Undead and eventually, a Fallen One."

Jonah dropped onto the bed, staring at his godfather in skeptical astonishment. "What? Where? I have an uncle out there?"

Marcus raised his hands. "Yes, you do, but–"

"I want to meet him."

"All in good time."

Jonah was finding it hard to get his head around this. He felt betrayed by Marcus. "Why didn't you tell me?"

"Your father and his brother never agreed on anything, including your birth. He had nothing to do with your life, which was strictly his own choice."

"He never wanted to see me?" When Marcus reluctantly nodded, Jonah's growing interest in this man waned. "Is he also part of the Alliance?"

"Yes, and Jonah, I'll tell you about him, but not today." When Jonah crossed his arms and frowned, Marcus added, "I'll reach out to your uncle and see if he wants to meet you. Okay?"

Jonah nodded. This was so busted. The more he thought about a man who never came forward, especially after his brother and sister-in-law died, the more Jonah decided he didn't want to meet him. "Don't even bother."

"You're angry now, and you have the right to be. Once I contact him, we can decide then." Marcus began kneading the back of his neck, a sure sign of agitation with the subject. "This leads into my next topic. The time is coming when the things your parents and I did to protect you must end."

"You mean protecting me from the bad guys?" Jonah snapped, still visibly angry. "They've been coming around anyway."

"I don't mean that. But even there, you're protected in ways you don't appreciate." Marcus took a deep breath. "No, I'm talking about the work and politics of the Alliance itself."

"The Egyptian Wraith told me I was a big weapon."

Marcus winced. "That was a bit much, but you do have powers. Soon, you'll take your place in the Alliance's mission." Marcus peered into Jonah's eyes. "I'm uneasy over your familiarity with this Wraith. They can be very dangerous."

"Not him. He's helped me all along by telling me about the potions. He also fought with us in the Underworld. And…" Jonah swallowed. "He's my ancestor. That's why he helped me," Jonah added as he realized something else. "That's also why he worked with Deyanira at first, just to get close to me."

Marcus blinked in surprise. "Isaiah never mentioned…"

"Maybe my dad didn't know. Like you said, I'm different." The statement didn't bother Jonah anymore. And he wondered if that could have been the reason his uncle stayed away. *He didn't want me born.*

"Your parents wanted you to be a normal kid before that burden fell on you. I can support their point of view. I've tried to keep it that way, but we all knew it would come to an end eventually."

"What are you saying?"

"I think you've reached the turning point. Albrecht told me your block is gone."

Jonah recalled the experience in the Underworld. "My Reaper side could handle it all."

"That's remarkable, and only proves my point. You're a powerful young man."

A smile tweaked the corners of Jonah's mouth. "So, are you shipping me off to the Alliance army?"

Marcus laughed but it was relaxed. "No, Jonah. Nothing like that. You've proven you can do amazing things. People will want you to do more in the near future. Be prepared."

"Oh," Jonah muttered, considering his godfather's comment. He bet it had something to do with Alastor and the Hardliners. Everyone wanted to use him, it seemed. Jonah ignored those thoughts. They would only open up the memories and conversations with the helpful Wraith and remind him of his promise to Death. That scared him more than anything else.

He caught his godfather scanning him with a partial Reaper stare. Jonah didn't want to go there, not right now. He fully intended to keep his promise with Death, but he had no plans to tell anyone about it, not even Mike or his cousins. Well, maybe he could tell Kevin.

Marcus shifted and Jonah switched to something else. "Will you tell me about my dad's fall?" he asked.

"Why don't you come up to the office one Saturday? I'll tell you everything I discovered. Bring your cousins and we can show them around Washington. Okay?"

Jonah nodded, liking the idea. They could go during the coming winter break.

Marcus came over, gripped Jonah's shoulder, and held on, applying a little pressure. "By the way," he began, "you don't know anything about young Brandon being found on the rooftop of the school, do you?"

Jonah was ready for this. He had plenty of practice calling up feelings of innocence and denial. He did that now, hoping he could fool his godfather. But Marcus surprised him and didn't resort to a Reaper stare.

Jonah let out a breath. "No."

"Really? A custodian discovered the boy, screaming his head off atop one of the solar collectors on the high school's roof. No one could figure out how he managed to get up there."

Jonah didn't squirm because it suddenly occurred to him that he could be genuinely happy. After all, Brandon had tried to bully someone else and finally paid for it. He smirked, thinking about that. "What did Brandon say?"

"He claims Latrell's ghost grabbed him and put him up there." Marcus shook his head. "His parents are furious because a picture of the helpless young man has already gone viral." Marcus paused, giving Jonah a questioning look.

"Yeah, that means it's all over the internet," Jonah explained.

"Well, they threatened to sue and the administration fought back, saying that given Brandon's antics, it was more likely a prank by him and his buddies that backfired." Marcus glanced around the room. "We never took that mask that Kevin said you wore. Do you still have it?"

Jonah gulped. Not seeing any way out of this, he fetched the mask from the closet. Marcus held out his hand.

"Brandon's evil," Jonah said, handing over the mask. "Me and Mike caught him bullying someone else. He–"

"I understand." Marcus turned the mask over in his hands. Jonah wondered if his godfather planned to put him in the null-bands again. Instead, Marcus gave him a tired smile. "We asked you to stand up to evil. Still, you're pretty young."

Jonah stared at his godfather in disbelief. "So, you're not mad?"

"After all that you've experienced, I believe that if you had done this to young Brandon, and I'm not saying you did, you would have only done it out of concern for others and not as a way to show off your powers. That makes a huge difference."

"So, the wristbands again?"

"Why? You didn't confess to going after Brandon. That being said, something else could be appropriate at this point."

Jonah's stomach clinched. What would his godfather want this time? Something worse than the null-cuffs? He

Amulet of the Goddess   535

steeled himself for the bad news as his godfather peered at him.

"I decided," Marcus began, "a promise from you would help me rest at night."

Jonah gulped, relieved. "Seriously?" Then the complications occurred to him. What if Brandon got out of hand again, or one of his other buddies?

Perhaps Marcus could sense his conflicting emotions because he lifted an eyebrow. "I still have the wristbands."

"Okay," Jonah blurted out.

Marcus extended his hand.

After hesitating, Jonah grasped it. When Marcus arched a skeptical eyebrow, Jonah said, "I promise I won't do any more vigilante stuff."

Given his recent experience with promises, Jonah prepared himself for the physical reaction. A sharp prickle had already raced up his arm and settled in his chest. For a second, he thought he saw curly, thin lines appearing on his and his godfather's hands, almost like writing.

Did this happen every time he made a promise? Before he could read the letters, the writing disappeared in a muted flash.

Marcus nodded and released the grip with a satisfied look on his face. He returned the mask and patted Jonah on the shoulder for real this time. "Take care."

After his godfather left, Jonah leaned against his headboard, thinking for once in his life, he was okay with that promise. He did what he had to do. And as far as talking about his father, he was also okay with waiting. Jonah wasn't sure he wanted to go into his dad's history at the moment. He also found it interesting that he didn't want to meet his uncle, either.

What he needed now was a rest. The mundane, ordinary everyday teen stuff to worry about would give him a much-needed break. He could be the Deliverer some other day.

*

That evening, Lynn and Robert crowded into his room after dinner. Jonah prepared to tell them everything, including news of a long-lost uncle, when he caught the expressions on their faces. "What's up?"

Robert glanced at Lynn before answering. "Uncle Amos called our dad about Aunt Ruby."

Jonah gulped and decided it would only be polite to ask. "How is she?"

"She's back in Milledgeville," Lynn said. "Our uncle hopes one day she'll be well enough to come home." Lynn frowned, like that was the last thing she wanted.

"I guess Uncle Amos can't know about what happened, huh?"

"No," Lynn agreed, surprising Jonah when she smiled. "There's one good thing. Dad and Uncle Amos were considering celebrating Christmas together this year. That way, you can meet the rest of your cousins."

Robert brightened. "I haven't seen my cousin, Stan, in a long time."

Jonah settled back, listening to his cousins talking about his other cousins. Lynn apparently wanted to attend the same college as Stan. Jonah smiled, and the tension began to leave his body. It was like a dark cloud had lifted now that their Aunt Ruby was no longer on the loose.

He eventually told them about Marcus's comments and, honoring his promise to be open, he told them exactly what he did to Brandon and why. Robert and Lynn high-fived him.

"Good for you!" Lynn said.

The front door closed and a second later, Uncle James peeked inside Jonah's door. He held up a tub of gourmet ice cream. "Who wants some?"

Robert and Lynn raced for the door, leaving Jonah alone. He hopped off his bed and paused when he noted the Ankh of Life bookstore picture lying on his desktop. *Why did I leave it out?* The answer was obvious.

The picture represented his mom and all the adventures she, Omar, and Trueblood had undertaken. That place was a connection to her. Making a sudden decision, he plucked the picture off the desktop, opened his mom's lockbox, and slid it into his mom's picture album, instead of the brown envelope with the pictures of Aunt Ruby and her family.

It's my picture album now, Jonah reminded himself. Positioning the box back on the memento shelf, Jonah hurried to the kitchen. The prospect of enjoying gourmet ice cream with his family shoved all thoughts about his aunt and the Amulet of the Goddess clear out of his mind.

ABOUT THE AUTHOR

John Darr is a native of the state of Georgia. As a graduate of Columbus State University with a B.A. in Communications, and with work on his M.F.A. degree at Howard University in Washington, D.C., John has over twenty years of experience as a writer, screenwriter, independent filmmaker, and educational television producer. He loves long walks in picturesque locales, playing tennis, and helping others realize their creative dreams. John currently resides in Arlington, VA. Visit him online at www.johndarrbooks.com.

www.ingramcontent.com/pod-product-compliance
Lightning Source LLC
Chambersburg PA
CBHW022010300726

48970CB00003B/823